RIVER'S LOST

RIVER'S END SERIES, BOOK SIX

LEANNE DAVIS

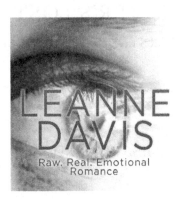

LEANNE
DAVIS
Raw. Real. Emotional
Romance

River's Lost

This is a work of fiction. Names, characters, places, and incidents are either
the product of the author's imagination or are used fictitiously, and any
resemblance to actual events, locales, or persons, living or dead, is entirely
coincidental.

Print ISBN: 978-1-941522-45-5

River's End Series, Book Six

Edited by Teri at The Editing Fairy

Copyediting: Jeannie Brooker

Cover Designer: Steven Novak

Methow, Washington is the real location of my fictional River's End. In the summer of 2014, the largest fire in Washington state history burned through it and decimated the valley my family had owned property in for forty years. Fortunately, the fire only touched the very tip of my family's property before the wind shifted downriver and spared our land. We were so lucky and whenever I go there, as I stare at all the burned land surrounding our property, I am eternally grateful that the structures my grandfather built still stand today.

CHAPTER 1

*N*O! JOCELYN JANTZ SILENTLY screamed. Then another one. Only this time, she screamed out loud, "No! No! Nooooo!"

The pain. Oh, God! It was excruciating. She'd read all about it. But no one could begin to describe *this*. She cringed and groaned through her agony. Trying to breathe. Trying to forget. Trying to deal with *it*. But she couldn't. Beads of sweat broke out all over her forehead and trickled down her face. Tears pooled in her eyes and filled her eyelids. She leaned forward through all of it before tossing her head back and resting it on the ripped fabric of the couch. Her sense of imminent defeat threatened her confidence. Her fear was real, and it tasted like the coppery flavor of blood on her tongue.

She couldn't do this by herself. She was so scared. She needed help. Lots of it.

But whom could she call?

She knew. The only people who actually cared about her. Or at least, she could rely on their sense of decency to be sure they would come to anyone's aid who needed it, even if it were her. But then… they'd know her secret. For real. And then? What if they…

No, she could not call any of the Rydells.

With the next contraction that ripped through her body, she cried tears and moaned as her entire body shuddered. It wasn't supposed to be happening yet. She was all alone and stuck out there. She never foresaw this occurring. Why did the baby suddenly try to rip its way out of her abdomen without any warning? She thought she'd have time, plenty of it, to get to the hospital. She planned to allow herself ample time to deal with her contractions under the watchful eyes of doctors and nurses.

Yesterday morning, she felt the first pains. She went to the hospital but they told her to go back home because she was having something called Braxton Hicks contractions. Bottom line to Jocelyn was that she hadn't been in true labor, and therefore, couldn't really be in any pain. She ground and gnashed her teeth over the next twenty–four hours as the stupid Braxton Hicks contractions kept her awake. Over and over, they pushed her threshold of pain to its limit. She winced every time she wondered how she could handle true labor if she couldn't bear the fake contractions. She'd just fail at that like she had failed at so many other attempts in life. But… there were so many women who successfully went through it and didn't fail. She wasn't all that special. But why did it hurt so much? Like a fire being set inside her. She gripped her swollen belly as another cramp seized her body and made her lean her head back while she screamed out loud.

That one couldn't have been fake. It just couldn't. When the tightening squeezed her lungs in half, she waited until it finally eased before she crawled over to the phone. No cell phones worked in the remote area where she lived. She had only a landline that was connected to the wall. The closest people to her, the ones who hadn't been totally burned out from the fire last summer, were the Rydells. Many of the residents never returned after the fire. The giant Rydell ranch property spread out over the valley below where she lived. Her cabin, or rather, shack, was perched way up in the hills above it. There was not a soul visible for miles from where the small shack clung to its foundation in the middle of the mountain.

The phone rang and she moaned as a new pain started to crest. Erin. Allison. Kailynn. Please, God. Please, let one of them answer.

But no such luck. It was a man. And none other than Jack Rydell who answered the phone. She had called the main ranch number, the one they formerly used for the resort, which burned down in the fire's path, and now wasn't open.

"Jack?" she gasped out before lifting the phone away as an excruciation pain managed to steal her breath and voice. She cried out loud in a heartrending wail.

"Hello? Hello? Who is this calling? What's going on?"

"It's J–Jocelyn…" Another one. "P–p–please…h–h–h…elp me," she squeaked out before an overwhelming contraction compelled her to grab her belly again. She dropped the phone and curled up in agonizing fear. *Oh, God.* Was she dying? Was something bleeding out inside her? There had to be a reasonable explanation for her to feel so bad. Why couldn't she seem to gain control? Why did she have to writhe on the floor in pain all alone? Far from any help or support and no clue of what she should be doing.

Real terror started to consume her. Women did still die during childbirth. Sometimes, freak things happened and the woman simply died. She was all alone. She had to be in labor, or at least she thought she was, and nobody else could know. There was no one to help her. There never had been really, which was cool to Jocelyn. She took care of herself. Always had. Always could, or so she once believed.

Until this… happened.

The terror she felt now, at this moment, was exponentially worse than the moment she learned she was pregnant. Unplanned of course. Unwanted too, so she walked around in a daze for several weeks. What would she do about the baby?

"Ben…!"

Screaming his name from her lips, she didn't know if she were enunciating it out of her present need, or want, or longing, or fear. Perhaps it was hatred and repulsion. Maybe she would seek revenge for what he'd done to her and left her to deal with alone. Alone. Squirming in pain like an injured animal left to die on this dirty, dusty floor. How long did she have to wait before anyone found her? How much longer did she have to endure this cruel anguish?

The fear of losing her baby and dying, then lying there for days or weeks, made her turn to her side as she clutched her swollen belly. *Oh, God!* She shouldn't have stayed at the shack. No. Big mistake.

But then… where else could she go?

Closing her eyes, the acuteness of the pain relaxed into a dull throb. She fell exhausted on her back. Lying there with her knees up as far as her bulk would allow, hot tears streamed from her eyes, falling onto the floor below her. She was too exhausted and too famished to even care what became of her now. She hoped she could just drift off and succumb to her exhaustion, letting it take her away.

Did she sleep? She wasn't sure. She seemed to be in and out of consciousness, or so she thought.

What was that?

A noise. A vehicle! She jerked and tried to sit up but the pain attacked her again.

Yes. It was a car engine. Stopping, and shutting off. And she even heard a door slamming.

Footsteps and then loud banging on the front door. Thankfully, a voice yelled out with firm authority and concern, "Jocelyn? What the hell is going on in there?"

Jack.

She closed her eyes. Squeezing her eyelids together harder, she thought, *Oh God, Jack came.*

"Jack…" she called out. Her voice was weak, and her chapped lips cracked and bled as she opened them to call him.

Silence; then the door jingled, but it was locked. *Shit.* She shouldn't have locked it. But… no. Jack smashed the front door open. If she could have mustered the energy, she would have, no doubt, cheered him on.

But she wasn't okay.

Jack was there. He stopped dead for a moment in the doorway when he spotted her. Then… he was instantly on his knees beside her, his hands kindly supporting her back. "Jocelyn. Oh, God… you're not all right. Oh, God."

Help. Someone was finally there at last. Something inside her released. She wouldn't die alone. That thought gave her the strength to hold on. She wasn't alone anymore. She didn't realize how much his being there meant to her.

But then…

"Damn it, girl. You're having a baby. Why didn't you tell us?" Jack was rushing all around. First, he tried his cell phone. She was too tired to tell him it wouldn't work. Then he was on her landline, calling for help. Screaming into the receiver, he commanded whomever was on the other end to respond. His voice was filled with fear and panic. She understood. She felt that way too.

She remembered how Jack was always so kind to her. Ever since she was just a kid, he'd been generous to her. He gave her a job and riding lessons for free. And let her hang out at the ranch as often as she showed up. He didn't know why she came so regularly. He also didn't know about things like Cutter Johnson, and why she so desperately needed to get away from her own "home." But Jack let her stay there all the same.

His hands gently touched her cheek and her forehead. Was he checking for fever? Maybe. Then he clutched her shoulders in a kind of hug. "You'll be okay, honey. We'll... we'll take care of you. I'm sorry to warn you, but I think I'm going to have to get real personal with you and real fast. Erin's on her way. But I'm not sure that will help. I'm not sure there's enough time. Allison... she's on the line. She's done this before. She's gonna talk us through this. Okay? You'll be okay."

She could have sworn he gulped when she suddenly grabbed his hand in hers and squeezed it hard as the unparalleled pain shot through her again. She squeezed his hand until his bones nearly fractured. Moaning and groaning, bullets of sweat broke out all over her skin and streams of tears rolled down her cheeks as she gritted her teeth. She was crying out like an animal, making strange grunts through her mouth.

Vaguely, somewhere in her mind far away, she heard Jack talking on the phone. His gentle hands touched her again, but were hesitant. She could almost feel his anxiety as he started to help her out of the sweats, which were the only pants that still fit her. "I'm sorry, Jocelyn, but I need to help you right now."

She nodded, closing her eyes, uncaring what Jack saw. Clinging to his voice and his presence, all modesty fell to the wayside. *She wasn't alone. She wasn't alone. She wasn't alone.*

Then it happened. And so fast, she couldn't prepare herself for it.

"Oh, motherfucker," Jack muttered softly once he realized what was happening. Then his voice grew louder and more panicked as he jumped back and screamed into the phone, "Oh, shit. Allison! I can see the baby's head."

She reached towards him, silently pleading him not to abandon her then. But he wouldn't have. He came right back and turned her over onto her back, saying gently now, "I'll be right back. Gotta get a towel and some water... Just don't move."

She might have considered smiling her appreciation in response if the situation weren't so lethal in her mind.

When she felt the cool water on her forehead, she opened her eyes. His compassionate eyes stared down at her as he said, "Okay, Jocelyn, we're going to do this and do it right. Nothing I can't handle. I've delivered dozens of foals before. How different could it be?"

Finally, a tight smile tugged at her mouth. He waited until she slowly nodded her agreement.

She was miserable. The pain didn't relent and it didn't get any easier. But her fear subsided, allowing her to find a new level of pain tolerance. The energy she thought was long depleted and buried suddenly resurged through her. Jack helped by talking to her and guiding her. He was her private nurse, doctor, mother, and coach.

Halfway through the ordeal, the front door burst open and Erin entered. Looking every bit as harried and wild as Jack, she pressed her lips together and went right to work assisting them, and taking over the more intimate details. Jack had already disconnected Allison and called 911, who forwarded his call to a doctor. And an ambulance was on the way. There was an ambulance coming for her!

She might not die after all.

But no one arrived in time.

She gave birth on the floor of the shack.

It all ceased to matter. Every single tear, scream, pain and mess of the experience all faded and dissolved when Jocelyn heard her baby cry. The healthy newborn cry of *her baby*. Erin held the baby in her hands and tears streamed down both their faces as they stared in wonder at the miracle. This tiny creature that seemed to magically emerge from her body, never mind how it nearly ripped her in half.

"It's a baby girl. You have a daughter. You did it! You did it, Jocelyn. She's a perfect baby girl."

There was a rather disturbing, ugly goo all over the baby. Blood and a strange, white substance that Jocelyn didn't recognize covered her daughter. Something her body must have created. Flopping back, she was exhausted but grateful as she smiled up at the ceiling. She floated mentally out of the shack and the sad circumstances of her life, so lost in the magic and wonder of her daughter's birth. She was no longer in the tiny hovel, but somewhere else. Somewhere beautiful. Somewhere special. She was beyond all those things that bothered her before, and all because she had this baby.

Erin came over to her, clasping her hand and pulling her hair back from her sweaty face. "You're okay, honey. You're okay. Help just arrived."

Chaos ensued. The headlights and warning lights of the ambulance made weird twirling reflections on the interior of the room. People she did not even know knelt beside her, finishing what Jack and Erin started. They put an IV in her hand and attended to her body. After wiping her baby clean, they placed her on Jocelyn's chest.

Minutes went by as the professionals treated their patient proficiently. It was so calming to watch them. She might not die from childbirth. She actually believed it now as they gave her fluids and medicine while checking the vital signs of her baby. Even her bruised and battered vagina received proper attention.

Then everything was calmer. She lay on the gurney. Ready to be taken to the hospital. The Rydells stayed right there with her, and Erin kept hold of her hand while comforting her like a mother would. Jocelyn didn't know, since she didn't remember too much about her mother. Erin was too young to be that for her. They were maybe only a decade apart in ages, but right now, she felt like curling up against Erin's chest. She thought she might find the help, affection, and understanding she'd been denied for her entire life. Which again, was cool. She wasn't a touchy–feely girl who needed shit like that normally. But... maybe right now, she did. She hated to admit she wanted that. So much fear and shock for the day left her dazed and unsure of what happened to her. She shook off her perceived need for parental caring. She knew it was not in the cards for her.

Until... until she looked into Jack's eyes.

He was staring at the newly cleaned baby she held. All wrapped up, now it seemed too civilized compared to the last hour... and all the others before that. All that primal, dirty, blood and guts was the epitome of life and all it entailed. Not sweet–smelling blankets and a rosy–hued baby.

Then Jack lifted his stunned eyes to hers and she met his gaze. Her eyes grew big and fearful. Somehow... he knew. *How?* Her tired brain could not figure out how he knew. *How did he guess?*

"She looks just like him." Jack seemed crestfallen. He rubbed a hand over his face. "Ah... shit. The night of the fire... he... This is what Ben was running from. Now I see what he's dealing with..."

Erin glanced up at Jack's odd rambling. "What?"

Jack looked at Jocelyn and she bit her lip, nodding slowly. Jack's head kept shaking. "She looks just like him. Just exactly like Ben when he was born."

"Who?" Erin inquired.

"Ben." His voice sounded raw, scraped of all emotions. "Did I just deliver my own granddaughter, Jocelyn?"

The words Jack spoke stabbed her heart. She finally nodded in the affirmative as she tried to explain, "Yes. But please… please, don't take her from me…please…"

As she was wheeled out to the waiting vehicle, she didn't hear his answer. She was crying, and clutching the baby she never wanted but would never, ever think of giving up now. She tightened her arms around her baby. *Her baby.* She'd die before she'd let the rich and powerful Rydell clan take her baby away from her. Ben be damned! This baby was hers. Forever.

She kissed her daughter's head. "I love you. I won't let them take you from me. Never."

Her quiet baby's eyes stared up at her in rapt wonder, and she believed right down to her toes and in the depths of her heart, that for the first time, someone she loved finally loved her back.

CHAPTER 2

*B*EN RYDELL SNIFFED THE fat line of white powder lying on the mirror up his nose. It hit him fast and hard. He leaned back, sighing his contentment at the instant relief that miraculously filled him. He tucked his bulky back against the headboard of the bed in a dingy, no-name motel room in which he'd been living for a few weeks now as he waited for the drug to work its magic. It helped him so much. His thoughts drifted away. He shouldn't continue to indulge this vice. He seldom went for the hard drugs because it was a bit like playing Russian Roulette when it came to potency. Knowing that, he believed he could control it. Sniffing the powder up his nose once in a while didn't hurt anyone. Especially him.

Memories—sometimes they invaded his brain and refused to leave. Today was one of those days. And rather than doing something violent or risking the welfare of others, as his sudden, red-hot, burning rage ignited and he wanted to literally hurt the next person he saw, he retreated into his solitude and self-medicated in order to forget. He just wanted to chill and stop hurting. He mostly relied on alcohol and marijuana, the occasional OxyContin or heroin. But those weren't very often.

He let his mind drift and looked up, unseeing, almost numb as he floated with the shadows that made strange shapes on the white popcorn ceiling. An ancient water stain, yellow and grayish, captured his gaze, holding him riveted. *Nice.* It was so nice to float. He could finally forget and not be Ben Rydell for a while. He could pretend not to remember Marcy. His wife.

He could forget about the abominable, callous man who chose to engage in sex with another woman while his wife burned to death.

THE NEXT MORNING, Ben awoke with a jerk. He glanced out the window. Shit! He was late. He got to his feet and a wave of nausea filled his throat with bile. Damn. His body didn't respond well to foreign substances. He didn't have the stomach for it. Oh, well. Grabbing his jeans, he slipped the dirty, crusty things over his legs. With his hard–hat in hand, he tromped out the front door and headed towards the pipeline.

Shit. The sun was blinding. *Fucking Montana.* He spat and leaned over the door of his truck. Fuck. He was ready to hurl. He stepped away from the truck before heaving out his guts on the side of the parking lot. It gradually soaked into the gravel. Rising up slowly, he wiped his mouth with the back of his hand before spitting out more of the foul residue from his tongue.

Putting his sunglasses on, he sped out of the motel parking lot, headed towards the job site. He pulled in only fifteen minutes late and still got his ass reamed out by the foreman. Ignoring it all, without apologizing or listening, he started work. So what if he was fired? Let the old, fat, bald prick fire him. He'd just move on. Hell. It sounded heavenly.

Years ago, the discovery of oil in Eastern Montana made overnight millionaires out of many Montanans and provided new jobs across their forty–plus oil fields that were now up and running. Ben decided it had good prospects for a guy drifting around like him. And now there were barely any rooms available for rent as men just like him filled all the vacancies at the numerous motels around the area. Naturally, that was owing to all of the stable, good–paying jobs. Ben wasn't technically a good or stable worker, and certainly did not deserve such a fine and decent job, but he took the opportunity nevertheless.

His day began on a crew assigned to maintain the oil wells. His stomach heaved occasionally and his breath was foul–smelling. With aching eyes, he barely managed to keep busy.

Only a half hour later, a voice interrupted him. "Ben?"

He froze. He dared not move when a familiar man's voice sounded from behind him, maybe only ten feet away. He wondered if the person had been standing there for a long time. No doubt. Watching him. Judging him. Perhaps even relieved to find him. His shoulders sagged as his heart lifted and then fell. No! Damned old bastard. How could he pinpoint his location? He didn't turn around or even acknowledge the voice. He didn't say hi, or even use his name.

Labor in the oil fields was competitive even for an entry level grunt–work position, which was termed a *roustabout*. Ben, however, managed to get on.

"You're wasting your time by coming here. I'm not going home. Ever."

"Can you turn around?"

He didn't. "I gotta work." He stepped to the side and started heading to another station.

"Ben, please. We need to talk."

"I have nothing to say to you. Go home. I didn't ask you to come here."

"No. I realize that. But there're some things you need to know."

What more could there be? He had nothing left after his wife and home burned up. They were both reduced to charred, blackened ashes. Yeah. Now, there was nothing he needed to talk about or return to. His only intention was to never lay eyes on any of it again.

"I realize you're grieving and having a hard time, but, Ben. I need to talk to you."

"I'm working. Leave it, old man," he replied in an ugly tone. Only a year ago, his dad would have instantly taken him to task with a stern lecture about respect. A year ago, Ben would have cowered in remorse because he cared what his dad thought and felt then. He'd have taken his dad's message to heart and applied it in how he acted and spoke. Now? He didn't give a shit anymore. Too little. Too Late.

"No… really. We need to talk. *Now.*"

Always the heavy. The commander-in-chief. Ben sneered as he suddenly whirled around and almost attacked his dad, standing there, all clean and neat in creased jeans and a freshly pressed shirt, which he had tucked in. He shoved his dad, backing him into the building behind him. "You can't come here and order me home. I'm not your fucking child anymore. I'm not your damn employee either. You aren't the Great Jack Rydell here. Look around you, no one gives a shit who you are here. Or that I'm Ben Rydell. You're out of your element, away from our nothing valley. In other words, Jack Rydell, you ain't nothing. Not a goddamned thing. So don't try to tell me to turn around. Or what to do. Leave, *Jack*. Just fucking leave me alone!"

His dad, to his credit, didn't attack him in response. Gripping Jack's flawless shirt in his fists, Ben jerked on it as he pushed his father forcibly away. He kicked the dirt at their feet, covering Jack's boots in it.

Turning, he started to walk away. *Fuck my dad! Fuck this place! Fuck this job!* He'd take off again. Now that he'd been located, he'd simply get lost again. He had no idea how his dad managed to find him. With only a damned backpack to his name, Ben was careful and hadn't touched a single credit card in all the months of his idle wandering. After selling his fancy–assed truck right after leaving River's End, he bought the heap he now drove and even had enough money left over to survive on for several months. No work, just wandering aimlessly.

"Jocelyn had a baby." Ben stopped dead and his shoulders hunched forward. He stared down at his boot tips but didn't turn around. His stomach clenched. *No! No! Hell, no! A baby? What? How? Just no!*

"Your baby, Ben. A baby girl." Jack's tone was much softer, gentle almost.

Ben clenched his fists and turned away, walking a little further before he replied over his shoulder, "It's not mine."

"Really? The baby looks just like you. She's definitely yours." Jack's tone was quiet and severe. His upstanding father, no doubt, would be atrociously disappointed about who and what his son had become now. Ben sneered at the thought, nearly reveling in it. He'd always been his father's little clone, the apple of his eye, striving all of his life to earn the respect and love of the great Jack Rydell.

Not so anymore.

A baby? His heart skipped a beat. He swallowed the spit that his mouth kept salivating. *Shit.* But... no. No. What were the chances? That could only mean that it... the... *the thing* was conceived on the night of the fire, the same night he regrettably had sex with Jocelyn Jantz in his feeble attempt to punish his wife, while his wife, at the same moment, was being burned alive.

Truthfully, however, it wasn't exactly that way. For months leading up to that night, Ben had been experiencing odd, unexpected, almost unexplainable feelings toward Jocelyn. They had been friends since childhood, so long, he couldn't remember ever *not* knowing her. She spent a lot of her free time with him and his uncle, Joey, since her age placed her smack dab between them. Best friends for years, Ben connected with her in ways he couldn't with anyone else. He could talk to her from his heart, which he didn't dare to do with anyone else. She had the unique distinction of being his closest female friend. He trusted her and could tell her anything, describing his feelings and confessing things he would never dream of telling another guy, not even his brother. As his marriage dissolved and became increasingly hostile, he liked hanging out with Jocelyn, who ran the resort café. He began eating lunch there almost daily just to see and talk to her. After work, they went to the beach in the summer or messed around in the snow in the winter. The ranch had plenty of snowmobiles so he and Jocelyn often rode them, or sledded, or competed in snowball fights. She could give and take it as well as any guy. But afterwards, they usually ended up talking for ten minutes or several hours. It depended on their schedules. Their conversations were always natural, always real, and always honest... And it never failed to make him feel better.

Eventually, his thoughts about Jocelyn seemed to invade his mind more often. Weird thoughts that he never experienced before. He knew he was much more aware of her presence. Whenever he was with her, he began physically noticing her. His stomach reacted by knotting or fluttering with anxiety and nerves at encountering her. Even his skin prickled in awareness at her presence. The feelings Ben had towards her were manifesting in unique ways.

However, he was already married.

Despite his guilt, he knew he had begun hating the woman he married. And in the end, right before she died, he demonstrated how much he despised her.

Nooo! The pressure in his head was blinding and instantaneous. It was the reason why he could never think very long about it. He almost fell to his knees. Noooo! The ghastly images kept flashing through his weary mind. He pressed his throbbing temples. Once again, his dad's annoying, familiar voice evoked the memory of his old life, intruding on his new way of living, a way that didn't hurt so damn much, or cause him unending, merciless pain.

"You need to come home, Ben. You need to—"

With flippant ease, Ben glanced at his dad, shrugging his shoulders as he replied icily, "You raise it. You and Erin raise the damn thing if you care so much about it."

Silence. Somber, disapproving silence. Ben smiled as he thought, *Yeah, Daddy, I ain't the son that you remember or want any longer.* No way could Jack Rydell admit his defeat. He wasn't strong enough to handle a son like Ben. Ben was a failure. Something Jack could never tolerate. His son turned out to be a complete disappointment, and that reflected on Jack. Ben sneered with cruel pleasure at the knowledge.

"No. That isn't an option. Jocelyn plans to raise the baby by herself. You just need to—"

Ben whipped around, interrupting him, cocking his eyebrow and replying, "I need to what, Jack? Be a good, upstanding citizen? Do everything right? Fulfill my responsibilities? Make good on all my debts? Sorry, but I tried that once, and you know it didn't go so well for me. So no, I don't care to repeat that mistake. I won't. Goodbye, *Jack*."

Jack's voice trailed after Ben with a deep sigh. "I'll sue you and have your wages garnished. You can't abandon her like that."

He didn't know which "her" Jack was referring to, Jocelyn or his baby. Ben stopped dead again. The old bastard refused to give up. He raised an eyebrow. "Do whatever you want." He chose to ignore him as he wandered back to his station to return to work.

It didn't matter. He was doing the... *the thing*, the baby, a favor by staying as far away from it as he could. He would not help it. She... *it*... was better off by far without him in her life. Besides, having him and Jocelyn Jantz as her parents was a huge liability. What the fuck kind of chance did the baby stand to receive from this life anyway? He sneered. Not much of a future, and that was for sure. Ben stood back to observe the giant machine. He was assisting a mechanic in adjusting the hydraulics. *Poor little bastard was fucked even before it was born, literally and figuratively, wasn't it?*

LATER ON, Ben pulled into the motel room. Nearly groaning, he leaned his head on the steering wheel. There was Jack, sitting on a bench in front of his motel room door. He hopped out after a long pause. He had to go inside and face Jack again because he needed his backpack and the drugs he'd paid good money for. Ignoring Jack, he unlocked the door.

"How'd you find me?"

"Just asked your foreman."

Fucker. Ben thought as he shoved the door open. It was gloomy and dark. Drug paraphernalia was scattered all over the unmade bed and on the dresser. Empty food containers were strewn haphazardly all over the small table and some of them spilled onto the floor.

"Does it help?"

Ben turned, confused by Jack's blunt statement. He was unsure of what Jack was referring to. Ben's bad attitude? His disrespect? What?

Jack nodded towards the drugs and walked forward, pointing at them. "Does that help you forget?"

Jolted from his apathy and simmering anger, he watched his dad rifle through all of his drugs. But instead of recrimination, outrage, disgust or panic at learning that Ben was using drugs, Jack merely asked Ben how it felt? That was so *not* Jack Rydell. Ben snatched the stuff from Jack and shoved it aside. "Yeah. It actually does."

His dad sat down on one of the side chairs and sighed heavily as he leaned forward, his shoulders slumping. He stared down at his hands clasped before him as he nodded. "I could see where that would provide you with some relief, then."

What. The. Fuck?

Ben finally looked at his dad. He really looked closely at him. Jack didn't appear like Ben remembered him. His face was drawn and haggard. Gray had replaced all the dark red hair at his temples. His weight was visibly less and odder still, so was his muscle mass. Something reached inside Ben's gut and tapped him. Was it fear? Towards Jack? Did he still feel a sense of responsibility? Towards his family? His father? Was he capable of feeling anything still? Could he ever expect to again?

Rage. That uncontrollable, dangerous, untapped rage.

"Have you been sick?" he asked, reminding himself he didn't care. Life happened. Shit happened. So what? If Jack were really sick, he'd either live or die. One simply had to accept the outcome, either way. You had to move on.

"No. Not really. Just… still having a hard time. The fire… It really changed things."

Strangely, Ben was surprised that Jack didn't mention it was because Ben was gone. Honestly? Ben assumed in his more lucid, caring moments that his sudden disappearance would most likely ruin his dad's life. But to hear Jack talk, it was like Ben wasn't the main concern right now in his life. That thought almost offended Ben, but he shook off the urge to ask *What things got changed?* The undeniable, age-old desire to help his dad, and to find out about all the people of his happy childhood burrowed into Ben's gut.

But no. He refused to be like that anymore. That's what hurt the most. Caring. Loving. Belonging to things and people. Jobs. Relationships. All he received was pain and destruction for his effort. So what was the point of it?

Jack motioned towards the drugs. "What is that?"

Ben eyed his father, crossing his arms over his chest and leaning back against the lip of the dresser. "Heroin."

Jack just nodded. "And the other?"

"Marijuana."

"That doesn't seem as bad, I guess, I mean, the marijuana. And although heroin is a strong opiate, maybe it's not as bad as methamphetamines. Always heard that if you tried those even once, some people get hooked on them." Jack stared down, keeping his voice neutral, and sounding merely inquisitive. Acting as if they were back in the old days, casually discussing the best way to approach a difficult horse to train. "Then again, I guess I've heard that caveat with heroin too."

Ben kept his facial expression unreadable, but for the first time in months, a shock-like disturbance passed through him. Was his dad suddenly endorsing drug use? Was he saying that marijuana was the better choice? Why wasn't he losing his mind at discovering his son doing drugs? Heroin! That was no small opiate. It was really bad, judging by most parents' standards. Yet his dad, the staunchest, most upstanding man Ben had ever known, thought it was not so bad?

"The marijuana just relaxes you, right?"

"I guess so." Ben restrained the urge to reply that nothing relaxed him. Nothing was strong enough to let him sleep. They could only barely take the edge off his pain. And temporarily erase his rage and self-hatred.

His dad's tone held no anger or passion. It was odd and disturbing, as if Jack were merely curious about what Ben was up to and how the stuff worked. "Sometimes, I imagine that would be a relief."

Ben shifted his feet, uncrossing them. "What do you want, Jack?"

"Want?" Jack lifted his head and stared at Ben. "Yes, that is funny, isn't it? How often I used to want things and always thought I controlled the things I requested. I guess that fire taught us both the irony of that kind of thinking, huh?"

"Jack...? I don't want to do... this... " Ben ran his fingers through his hair, pressing the ache in his head and eyeing the drugs. Recalling anything that shot him back to the moment of the fire's conquest, and the knowledge of what he'd done, as well as what happened to Marcy, made his brain hurt like it was about to burst into flames, or explode out of his head. It literally killed him to remember the event. He chose NOT to remember. Self-medication in the form of painkillers was a convenient therapy.

His dad's lips compressed. "I never wanted you to endure such pain, you know? The pain of losing a wife. I also had to survive that. I just never dreamed my son... would be destined to bear it too. Your mother. Your wife. It's okay,

Ben, I get the disdain you feel toward me. I deserve it. I expected a lot. I promised you that if you worked really hard, and lived the right way, only good things would ensue." His attempt at laughter resulted in a sneer that quickly soured. "I told you that somehow life would be *fair* to you. Funny, but losing my parents, my mother, my father, *and* my wife didn't teach me the lesson that life isn't fair. No, it's brutal, random, and cruel. It took my son experiencing those same things for me to finally understand. All my advice and all of my expectations were just shit, weren't they? Really, Ben, I understand if you hate me. I mean, I have to say that everything you've done and are doing right now pretty clearly illustrates that. I didn't prepare you for anything like this."

Ben kept his face neutral, his stance frozen, but his mind was practically short–circuiting. He didn't recognize this pathetic man before him. Tired. Old. Depressed. Hopeless. Broken. Jesus! Jack Rydell was acting as if something were irreparably shattered inside *him*. How could that be? No! Jack was always the strongest man, emotionally and physically, from his eternal commitment of doing right instead of wrong, and universal fairness and justice, to God and his spiritual responsibilities. More than any other man Ben had ever known.

"You now know where I was that night." Ben nearly bit his tongue when the sharp statement popped out of his mouth, despite his intentions to send his dad packing.

Jack nodded. "Yes. I understand more now of what happened to you."

"I was fucking Jocelyn while my wife was being burned alive. You understand that, right, *Jack?* You have that image clearly etched in your mind?"

Jack didn't even wince at his graphic depiction. Never before would he have allowed Ben to talk that way about anyone, and especially a girl with whom he'd grown up. Ben used to like her and respect her as his friend. Jack had mentored and facilitated her in any way he could. She had worked for their operations for more than a decade.

"Yes, I understood it the instant I saw the baby girl's face."

No. He banished the image. Calling *it* a *she.* The picture Jack's soft words painted in his mind was quickly obliterated. The—*the thing*, the baby, would always remain *it* and was far better off without him. He had nothing to give *it.* Nothing left for it but anger, rage and self–disgust. He was so vile, how could he help a tiny baby? His place in life had become the gutter. *It* could not be his child.

"I understand, Ben. You're not Ben anymore. You're not the son I raised. You think this ruined you. I know you, son. I know exactly where your head was over these last nine months. That's why I didn't try to find you or help you. I understood what no one else did; I couldn't help you." Jack shrugged. "And that made me realize I can't help anyone. My constant need to prevail was all an illusion. Not feeling that way anymore."

"Where is Erin?" Something stabbed Ben in his gut. Fear. Concern. Something besides his selfish, burning rage for the past nine months. His newfound interest in someone else nearly floored him. Who was this shell of a man collapsing right in front of him?

"She's at the ranch. She was going to come with me. I begged her to stay home and just let me see you. I honestly didn't have it in me to deal with her coming on this trip."

"Are you... are you still with her?"

"Yes. Sure." But there was no passion in his father's terse reply. His dad loved Erin, his second wife and Ben's step-mother. Ben liked Erin too. He had nothing against her. She made Jack happy, but never in the half dozen years they'd been together had Jack talked about her with so little passion, care or protection in his voice.

"What the fuck is going on with you?"

He shrugged. "Ian's running things at the ranch now. Kailynn had a big, exciting job lined up in Seattle, but she let it go so they could move back home for good. Her old man, you remember Chuck? He lost his trailer in the fire and now lives with them. He's around the ranch a lot. You know, he's disabled. We chat quite a bit. He knew my dad, too. They were good friends. So we talk about Dad a lot. That's kinda nice. Anyway, Ian's gotten things moving along. Did you know the main house burned? Yup, it's all gone. Just charcoal and ashes. The fireplace was all that was left standing."

The stabbing hurt he felt flummoxed Ben. No, he didn't know the main house had burned. Instantly, his mind was a stream of memories from his childhood: his mother, his father, Charlie, and Joey. He pictured the fireplace, and a roaring, warm fire along with the sense of safety that persisted throughout his childhood. Even after his mom died, his dad's unfailing love and support fortified him in that house. Along with the love and support he got from Ian. Shane. Joey. And Charlie.

Ian was running things now? No! They ran it all together. Either Jack was their leader, or they both did it together. Never before had Ian offered to run the ranch. What the fuck was Jack talking about? "What are you doing then?"

Jack shrugged. "Kinda taking a break. You know, Erin's really good with the horses. You remember how much she likes them. She and Joey train the horses together. And Shane does too. Funny. He takes care of the horses too now."

Funny. Shit. No. It wasn't. Taking a break? His dad was what? Not taking care of his horses? The ranch? Besides his sons, Jack lived for the horses. Shane was helping to manage the ranch for his dad? At least three men were necessary to equal one of his dad. The thing Ben could never live up to was the long, tall, strong, competent, and yes, necessary umbrella his father used to shield him.

"What about Charlie?"

"Oh, he's good. Going to school. He spends all his time with Cami. I think he misses you. I don't know. He doesn't say too much about anything. But then, he was always so quiet anyway."

His dad was not freaking out to make sure Charlie was okay? Who the hell was this man sitting before him? Ben shifted his ass on the dresser, his former apathy starting to melt in the face of such shocking circumstances which the strange man he now saw revealing to him.

Instead of glimpsing Ben's surprise and utter disbelief at what was going on at his home in his absence, Jack didn't even glance up to see how Ben was taking any of it. With a long sigh, he stretched his legs out and said, "I delivered her. Your daughter. Jocelyn didn't tell anyone else. She called the resort number that night, screaming in pain. Shocking is an understatement when describing what I found. I went up to the shack she lives in. Have you ever been there? Way worse than I ever dreamed. It's garbage, actually. Anyway, there she was, in full labor and all alone, scared and hurting. Frightened right out of her mind. I had to go south and take care of business. I just pretended she was a mare foaling, you know? It worked. No harm, no foul. And then I saw her perfect, little face."

Ben cringed and turned away after hearing what his dad described. No. He refused to imagine Jocelyn in pain or having a baby. Or his home. It burned up. It was gone. Ian was in charge now. Jack? What was Jack doing anyway? Where was Erin in all of this? Fuck. It was like the world had turned upside-down since the awful night of the fire. Ben's response was to do drugs and run and hide. He'd become a shitty worker, and his dad? His dad was not working?

Jack shifted around again, still not lifting his head up to see Ben's reaction to his almost monotone explanation of what had happened there since Ben's disappearance. "Well, it'll end up being a legal issue at the very least. You know? You'll have to pay child support if nothing else. And if you saw the shack where the poor girl lives, you'd agree that's the least she deserves. I didn't know she was that poor. She'll probably be released from the hospital soon. She just had the little girl three days ago. I had to come here to tell you, I hope you see that. And I really think you ought to at least help pay for her delivery bill. The baby, I mean."

Ben's mouth dropped open in astonishment. Was his dad suggesting he could do the minimum by sending her payments for his child? His dad said that? How the shit could this be Jack Rydell? Ben blinked several times in disbelief. His dad didn't care anymore if he came home to meet his own damn offspring? His baby? His *daughter*?

No. He refused to take on that kind of responsibility. It was too much for him. He was not ready to be the father to anyone. Much less, the cursed, biological result of what he and Jocelyn did to Marcy.

Jack heaved himself to his feet. "Well, I think I'll go lie down. I got a room here too. I hope you don't mind. I have to think on it all." He didn't wait for Ben to answer before he walked out the door.

Ben's jaw stayed open as he stared after the man he no longer recognized. Ben thought he'd changed, after what he'd been doing for the last nine months, but he never expected to see so much change in his father.

CHAPTER 3

*J*OCELYN GLANCED UP AFTER hearing the soft knock on the hospital door and figured it was some Rydell or another. She drew in a deep breath for courage before she invited them in. There was no ignoring them any longer.

Joey and Erin Rydell walked in together. It seemed so incongruent for a minute. Years ago, they'd been sleeping together. Jocelyn knew all about it. In a matter of weeks, however, Erin was with Jack and Joey had enlisted in the Army. Now? Since the fire, Joey and Erin were together a lot, taking over many of the horse training responsibilities. Ian, the second brother after Jack, was in charge of all the ranch business, handling the insurance claim and deciding how and what to rebuild and in what order to accomplish that. Ian determined all the details, logistics, and facilitating involved. Shane, the third brother and one–time biker, who avoided all things equine, now pitched in too, as did almost everyone else who was formerly involved with the ranch. Rebuilding the salvageable units and clearing the charred land from all the rubble and ruins, as well as fixing the fences and caring for the horses, were jobs that belonged to everybody, and everyone pitched in. Jocelyn included. From the very start of their overhaul, she'd been in on it.

A few days after the fire, she came to the ranch. She'd already heard the news about Marcy and Ben. There were no words to describe how low her emotional state was. She fell to her knees and began puking when she first heard the news. It even made the national news, and like the rest of the valley residents, Jocelyn was listening for updates about the fire. From a battery–operated old relic with barely any signal, the radio provided just enough information for her to understand what she had done.

Mustering her grief and disgust with herself, she headed to the ranch the day after the valley was given the all–clear to return home from the evacuation. She, like everyone else, gaped in horror at the meager charred remains of the ranch. So much of it had burned to ashes. So much more than anyone ever predicted. It wasn't all gone, of course. And more than half the buildings were still standing. But no one expected so many to burn, especially the main house. The house that had become the café where Jocelyn worked.

It was her first real, legitimate, and demanding job. She loved her job there. It was exciting, dynamic, and gave her a degree of authority. Every day, she met new guests to serve and interact with. She also ran the staff who answered to her directly as she coordinated, managed, and assigned their tasks. Turned out she was more than just a decent leader. She had no problem getting her underlings to work while also earning their respect and admiration. She liked being the one in charge of ordering food and figuring out the necessary quantities, which turned out to be another hidden talent she discovered: she was a champ at inventory evaluation.

But the café and all it involved were burnt to the ground.

The same day she witnessed how much of the ranch was burned, she also learned that Ben had taken off without a word to anyone. Other than a quick *See ya*, Ben vanished from River's End and Jack had all but vanished inside his house since that day. No one knew about Ben and Jocelyn and she intended to keep it that way forever. Forget it. Bury it. Deny it. But nature had a different agenda. At first, seeing that Ben was gone and the entire valley was flattened to a blackened plain, she approached the Rydells in need of both security and money.

The popular resort that employed her for the last four years was gone too. They lost half the cabins, and the formerly manicured grounds surrounding them were ruined. Ian told her right off the bat that it would be close to two years before the resort and ranch could be up and running again. He insisted they would get there though. And if she was interested, she was invited to be a huge part of it. Of course she was interested. As if she had any other options. Ha. No, for Jocelyn, it was either the Rydells or traipsing off all alone to apply for a low-level entry job and receive crappy wages. With the Rydells, at least she had a chance of acquiring higher wages as well as continued job growth.

In the meantime, there was plenty of work to do. Jocelyn participated in everything, from putting on leather gloves and carrying out the charcoaled debris to rotating the sprinklers and irrigating the parched crops in the insidious heat of that summer. She was up for it and had worked long, hard hours for the Rydells most of her life. In the aftermath of the fire, an unparalleled upwelling of community support and companionship provided the inspiration to rebuild. Some families were living on the Rydells' land in cabins that survived the inferno. Many other families were displaced.

The fire swept through so fast that many people didn't have enough time to get anything and only had the clothes on their backs. Many were also underinsured and could not rebuild. Others simply chose not to and left the town for good. The once popular valley had lost many of its former residents.

Everyone seemed to be walking around in a daze. The citizens who witnessed the fire or were unfortunately caught in it, like Jocelyn, possessed a collective sense of surreality toward their lives as the summer finally waned. No one knew what to do. Everywhere, as far as the eye could see, were harsh reminders of the devastating loss. The ugly brown landscape, devoid of all its former vegetation, and scrub brush, as well as bitterroot, sagebrush, and prairie grasses, told a horrifying tale. So many trees were reduced to being half–burned or completely blackened corpses.

Jocelyn clung to the Rydells. They were all she had left in the world, although they didn't know that. She never acted needy towards them or told them anything about her personal situation so they didn't have a clear picture of her utter reliance, as well as loyalty towards them.

Her mother ditched her when she was only thirteen. She had no qualms in leaving Jocelyn with Cutter Johnson, a man whom her mom always called her "uncle" even though he was never that. Her mom dutifully screwed the burly, old biker and in return, he allowed Jocelyn and her to stay in his shack. It was a clumsily nailed together monstrosity of fiber-board and uneven planks, along with all the other wood scraps Cutter managed to pull off the different construction sites he occasionally worked on. Even Cutter referred to his hovel as a *shack*.

That shack turned out to be Jocelyn's only home.

Her mom ran off while Jocelyn was at school one day.

Jocelyn started living there when she was ten. Now, at age twenty–four, she'd never considered anywhere home. No. Nope. Certainly not with Cutter. The grizzled old man. Perhaps he was age fifty when she first met him, with long hair, and a stringy beard that ended mid–chest. He was all gray and big with bushy eyebrows. He drank until he passed out every day and his broad face had a big, bulbous nose that nearly glowed in an eerie reddish and purple shade. Ma had plenty of boyfriends too. Other ones. But none of them would let her live with them. So Ma kept Cutter happy enough with her sexual favors while Jocelyn cooked and cleaned and did his laundry. That was their share of the rent, he claimed.

After three days of looking for her mom, Jocelyn finally concluded her mom had simply ditched her and left her with "Uncle Cutter." The lecherous way he looked at her as she got older made him the furthest thing from an uncle she could imagine.

She attended school with Joey and Ben Rydell. Joey, Jack's youngest brother, was two and a half years older, and Jack's son, Ben, was two years and two months younger than she. She'd been good friends with both boys since elementary school. When she started working on the ranch, she often stayed late to hang out with one or both of them. It was her safe haven from Cutter's shack and served her for the majority of her life. She'd only go back to Cutter's to sleep.

She avoided any encounters with Cutter at all and stayed because she had nowhere else to go. If he kicked her out, she would have begged for mercy on the Rydells' doorstep. There was nowhere else for her to go. Ma never mentioned where she came from, who her family was, or who her father was. She had no clue about her brief history. Without Cutter, she would have been orphaned and homeless, eventually relegated to foster care. She heard the stories, and who wanted that? The only security and constant in her life were River's End and the Rydells.

More importantly, River's End was her home. She knew every back road, valley, hidden lake and trickling stream. She knew each bend of the river and every ripple in the water. She spent all her time outside exploring the vacant, empty land that comprised the Gunderson Hills. She hiked, waded, climbed rocks, and swam. Were it not for all the space and outside activities, she'd have surely withered up and died.

Luckily, Cutter left River's End a lot. He rode his bike and disappeared for long stretches of time. That was the only relief Jocelyn got.

She moved out from Cutter's to rent a room in a lady's house after she graduated. It was located about a mile beyond River's End. It wasn't much, but so much better than the shack. Unfortunately, that house burned up in the fire. The few possessions she had were also incinerated. The money she managed to save was used to replace her lost items and start preparing for the coming baby. She had no renter's insurance so she received no help. After the fire, she returned to Cutter's shack. How ironic that she ended up staying at the shack.

Against all odds, the flimsy shack survived the fire. Jocelyn looked for it after the fire moved on, and paused on the hill below when she spotted it, standing unscathed against the otherwise black hill. Firefighters protected the area and managed to save many of the homes. She didn't mean to belittle their efforts and sacrifice. But she couldn't decide if she were happy or sad to see that the shack had survived the fire. Entire ranches, generation's old farm-houses, and large vacation homes were lost, yet this hideous shack survived? With a heavy heart, she made her way up to it. The scorched ground beneath her feet crunched as she walked across the drive and finally ventured inside.

How ironic. So many acres had burned and so many families, over three hundred, were ruthlessly displaced and yet, Jocelyn ended up back in the shack because of the fire.

Pregnant. That stunning fact left her shaking in fear for days. How could she be a *mother*? There was nothing about her that appeared motherly. At the time of the fire, she had a pierced tongue with a stud in it. Her short hair was recently shaved into a design in the back. The end's of her hair that was not shaved were finger–length and spiked up with bleached blond tips.

Now, she was pregnant. And nothing about her or the unfortunate circumstances of conception represented her ideal of a blessed pregnancy. Especially around this small–minded, conservative town.

She couldn't be a mother. But she was about to become one.

She was perhaps in some denial for many months. The pregnancy was relatively easy on her body and she managed to continue all her normal stuff. She wasn't reckless or stupid after all, but practical. And staying healthy for her baby was her first hurdle. She consulted the doctor and followed all the usual prenatal recommendations.

Second, her baby couldn't have a mother with a freaking barbell in her mouth. She removed it, as well as many more piercings. The holes were mostly closed up in her tongue and ears. Only the faintest impression of them remained. Her hair had also grown out to a few inches on top and the bottom part began to fill in. Conveniently, the top strands flopped down and covered the area where it was shaved. She let the coloring leach out of it so she was closer to her true dirty–blond color.

She tried to tone herself down; most of all, she didn't

want to embarrass her own child. Not like her mother embarrassed her. But in all honesty, she'd have clung to her mother any way she could have had her. She'd have given anything for her mom to come back and not leave her.

Jocelyn clutched the small bundle in her arms, now fast asleep, all swaddled up in a white blanket with silk edging. She would never leave her daughter. Or let her believe she wasn't good enough for her mom to stay and raise her. Her baby would never cry herself to bed at night wondering why her mom didn't like her. Jocelyn wanted her baby more now than *anything* else in the world.

No, her baby would never suffer from the pain of doubt or self–hatred.

That is, unless the Rydells found a way to take her away from Jocelyn.

With a deep breath, she finally met Joey and Erin's intense gazes. Erin skirted around the bed and came towards Jocelyn's head with a soft smile on her face. "You two look much better in here than you did on the floor of the cabin. I'm glad you're safe and okay, Jocelyn," Erin said as she ran a hand over Jocelyn's forehead as if to check her temperature. It was such a simple, gentle, motherly gesture. So soothing and comforting. Appreciated by any young girl, a gesture she should have received from her own mother, but never once did. Jocelyn made a mental note of it, deciding it was something she could do for her own daughter. Her mother had never done anything to calm or comfort her. Truthfully, her mother didn't seem to know how to do *motherly* things for Jocelyn. So Jocelyn had never learned.

The choking realization of how much she didn't know about childcare often made her respiration escalate before she felt dizzy. That had happened during many moments over the last nine months. She didn't even know the extent of her ignorance.

But the baby began to grow all the same. It didn't require much from her either. Just eating regular meals and exercising and taking some prenatal vitamins. She did all that anyway. But what about afterwards? When the little being inside her was born? She had no idea what came next, and no skills to prepare her; the ensuing fear of it all overwhelmed her at times. She had no one to turn to and no one to ask.

Until now. Erin and Joey came over to visit her.

"I'm glad she's okay," Joey said from the other side of her bed. He stared down at the sleeping baby, studying her perfect face. His smile was genuine and soft. "She's so beautiful."

"Thank you, Joey," Jocelyn replied, blushing to the roots of her hair. They had been friends for more than a decade. It humiliated her to realize she conceived her baby with Ben on *that* night, of all nights. But after giving birth on the floor of the shack with Jack acting as midwife, well, that was much more humiliating to remember as she faced Joey now.

He leaned closer and his lips brushed over her forehead. Sighing, he stared into her eyes. "You should have told me, Jocelyn. You should have come to me. You know I'd have helped you, don't you? You should have never chosen to do this all alone," he said softly. So polite. She closed her eyes. Years ago, she might have wished that Joey was the object of all those mushy, girly, crush–like feelings she had. But it wasn't Joey. And Joey didn't feel that ways toward her either. He all but considered her another dude to hang with. Just as she tried to project to the world. Except when it came to Ben. But of course, even to Ben, she was Jocelyn Jantz—girl jock. She was the tomboy, dude, gangsta–wannabe. She often worried that no one from River's End could ever fall for her. Especially the only person she wished would fall: Ben Rydell. She had a hard time trying to resist being taken in by him. He always treated her with the utmost courtesy, humor, and care. His sense of humor was never sarcastic or mean to Jocelyn. Of course, other guys made fun of her and some said she was a *dyke*. They called her "Joe" instead of "Jocelyn." They shoved her like they would have done to another guy. But they were worse than that too; they mocked her.

She was criticized for the way she dressed, having short hair, and doing unique dance moves. Her discomfort with anything traditionally girly earned her a "butch" reputation. High school was the worst of it. But Ben stuck by her side always. He helped her keep her sanity after school by insisting that she forget all the jerks who gave her crap. Ben thought she was cool. Was it any wonder, then, why she'd fallen for Ben Rydell? So many years ago. When was it exactly? Perhaps when he was about sixteen or seventeen. Yes, probably that long ago.

But Ben only had eyes for Marcy Fielding.

Ben was Jocelyn's best friend, however. Never Marcy's.

Tears filled her eyes. She sniffed, sucking in the snot that instantly blocked her sinuses. She shook her head. "I couldn't tell you, Joey. The circumstances and all... You heard about them, right?" she whispered before the rush of heat engulfed her chest, neck, cheeks and climbed all the way up to her forehead. She could not bear to look into either Joey or Erin's eyes.

"I understand everything, all the more reason why you should have told me—us." Joey kept his voice quiet and soft, showing deference to her sleeping infant, not to mention the delicate subject matter.

She sucked on her lower lip. "I didn't mean... for any of this to happen." She gently lifted her baby in her arms to indicate what *this* was. "Or what we did that night."

"You didn't have a crystal ball, Jocelyn. There was no way of knowing what could happen. The fire did a lot of damage and broke a lot of people's spirits and hearts. But there was no way for you to know Marcy would end up dying that same night."

"But the point is I—we..." She had to shut her eyes. There was no way to say what she had to without stating the obvious. Something her brain ultimately shied away from admitting. She was having sex with a married man whose wife was in the near vicinity. She dropped her chin to her chest, mumbling, "I'm so ashamed."

Erin continued to stroke her forehead. "Well, Ben was the married one. Ben had the wife. He chose to get involved. It's tragic, I don't deny that. But something this awful, miserable, heartbreaking, and honestly shocking can't be dealt with all alone. Oh, Jocelyn, how could you not come to us? You know we would have helped you."

"I was afraid you'd take her from me," she mumbled, tucking her chin down further in visible shame.

Joey leaned over her and put his index finger under her chin to lift her gaze back up. "No one will ever take your child away from you. I hope you understand and believe that. First, there is no way we *could* do that, even if we wanted to, which I can assure you, we don't. You are her legal mother. Now and forever."

Forever. His words made her heart swell. The shocking term of eternity. She'd never had anything *forever.* Whenever she started to imagine herself being responsible for this baby, she felt terrified. Hearing Joey announce that no one could take her baby from her *legally* was beyond intoxicating, exciting, and elating. Her heart burst with hope. Her baby...

"Joey's right. Nothing and nobody will separate her from you. Not even Ben. We would never let that happen."

"I just didn't know how to explain it to anyone. It's such an ugly story." Her voice broke and she shook her head. "How can I ever tell her what happened that night? And how she came to be?"

"Easy. You don't. You don't tell her anything. Some things aren't important. How she came into this world doesn't matter; that you had her is all that's important. Concentrate on that. Okay?" Erin said and her tone sounded so firm and sure.

Jocelyn glanced up at Erin, feeling so unprepared, knowing she possessed so little advice, guidance, reassurance, and support. How was she going to raise a baby if she didn't know any of these things?

"It was always Ben for you, wasn't it?" Joey asked as he backed up and sat down in the chair nearest the bassinet.

"Yes." She shrugged, pinning her gaze on the delicate, almost invisible fan of her baby's eyelashes on her lower eyelid. Compelled by an irresistible urge, she leaned forward and pressed her lips to the baby's soft forehead. She slowly inhaled the sweet scent, so unique and strong, reminding her of something innocent and original. She let the aroma fill her nostrils. She had no idea. None whatsoever. The bond she felt growing inside her. The unconditional love, the fierce protectiveness, and the undeniable need for her. Already. The gnawing it created inside her, like it could eat her alive. How could her ma have ever made the terrible choice to leave her? Why hadn't she felt the same desperate need for Jocelyn that she felt now for her newborn? Already, Jocelyn would rather die than live without her baby.

Joey leaned back and laced his fingers through his hair. "This must have been a very confusing experience for you. I'll forgive you for temporarily forgetting how much you mean to us: me, Jack, and Erin. All of us, actually. Just remember, you're not alone now, Jocelyn. We will always stand by you and help you, we promise to take care of you both."

Jocelyn shook her head. "I didn't do this just so I could become your next charity case."

"Oh, honey, you have no idea how hard having a baby is. No one can do it alone. Allison is one of the most capable people I know and even she couldn't do it. She's at the ranch now and more than willing to help you in any way you need. She can teach you all the basics of newborn care. I'm sorry, I can't compete with her. She's the go-to guru for babies.

"And as for your care, I saw that shack. How did you manage to keep that horrible secret from us all these years?"

Jocelyn averted her gaze from Joey. "I was just glad to be able to come to the ranch. It didn't really matter where I came from."

He cussed under his breath. "And Ben and I were too freaking self-absorbed and self-indulgent to even notice."

"You were both good friends to me. Don't ever doubt that."

"Oh, but I am doubting it. You could have died on the floor of that filthy wooden shack that barely has indoor plumbing. I more than respect what you just went through and feel ashamed that you had to. All of us were blind not to notice *you.*"

Erin nodded. "We would like for you and your baby to come back and live in Ben's apartment. He's gone now, Jocelyn. Marcy's gone too. It's just sitting there vacant. No one's using it. You gave birth to Ben's child, giving you every legitimate reason to live there. And even more than that, you work here too. You're a valuable and loyal employee. You've worked for the ranch and Jack reliably for more than a decade. Consider this a perk if you prefer not to feel like a 'kept' woman." Erin glared at Joey as he started to sputter and interrupt.

"There is nothing wrong with asking for help. Considering you're—"

"You're a Rydell, Joey, and therefore, you've always lived a privileged life. You don't know what it's like to feel helpless, lower than shoe–scum because you need help. Don't forget, I too was 'kept' by them. It's nothing to be ashamed of either. You're just being offered a residence in the same location where you work. Like the other survivors from the valley fire, you were burned out, and it isn't easy to pick yourself up again, especially when you're starting from scratch. You do still work for us. And that shack is no place for you to raise an innocent baby. There is no insulation, it's always too cold or too hot. It's not habitable, Jocelyn. Not for you or a newborn. Think of your baby."

Think of your baby.

Jocelyn sucked in a breath. That was something new. Thinking of someone else's needs. She held Erin's gaze before she dropped her head down. Erin was right. The shack was no place for this beautiful, new, unsullied baby to grow and thrive. It might have worked for Jocelyn, but it was not good enough for *her baby*.

"Okay."

Erin rubbed her forehead again. "Thank God," she sighed. "Jack left this morning to look for Ben. He's somewhere in Montana. Been there for a few months now. I didn't know Jack even knew where he was. I'm shocked actually that he didn't go after him before now. But as you know…"

"Jack hasn't been himself, not since the fire."

"No," Erin agreed softly, glancing up at Joey as they exchanged a look. "Things have been weird and off, some-times even awful since the fire, for more people than just you. So this? This baby? She is not awful, weird, or off. Okay? She's a freaking miracle, and I, for one, feel blessed to have her."

"He might be coming back." Jocelyn tried to keep the tremble out of her voice. She didn't want Ben to return now. She could not picture the moment of having to see him again.

"Of course, Jack will bring Ben back with him. I mean, that's the only decent thing to do."

Jocelyn tried not to gasp. It was true. Common decency demanded that she tell her baby's father about his daughter. But in her defense, she had no idea where to find Ben. She had not heard from him since the night they conceived the child. In all honesty, it was really such a weird twist of fate to learn that they did conceive her. Ben even used a condom from his wallet *that* night. Without any question, Jocelyn knew they had protected sex. That's why it was such a blow to discover this was the result.

"Ben will come back. He'll be there for you, and for his baby. He'll find a way to deal with his grief and surprise. I mean, it's Ben. He's as solid as Jack." Joey's tone sounded as if he had no doubts. Jocelyn's stomach cramped at the thought. How? How could she face Ben? After what they did? What they engaged in that night? How could she look him in the eye ever again? The image of what they were doing while his wife endured the most gruesome death imaginable was too much to cope with. She knew Ben remembered that night as one of betrayal and hatred.

Of course, it hadn't started out like that.

"So we're going to get an infant car seat. And some other basics and essentials. We'll help you get home too. When will they release you?" Erin asked.

"I have all that already. It's at my place. If you could stop there first and get it, along with my car, I'd appreciate it. I was prepared for most of this. Everyone else was surprised except me."

Joey leaned over and squeezed her shoulder. "That's the Jocelyn I know and rely on. Of course you were prepared. Yes. We will get all your stuff and your car."

"They said I could go home tomorrow morning." She had

stayed longer than most new mother's due to the fact they had a hard time keeping her baby's temperature stable.

"Then tomorrow it is." Erin's tone was firm. She hesitated before she asked, "Have you thought of a name yet?"

Glancing at both of them, Jocelyn shrugged. "I was thinking… maybe Lillian. But perhaps that's not appropriate…" She wimped out as her voice faded.

Erin's smile was gentle. "After Lily? Ben's mother. Of course, it's appropriate. I think it's a beautiful name."

"I don't know. He might hate knowing I chose it."

"Are you kidding? It's *his* daughter." Joey countered with something close to disgust in his tone.

"And I didn't want it to bug you either, Erin, considering she was once married to Jack."

Erin smoothed Jocelyn's forehead again. "First and foremost, she was Ben's mother. Of course I don't mind. I have not forgotten for one moment the mother of Charlie and Ben. I fully respect her place in their life and in Jack's. So I think it's the loveliest gesture, Jocelyn, and Ben better appreciate that."

"Okay. Then yes, I'll call her Lillian."

"Rydell?"

Jocelyn's eyes lifted to Erin. "Um. I don't know. I hadn't thought that out. But legally, I suppose that would be the case. Lillian Rydell." It made her heart swell. Never in all her fantasies of being with Ben could she have foreseen a scenario such as this. His baby. Her baby. His mother's name on her baby. And Marcy. Marcy still stood between all of them. But it hurt too, knowing her baby didn't have the same name as she.

"Fitting. I didn't have the same name as my mother either," she muttered more to herself than to Joey and Erin.

"Pardon?"

She glanced up. "My mother claimed she gave me my

father's last name, which is Jantz. Hers was Waverly. I didn't know my father. Not for even one day. My mom was fourteen when she had me. I grew up and never had the same name as my mother either. It bothered me when I was young. Like I didn't really belong to anyone that I knew, you know? Just as Lillian's name now won't belong to me either. I just never meant for any of this to happen."

Joey leaned down and kissed her forehead. "Rest. Relax. It's done and over, okay? You aren't your mother, and you're not fourteen either. You are strong and you can handle this. The Jocelyn I know and admire can handle anything. Remember her? One day at a time from here on out, and remember this: you're not alone. We're a big damn family and that can only benefit you."

Her lips compressed. "I don't remember her right this moment." Lying supine in a hospital bed after having given birth, she was holding a sweet–smelling, tiny girl. No way. There was nothing even remotely Jocelyn–like about that scene.

Her mind drifted as Joey and Erin both left, but not before they planted kisses on her forehead and left plenty of assurances they would be back tomorrow. They'd help her go home. They discussed the necessary supplies, formula, diapers, wipes as well as the logistics of how to get Jocelyn and her baby settled in. She shuddered. Imagine going to live on the ranch.

She'd never had a real home. The wilds of the hills and fields, the river and mountains of River's End were the closest thing to home for her. She didn't look or act the part of a native from River's End. Jack, Ian and Ben sure did with their cowboy hats, boots and country music blaring from their pickup trucks. She may not have dressed the part either but she belonged in the wild backcountry of her hometown. It was all she had. It defined who she was.

But it wasn't exactly newborn–friendly.

Her eyes fluttered shut as her baby slept quietly in her arms.

That night, the fire night, haunted her for the first time in nine months. She never analyzed it. She never allowed herself to experience it.

She flopped her head back onto the hospital pillow and stared up at the white tiled ceiling. What did it matter anyway? It was adultery. Tawdry. Wrong. Everything about that night was bottled into a shameful, treacherous mistake. A betrayal of everything decent in the world.

Even if Lillian were the epitome of everything decent in her life.

When it happened, they hadn't even talked about Marcy for hours. They were talking about *them.* Laughing, flirting, and having fun. Almost… almost like what a first date might be. The moment, where it all started, was as unplanned and startling to Ben as it was to her. It was like they finally looked at and saw each other, or rather, *he* finally looked at her and saw something he'd never seen before.

She'd faltered in those moments under Ben's scrutiny and attention. She forgot all of the reasons why she should not have been with him. She did not feel she was being used as Ben's instrument of revenge. In that critical moment, she never imagined she'd end up pregnant and soon become the most despised woman in the valley.

Of course, she never dreamt Marcy would die either.

They had sex. Whatever label and nasty name you want to call it. But in those precious few moments together, it didn't feel like anything so negative. She thought they'd simply found each other at last and could finally express their thoughts through touch, kisses, and mutual affection. They communicated their words through their hands.

She never intended to entice a man to cheat on his wife.

She never dreamt of what would happen next.

In her former brief flashes of her fantasy, Ben could eventually divorce Marcy, and she might stand a chance with him. A real one. A grown-up one, like they'd never had before.

Jocelyn wiped her tears again. She vowed she'd never tell anyone. But now? People were finding out on their own. She'd have to live with that, facing the public gossip and scorn not to mention, Ben. She never intended to do anything so terrible or live the role of the other woman; certainly not to besmirch, and literally spit in the face of a dead girl. She might have hated Marcy in real life, but she never wished for her death. And now, Jocelyn could barely tolerate the knowledge of her part in the whole affair.

Lillian slept soundly in her arms. Jocelyn nearly burned up with shame as she began remembering that night, while this innocent angel, the living result of that night, slept silently in her arms. Yin and yang. Heaven and hell. Sin and redemption. All those things were symbolized in this tiny bundle she held in her arms.

No. Lillian's birth was not a sin. She wasn't even a mistake. She wasn't an instrument of betrayal or a means of revenge. And no matter how many people frowned and gossiped about what Jocelyn did, she'd spend her last breath making sure that no one scorned Lillian or blamed her for her mother's sin. Lillian could never be exposed to those thoughts. She didn't deserve it. Jocelyn jiggled her baby slightly, suddenly afraid to admit the feelings she experienced. No. She had to bury them. If Ben came back, it would never matter. That night was the means and Lillian was the end, and nothing else. It meant nothing else. Nothing good and nothing evil. That is how she'd remember that night. And no matter how long it took her, she'd make sure that everybody else knew it.

And as for Ben? He didn't matter anymore. Not to her. He

had no effect on how she thought about her daughter. He might, someday, mean something to Lillian. Jocelyn didn't plan to hold her breath while counting on that, however.

Only her sweet baby mattered to Jocelyn now, and nothing else.

CHAPTER 4

*H*IS DAD DIDN'T LEAVE. Ben walked out of his room, groggy and hungover again, only to find his dad sitting out on the bench. He didn't turn at Ben's disheveled appearance. He merely sat stock-still and stared out over the pot-holed, dusty, partially graveled parking lot. There were four trucks, including his own inside it. What the hell? Why wasn't his dad all over him, strong-arming him to come home? That's what his dad usually did. He ordered and commanded everyone, and those who heard it jumped to. If they ignored him? His dad would keep hounding them until they obeyed.

He leaned back against the door of his room, closing his eyes to block the bright sunshine. He tried to shut out the familiar feeling of his dad being there. He almost walked right on past him and got into his pickup, but still, Jack sat there silently. With a sigh of resignation, he stopped and sat down next to him.

Jack's eyes were closed. He opened them and glanced at Ben. Ben could see the fatigue in them and the redness. Did Jack get drunk last night, all alone in his motel room? Just like Ben? Ben shook his head, somewhat unsure how the hell that could have happened. "I need to get to work now. Are you leaving today?"

Jack shrugged. "Not sure. Maybe I'll just stay here for a little while. Slept pretty well last night. It felt good. Mind if we get some dinner together?"

What the hell? What kind of manipulative shit was Jack using? But twenty-two years of constant training couldn't alter Ben's deference, despite all his efforts to change over the last nine months. "Whatever you want to do, Jack."

Hearing his sarcasm, Jack merely lifted one lip. "You would shock Erin right now. She called and said Jocelyn's being released this morning."

"Where's she going? To our home? The ranch where she's always worked and most likely wished she could belong to? I guess I was the perfect solution for her to get what she wanted, huh?"

Jack shook his head. "No, son. If you recall, it was your wife who did that. Not Jocelyn. But it's ancient history now, huh?"

Ben's mouth gaped in astonishment. Jack never once criticized Ben for choosing Marcy as his girlfriend. Not since they were teens and his dad and Erin caught him and Marcy trying to have sex for the first time. He managed to shame them enough that time to delay it for two more years. Ben hooked up with Marcy during his senior year of high school. From the moment his dad found out, he kept quiet about it. Ben sensed his disapproval nonetheless. He was sure his dad didn't want Ben to get married to her. But to outright insult her? To actually suggest he believed she was after Ben for something besides love? Jack simply stood up and walked into his room without glancing at Ben again for a reaction or an answer.

Who the hell was this stranger?

Dejected. Tired. Ben dragged his sad ass to work. He only received two chew-outs by the foreman. He used to be the star worker on any crew, the one that outdid every other worker and followed the instructions and codes flawlessly, as if he thought he could earn extra credit. But now? Nah. He just did the minimum required and earned enough to keep eating. He irritated his foreman on a daily basis with his lackluster performance and apathy. Ben had a hunch he'd be getting kicked to the curb pretty soon, and it didn't matter to him anymore. He was ready to move on anyway.

He sighed at seeing Jack's truck parked there all big and black and bad-ass. His dad's one indulgence was driving new trucks. Every few years, he bought himself a newer, better, blacker truck. That was his one guilty pleasure, since Jack wasn't exactly extravagant.

Jack opened his motel room door and lounged against the doorway. Ben got out of his dusty truck and approached him. His dad's gaze traveled over him. "Hangover ease up any?"

He noticed? Ben had never done anything to excess in front of his dad. Not alcohol. Not swearing. Not women. Certainly not drugs. Now? He'd obviously surrendered to all of them. He had to in order to live with the knowledge that the woman he vowed his fidelity to for the rest of his life was burning alive while he was having sex with someone else. Someone who now had his baby to raise.

The images of Marcy kept trickling in no matter how much he tried to banish them. He almost begged the thoughts to have mercy on him. Just to leave him alone. Let him be. Let him live. He didn't want to go back there. Back in time. And that night. When he was Ben Rydell. Married to Marcy. Using Jocelyn. And he definitely did not want to go back to River's End.

But there was a baby now.

Which meant, and Ben knew it, that somewhere in his

heart, the urge to return home was irresistible; he had no choice but to go back. "Yeah, it finally eased."

Jack nodded, straightening up and standing beside the door. "Jocelyn named her Lillian. After your mom. She asked Erin and Joey's permission first."

Lillian. It—the baby—*she*—had a name. His mother's name.

"Who gave Erin and Joey the authority to give her permission?"

"There's no one else to ask now, is there? And it's her baby. She can name it whatever she chooses. Look, I get this is a shock, and all that, but you did have sex with her, whatever the circumstances, and things like this do happen. I have to go back home. I meant it when I said you owe her a financial responsibility at the bare minimum. I will see to it that you honor that debt if you try and disappear again. But other than that? I can't tell you to do anymore. I'm asking you though, will you just come home? Don't you want to meet her? Lillian Rydell. Jocelyn gave her your name. Anyway, come back with me and meet her, and then you can decide what you're going to do about it." Jack shrugged and added, "Or not. I think it could go either way with you, nowadays."

Lillian. Lillian Rydell. His daughter.

That meant nothing to him. However, only a year ago, it would have meant everything. But a year ago, Marcy would have been the mother to his child. Not Jocelyn. So why was his father half expecting him not to come home and do the right thing? He seemed to have half the energy, interest, and potency that usually characterized Jack Rydell. In many ways, his transformation left Ben feeling almost bereft. Where was his former passion? His compassion and concern? The interest he always demonstrated in whatever Ben did? For his entire life, Jack's word was the law, and the one goal Ben always held most dear was to please his dad.

Make his dad proud. It was a hard habit to break. Now? At the most vital, pivotal point of his life, when he was facing real circumstances with lasting consequences, Jack was almost shrugging his shoulders, saying *Whatever?* He seemed to have little or no expectations of Ben. It was as if he'd entered some kind of alternate universe.

Ben expected Jack to start ordering him to act. Telling him to square his shoulders and fight Jack if he disagreed with him. His always-present anger was eager and ready to lash out. But now Jack looked too damn tired to even argue with him. He wanted Ben to come home, but seemed resigned to let Ben do whatever he decided without much of a protest.

What the fuck was this?

"I don't want to go back there."

Jack closed his eyes, his shoulders drooping. "Please, Ben. You have to understand, you must come home. At least once. Just to… you know, figure out the baby thing."

Baby thing? Ben could not fathom why his dad wasn't pressuring him to step up and be a father. Help Jocelyn. Be the man that Jack raised him to be. But then again, Jack didn't raise him to be a liar, or a cheater, or a man who would father a baby outside of his marriage. Let alone, the grim circumstances that surrounded Ben's cheating and subsequent death of his wife. The unforgivable, unparalleled circumstances.

"Besides, I promised Erin I'd convince you to come home. It's the least I owe her. Things have been… not too good for a while. I'm asking for just a small amount of your time."

It was not the reasoning Ben expected to hear coming from his dad's mouth. What the fuck was wrong with Jack? Or Ben for that matter? He glanced down at himself. Dirty clothes, unwashed, and not just the dirt he got from work. He had food stains on the once-white T and stunk of BO and booze and marijuana. He sighed, closing his eyes. Who was he anymore?

"Yeah. Not much choice, huh?"

Jack indicated the negative. "Not really, no."

His subsequent agreement came in the form of a jerky nod.

~

JOCELYN FOLLOWED Erin inside the door. Her stomach twisted in revulsion as she entered the living space, which was fairly recently occupied by the now deceased Marcy Rydell. They were living above one of the outbuildings. It was originally a loft, which they converted into a one-room apartment. There was a bedroom and a small bathroom. The kitchen and dining room were combined and the couch and TV area sat right next to it. The windows looked out towards the river. It was small, cozy, and flooded with natural light.

Nothing less than a palace. Jocelyn had never seen, much less lived in anything like it.

"We moved all of their stuff out months ago. It's being stored at our place. Really, Jocelyn, you belong here. Don't look so sick about it."

Jocelyn cuddled Lillian against her chest. At a loss for words, she simply nodded. "It's so nice."

Erin scoffed. "Marcy never thought so. She wanted to live in the main house."

"I know. I always heard that. I didn't know you did."

Erin shrugged. "What could I do? Or say? Late-in-life stepmothers have to watch their p's and q's when it comes to late-in-life stepsons. I refused to lose Ben by divulging all of my complaints about her."

"I felt the same way."

Erin smiled. "Well. I did know that. I don't think anyone within fifty miles didn't know."

"I so regret every rude remark, snarky comment, and gossipy tidbit I ever said about or to her. It makes what I did, and how I ended our feud, so much worse."

"There are a lot of people who have plenty of regrets since the fire. There was no way you could have known. And Marcy was a difficult person to be around for much longer than a brief conversation."

"You noticed that too? It wasn't just me?"

"Oh, sure I noticed. Again, Jack and I just kept things like that to ourselves; we were so unwilling to push Ben away because of her unpleasantness. We felt he needed our support all the more for how difficult she turned out to be."

"It still makes none of it right. No matter how 'difficult' or whatever she was. Stealing her husband on the night she died? No one could have deserved that ending."

"No. We agree on that. But don't allow the ending to rewrite her whole life. I'm sure you can't forget her attitude. Her sense of entitlement. And how she used people with so little thought or care, including Ben."

"But it almost seems like making up justification for what Ben and I did."

"Maybe it is. However, it's also the truth about her. But *you* didn't kill her, Jocelyn. Remember that." Erin came closer. "Let's discuss maternity leave. You need a few months off, you know, to nurse and bond and take care of Lillian and heal. We'll be around… Kailynn and I, and most helpful of all, Allison. In fact…"

The sound of footsteps preceded the opening of the door before the red-headed Allison Rydell, Shane's wife and Ben's aunt, appeared. She smiled warmly at everyone. In her mid-thirties, she had just given birth to a healthy baby only three weeks ago. Now baby Iris was cuddled snugly against her chest in a wrap–around, rather elaborate sling.

"Hello, Jocelyn." Again, such a kind voice. As if Jocelyn deserved it. Their unsolicited respect and help, not to mention their endless patience made her almost feel as if she were a deserving new mother.

She tightened her grip on her baby. She didn't deserve it, but her baby did.

"So? Let me see her." Allison's smile was wide and welcoming. Motherly. There was so much of that maternal vibe flying around here, and being directed toward her. So much that Jocelyn fidgeted under their rapt attention. Her life lacked any motherly gestures directed towards her. Jocelyn held Lillian out towards Allison, who did the same with her own newborn, Iris. Jocelyn shuffled her feet, suddenly unsure of how to respond. She lacked the experience to share any newborn and mothering tips with another woman. She was twenty–four years old, but right then, she felt more like sixteen when it came to that subject.

"If you need anything, *anything at all*, please call me. I'm here on the ranch too, always around. Just taking care of the girls, so I'm happy to help you in whatever you ask." Her cheerful smile wavered. "Last year, I could have given you an entire wardrobe and every gadget you could have ever contemplated having for a baby. But…"

It burned in the fire. Sitting on the couch, *Marcy's couch*, Jocelyn couldn't help sniffling as the unfamiliar knot of emotions lodged in her throat. No one had ever offered their help to her before. And she winced at how many times in the last nine months she'd heard the word "burned." Far too many. Jocelyn nodded. "I'm very sorry you lost everything."

She and Shane were currently living in what was previously Joey's house. They were nearly done with the rebuilding of their house, which also burned in the infamous fire of last summer. They lost their entire household: furniture, clothes, pictures, baby equipment and Allison's most cherished family heirlooms.

Allison lifted her face and dabbed her eyes. "It's so dumb, but it still makes me cry. It's not the worst thing that's happened to me. It was all just stuff before, things. But..."

"They were *your* things, and *your* stuff. Your family's entire life's belongings," Jocelyn supplied in sympathy.

"Yes. As grateful as I am that none of us were hurt or worse, it sometimes doesn't ease the reality that something pretty big and tragic actually happened. I mean, in a matter of only minutes, both Shane and I lost thirty–plus years of keepsakes and memories. And Rosie's stuff? All gone. Sometimes..."

"Just because someone else might have no feet doesn't change how you feel if you have no shoes," Jocelyn quoted. It was one of her favorite sayings that she'd ever heard.

"What?"

"Well, if you don't have shoes, your feet will eventually be cold or bruised or blistered, right? You'll suffer without shoes. Maybe even get frostbite. Whatever. Well, obviously you're better off than someone who lost both of their feet but that doesn't negate or diminish the fact that you still need shoes. Or you are doomed to endure the consequences of not having shoes, right? The person without any feet might have even worse and different problems, but at least, they won't have cold, blistered, bruised or frostbitten feet, right? They don't need a pair of shoes. You do."

Allison's bark of a laugh was gusty and long. She finally leaned over, roaring so hard that tears came to her eyes. "That's morbid and terrible. But also a wonderful illustration of this. Sometimes, I get so tired of having to convince myself how grateful I am, but you know? My entire house, my lovely home, burned up right before my eyes. Every dream and design and all the time, energy, resources, and money we invested burned up in minutes. Yes, we grieve for our home. And our stuff. We're all fully conscious and aware of how bad it could have been, but yes, it still did happen and we lost a lot. It uprooted everyone and caused havoc in our lives. People who have never watched their entire lives burn up in front of their eyes have no idea how cruel, random, and merciless it is."

"And so many from here were victims," Jocelyn agreed quietly.

She stared at Lillian when they left a half hour later. Everyone fussed and baby–talked to Lillian. They offered Jocelyn meals and sincere comfort as well as a break. Lillian was awake, and her eyes were huge, like blue coins in her small, pink round face. She had fat cheeks like a cherub, all rosy. There was only the hint of hair on top of her head. A faint red patch of peach fuzz. Red. Like Ben.

Jocelyn silenced her brain. No! Lillian simply belonged to her.

And beautiful? Lillian was the most beautiful sight Jocelyn had ever beheld. She kept staring at her, losing minutes, and massive blocks of time spent merely gazing at Lillian. She loved watching her arms move all about, while her little fingers and toes jiggled back and forth. She would often startle in sleep and her entire body would jerk in surprise, making Jocelyn smile to herself as waves of tenderness overtook her. In only a matter of days, Jocelyn could not imagine herself without Lillian in her life.

There was so much for her to remember. So many little details. She learned the different ways to wrap Lillian snugly in a blanket. The schedule for how often she ate and slept as well as changing her diaper had to be followed. Not to mention the more serious concerns, like SIDS and her inexplicable phobia of driving in a car now. She never felt her heart clench so violently in fear and it happened to her about a dozen times in the last three days. Every single time she woke up, she frantically checked on Lillian to make sure she was still breathing. Her heart climbed up into her throat until she knew she was fine. Then, every single muscle in her body would relax.

Her attempts at breastfeeding felt odd. There was something not right about it. Jocelyn's boobs were huge compared to what they normally were. Hard as rocks, they were as painful as an infected wound. Swollen to the point of bursting, her milk didn't seem to come out right. Her embarrassment at her ineptness kept her silent that first night in Ben's apartment. No matter how many times she tried to get Lillian to latch on, something wasn't working. Lillian would latch on with her gums and then unlatch before screaming in frustration and hunger while Jocelyn cried right along with her in despair, unsure of what to do next.

She sat up on the couch with Lillian crying in her arms. What was she doing wrong? She didn't know. But Lillian kept crying and her swollen boobs kept aching. Stretched to the point of leaking like a faucet, they squirted out pin streams of milk. And then, nothing. Except they hurt.

She survived two more days breastfeeding, or trying to, this way. She hadn't showered since leaving the hospital and scrounged whatever food Erin kindly left for her, while jiggling, walking, and doing her best to soothe Lillian. When anyone came to check on her, she lied and claimed Lillian was crying because she had just woken up .

What was wrong?

Finally, she knew she had to overcome her own guilt and ask for help. Guilt prevented her from depending on any of the Rydells. But her stubbornness wasn't helping Lillian. And her pride no longer ruled anymore, not where Lillian's welfare was concerned. Dejectedly, she wrapped Lillian up tightly in blankets.

With a sigh of defeat, she went to Allison's front door and knocked, feeling timid and unsure. Her face burned up with shame when Shane answered. To her surprise, not a trace of surprise or shock at her presence showed on his face. Just a welcoming smile. "Hey, there Jocelyn. Come in. Come in. Let me see the little angel."

Shane was a huge man, and tattooed and intimidating. He was the antithesis of Allison. Jocelyn often wondered how those two ever got to the point of having sex, let alone getting married and having kids. Shane used baby–talk, which was at the least startling to hear coming from him. Lillian, however, was not consoled and simply cried some more.

Shane grinned. "I bet you need Allison. Let me get her and give you two some privacy, okay?"

Jocelyn nodded, eager for Allison's advice and the privacy. She was grateful to see he was smart enough to offer it. He left and Allison came down the hallway a few minutes later. "How long has she been crying like this?"

"Since I saw you last."

Allison nodded. "How's the breastfeeding going?"

"I don't know. I mean I try… but she won't stay on. It's… it's so painful."

"Can I see? May I watch how you do it? Maybe she's not latching onto you right."

Jocelyn suffered three shades of embarrassment but sat down and took Lillian on her lap. She tried to remember all the tips the nurse at the hospital showed her. She tucked Lillian's head up with a pillow provided by Allison and lifted her shirt up. Wincing when she aimed her boob into Lillian's small mouth, she urged her to suck and Lillian opened her mouth but something didn't work. She grew frustrated and turned a deep shade of red while Jocelyn cringed as she watched her cry harder.

"Oh, honey, you're all engorged. She can't latch on because of it. See? It's nearly flattened your nipple right out. Here, I have something that will help you. The same thing happened to me with Rosie."

She came back with a little plastic thing that looked like a miniature sombrero. "It's called a nipple shield. I had to go back to the hospital with Rosie when I got so engorged and she wouldn't latch on correctly. I used this for just a few days each time I nursed her until my engorgement lessened, and my milk supply regulated. Eventually, my nipples became soft and puckered, the way they are supposed to be. This little gadget worked wonders for me. Would you like to try it?"

"Desperately. Anything to help ease this is a pure godsend."

"Just put this over your nipple. Switch boobs and start feeding her often until your milk supply starts to regulate. It will too, honey. Just hang in there."

Jocelyn obeyed her instructions despite initially heating up at all the nipple talk. This was with a woman she'd only discussed pleasantries or problems at the ranch before now. She was Ben's aunt and Joey's sister–in–law, but always had been an authority figure to Jocelyn, who felt so embarrassed still. "This will allow her to stay latched on and ease your engorgement."

Jocelyn nodded, hot tears filling her eyes and her lips trembled. "I had no idea…"

Allison was sitting near her and noticed her tears. "Oh, hey, Jocelyn, you're okay. I swear. I had no idea about that either. When I had Rosie, I learned how hard the first few weeks with a newborn can be. You're not alone or imagining it. It's so hard. And especially when any little thing goes wrong." She gently rubbed Jocelyn's shoulder. "I swear to you, it will get easier. You'll get the hang of it all. I promise. And soon, you'll be able to shower again."

Jocelyn's smile was self-deprecating as she lowered her head. "Yes, I haven't figured that out yet. She hasn't quit crying so I was afraid…"

"Call on me. Or Erin. Kailynn. I'm serious. We're all right here. Not even a mile separates all of us, right? We need to use that to our mutual benefit."

"It's hard when you feel like an imposter."

Allison's smile faded. "Jocelyn, no one intends to punish you for what happened. Don't forget: Lillian is right here. Huh? There is no use crying over what should or shouldn't be. If you insist on crying, then let's cry over what's going on right now, today. We can both cry over how exhausting these tiny creatures you love so much are."

Her lips lifted into a small smile. "It is. And I do love her."

"Switch breasts now." Allison nodded. Jocelyn did and relaxed slightly when one breast already felt less full.

It was an odd feeling, almost like gravel beading up inside the skin of her breasts. "Why did this happen?"

"Because your milk came in and your body's trying to regulate it to the baby's needs. Too much. Too little. Somehow, you produced too much, and Lillian wasn't able to latch on and get enough, which only made the problem worse. Not your fault. And fixable."

"It's already feeling better."

Allison smiled. "Good. Now, when you're done with her feeding, why don't I take her while you go and have a nice, long relaxing shower? And you can do this fun thing called 'expressing some milk.' Do it often and it's easy in the shower. It'll help relieve the swelling and soreness." She went on to explain what to do. Still blushing, Jocelyn felt no longer bad-ass or tough. Becoming a mother had her discussing private body parts and their functions in ways she never dreamed of with near strangers.

"I can't ask you to watch her."

"Well, yes, you can. And then later on, when I need you, you can return the favor with Iris. That is, if you're comfortable doing so."

"If you trust me, I can."

"Of course, I trust you. We're both here with newborns, so who better to help each other? Besides, they'll grow up like cousins. If you stay here, that is. And I hope you decide to stay."

"River's End is my only home. I have nowhere else to go. And no reason to go. Other than perhaps the gossip that might haunt me and therefore Lillian."

Allison shook her head. "We won't let you be driven out of here by small–minded hens. This is not the last century, Jocelyn. Okay? Now, go have a hot shower. Take a break. We'll be fine. Look at how content she is now." And she was. Lillian had quit crying and was looking around, staring up at the ceiling. Jocelyn nodded, hurrying into her temporary apartment, but feeling quite odd to be suddenly without Lillian. But she successfully breastfed her. Her breasts still hurt, but a degree less than before, and she was relieved to know Lillian was finally receiving proper nourishment. During the hot shower, she expressed more milk by following Allison's instructions. When she came back, she was clean and her breasts had considerably less burning pain than they did hours before. She felt so refreshed, she could face the coming night.

Each night was turning into a unique experience. Lillian cried most of the nights so far, and Jocelyn had to walk her throughout the wee hours. She often felt particularly lonely to be up at those hours, alone in *Marcy's apartment*. All her sins tripled in magnitude and scope at night, which seemed longer and darker and lonelier. Tonight, with a full tummy, maybe Lillian would sleep longer.

"Is she sleeping through the night at all?" Allison asked when Jocelyn started to leave.

"No. But maybe now that she can nurse properly, it'll help her sleep."

"Yes. She might also have her days and nights confused. Hang in there, Jocelyn, it all evens out. In the meantime, I'll contact Erin and we'll both be happy to take turns at giving you a few hours in the day to nap, shower, and eat. You have to take care of yourself too, you know. You've heard of post-partum blues, right?"

"Yeah, the hospital told me all the signs to watch for."

"Yes, it can occur to anyone, at any time. It's a hormonal imbalance thing. So don't think you're all alone and don't have anyone to relieve you. I always had Shane. But we'll help you."

Shane walked in just as Allison was finishing her sentence. He nodded. "Hell, yes. I've been known to calm a crying infant or two. I can help you too."

Jocelyn's cheeks burned up with shame and gratitude. Imagine Shane Rydell playing nursemaid to her daughter. But then again, why not? He was usually around and had two small children of his own. Jocelyn guessed he knew more than triple what she knew about babies.

"I can't thank you enough."

"Rydell. Her name is Lillian Rydell. She belongs here, same as the rest of us. No thanks necessary. Simply what should be," Allison reassured her.

That evening, Kailynn came by with a premade dinner, and enough leftovers for the next several nights. "I am clue-less when it comes to newborn care, but I can cook the hell out of any kitchen, so that's my contribution," Kailynn explained.

Jocelyn shook her head. "You don't have to do anything. I mean, I can't tell you how much I appreciate it, but…"

"It's family. Actually, no, it's out of friendship. You're a friend to so many Rydells here. Joey. Me. And none of us had a very clear picture about the few family members you do have. None of us realized how alone you were in the world. So, to hell with any guilt. You realize, I hope, that I was once the Rydells' housekeeper for years. I earned my family's primary wage. My two brothers made their living by working at the ranch. The Rydells also helped me then, and elevated me to where my family is today. So actually, I do get it, Jocelyn. And taking care of a newborn alone? No. I can't imagine. Don't feel guilty for a little bit of babysitting and meals." Kailynn shook her head. "No. Our help is always offered to anyone in need, but especially to you."

And so they helped her. There were many long hours, about nineteen per day where Jocelyn was alone with Lillian, but that brief window of help they provided managed to keep her sane. Being a mother to Lillian was an exhausting endeavor of which she could not imagine doing without that break. She lived for the temporary respites. The adult company, lively conversation, heavenly showers, and the advice. Most of all, the meals and gossip. It helped liven up what would have otherwise been a completely isolating experience. Having worked at the Rydell River Resort for the last four years, she spent her days interacting with all types of people who were guests of the establishment, along with the Rydells. Being alone in an apartment wasn't something she ever experienced. When she wasn't working, she usually hung out with her friends from around the valley. She went swimming, hiking or dancing. She'd never been so sedentary in her life. Nor felt so exhausted either.

But a week into living on the ranch, Erin suddenly ran up to her door and exclaimed, "They'll be back today. I just wanted you to have all the forewarning and notice you could."

Jocelyn nodded. Her stomach clenched with sharp cramps. She didn't want Ben to return. But then again, it was Ben's home. Ben's family. Ben's ranch. Not hers. She was the first to admit how much she needed and valued the women of the ranch's help. Well, and Shane too. He came by twice and stayed on while she went to her shack to grab some things as well as the gear she had collected for Lillian. Even Joey took Lillian for an entire evening when Hailey, his girlfriend, came to visit. So really, it wasn't just the women. Ian dropped by occasionally and checked on her too, all of his own accord. When he went to the store, he always asked her what she needed. At first, she'd been too shy to request things, but finally, she gave him a list of supplies. He returned with everything and refused payment.

He grinned and confessed, "I'm a little terrified to be left alone with her," nodding towards Lillian, who slept in Jocelyn's arms. "I'm not like Shane, but when she's a bit older and I don't have to worry about that neck thing with babies, well, I'm your man then. My worst fear is breaking them until that time. They're so fragile and delicate at this age. But I promise I'll be here for you in the meantime, and I'm happy if I can provide you with any essentials."

She had committed a sin, a moral crime in how her baby came into existence and now, all the Rydell family did was support and help her. Their kindness, along with their entire attitude toward her, were based on respect. Friendship. Concern. Worry. Care. They faithfully kept watch on her for signs of depression or being overwhelmed. One day, Lillian didn't sleep the entire day and cried incessantly, so Erin ordered her to leave. Erin took her while Jocelyn simply walked down the road, clearing her head, and savoring the quiet repose. By the time she came back to her still–

screeching newborn, her temperament was fully restored, her stress levels were visibly reduced and she managed to continue holding and soothing the crying baby until she successfully calmed her down.

Erin also knew how to soothe Lillian, which Jocelyn often observed. "You're so good with babies. How come you and Jack never had any?"

Erin smiled, letting her gaze drift off towards the river. "I don't know. Maybe his age, or his two older children. My dyslexia. I've spent the last six years figuring out how to even learn how to read. It was the main focus for me and I didn't consider much else. Honestly? Dyslexia is a disorder I wouldn't wish on anyone. It's hereditary."

Jocelyn's gaze sharpened on Erin, rather astonished at her reasoning. "But you'd know what to do now. You could find out early, and not let your child suffer like you did. Was it really that bad?"

"Yes. It was." She shook her head. "I don't know, I think I could enjoy helping you with yours, Jack's grandchild. And that could be enough maternal bonding for me. I love this ranch, the horses, and this lifestyle. I don't feel that having my own children is necessary for me. I have Charlie and he's been more than enough to participate in raising."

"You're always so diplomatic."

"Again, late–in–life stepmother. I had to know my place. We took it slow, and I never assumed I could replace their mother or any of their memories about their mother. Their birth mother, I mean."

"Still, Erin, you're really patient, and kind and loving. I think it's a shame you don't pass those positive traits along to your own child. Maybe even the dyslexia, since who better than you could turn it into a positive experience?"

Her laugh was bittersweet. "I never once thought of it as being a positive experience. But thank you all the same."

Jocelyn really didn't want Ben to come back. As she remembered the circumstances, dealing and sorting through how Lillian's conception came to be, she was more convinced that Ben and she shared nothing, except for *that.* The sin was the only thing between them. They betrayed Marcy and everything moral and decent. She didn't want to share Lillian with Ben.

Besides, the pinching pain in her gut was fueled by her dread. Her reluctance to face Ben Rydell after their last encounter was so tangible, she could taste it. She remembered her last words to him. At the time, she didn't understand their lasting effects.

Closing her eyes, Jocelyn relived her last and worst memory of Ben Rydell and her.

CHAPTER 5

~*Night of the River's End fire– August 14^{th,} the previous summer*~

JOCELYN COME UPON THE group of teens and twenty–somethings, all milling around together on an old logging road, well away from the prying eyes of adults and cops. There were quite a few underage high school teens as well as older crowds of people like her. The sun was setting behind them and they were up very high, on a flat spot that overlooked the valley below. There had been several lightning strikes across the state that occurred the night before and several fires were reported. In deference to the extreme heat, as well as their collective weariness of fires, there was no bonfire lit that night. But the loud music blasted from the trucks as beer and food were passed around liberally. It was an hour or so before she even noticed Ben Rydell and soon afterwards, Marcy. Ben could never escape Jocelyn's notice. If he were within a mile radius, she always seemed aware of him. He wasn't smiling now, however. His expression was grim. He took out a black flask and downed half of it, his throat vibrating as the intoxicating liquid disappeared. So not something Ben would usually do.

Marcy Rydell. Her name left Jocelyn's tongue tasting bitter, as if she just bit down on a coffee bean. She hated the girl, detested her interest in Ben, and nearly became ill whenever she thought about Marcy having Ben's name. His legally binding name. Forever. Amen. Why not? That was how the Rydells rolled. They were the equivalent of commitment. Life and all of its responsibilities were real to them. They didn't make mistakes or get divorces. There was no feasibility whatsoever that Ben could free himself of the leech that Marcy turned out to be. At least she was in Jocelyn's opinion.

But Marcy used all her skills and sexiness on Ben to land him in high school. She first dazzled Ben when he was about fifteen. Then, however, he backed off from her advances. In his senior year, he suddenly fell in love with her. Nauseating, sickening, cloying love with her.

Marcy was a narcissist. Her excess ego shone from the top of her shiny, platinum head to her tiny, pointed feet. She was all about herself. It was not merely sour grapes on Jocelyn's part. She had known Marcy since they were in grade school. Hard to believe they were friends until Marcy entered high school, and her true nature gradually emerged.

Yeah, they both had rough childhoods in common, the fact that first bonded them. Marcy's father was mostly absentee while Jocelyn's mother was also gone. Marcy's family was just as backwoods as Cutter Johnson's shack. Marcy had no money, and neither did Jocelyn. They often sneered at the more gifted and privileged teens around them.

Including Ben Rydell.

Jocelyn never did it in a mean way. He couldn't help all the privilege he grew up with. Sure, he was aware of it and didn't feel the need to apologize for it, but he also didn't squander or flaunt it.

Marcy did not like the Rydells. Those rich folk with all their money and vehicles and horses and land. Freaking *Barons of River's End,* she used to call them with a sneer.

Meanwhile, Jocelyn had been growing closer to Joey and Ben as she worked on their ranch and they soon became good friends. By then, she'd witnessed how abusive and opportunistic Marcy had become. Jocelyn didn't like that about her and eventually ended their friendship.

She was floored when as soon as they graduated high school, Marcy became his freaking fiancée. How could that happen? Who does that? Who nowadays would choose to get engaged at the end of high school? It was totally incomprehensible to Jocelyn. She assumed, like most of their friends, that they were going through a brash, romantic phase and would no way actually do it.

One year later, on a weekend in July, they disappeared without telling anyone and came home married. It was a shocking development that rippled throughout the whole valley.

The news broke Jocelyn's crusty, hard heart. That was her last glimmer of the one boy who had ever been really nice to her, and bonded with her, and cared about her as something more than just another dude, or a friend or a good time to drink and party with.

The first year went by and Jocelyn didn't fail to notice the cracks and fissures she observed in Ben. She heard their loud, screaming fights because Marcy always did it in public, when they were out with their friends, or even in front of his family. Ben was always quiet and tolerant of her unreasonable yelling. He usually tried to soothe her, and apologized and begged her to go somewhere private where they could discuss it. But Marcy didn't do anything in private.

She was unhappy that she could not live in the main ranch house. By marrying Jack's son, she expected Ben to live there, but they converted it into the café and extra rooms. That was not acceptable to Marcy. Ben worked long hours on the ranch, as did all the Rydells, and Marcy's job at the resort was working with Jocelyn. Marcy resented, hated, and detested everything she had to do at the ranch. Jocelyn not only witnessed, but also listened to the scathing insults and relentless verbal attacks Marcy hurled at Ben and Jack, as well as Ian, Joey, and Allison. But especially Erin. She detested Erin. Who hated Erin? The only reason Jocelyn could find for that was jealousy. Erin lived in the nicest house and had seniority over the whole ranch, which Marcy believed should have been *her* position. That was just nuts in Jocelyn's opinion.

But that was how Marcy thought. Jocelyn wondered when Ben was first introduced to his *real* wife without her usual camouflage.

Fewer smiles and little laughter were coming from Ben's mouth nowadays. He often appeared tired and stressed, too much for a man only twenty–one years old. He acted like a weary, old henpecked hubby, married before he could even legally drink.

But tonight, wow! He drank. The flask was drained dry before another appeared. Jocelyn observed him at first but didn't dare approach him. She was hanging out and talking, drinking a little, until a song she loved came on from one of the trucks. It wasn't country but a smooth pop song. She stared kicking it around a bit. She was known for doing that. If she liked the music, her body reacted. She'd never had one formal dance class in her life. Yeah, as if River's End even had a dance class to attend. Nor the money, time or interest of anyone who could provide such a thing for her. No. Nah.

She used her phone to hook into the Rydells' internet and

watched the world of hip–hop and street dancing that she'd have loved to be part of, if only she were born anywhere else. But she could mimic it like a pro. She could twist her body and kick off rocks or stumps in easy jumps and turns while gyrating on the ground.

She could pop–and–lock and also manage the controlled movements of slower styles. She was stronger than most girls her size and part of what kept her that way was her gymnastic ability to capture the moves. She wasn't shy, and did it often at parties, or wherever someone asked her. It usually drew everyone's attention, even those who had no idea what she was doing or disdained the genre. She could hold on to a beat and tweak her body fluidly to smooth flowing slides or heavy stomping moves. It depended on the music. She could also control her feet and hands separately and increase the small moves to large ones.

Anyway, sometimes large crowds of people put the music on just to see her latest moves. It was her one claim to fame. So yeah, she kicked it when anyone asked. Nothing all that new. She drew a crowd around her instantly. Most couldn't copy even one of her arm flicks. Girls would try to gyrate and look sexy, like they were really into the music by raising their hands up, waving their arms, and flashing their mid-sections while trying to catch a beat. They all looked like spastic rejects trying to do basic aerobics in Jocelyn's opinion. While they tried to keep up with her, she was the star, always in the center and actually moving.

Ben edged closer, mesmerized by her like the rest of the crowd. Sitting on the tailgate of his pickup, he suddenly got up and left. Jocelyn spotted Marcy and him walking off into the shadows. Marcy walked away and Jocelyn lost sight of her. She tried to return to what she was doing. There was never any choreography for her, just freestyling, and it all worked.

Ben returned without Marcy, frowning, and drinking some more. He sat down again and watched her. She always knew when Ben watched her. Finally, the song changed and she stopped her performance, waving people off as beads of sweat rolled off her cheeks. She wiped her face, dislodging her hat before tucking it back on and going over to where Ben sat. Other people slowly drifted away.

"'S'up, Ben?" She nodded her head and he waved at the tailgate as if inviting her to sit.

"Hey, Jocelyn. Need a drink after that? Pretty impressive as usual."

She took the flask and tipped it up to her lips, not to drink it as much as just to share his germs. The totally girly urge and excitement of putting her lips to the warm mouth of his flask had her stomach pinching with nerves. She hated when she turned that way around Ben. He was married. Worse than not being into her, he was *married*. She nearly shuddered at the words. She drank too much and practically choked on the dark rum. Holding out her hand, she gave it back to him as she sputtered and coughed. He laughed and grabbed her hand, pulling her closer. His wide, warm hand gently patted her back. "I forget sometimes that you're not as tough as you look."

She scowled up at him in the night shadows. "Fuck off, Rydell," she said, smiling, with no real heat in her words.

"I always appreciate how you don't bullshit. No games. The last move you did there new?"

"Yeah." She sat next to him, fidgeting with her cap. She pulled it lower so her face and the stupid blush all over it were hidden. Her heart skipped a beat. He noticed. Why him? No one else did. No one else even realized how hard she worked at that.

He bumped her with his shoulder. "Why the hell don't you get out of here? Do something lucrative with that shit?"

She scoffed. "Do what? I have nowhere to take it. It's just a party trick."

He drank and she felt his gaze fastened on her. "Nah. It's more than a party trick. It's like a… a lifestyle with you. The clothes, the attitude, even the way you move all add up. Like you're ready to start springing off every hard surface you can find. You don't belong on a ranch in the country. Horse country. This place."

"But you do?"

He offered her the flask again. This time, she took only a sip.

"Do you question that?" He took off his cowboy hat, showing it to her as if to illustrate his point and tossed it up so it landed behind them. "I'm the antithesis of you."

"Yeah," she said with her head down. He was too. Tragically, that's what kept him from seeing her as anything but a friend.

"I'm serious. Why don't you try to do something with that? You're insanely talented."

She scoffed. "With what money, Ben? The dollars I save from the tooth fairy? Nah. I'm too old. It's just a form of fun and exercise now."

He leaned over suddenly and his hand touched her hand. "That's a shame, you know. You are special. Different. Like no one else I've ever met."

She stared up at him, startled because his face was inches from hers. His gaze started on her forehead and dropped down, scanning her features. What did he see? Her heart launched up into her throat and her pulse quickened. She pushed him, relieving the odd tension of the moment and putting them back on solid ground, kidding around, and just friends. "Yeah, duh, I'm different because I don't wear dresses."

He smiled. Her breath caught. His smile was ever–so–

slow as it slid up to his eyes. Those blue eyes, so deeply set and wide with dark lashes and traces of auburn. "Or makeup."

"Or perfume."

"Or jewelry."

"Not true." She clicked her tongue. He laughed out loud when he stared at her tongue in her mouth. The small barbell she wore clicked on her teeth when she clacked it against them.

"Okay, not true. Not the usual jewelry girls from around here wear, then."

"Or high heels."

He'd often commented before on how nice it was to hang with her because she didn't take long to get ready or spend all of her time fussing and preening in the mirror. No time spent adjusting her makeup or teasing her hair. No guy cared why any girl actually did all that.

"Or a bra."

She slapped his arm and rolled her eyes. "How the hell would you have any clue about my undergarments?"

"'Cause you don't." His lips curled up into a smug smile as his eyebrows rose.

She crossed her arms over said area, knowing it was a reference to her A cups. So yeah, she didn't often wear one because it did nothing for her figure.

"Always the dude right?" she muttered, adding a vicious, sarcastic tone to her voice.

His smile faded. "No. Not at all what I was thinking."

She froze, looking down and flaming in color. He took it to mean she was offended when really, she was merely speechless that he was acting like he might have been flirting with *her*. "Hey, Jocelyn. I'm sorry. I wasn't mocking you. I was simply commenting like a guy and noticing things that married guys shouldn't notice. Okay? It wasn't an insult."

She shrugged. No one else ever considered her feelings or that they might get hurt. It was nice of him to care. She still couldn't look at him. He sighed. "I don't think of you as a guy."

She shrugged it off again. Swinging her legs, she turned her head away to stare into the night. "Ah, hell, Ben. Everyone's still trying to figure out if I'm a lesbian or not. A dyke. The local transgender. Which makes me a freak, right?"

He suddenly turned and put his face right up to hers. "No. Damn it, Jocelyn. No. You always do that. Deflect me. I don't think about you or wonder what you are as if you're some kind of freak I can't figure out or relate to. If you are a lesbian, I wouldn't know now, would I? I don't assume it. You've never told me that. And no one should call you names regardless."

"What would you do if I were?"

He frowned. "What do you mean, what I would do? Nothing. Listen to you. Note it. Remember it, I suppose. But do? There'd be nothing for me to do."

"You'd just accept it?"

"Accept what? That you're the easiest person I've ever talked to and talented as all hell? You're smooth and cool and you make me feel like the country hick I am, but surprisingly, you still embrace me as your friend? Did it ever occur to you that I feel lucky you acknowledge me? There isn't anyone as cool as you around here."

"That's a load of shit."

"No. It's not. You're the only one who doesn't see that."

She let out a stunned breath. "Umm… well, just so *you know,* I'm not a lesbian. I—I like guys."

"Yeah? Anyone in particular?"

"Yes," she whispered, quickly looking down.

Ben bumped into her, good naturedly. "Lucky guy. You're not going to tell me his identity?"

She swallowed and shook her head. "Yeah. So lucky. And no, I'm not. What are you doing, Ben? We don't talk about stuff like this. Where's your wife tonight?" she tossed out with a sneer.

Marcy. Marcy. Marcy. She had to get back on track. Remember not to flirt or like each other, as Ben had a wife. A freaking, damn wife. Like some kind of old rancher, he sometimes talked as if he were already dead and buried. His life over and long behind him.

He drank liberally. "She left me. Maybe for good. But she's definitely mad at me."

Her heart bumped. His sneer said his story and feelings. "What did you do?"

"I talked. I walked. I glanced around. How the hell should I know? You name it and she gets pissy at me for it."

Jocelyn's throat went dry. Ben never, not once, commented on Marcy or disparaged her behavior, no matter how blatant, loud, and embarrassing it was.

"Well, maybe you should behave better." It was a weak and lame thing to say. She didn't know how to reply without her heart's desire dripping from her words and her tone of voice. So she had to play it casual. She had to pretend she was Marcy's advocate or her true disdain and feelings would be evident.

Ben pulled a leg up. "Yeah, I should." Turning towards her, his eyes glittered with something new, something she never saw before in Ben's eyes. Silence accompanied his expression and lasted way too long.

Puzzled and feeling hot with his gaze fastened on her, she muttered, "What?"

"You know, don't you?"

"Know what?"

"That I'm a fucking idiot. About my *wife.*"

The way he said "wife" with a sneer made Jocelyn flinch.

It was so odd hearing Ben talk like that. He never used to swear. Ever. She'd heard him cussing a lot in the last few months, oddly enough. And as for Marcy? Of course she knew. She'd known every guy Marcy was sleeping with since the girl was a freshman in high school. She hoped and prayed that Marcy would stay faithful to Ben, but in her short sexual history, she never seemed to value fidelity. Jocelyn shrugged, trying to evade his question.

His laugh was bitter before he drank more. And then even more. "I heard about it, you know."

"What?"

"All the shit you give Joey about Marcy. How she doesn't work and she's lazy. How she uses me as an excuse to avoid the few duties she does have to do. I've heard what you think of her... and me, for marrying her." He drank and smacked his lips before wiping them with the back of his hand. "Yup, all kinds of gossip around here, and lots of it revolves around the never–ending hate feast between you and Marcy. So tell me, Jocelyn, why? Why do you despise her so much? I agree she is lazy and doesn't do a good job for the ranch. That's why I'm embarrassed, and my dad is disappointed, while Joey is frustrated. But why do you hate her so much?"

Jocelyn tucked her hands under her armpits, crossing them over her chest, just under her breasts in a protective huddle. "She treats me like I'm that freak we just discussed. She's been the worst about it, for a few years now."

"I've never heard her say anything."

"Of course not. She hides it from you." The words burst out of her lips. Jocelyn gritted her teeth and looked down. Damn. She could not add to Ben's anger or his doubts about Marcy. It was his marriage. "She's not stupid. Contrary to the act she perpetuates, all that breathy sweetness? It hides a sharp mind, tongue, and perpetually conniving schemes."

"Why?"

"Why what, Ben? Why you? Why is she that way? Do you really want to know the answer to that?"

"Yeah, might be nice to understand why she chose me as her loser target and general shmuck."

"Because your family is rich, of course."

"We're not rich. If we stop working, we'll be broke within a year. Takes a lot to keep a place like ours afloat."

"Yes, but she sees the potential there. The land. So much land. And you are a well-respected, founding family. Your family is the backbone of the valley and around here. The biggest fish in this pond. She wants the prestige, the power, the respect, and yeah, the money. Why? Because she grew up as poor as I did. It's… jealousy. She wonders what it would be like to be you."

"But you'd never use me like that."

"No." She glanced at him, then away. Something pinged in her heart that he at least remembered and knew that much about her. "I wouldn't."

"She pulled my strings like a puppet, didn't she? I was such a wimp. I was all 'Sure, Marcy, whatever you want' about everything she asked for. I was so bug-eyed and proud someone like her wanted someone like me. And in the way that she did. I thought—"

"Did something happen? Where is all this coming from?"

His gaze wandered off. "Don't play dumb. You, of all the girls I know, can't pull it off."

Her heart hurt for him. Humiliated. Embarrassed. Young. He was so young to lose his once bright-eyed view of the world. She dropped her eyes to her knuckles and cracked them as she nodded. "Yeah, I know."

He didn't react. Silence filled the minutes between them. People had wandered off. They were all alone. Finally, he softly asked, "Not the first?"

Squeezing her hands into fists, Jocelyn wished she didn't

know the answer. She didn't mean to. But she was well known in many circles around the valley. Gossip was a cherished hobby of the locals in the area and Marcy Rydell was a favorite topic. "I'm sorry." Why was she apologizing? She wasn't sure. Being the messenger still felt somehow like she was complicit in what Marcy did.

"Why didn't you ever tell me before?"

"Because you wouldn't have believed me. Love blinded you. I knew you'd end up simply hating me and I refused to lose your friendship over *her actions*. Besides, why are you asking me? It's not like we're friends anymore. She doesn't confide in me."

"I realize now you were the only one who knew the truth. How many?"

"I don't know for sure. At least two. What… Where is this coming from? I just saw you talking to her."

"No, she followed me here and I told her to leave and go screw herself and die. I wouldn't grieve."

Her heart jerked. Shock. Yes, honestly, hearing Ben— mild, easy-going, almost innocent Ben—speak like that, alarmed her.

"You didn't."

"I did. She ran off from Ian's wedding. She was mad at me, accusing me of flirting with Hannah Campbell. Right? As if. I let her go. Only something didn't feel right. I drank with Joey for half the night before I sobered up long enough to go find her. I found her."

"How?"

"I tracked her phone. Found her with Jeff Olson. I mean *found* as in *I saw*. There she was, screaming insanely. I assume that goddamned drifting loser pleasured something inside her I could not. The part I must assume now that I never did. Too boring. Too what? Wimpy. Ordinary. Working my job every single day, following my family's rules. Being the same as always, day in and day out." He shook his head. "I probably deserved it."

"You didn't deserve it," she hissed, her tone sharp and quick while shaking her head back and forth.

He glanced her way. "Anyway, I don't want to talk about her anymore. I just… It's always about me. How are you? Tell me something to make me forget my crappy character judgment."

She released the rigid set of her shoulders. "I work. I watch dance moves. I try them. I listen to endless music. That's the extent of my life."

He let out a short laugh. "Yeah, that's my life until now with Marcy, but you? You're not like anyone else. Tell me, what was that last little thing you do there with your arms? How do you figure that out?"

He managed to draw her into conversation, despite having just revealed the most shocking reality she could imagine. He knew Marcy cheated. Jocelyn believed it, and was almost entirely sure of it but had never witnessed it with her own eyes. Though there were times, Marcy hinted at it to Jocelyn for, what? To challenge her? Somehow show her up? Taunt her? Jocelyn didn't understand Marcy's motivation in not hiding her adulterous trysts better, but then again, she was only twenty–one and the way she and Ben were living seemed like an old married couple in their sixties. Maybe Marcy was just bored. Maybe she couldn't handle the commitment. All the excitement and shock of their young engagement and marriage soon started to wear off and no one really cared anymore. People were busy with their own lives, going off to college or landing their careers and Ben and Marcy were trying to set up house. They were expected to dig in with both hands and make it work now. So not the glamourous lifestyle that Marcy Rydell thought was in store for her.

Ben was the only person who ever asked about Jocelyn's dancing. How she did the moves, and why; he always seemed impressed how easily she could do it, regurgitating what she saw on the internet. Just knowing that he listened, cared, and acted interested was flattering to Jocelyn, considering she had no other claim to fame. The rest of her life was involved in the work she did for *his ranch* and restaurant, which she'd been doing for the last decade.

So they talked and their conversation descended into silly things. They got quite drunk together and everything became outrageously funny to them. They were off all alone, under the stars that could periodically be glimpsed through the smoky sky.

"You just snorted." Ben pointed out with a huge grin. He leaned up on his elbow. They were lying on the bed of his truck, staring up at the sky, spending the last half hour discussing the virtues of mixed drinks versus straight alcohol.

She wrapped her arm over her face to mask her laughing even harder and began snorting again. He leaned closer and tugged on her arm. "You are always a surprise."

He was right next her, above her, and staring at her. They were smiling, laughing, but after his statement, things became somehow serious and quiet and even sincere. Her smile faded as her arm slowly lowered to her side. He reached over and touched her face. The act, so soft and subtle and small, had never happened before. She held her breath, suspended by his fervent gaze directed on her and only her.

"How do you figure? There's nothing surprising about me."

That smile of his grew even fuller and made his eyes twinkle. He shook his head. "You appear so tough, but there's so much about you that isn't. Something unsure. It comes out all the time when you have to do anything new. Like when you snort and it embarrasses you. While anyone who meets you for the first time would think nothing embarrasses you. But so much does."

"It's just you, Ben. I don't like to be embarrassed in front of you."

His face was still leaning over her and his neck jerked back in surprise. "Me? Why? You've been my best friend for years, ya know? There's nothing that should embarrass us. I missed you when you graduated high school." She'd graduated two years before he did.

"I didn't know that."

"Look at how crappy my judgment got without your influence. You're my best friend."

"I know we used to be." Her heart dipped down to her toes. Always his *friend*.

"What? Aren't we anymore?"

"It's the rare boy and girl who can be best friends."

"That's what's so awesome about you. You're the easiest person to be around." He moved to the side quickly but remained right next to her.

"Yeah? I'm not a puppy, Ben."

"I doubt I said that. Or thought that."

She hunched forward, gripping her toes and resting her head on her knees. The air was still warm and her legs were bare. His hand slid over her neck and crept up into the back of her hair. She shaved it short just last week, with a pattern of zigzags. Her top layer was finger–length and spiky and weird. His fingers touched the shaved part, sliding over it, feeling it, and even patting it.

She tilted her head towards his exploring fingers. Shivers broke out over her arms and her insides trembled. It was innocent. Innocuous. But a fiery heat drifted over her instantly. He'd never touched her like that before.

"I always thought you liked Joey."

His statement was quiet, and right near her ear. It startled her. She flipped her head to the side, facing him head on. He stared into her eyes. There was enough moonlight for them to see each other, but enough darkness to hide the awkwardness of the moment. The color predictably began infusing her cheeks.

"Joey? What? Why?"

"Because you guys were such good friends. Honest. You told him what you thought. Not me. I was what? The annoying little brother?"

"No. Never."

"If Joey had a girlfriend or a wife who was cheating, you'd have told him. Why not me?"

She pressed her lips together, shutting her eyes. Tears filled her eyelids. Several escaped and rolled down her cheeks. "Because I did feel like Joey was my brother."

"Not me?"

"No." She barely breathed the word. "Not you."

His hands touched the back of her head and she kept her eyes shut. For four years, she had fantasized, daydreamed, hoped, and hated herself for wanting this boy, now a man, with her now. Wishing and hoping that someday he'd realize the mistake he made at such a young age with Marcy Fielding. But not like this. He was drunk. He was hurting. He felt betrayed. He still loved Marcy.

But his hands felt so gentle. They slid over the back of her head, as if the texture appealed to him, rubbing his palms over her short, soft hairs and gently bringing her face closer. "Why the tears?"

"Because your heart is broken, and you're about to break mine."

"I didn't know I could." Their voices were muted, as if

maybe by not enunciating the words, it would make it less real.

His mouth was hovering over hers and she could feel the warmth of his breath, and smell the strong, acrid scent of booze. When his mouth touched hers, the tears flowed harder. It was the moment she'd always prayed for and anticipated. The moment she did not deserve. The moment she'd do anything to hang on to and cherish.

Her mouth opened to his and his tongue entered. It was so soft, easy, and exploratory. His hands kept gripping the back of her head. He tilted her mouth under his better. She kept her eyes closed and pretended, for just a moment, he was kissing her because he wanted *her.*

His mouth lifted off hers and they both exhaled loudly, mingling their breaths together as they were only a few inches apart. His lips brushed over hers again as his thumbs moved over the nape of her neck. He pulled her closer, twisting her body so she was facing him until he was on his knees. Lashing their arms around each other, their lips met harder and faster before everything around them faded away.

It was just the two of them there in the silence of the night. The peace of the dark. They kissed on and on, moving their lips together, opening and closing their mouths as their tongues touched and twisted and tasted the other. His arms never left her, placing his hands on her neck and hair before slowly letting them fall down her back. He had big hands, and the hard calluses rubbed her soft, bare skin. He paused long enough to lift his head, his eyes blazing on hers. He stared at her and slid both his hands to the bottom of her shirt, tugging upwards, and never breaking eye contact with her except when the shirt got in the way.

Her bare chest had two small bosoms. Firm muscles defined her abdominal wall and arms. His breath caught as he lowered his face to her clavicle and kissed her. His arms wrapped around her, pushing her against his chest. A few minutes later, his hand slid to her stomach, rubbing up and down on her muscles there, making her stomach flex with nerves as her response to his erotic exploration made her tingle everywhere. He brought his hand up to her small breasts and rubbed the right one back and forth with the flat palm of his hand. Her nipple sensitized immediately and she moaned into his mouth. Using his thumbnail, he flicked the end of her nipple as his mouth aggressively came down on hers and he nearly bent her backwards over his arm, which was all that was supporting her. His tongue was deep inside her mouth and her entire body became as limp as wet spaghetti in his arms when he kept pebbling her hard nipple.

Then, ever-so-gently, she reached under his shirt. Her hands hesitated, feeling suddenly unsure. She touched the warm, soft skin above his belt. His chest lurched in response, making him gasp. She slid her hands on his stomach, grazing over his flat nipples and rising up to his shoulders.

His mouth nuzzled her neck and ear as he kissed her lips again and her hands fumbled with his belt buckle and the snap of his jeans. Slowly, she peeled them back, pushing as far as she could reach while keeping their lips sealed together.

Shifting his hips around, he lifted his butt up to allow her to pull him free of his clothes. He released her and his hand drifted down her chest, while his mouth glided over her breasts and he kissed her stomach. His hands felt warm and soothing as he pulled her shorts down and they slid off her legs. He included her underwear with them. His gaze centered on her lower half, which was barely visible in the kaleidoscopic shadows of the dark. His hands were gentle, and so soft when he moved them over her thighs, waist, hips, and butt. She shivered at the intimate contact. Exploring her wet, eager opening with his fingers, his mouth returned to hers. His fingers entered her and she gasped at the long awaited, much craved, and dream–like contact. Her sounds were muffled by his insistent mouth. So long, for years, she fantasized about this, imagining the romance and discovery. Shutting her eyes, she could block out everything else but this. There were no other people around. No Marcy. No right or wrong. And her body was willingly opening up to Ben Rydell in all the ways her heart desired from so long ago.

He stopped to dig his hand into the pocket of his jeans before bringing out his wallet. Then he seemed to fumble around for an eternity before he finally found a condom and slipped it on. She stared up at him in disbelief as he positioned himself over her. They paused for a long moment, their eyes riveted on each other. He reached down and touched her cheek in a gentle gesture. It didn't surprise her at all. She almost expected and could have predicted that Ben would do something at odds with everything else about that moment and what they intended to do.

When she felt the tip of him nudging her entrance, her body moistened with want and he rubbed against the wetness there, exclusively lubricated to welcome him, an urgent invitation to put his body inside hers. He slid into her, his eyes holding hers as he sunk inside her completely and they both gasped. All they could do was moan softly at all the warm, hot, passionate, good feelings.

His gaze was hot on her face and he moved his hips gently at first, then harder. She lifted her knees and he settled better against her, tilting her hips just enough to maximize her comfort and pleasure. His mouth dropped back to hers and their lips clung together as hot and connected as their lower halves. She hung her arms around his neck and held him. They moved together with subtle, quiet sighs and murmurs of wants and needs being explored and fulfilled.

Her body started to spark and explode with pleasure as Ben filled her up, hard and long, tightening his grip around her and holding her against him as he pushed deep inside her.

The air was still warm but felt cool against her sweat–slick skin. She lowered her knees and Ben lifted his hips off her, moving to the side as he pulled her against him to his chest. She curled up, and he surprisingly touched the top of her head with his lips.

She closed her eyes. The hard face of reality regrounded her. "What did we just do?" she finally whispered.

"I don't know," he replied softly. He tilted her a few inches from him, so they could look at each other. Both their gazes were filled with regret. Confusion. And caring. She sensed his regret in the energy he now released as he so gently rubbed her back. It was at odds with what should have been a cold, empty fuck to avenge his adulterous wife. It didn't feel like that at all to Jocelyn. It was between them, and only them. "I didn't plan this."

She buried her face against his shirt, which was bunched up around his neck before he put it back in place. He smelled of suntan lotion. She sniffed deeply, relishing the scent, *his scent*. It was so familiar. She'd often hung closer to him just to catch a whiff of it. "Neither did I."

Silence made it strange and awkward but still, neither moved. "Jocelyn?"

"What?"

"I'm going to have to tell her."

"Yes. Of course." Jocelyn readily agreed, but her heart was protesting and squeezing in physical pain. She wanted to scream, *Tell her what?* What they did? Or how he felt about what they did? And what did he feel?

"It's not going to be pretty."

87

She scoffed. "No, I guess nothing can make this situation pretty."

"I'm sorry for that."

"For this? Are you sorry for this?"

"I'm…" he sighed, shaking his head, "completely confused by this." Her heart dipped in response as he muttered, "Except, for some reason, it doesn't feel nearly as wrong as it should. Jocelyn, I think I have strong feelings towards you. Maybe I have for a while. I think—"

But Ben never finished his words. Far off in the distance, a collection of loud voices and shouts finally came within hearing. One word was repeated over and over: "Fire!"

They jerked upright, separating instantly. Glancing nervously around and then at each other, they frantically began adjusting their clothes.

The desperate, shocking scream echoed all over the area as the former partiers all began screaming in unison as they scrabbled around to vacate the area. The spotlight of emergency trucks along with firefighters dominated the scene and began to evacuate the area. They explained that the fire had merged with the one up north and turned back. The thick smoke was making it hard to breathe when the firefighters spotted the kids who were partying and ushered them out of the mountains, as if the jaws of hell were snapping at their tailgates.

Jocelyn went with Ben in his truck, but neither of them spoke. It was too hurried and frantic. Then… his mouth went grim. They stopped several miles down the main highway at the north end of the fire command center.

Ben parked and stared out at the streams of panicked people around them. Jocelyn held her breath, pinching her fingernails into her palm to focus on something besides her fear and grief. "Marcy went up the road further. With… Jeff Olson." Ben's voice broke as he said that name. The name of

Marcy's lover. The man she was cheating with. Ben had this information the entire evening he spent with her. It put a completely new spin on it for Jocelyn. Ben shook his head as if doing a reset on his thoughts. "I told the fire crew I have to go find her. It's just... Years ago, I told her... I told her I'd always love her and be there for her. I have to go find her."

Jocelyn stared out the window, her heart ripping open and nodded. The restrained tears began streaming over her cheeks. Jeff Olson. Jocelyn's head spun as she realized why tonight had happened. "I know, Ben. I know what you promised her." The irony was not lost on her. She witnessed their entire courtship and marriage and now? *She knew.*

"Jocelyn, I..."

She gripped the door handle, cutting him off, "Go find her. It—it'll be okay. None of this ever happened, right? We were drunk and stupid. She'll forgive you. Because you're going to forgive her. You're going to forgive her relations with Jeff, and she will forgive you for your relations with me."

"What about you? How do you feel about this?"

She flashed a false smile. "What about me? You know how I feel about Marcy. This was just an easy way for me to rub it in her face."

His jaw tightened. "You don't mean that. You didn't do it for that reason."

"Didn't I? What makes you so sure?" She was lying, of course. He should have known her well enough to understand that. But tonight? Everything felt surreal and it would have to be banished from both of their memories. It felt better to protect her heart than to believe he would actually leave his wife for her. It was essential that she regard this as nothing, even if it were *everything* to her. She needed to make sure she didn't pine for a man who didn't really want her. He would never put her above his wife, right? Ben was just angry, confused, even if he only now just realized she was easier to be around than Marcy. Of course, it created some confusing feelings but no way were they strong enough to extract Ben from the commitment he'd already made to the woman he claimed to love.

"Just go, Ben. Go out there and find your wife." She clicked the door handle, got out, and hadn't seen Ben since that night.

CHAPTER 6

*J*ACK AND BEN TOOK a full week to drive back to River's End. First, Ben had to arrange for his foreman to sell his truck and send him the money for a small fee. Then, oddly to Ben, Jack meandered home. He chose off–the–grid roads and wove across much of Montana instead of taking Interstate 90 and flying straight through it.

"Never seen much of Montana before. Might be my only chance," was Jack's response when Ben questioned him. Most of the long journey was quiet as they drove in Jack's pickup truck. It could have taken a day, maybe two, but Jack refused to drive more than three hours a day. They stayed in cheap motels and had separate rooms. Jack slept a lot. He frequented the quaint taverns they found in the little towns they passed through and Ben went right along, with nothing else to do. Yet, Jack didn't try to talk to him. They were physically together. But not mentally.

One night, in a dark, murky tavern, fresh beers before them, and the smoke all hazy around them as there were no non–smoking laws observed there, his dad said, "I told Erin we were taking so long getting back because you were dragging your feet. I was having a hard time getting you to commit, so just in case she asks…"

"You told Erin I'm the reason we're taking so long?"

Jack shrugged. "She asked. She questioned it finally. She thinks we should have been home a few days ago."

"Well, yeah, we could have," Ben grunted, drinking liberally. "Why aren't we?"

"It's kind of nice to be away. No chores staring at me. No charred remains. No horses. No… hopeful expectations. Now I can see the benefits and the appeal of disappearing into nowhere."

Ben leaned back in the booth, crossing his arms over his chest. "You appreciate this? What gives, Jack? What the fuck is wrong with you? The Jack I know would have been storming after me, shaming me for not racing home to attend to my daughter. The Jack I know would have condemned me mercilessly for running away. Shirking my duties. Worrying everyone. The Jack I know would have tried to put me in rehab if he found *heroin* in my possession. And not simply asked what I liked about it! What is wrong with you?"

Jack leaned back and scrutinized Ben. Nodding, he swallowed before he replied, "The Jack you know is dead." His tone sounded as dead as his words. Ben flinched. "As is the old Ben I once knew. Right? As cold and dead as Marcy."

Ben jerked upright. "That was a shit–ass thing to say to me."

"It was. But your entire demeanor is shit–ass, so what does it matter?"

"Why are you lying to Erin? What the hell is that all about?"

Jack shrugged, picking at a napkin and hunching forward, then he sighed. "She keeps looking at me, with hopeful eyes, each day, just waiting for the old me to return. That's the way she wants to see me, I guess. I disappoint her every single day when the old me never returns. She doesn't say anything, mind you, it's just a silent expectation. I'm tired of that look. I'm tired of disappointing her. I'm tired of failing in her eyes. So it's been nice just traveling on the road. You don't expect anything from me and neither do you want to talk to me. Everyone, Ian, Shane, and especially Joey are looking at me the same way as Erin. Waiting me out. Hoping and praying, no doubt, each day I'll bust out and be myself again. That's what I'm being told all the time anyway. That I'm just not myself."

"And what about the other son you're supposed to be raising? Charlie? Where does he fall in all of this and why don't you give a shit anymore?"

Jack's back jerked upwards. "Oh, like you give a shit about Charlie? I do give a shit about my other son. Far more than you care for the daughter you call 'it.' I'm just... exhausted. I can't muster the energy to care about very much anymore. You know? Not like I used to. What's the point?"

Ben didn't have an answer. He didn't know what the goddamned point was either. Hunching forward, he shrugged. Even if he felt that way, he never dreamed his over-achieving father would. "So you're not ready to go home and you're blaming it on me."

Jack grunted. "As if you cared. I still care enough that I don't want to lose my wife. I just need a breather right now maybe, you know?"

"At least you still have a wife," Ben mumbled.

Jack took a sip and slammed the half empty glass of beer down, making it slog up and down as he replied, "You didn't want your wife anymore. Don't act like you were in a healthy, positive relationship. Otherwise, there would have been no interest in Jocelyn. I'm not condemning you because there is, but let's not go back to that bullshit politeness and fake euphemisms for what you and Marcy used to be together."

He eyed his dad. "Does Erin know you talk like this?"

Jack scoffed, shaking his head. "No. And you're not going to blackmail me over it either."

Ben frowned. "Why the fuck would you think I'd do that?"

Jack waved his hand towards Ben and replied, "Why? Just look at you. What you are now. So hell, yeah, I think you'd do that. I don't know how often you do the drugs I saw in your hotel room. Much less, how much your habit costs you."

"Well, shit, Jack, why the hell would you care? The way you talk, we should just go off together and maybe vanish and never go back. Leave the ranch and all its problems to Ian, Shane, Erin, and Joey. Why the hell do any of them need *you*?"

Instead of reacting to Ben's rising tone as he stood up, Jack stared down harder at his beer and said in a gentle voice, "That's exactly what I keep trying to convey to all of them. They don't need me anymore and I don't think I want to be needed so much either."

Ben sat down and swallowed the rest of his beer. His stomach churned as his heart raced. What the hell was happening? Who was worse off emotionally? Him or Jack? Before his dad showed up, Ben would have said he was worse off, but after listening to Jack? Maybe they weren't so far apart in their situations and emotional turmoil. Like Jack, at the very core of his dilemma, Ben didn't want to be needed anymore by anyone either.

Jack stood up and tossed a bill down for the drinks. "I told Erin we'd be home tomorrow."

Ben was startled by his announcement and glared up at Jack. *Tomorrow?* His stomach cramped at the close proximity of the prospect. For a split second, he considered simply vaulting over the high–backed booth and running as fast as he could away from his dad, just to avoid going home. He'd had a whole week to get used to the new reality although he didn't feel even remotely ready. Talk about avoiding responsibilities. Like father, like son, history seemed to be repeating itself.

BEN STARED out the passenger window, avoiding the view in front of him. After all these months, they were back in the valley where he grew up. Sunshine streamed down over it all, making everything glisten in the six o'clock evening sun. But the landscape was as foreign as the moon, like the rest of the land where Ben had wandered over the last nine months. It did not, even remotely, resemble the place where he'd grown up. Every square inch of land that hugged the highway, and both sides of it, climbing from one rolling peak to the next, was nothing but burnt, charred, scarred land and unidentifiable rubble. It was breathtaking to behold both in scope of how much land it was and the sheer volume of destroyed structures. Fascinating but in a horror movie kind of way. Over the years, Ben had passed through many areas where hundreds or even thousands of acres had burned up, but nothing could compare to the fire that engulfed and devoured the entire valley and horizon for as far as one could see.

Ben didn't comment or even twitch but somehow, his dad sensed his shock. "It looks like this all the way up to the Columbia River."

"That's a lot of land."

"From one horizon to the next."

Ben twitched his butt, jerking on the smooth leather seat.

"How did it manage to burn the house? That should have been the safest place around here, what with all the green fields surrounding it."

Jack shook his head. "It was... unspeakable the day it happened. Utter chaos. Fast too. So fast, people were fleeing with nothing but their cars. I've heard so many sad stories since then. A guy pulled off in the middle of an alfalfa field and watched one fire converge with another before burning all around him. All he could do was sit on top of his car, trapped, trying not to inhale the smoke and toxic gases, and wait it out. So many tragedies like that. It's a goddamned miracle more people—"

His dad stopped talking abruptly. Ben didn't turn his head towards him as he interjected, "Didn't die?"

Jack cleared his throat. "Yes. The fire burned so hot and fast, live sparks and embers flew up into the sky as high as you could see. Like tiny whirlwinds of fire. Sparks stayed lit and touched down in places up to a quarter of a mile away, instantly burning as soon as they landed. Everything was so tinder dry and explosively hot, it was as if all the land was doused in gasoline just waiting for a lit match. Other spots where the fire crept in were the ditch lines, the few that were all dried up made an easy artery for it to follow before finding more fuel to burn."

"What else?" Ben finally asked.

"Allison and Shane's house was lost."

Ben whipped his head around. Preoccupied with his own distress and apathy, he forgot to ask about the rest of the family. The verdant ranch was so lush when he left, Ben figured the fire just swooped right around it, maybe singing the perimeter. But not... burning the whole thing up. His heart hurt. They just built their house three years ago. "Where did they go?"

"Staying in Joey's house for now and rebuilding as we

speak, but they lost everything they owned, Ben. Just the pictures they put in their computer clouds are all that's left of their memories."

"I didn't know."

"Allison had another baby too. I just now realized you were gone before she even announced her pregnancy."

"Holy shit. Shane has two kids now?"

"Two girls. Rosie and now Iris."

Two daughters. Ben could hardly realize that Shane had one daughter. Then the reality sunk into Ben. He had a daughter too. He, Ben Rydell, was a father. The sharp knowledge struck through his head like a spike banged into his skill. How? How could this be? Talk about not being able to picture someone, he couldn't picture his own daughter. "Where did Joey go?"

"Living in Erin's, and then in AJ's old trailer."

"Thought maybe he went off with Hailey. Did that romance fizzle out?"

"No. I figured it would have by now too. They're dating long distance. She comes to the ranch nearly every weekend, and he goes out her way every so often."

"What about her kids?"

"Brianna finally came to grips with her behavior and made some kind of peace with her crush on Joey. She quit lusting after him and became best friends with Cami."

"Kate and AJ are good then?"

"No, Ben, they're not. Their manufactured home exploded and disintegrated. Gone. AJ's first and only real home that he barely enjoyed for about a year."

"Did they leave the ranch?"

Jack's mouth twitched. "No, my indomitable sister wouldn't pull Cami from school. They lost everything too. Kate had some stuff she left back in Seattle, but anything of value to either of them was burned up. Including everything

Cami cherished from her dead mother. Kate got a mobile home brought in almost immediately, and they are also rebuilding. She stays in Seattle more often than before, a few days per week now. It's been hard on both of them too."

Ben's heart twisted and ached. How long had it been since he felt something painful in his heart? He wasn't sure. But they were his family. For two decades, they comprised his entire world. He never considered them suffering or having to endure so much hardship. "Ian? Kailynn? What about them? Did they lose their house too?"

"The houses along the river fared pretty well. But Kailynn had to give up the job she spent four years in college trying to procure. Her dad's place burned, and of course, her brothers still lived there, so now her dad, Caleb, and Jordan live with them. Ian quit his other job too."

"Not exactly newlywed heaven, huh?"

Jack fell silent. Finally, he muttered, "No. God, Ian's wedding... It seems centuries ago, huh? Not even a year."

Ben shut his eyes for a split second as the warm feeling of home and connection and family filled him. For a moment, he forgot all the anger and pain of the last nine months. Ian's wedding... That day, that weekend, just before the fire broke out, and the entire family was gathered at the ranch, all together for the first time in about four years. There was such a celebration and fun and laughter, kinship, and love. Things were golden for a few hours that day. Then? Then, it was like a nuclear bomb exploded and pummeled them all into darkness.

"I didn't realize how many lost their homes. I mean, I heard most of the reports on the news, but I never considered us, several of us, in fact, would be included in the list of victims."

"The resort shut down. Half of that burned too."

"Fuck. How do we earn money now?"

Jack was silent so Ben glanced at him. "Jack?" he prompted.

"I—I don't really know."

He jerked around. "What do you mean, you don't know? Then who knows?"

"Ian? Shane? Joey? Joey's really stepped up. Lost his job, of course, without the resort, so he wants to get it up and running again as fast as possible. Anyway, I mean... you should ask one of them."

"Why don't you know the answer?"

He shrugged. His hands tightened on the steering wheel. "I just don't know."

"What? What is all this passive bullshit? *You don't know.* Find out. Since when aren't you the one in control of every facet of all the Rydell operations? Down to each nook and cranny, and every sheet of toilet paper we need to order for the guest cabins."

"Look around you at this. This ugly, blackened, wasteland. That's what I've been staring at for the past nine fucking months, Ben!" For the first time in all the days they'd spent together, Jack's tone of voice rose with some kind of feeling finally inserted into it. "I step out onto my porch and get to stare up towards the charred remains of the house, *your mother's house*, and everything beyond that. It's all burned too. You disappeared. Gone. My older son. I had no idea how you were. What was I supposed to do, Ben? Jump in? Save the day again? For what? For what possible reason? The next tragedy will come with or without me, right?"

"Because you set it up. You were our leader, Jack. Always. Except for Ian, you are the only one we all, every one of us, rely on in times of crisis and trouble. So now, you're saying you're just done? Life's gotten too hard for you?"

Jack's jaw clenched and he shook his head. "Yeah, Ben. That's kind of how I feel. It's too damn hard this time."

"And what does everyone else say to your claim that it's just too hard?"

He stole a glance at Ben. "As if I've told anyone else."

"Then why tell me? Why should I be the one to know?"

"You were hungover the first time I saw you. Your shirt was stained with vomit and food and sweat. It hadn't been changed in days. You don't shower, shave or take any hygienic care of yourself on a regular basis. The way you look is how I feel. Maybe I can tell you how I feel because it's not like we're Jack and Ben anymore. We're just two guys whose lives got all fucked up. I don't know, but it's like I can finally be totally honest, completely real in my assessment because you are just as miserable as I feel."

Ben stayed quiet for another mile before he muttered, "I thought you'd be furious at me. Ordering me to come back and accept my responsibilities like the man you think I should be."

"How can I expect that of you when I can't do it either?"

"What about Erin?"

His fingers flexed. "What about her?"

"Are you, like, planning to leave her or something?" His throat felt tight even asking such a personal question. Seeing his dad with his second wife convinced him that no matter what happened in life, second chances did exist. It seemed so real. But that was before. Before everything was snatched away by a cruel act of Mother Nature.

"No. Shit. I just—no. Why do you think I don't say anything to her? I'm trying. I want to get back to where I used to be. Be the man I once was. I can't seem to find the path to get there. But this has nothing to do with how I feel about Erin."

"She… she needs you. You know?"

"I can't believe you give a shit about Erin, or anyone, really, to worry about what I do to them."

"She was always good to me. And to you."

"She doesn't need me anymore. I seem to need her more nowadays. If not for her and Charlie, I probably would've just walked away from it all." He shook his head while blowing out a long breath. "I've never said that out loud before. Thought about though. Obsessively. But damn. It feels kind of nice to admit it to someone."

Ben glared at his dad's profile, thinking how much he lost, and how he screwed up his life and his self–image and reputation and self–worth. Ben always understood that at some point, he'd have gotten his life together again well enough to come home. It remained a solid fact to him. As Jack Rydell's son, he possessed part of a family ranch, and had a home, a forever place to live, no matter what he did or thought. He had the luxury of always knowing his home awaited him. But to hear his father speaking like that, when his dad was supposed to be the same as he was when Ben left him, bothered Ben. Waiting. Longing. Hurting over Ben's absence on the ranch. Why wasn't he demanding for Ben to come home and be the way *he* used to be?

"And what would you do, Jack? Where would you go? Where do you think you could possibly go and find peace?"

Jack's gaze jerked to Ben's. "I don't know. It's not like I have that choice. Not like you once had."

"What do you mean?"

Jack sighed. "I wished all the chances I never had in life would be offered to you. Going to college or getting a job outside this valley. All that stuff you were saying before, about a whole other world and another kind of life beyond our valley? It's true. We are nothing compared to other places. Imagine, getting to just go wherever and be whatever. I wanted that for you and Charlie. I worked the ranch so there was no reason you'd have to stay here, unless of course, you wanted to. Not like what happened to your mom and me. But then…"

"I got married just like you did."

"Yes. And there you were, struggling and settling down to your life for the next forty years."

"What are you trying to tell me? You regret your life? Mom? Me? Charlie? The ranch? What did the ranch and us keep you from doing? You never once mentioned anything else you ever wanted. You practically breathe those horses. Don't try to tell me this was all an unspeakable burden you were forced to endure for the good of your family who never allowed you to do your own thing. You chose this too. You *loved* this. What in the *hell* are you talking about now?"

Ben's distress was visible. But he could not listen to his dad trying to rewrite the childhood he adored and remembered. His dad lived for and loved the Rydell River Ranch. Now was he saying that devotion had it limits? And was fraught with burdens? Ben's stomach hurt and he pushed his fingertips through his hair before rubbing the rough scruff of his beard. He hadn't shaved in so long, the hair had all filled in. It wasn't really a beard but looked like he just hadn't bothered to groom himself. His red hair was too long and his beard too scraggly over his cheeks and throat and chin.

"Of course I don't regret you. Or your brother or Lily. Or Erin. You're right, I always loved the horses. But all the ranch work? No. Nah. I liked to train the horses. Period. I am always curious to see what I can teach a horse to do. But I don't like breaking the stable horses for tourists to ride and turn and stop and go. It's like having a CEO do clerical work to me. I always wanted, and used to dream about another career when your mom and I first got married, before my parents died. It was running a horse rescue facility."

"You what? Are you having a mid–life crisis? Is that what all this shit is?"

Jack threw his head back, laughing. "Maybe. Maybe I am, Ben. Maybe I'm just your typical middle aged man whose life is flashing before his eyes. I am just catching a glimpse of all that I haven't done and always wanted to do, yet I was so busy, the years passed by. You know what I mean, right? Like one of those outfits that work with rescues horses? The Bureau of Land Management takes them off the range, wild mustangs that need lots of coaxing, patience, and training before they can be ridden. Or horses that are rescued from terrible circumstances by abusive or neglectful owners. Some are so mishandled or mistreated, they have to be put down. I could coax them back to accepting humans again. I could train them to be good horses again, horses that someone would adopt and give a good home to. I know I could save them because I know how to train them. Right now, I'm training horses for paying customers, stuff I can do sleep-walking, and never mind the shows and tickling the crowds with cute parlor tricks. They're cool, sure. But I used to do it just for fun, you know? See what I could get out of every horse. It became such a big thing at the resort and never ceased to amaze everyone. But it's not what I actually wanted to do with those skills. I prefer to save horses. I love horses, Ben. That's probably the only thing I haven't ever wavered or waffled on. I freaking love those gorgeous, majestic creatures and I feel blessed with some kind of gift every time a horse responds to me. But I have this ideal, younger version of myself, saving dozens of horses. Doing it the right way. I always hoped I could find a way to make it my life. But after your mother died, there was never any extra time. There was you, Charlie, Joey and even Shane. There were so many other priorities to do."

Ben's mouth dropped open. He didn't know his dad dreamed about saving and rescuing horses that others had given up on. Ben shook his head. "Are you serious?"

Jack's smile was small. "Yes. That's what I dreamed of doing in my youth. So you're correct; I always wanted to live on the ranch and be part of it. There is nowhere else I ever wanted to live or go. But my fantasy was a little different. If Dad hadn't died... Yeah, once there was a real chance it might have happened. He ran the operation. I worked for it. I was a far better trainer than he, and he preferred the breeding and boarding side of it. You've always known where my heart lies. I don't know, maybe all this shit just brought it up. Or maybe I am having a goddamned mid-life crisis. Stop me if I tell you I have to go out and buy a toupee and a cute little sports car."

"That's too cliché. Which you've never been. So maybe... this *is* it. Have you told Erin anything about it?"

"Over the years, I've talked about rescuing horses. It just never happened in the big way I envision. We get one here and there. But in terms of doing that right now? No."

They turned off onto River Road and both of them fell silent. It was more than shocking and real to see all the landmarks Ben recognized and memorized since he was a boy now all burned up. Much worse than talking about it or hearing stories on the news. The hills above the road were mostly barren with tiny blades of spring grasses and wild flowers filling in the now empty land, a welcome relief from the browns and blacks beneath it all. The trees were stripped of their foliage, stabbing the air with their ugly, spear-like branches. Like pitchforks piercing the blue belly of the sky.

The old resort and ranch signs were gone when they turned into the ranch driveway. The driveway soon became a blooming cloud of brown dust that plumed like foggy smoke several feet into the air. Jack's black truck roared down it, spewing thick layers of dust as he turned and skidded to a stop where they used to park, when the main house was their home.

Ben didn't expect the shock he felt. After all he'd witnessed and ruined, he thought nothing could penetrate the layers of anger and rage he felt or turn it all into a cold, hard, brittle shell. But the house he loved was gone.

It was jolting to his eyes to scan the land before him and see merely an empty field. Once, a gravel parking lot skidded into a blanket of green grass that spread up the knoll where the house used to sit. Reaching the base of the long, luxurious wraparound porch, the logs, glass, and metal roofing created a unique transformation of ranch house to resort. The ranch house stood there for decades. Ben's entire life.

It was simply gone. A grassy, empty lot.

Ben's breath stalled and he felt like someone kicked him in the gut. He didn't think the pain from that night could still affect him.

Jack put the gear shift into park and finally shut off the diesel engine. Quiet pervaded the cab. Jack stared ahead and Ben could hardly breathe. There were no words to describe the peculiar sight before him, the place that *should* have had his home sitting on it.

"Makes you think of your mother, doesn't it?"

Ben shut his eyes to his dad's soft words. Yes. It made him immediately think of his mother, as well as his dad and Charlie. Before. Before she died and they weren't a normal, typical happy family. Before she died and left him. Before the gut-sickening pain began haunting him. Ten years old. He was only ten years old when she died. He was too fucking young.

Jack cleared his throat. "Erin, Allison, Shane, and Ian are all sad; everyone's sad it's gone. But... they... It wasn't their family home, was it, Ben? It was ours. Huh? You, me, your mom, Joey, and Charlie. I think Joey feels like we do. But you remember scenes. Like your mother working in the kitchen or tucking you into bed at night. You remember the way she stuffed her feet into those ridiculous boots to run after me to help me with chores. Do you remember those days?"

A laugh escaped his mouth that startled Ben and he glanced at his dad. A laugh? But yes, how could he forget those boots? "She got them at the thrift shop, right? They were some kind of old boots used by the Inuit, right?"

"Mukluks, she called them." Jack laughed too, shaking his head, a rare grin splitting his face.

"Looking back, you could say they were the original Uggs."

"True. Except hers were so old and so ugly. Don't you remember?"

"Yes. I remember. You'd give her shit all the time about wearing them out in public."

"She thought," Jack said still laughing, "that they were so styling. And they were a size too big so she'd clomp around in them."

"Tripping on the stairs…" Ben said, smiling too.

"The throw rugs…"

"The toys we left out."

Jack's smiled slowly vanished. "Then I buried her in them. In the end, I loved them on her simply because they made her so happy. I liked to tease her about them, but I really I adored her in them."

Ben's stomach knotted. "Yeah, I remember." And he did. He closed his eyes, thinking of his parents together. Something Charlie never had. Joey? No. There was a distinct difference in how his mom treated Joey and how she treated Ben. He knew it, and felt sorry for Joey. Although his dad never favored his own sons over his youngest brother, his mom did. But he had a different perspective now, realizing the vast amount of responsibility his parents had undertaken when they were exactly his age now… Well, at least he was not so bent on judging them anymore. He couldn't even wash his shirt nowadays or shave his face. Raising a bunch of boys and running a ranch all by themselves? Never.

"Did you love Mom? Or did you regret getting married so young? Did loving Erin show you it was a youthful mistake?"

His dad shut his eyes. "I loved Lily, Ben. I loved her as much as I love Erin now. It wasn't an easy reconciliation for me to make. I loved her so much. I didn't think I could ever love a woman that much again. Maybe it's like having two kids. You think you can't love a second child as much as the first, but you do. You find room in your heart for both, and you don't compare one over the other. Yes, I loved your mother with all my heart. I never regretted marrying her. I sometimes wish our youth and the adult responsibilities that were foisted on us weren't quite so severe. It was a lot for us to handle. It wasn't fair. She had to care for Ian, Shane, Joey, you, and later on, we had Charlie. But we wanted two kids."

"How come I never knew any of this about you?"

"I don't know. Maybe I didn't talk to you often enough. Like a person. Like a—a friend. You know? You were always my son, and I didn't want to burden you with my problems. Maybe I should have. You didn't come with a goddamned instruction book when you were born. Which, if you man up, you might just start to understand. Then add into the mix your mother. She was the link that knew how to handle all the emotional stuff, you know? Without her guidance and support, it would have been a lot harder."

"She'd knock you in the gut for making the sexist assumption you couldn't be sensitive and she could just because she was a girl."

Jack chuckled. "Yeah, she would have. I loved that about her. She didn't take shit from anyone. Not even me. She could stand toe–to–toe with me, contrasting her opinion to mine, and work as many hours as I did. She wouldn't have been friends with Erin."

"She was not like Erin at all."

"No, she was very different from Erin. They don't have much in common."

"Was that hard?" Ben stared at his hands. When had he ever talked to his dad so intimately? "You know, going from one type of woman to another?"

"Yes. I did some stupid things with Erin. You witnessed some of them. I was never comfortable with change. And this change..." Jack motioned towards the emptiness before them. "Goes way beyond my comfort zone."

"Did you cry? I never saw you cry over Mom. You didn't talk about her much. Well, you talked about her as our mom, but never as your wife."

"I know. I kept that to myself. One of the first things Erin ever confronted me on was how I didn't share my grief. With you boys. And no. I didn't cry much. The night she died, I cried. Right over her body. I couldn't say goodbye. God, I couldn't find the strength to let her go. I could not accept she was dead. She was a strong, healthy woman. I mean, way stronger and more muscled and healthier than any woman I knew. And then she just got sick and died. Your uncle Ian pulled me off her and tried to soothe me." He scooched around. "I haven't thought about that in years, maybe never. Maybe that's the fucking problem."

"What?"

"I never hesitated in the scheme of things. I didn't... feel it. I mean, I felt it, and lived it, but I couldn't stop and grieve over it. There was so much for me to do. Always. So much to take care of. My parents died and there you boys were, and me too, really. I was still a boy. There was never enough time, or a single second when I didn't have stuff to do. There was no one else to take the lead. Maybe, this time..."

"Someone else can take the lead."

"Yeah, maybe. The thing is, I don't want to be the family

patriarch anymore, Ben. I'm just so damn tired. I look at this"—he waved toward the empty lot—"and I want to tear out of here and never come back. It was *her house*. Our house. Our dreams. Our family. And even that got ripped away from me. I never wanted to move from it. The house by the river? It's fine. But I built it for Erin. Only for Erin. But this..." He waved towards the charred field. "This was my *home*. You understand?"

"Yeah, I understand. I also took it for granted and assumed, no matter what, it would always be here." It was the only definition of home Ben had.

"Yeah, even if it were a fucking hotel and café or every other nauseating improvement we made, it still stood. I could always look at it and remember *our family*. I don't like it being gone. Everything else was gone: Mom, Dad, then Lily and you boys had to grow up without your mother. I just liked seeing the house sometimes and remembering things and people."

He shifted and stared at his dad. "You don't like the ranch anymore, do you?"

"I like the ranch. It's just, for a lot of years, I considered it my ranch. I had authority over it simply because there was no other adult in charge. And when Ian was old enough, he simply agreed with my decisions. For at least a century, the firstborn son inherited the ranch. That's how it went until now. If we'd kept that tradition, the ranch would eventually be yours. It might have happened if my dad had lived longer. But he didn't and the ranch became a collective endeavor, the legacy of all the brothers and my sons. I was the lynchpin of it all."

"But then it had to change."

"Yeah, we were grown men. I couldn't keep it as my personal vision. I had to include the rest of my family. I just wanted to spend my days exclusively with horses, Ben. The land is there primarily to feed and contain them. Honestly? That's the extent of my ambition. All those guests, and the mini–cabins and resort and café, along with the trinkets we sell, and river–rafting and snowmobile riding, all the other recreational things we do, or we used to do, were not my idea or my dream. Even when I started to get used to it, suddenly it was gone."

"More change."

"Yeah. And then, you were gone."

"This was about me too then?" He hated asking the question. It made him sound like a needy, little boy seeking his dad's approval and affection. But wasn't that the old Ben?

"Yes. It was mostly about not hearing from you."

"How did you find me?"

"I found you almost right off. When you were still using your credit card and before you sold your truck. Used a private investigator after that. So I knew what your new license plate number was. I always knew where you were, son. I just also knew I couldn't help you and you wouldn't want it."

He had no idea. Shock filled him. "Why didn't you use that knowledge?"

Jack shrugged. "I understood there was nothing I could do for you. That coming back here at my will would most likely make you hate me. I just had to let you go."

"If not for Jocelyn's baby…"

"I most likely would have never seen you again." His dad's voice was deadpan.

"Did you really believe that?"

"Yeah. I really did."

Silence filled the cab at his admission. They stared ahead at the empty sight where their house once stood. Maybe that contributed to his dad's drastic descent into depression and in *not* being Jack Rydell. "Maybe that's part of why you feel so disconnected from this place now."

"Maybe." His dad's tone was noncommittal, as if he wasn't convinced. Silence again.

"There's Erin," Ben said when he noticed her walking up towards the truck. Her hands were deep inside the pockets of her jeans. Her bare arms peeked through the long hair swinging around her shoulders. Her face was solemn. She looked almost awkward and unsure coming towards them. No doubt, she must have noticed when they pulled in a half hour ago and wondered what they were doing just sitting there.

His dad blew out a long breath. "Oh, fuck." He closed his eyes.

"What?" Ben's alarm grew. What now in this altered moonscape of post–apocalyptic fire? Would his dad start the truck and rush out of there like a thief, ditching all that once mattered to him in the world?

"It's not her. Not any of this. I love her. I need her. Turn away. I'm going to kiss her. I'm sorry if that causes you pain and all. I just… she thinks… I need to tell her…"

"Yeah, I'm sure she does think and you do need to tell her. It's okay, Jack. You don't have to avoid kissing your wife because I lost mine."

"One of these times, I'm going to sock you in the jaw for calling me Jack." His dad's lips didn't turn up a millimeter to smile at his cryptic remark. His solemn face remained tense. He tugged at his truck door handle. So did Ben. His dad stepped out and Erin stopped dead at the edge of the truck's bed.

There was a long, pregnant moment of tension as they both stared into each other's eyes. Ben had never evaluated his dad as a man before. Meaning, he had never considered his dad's marriage might need work or passion or that he could witness their obvious love for each other and be okay with it.

"Hey," Erin finally said. Her tone was soft and unsure.

His dad, with his fists flexing at his sides, moved forward in about four giant steps and swept the small body of Erin up into his arms, holding her against him and hugging her so tightly, she might not have breathed again. Ben almost grinned at hearing Erin's squeak of shock and surprise from the way his dad swept her feet out from under her. He watched his dad's arms as he leaned on the lip of the truck bed and kissed her. His mouth met hers in a long, hungry kiss that should have offended Ben as it was *his dad*. But maybe that was because he never let his dad be a real man any more than his dad allowed Ben to be. Something big must have shifted between them and Ben wasn't sure yet what it meant.

Erin responded as desperately, wrapping her arms around his neck, and letting minutes pass by before she finally struggled free and turned her face towards Ben's in a blush. "We... I mean... what...? *Where have you been?*" she finally settled on.

"Finding my way back to you," Jack replied.

He slowly let her feet fall onto the dirt. Tears spilled over her eyelids. "You scared me this time."

"I just needed a bit of... a pause."

"I know. I know. I know you do." Erin soothed him, cupping his dad's cheek. "I'll wait for however long you need just so long as I—"

"I love you, Erin. There is no doubt of that."

"Just everything else?"

Jack glanced at Ben and he had a feeling that was where his dad didn't usually answer directly. "Yes. Everything else. I needed a break. I needed to find Ben."

She wiped her wet cheeks with her knuckles, nodding,

and glanced at Ben. "I know you needed to find your son." She stepped away from Jack and walked around the truck bed before coming to a stop in front of him. Erin was a small woman and Ben towered over her. "Hello, Ben."

"Hi, Erin," he said, using a degree more of respect in his tone than he'd used with anyone since the fire happened. They had always shared a good relationship and not because of anyone else, just because they clicked.

She put a hand out and set it on his forearm, squeezing it. "I'm sorry about Marcy."

And so it began: the inane platitudes that meant nothing. That made him squirm, and he felt like tossing the temporary comfort and running away. He had to face it. The other problem he had was being around people he knew would ask questions. They'd comment and ask for his feedback. He'd have to start interacting eventually. Facing it. Dealing with it. Grieving over it. Instead of running away. Instead of surrendering to a permanent state of anger and just disappearing into the ether. Here, at least he mattered to people and what he did mattered. Here, he was relegated to finally facing it.

He jerked his head down and up in a rude nod and his throat collapsed. He couldn't speak. There were no words. His brain buzzed strangely, but there was nothing more to say. What he did to another human being. His head started to hurt again. His heart. His...

"Um, yeah, so I have no idea what's the best way to handle all this. But Jocelyn is about strung out with her nerves. We saw you pull in. We weren't sure what to do, and that's why I came up. She needs to get past this hurdle. Over this confrontation. So, I guess you ought to just go up there."

"Up there?"

Erin swung her gaze to Jack and licked her lips as she nodded. "Your apartment, Ben. We emptied Marcy's stuff and I gave some of it back to her family. As for the rest, I have it."

Ben was grateful to learn Erin had handled all of that in addition to the ranch and horses. Even now, his dad stood back at a distance, becoming quiet, dropping his arms at his side in total deference to Erin and her nurturing.

"There was nowhere else. It all burned, Ben. Everyone is displaced except for us and Ian and Kailynn. But they also have a houseful now. So... yeah, she's living there. *Temporarily;* she's very adamant about clarifying that point."

He opened the passenger door and grabbed his backpack, keeping his back to Erin. The pain rising in his chest began to suffocate him and the oxygen he craved seemed stuck in his throat. "Okay." But it wasn't. How could he go into that place? The place he formerly lived with Marcy. The last time he walked out of it, he was married, his life's path determined; maybe a rocky and bumpy path, but he believed it was his path to follow. It wasn't what he wanted now. He wasn't even the kind of person who could do what he came back for. His fear was very real. He was coming back to a... a baby? Another woman? A daughter?

"Alone?" Jack questioned.

"I don't see any easy way around it. But yes. Probably going alone is best."

Ben hiked his backpack onto his shoulder. "Yeah, okay." He passed around his dad and Erin, but felt their eyes boring into his back. He was glad there wasn't anyone else in front of him. He couldn't have dealt with a crowd or even another person. So much pressure was fraught in this encounter that he feared for his heart. The situation was unlike any he could ever have imagined. A more precarious, terrible situation was unfathomable and he put himself there.

His feet felt heavier with each step. Lifting the dead weight in the extreme gravity field he suddenly seemed trapped inside, his anxious nerves fluttered in his stomach. Something he thought dead inside him resurfaced. Feelings. His raw emotions overwhelmed him: dread, discomfort, and anger.

The stairs were located on the outside of the building. He started climbing up. Pausing, wincing, and trying to prepare himself. He could do this. He had to do it. There was no other choice.

He had to meet his daughter.

A wave of dizziness overwhelmed him and he almost fell off the landing onto the ground below him.

When he regained his balance, he set his hand on the doorknob and turned it.

CHAPTER 7

*J*OCELYN'S BREATHING WAS IRREGULAR and her chest hurt. Heart attack? Maybe. Considering the amount of adrenaline that pumped through her, why not?

Ben had been back home for half an hour. *Ben was back home*. Her heart was beating against her chest with loud regularity. Sure, he'd been there for a while but no one got out of the truck. Erin was standing with her when they drove up and they could see the ranch driveway from one of the windows. What were they doing out there?

It had to be due to the shock of seeing their family home in its current condition, or lack thereof, of course. Ben hadn't seen any photos of his home or the devastation the valley he loved and lived in had to endure.

"I can't take it anymore. I'm going out there to see what's up," Erin said finally after she grew too impatient from waiting for Jack or Ben to get out of the truck.

"Okay," Jocelyn said, her tone nearly reduced to a whimper. Her hands were clammy. Lillian rested against her chest, sound asleep. She fed her a while ago, then bathed and changed her into a soft lavender dress with matching little bottoms. Ribbons and flowers decorated the fabric and she smelled of sweet baby powder and freshly laundered clothes left to dry in the sun. Or at least, Jocelyn thought so. She paced the apartment. Keeping Lillian swaddled and close to her at all times, the little angel slept through it all. Jocelyn glanced down. Perhaps she should have taken the same pains with her appearance as she did with Lillian's. There she was, dressed in basketball shorts and a white t-shirt. She looked like she was ready for PE class. She flipped her short hair back only to let it flop forward again.

"It'll be okay. I mean it, Jocelyn."

"Yeah. I just want to get this over with."

"I hear you."

After Erin left, she paced the apartment some more. She gently nudged Lillian. Then she heard it. *Steps. Thumps.* Someone was just outside the door. The doorknob jiggled. She shut her eyes, and took in a deep breath. She could handle this. She'd faced much worse. She was tough. And strong.

Oh, hell, no. She'd never faced anything remotely like this.

They had a brief sexual encounter and never took a moment to make any sense of it. Their tryst was followed by loud screaming and evacuation orders before discovering that Marcy was missing and the ensuing chaos of updates from the command center and then nothing. Not a thing.

But in that time, something epic happened.

Now was the moment of truth. Except the door didn't open. She stepped closer to it. Waiting. Still nothing. Silence. Creepy, pervasive silence. She knew Ben was out there, less than two feet away, on the other side of the door, yet there was nothing coming from him. Nothing happened.

Finally, a soft tap on the door when he knocked.

Initially, she wanted to deny him access. She could have, too. This was her place. At least, for right now. She didn't want to face him. But she knew that was not an option. Putting her hand out, she touched the doorknob. Swallowing the lump in her throat, she sniffed. It was now or never. She had to do it. She earned this level of discomfort. She was responsible for this. Lillian was not to blame for anything and Lillian deserved to know her father.

She jerked the door open, suddenly feeling at odds with the gentle, graceful way she intended to face him.

Ben stepped back, surprised that she nearly yanked the doorknob out of his hand.

They stared at each other in a long, lingering moment, and their gazes collided. His eyes looked over her head, then at her face before carefully descending to the tidy bundle in her arms. He couldn't see anything but the blanket. Lillian wore a hat and her face was snugly burrowed against Jocelyn's chest.

"Ben?" His name came out as if she were being choked to death and gasping for her last breath of air.

His eyes returned to hers and he licked his lips. After another long, interminable moment, he said, "Hi."

Hi? All the months of agony, dread, fear, anger, and loneliness about that moment flashed through her brain. Seeing this man. Letting him discover the situation. And his profound response to this critical moment? Hi? Of course. What else would he have said? Did she expect him to fall to his knees in gratitude to be with her?

She stepped back. He hesitated at first but proceeded to stomp inside. He glanced around and she closed the door behind him. The click of the doorknob seemed to emphasize with loud condemnation that they were alone. Together. Finally. What now?

What was Ben feeling? she wondered. She couldn't see his

facial expression. She didn't know what he thought of seeing her belongings, and Lillian's baby paraphernalia and clothes filling up the space where his wife's stuff used to be. Jocelyn hadn't seen how it looked under Marcy's style, so she didn't know what Ben expected.

Ben slowly pivoted around and slid the backpack to the floor.

Jocelyn clutched her precious baby tightly to her chest, grasping the blanket in her fists. She found it hard to breathe and her skin practically boiled. This was so awkward, so terrible, and so unfair even in her worst scenarios. How wrong the situation was. Last time they spoke, they were friends. Last time they were together, they performed an act of betrayal to everything that meant anything to either of them. Now? Now, they had a baby together.

"I didn't know about... *that,*" Ben finally said. He was just standing there, shuffling his feet in silence, his gaze fixed on hers before glancing away.

That? Her baby? Their daughter? The human being in her arms. Lillian? He dared to call her *that?*

She bristled. "*She* isn't a *that.*"

He shook his head. "I know. I meant her. I didn't know about her."

"Of course, I understand you didn't know. But now that you do?"

"I'm trying to figure out what the hell to say to you. Sorry? Should I be sorry I was gone? Unavailable for it all? Or angry because you didn't tell anyone? There was no way I could have known."

"You wouldn't have known about it even if I told the entire valley. You were gone, Ben."

"It never occurred to me, not something like this." He waved towards her, indicating the sleeping baby.

"That and this. God, Ben. She's here. She's my daughter.

Yours too. But believe me, I don't give a crap what you decide to do with that knowledge. You had to know. I get that. But you do now and so far, your response was to take a ridiculous amount of time in coming back here and choosing not to call me. You could have called me at any point along with way, you know."

He crossed his arms over his chest. "I had no reason to call you."

"I meant after Jack found you and told you the news."

"Really? What could I have said over the phone? We can't even figure out what to do now."

She turned her head to the side, staring out the window towards the river. "I didn't trick you that night."

"I didn't think you did."

"You can't be angry at me about this part of it. I didn't want a baby any more than you did. In fact, I prayed very hard that I could learn to deal with it. But now that she is here, I wouldn't trade her for anything in the world."

He dropped his arms and shook his head, blowing out a deep breath. "It wasn't your fault. It was mine."

Flummoxed by his admission, she studied his down-turned face as he spoke, staring at his sneakers.

"We were both active participants," she muttered. Having violated their friendship, their hopes for a future relationship were risky.

"She... Marcy, I mean, in the past used to poke holes in the condoms I kept around. She wanted to have a baby. I kept saying no, considering how things were going. I think... I think she must've gotten to the one I wore that night. I'm sure it never occurred to her that I'd cheat. So you see, it's actually my fault."

Jocelyn's looked up and her head rushed with raw emotions. Anger. Shock. Relief. She was glad to know it wasn't her fault. The jolt of hearing *she* in reference to

Marcy, the dead woman, the one who formerly came between them, was a little harsh. Even hearing the word *condom* out of Ben's mouth had Jocelyn's cheeks flushing with heat. It never was that way between them.

What was the new norm for two longtime, childhood friends, who acted more like two guys together, when discussing their baby and other intimate things like sex and condoms? She took in a deep breath to steady her nerves.

Ben turned and flopped down on the couch, rubbing his disheveled hair. Jocelyn chewed on her lower lip, staring down at Ben sitting there slouched before her. Didn't he want to see his own child? Wasn't the curiosity killing him? She didn't get Ben. Who was this stranger before her whom she thought she'd known most of her life?

"Where did you go that night?"

She sat in the lone rocking chair given to her by one of the family members. They thought it would come in handy for soothing Lillian. She automatically began to rock back and forth, Lillian's warmth and weight in her hands bolstering her courage.

Ben stared at his feet. With a sigh, his shoulders jutted back as if he were steadying his nerves. "I drove around but was halted by the fire crew. Finally, I waited at the command center. The dispatches came in and I heard... I heard what happened."

She swallowed a lump of guilt and grief. The horror of his story didn't fail to upset her.

"The firefighter who gave me all the updates looked at me, and I knew. He turned to me and our eyes met and I instantly knew what he was about to say. I couldn't stay to hear it. I just... ran. I don't remember parts of it. I just took off running. I ran until I thought my heart would stop. Miles, I think. I remember smelling and tasting all the smoke. I finally walked back to my truck and got in. I didn't want to speak to anyone; I just started driving. I went faster and tried not to think. I could not think. I could not feel either. I just drove some more."

Tears fell over her eyelids. She could picture him so clearly doing that. The guilt must have nearly eaten his stomach alive. She understood only too well how suffocating guilt can be. She could only imagine his.

"I guess in most ways, I haven't stopped running yet. I try not to stop long enough to let it catch me." He lifted his gaze to hers. His blue eyes were haggard, stormy, and tortured. They were so full of emotions, Jocelyn reacted by clutching her baby closer. He looked so terrible. "Because I don't know what I'll do when it finally does hit me."

"That's why you left?"

"I didn't intend to come back."

"Because by being here, you think it might catch you?"

"Oh… it will catch me." His tone sounded hollow and defeated.

Jocelyn understood, perhaps more than anyone else. She dropped her gaze, unable to stand the bitterness, pain, guilt, and rage she now saw in Ben's once clear and trusting eyes. She hated how much he'd changed. The hardness she saw in his face and eyes along with the crushed slouch he now possessed made her sad.

After a long, uncomfortable silence, she whispered, "It's not Lillian's fault, Ben."

His gaze lifted off the ground and went from her to the bundle she held against her. "I know."

"I won't allow you to blame this innocent baby."

"I don't know what to do with her," he finally admitted. Jocelyn was startled by his statement… and the brutal honesty of it.

"You think I do? Until the moment I laid eyes on her, I had no clue either; then it all made sense."

His mouth was bracketed in lines of stress. He kept folding his hands and clasping them together. That small, nervous tic was endearing to Jocelyn and the only reason she didn't kick him out. His words and attitude were all wrong, but his visible anxiety showed something decent still resided in him. She had the same sense of discomfort, anxiety, and unsureness.

Something inside him might still feel *something* for her.

"Do you want to see her? Or are you going to just pretend she doesn't exist?" she finally spat out, unable to take his odd reaction any longer.

He nodded. "I know. I just don't know *how*."

"How to look at her?"

"How to do anything with her."

"You have to see your daughter," she said in a firm voice. "You simply have to. Or just leave now."

A small smile appeared on his lips. "That's the old you, the one I recognize. I don't even know how to talk to you anymore. You don't sound like the old you, either. Everything is all so fucking odd."

Nearly snorting, all the stress, worry, awkwardness, fear, and unease made Jocelyn's eyes fill with tears as she half laughed at the unique circumstances. "Oh, God, it's so fucking odd. How? How did we get here?"

Ben's eyes met hers in an honest and very real moment, and the knowledge of each other they shared passed between them. "I don't know. Honest to God, I've spent the last nine months trying to make some kind of sense of it and I can't, and then to cap it all off… this."

He nodded, slowly rising to his feet. Her heart beat faster as he stepped closer and she shut her eyes for a moment, unable to handle the intensity of his gaze. When her eyelids fluttered open, he was nearer to her, and his body heat seemed to singe her skin. She was so physically aware of him. He put a hand on the back of the wooden chair, just behind her head. His other hand rested on the armrest and he leaned over her. She nearly gulped out loud as she gently loosened her baby from her chest and lay her flat on her thighs.

Lillian made a face and startled at the sudden movement. The blanket slid down, exposing her chest and little hands to the cooler air. She scrunched up her face and lifted her hands up by her head before slowly settling back into sleep. Those kind of moments happened by the hundreds but never failed to keep Jocelyn entranced. She was captivated, and nearly smitten with her daughter while watching her sleep. She wanted to catalogue every movement and file it away for her heart to hold on to.

"This is our daughter, Ben."

Ben leaned closer. His profile was directly in her line of sight. His hair fell over his forehead and he started to tug at the blanket before he stopped. "I should wash my hands first. We stopped at a tavern earlier for lunch."

She sniffed and recognized the flat smell of beer on his breath. Wonderful. Lovely. But her heart was thumping hard. Why wasn't Ben melting? Or holding Lillian to his chest? Or calling her every complimentary adjective there was: lovely, beautiful, wonderful, adorable, cute? No words could capture the essence of the creature in her arms, but why wasn't he falling in love with her like she did?

"What do you think?"

"She's so… small."

Precious. Helpless. Delicate. Needy. Vulnerable. Theirs. She was also theirs and her entire well-being, safety, nutrition, hell, her survival depended upon them. How could that not slam through Ben's mind and stimulate his need to protect and shield her from everything and everyone who could possibly threaten her? Why wasn't that sense of responsibility that she felt not suffocating Ben? He was not falling to his knees or taking her into his arms.

"She weighed six pounds and one ounce when she was born. She's tiny. But healthy. Very healthy. She lost a few ounces shortly after birth, but is gaining them back. I guess that is normal."

"That's... that's good. I mean, I'm glad she's doing so well."

I did that. Jocelyn wanted to scream into his face. She successfully bore their daughter safely to term and delivered her whole and *healthy*. She happily nourished, loved, and cared for her so why didn't Ben feel like that? His words were so... generic. God. She could slam her fist into his face. How could he be so blasé with his first glimpse at the tiny angel he saw in Jocelyn's arms?

He didn't rise, but kept staring at her. Jocelyn had no idea what he was thinking. It wasn't how she pictured the moment. How could anyone look at this most perfect being ever born on the earth and not have a passionate response and instant attachment to her? She figured he'd need to hug her, hold her, and apologize for appearing so late in her life. Days late. Almost two whole weeks.

Was he angry at the circumstances that made her?

No, Ben was unsure, timid, and oddly apathetic about Lillian, but Jocelyn did not sense any anger; and that almost made Jocelyn want to hurt him. How could he not be passionate one way or the other about this child? Was he numb? Surely he possessed some feelings. Some recognition of his paternity, and his relationship to the most beautiful child of the century? Instead, he seemed completely unsure and so uncomfortable as if she might reach up and bite him. Why was he so wary and keeping his distance?

He straightened up and walked to the kitchen sink to wash his hands, acting for the first time as if he recognized the living space.

Lillian started to squirm around and yawn before her blue eyes popped open, as well as her mouth. Her face scrunched up and she let out a squeaky yelp and then another until she built up for a real good, lusty howl and then another.

"What's wrong with her?" Ben turned from the sink, quickly drying his hands. He stared in alarm at the baby.

"Well, I don't know exactly, Ben. I became a parent the same goddamned day that you did. I suppose she's hungry, or needs a diaper change, or simply a cuddle. Or perhaps, her stomach hurts or she needs to cough or fart or... How the hell do you think I know?" Jocelyn stood up as her voice rose in competition with the rising shrills of Lillian. "She's just a baby. She doesn't tell me what's wrong."

"I've never been around babies. Just Shane's. But I didn't take much interest. I mean..."

Jocelyn gritted her teeth. "Well, neither have I. Not once. I didn't inherit some kind of special *mommy powers* just because you had sex with me and fertilized my egg. I mean, for crap sakes, Ben, I know nothing about parenting either. I've been shown how to do everything and what little I know is purely from doing and trying. So I'm going to try something with her because that's all I can do; never mind that it's the hardest thing I've ever done."

Of course, she could not contain her anger. His sheer lack of gratitude for this baby once he made eye contact with her had Jocelyn fuming and roiling in anger. How dare he not fall in love with her at first sight? Here. Now. At this moment. He was her *father*. Jocelyn was her mother and despite being terrified and afraid of having a baby, the moment Jack showed Lillian to her as she lay on the hard floor of the shack, all she could feel was unconditional love for her child. One moment. One second. And Ben? Eh. His reaction was so unimpressed, stating how small she was. No.

No, that wasn't okay. Where was his love for her, toward her, about her? Where was the father he should have been? Just as she became the mother she now was? It wasn't magic. It wasn't based on preplanning or even wanting a baby, but once seeing that baby, the bond was established. And there was something drastically wrong with Ben if he could not feel that.

She turned and clutched her screaming infant and went into the bedroom, slamming the door. Her tears falling, she quickly changed the dirty diaper and planted Lillian on her breast. All the while, she glared at the closed door and her sinking expectations settled into a knot that lodged in her stomach.

CHAPTER 8

$\mathcal{B}$EN STOOD AT THE kitchen sink. His mouth dropped open in shock at the now empty spot where Jocelyn just stood. She left in a flurry and locked herself in the bedroom. What the hell? What did he do? He was simply washing his hands, preparing to touch the baby. Why would she fly off the handle at that? What did he say that was so wrong? He felt numb. Inside and outside. Even his fingertips didn't feel like they belonged to him, as if the sensations he received were being felt by someone else. It was like an out-of-body experience to return to his former place of residence and instead of finding Marcy and his previous life there, he felt oddly transported into another person's life.

The whole thing was an unmanageable disaster. And nothing could instantly turn it around into anything better. He had to face his own family as well as the judgmental residents of the valley. Yeah, all them too. He knew he had to stay. There was nowhere else for him to go or live, and any freedom he might have had prior to that moment was over too. Whether he wanted the child in the next room or not, it didn't matter anymore. It was over and done. Now he had to live with the consequences of his poor judgment.

A loud thump on the door interrupted his rambling, overwhelming thoughts.

He answered the door, grateful for the distraction. Charlie stood there.

Ben's heart was nearly crusted over in a layer of ice and stone. He sometimes wondered why he was still alive, but all of that fractured just a sliver at the sight of his cherished little brother. Now fifteen, Charlie had grown a little in the last nine months. He wasn't nearly as tall as Ben and Jack were. He had brighter red hair than Ben's auburn, dull-red color. Charlie had freckles and the same bright blue eyes as Ben and Jack. The family genes were distinctly represented when all three of them were together. He could not remember how many times he'd been told he was the spitting image of his father, only twenty years younger. It was impossible to count how often people said that.

"Hey, Charlie."

"'Hey Charlie'? That's all you have to say? 'Hey'?" Charlie's face didn't break into a smile. His gaze remained frosty and his lips turned down into a mean scowl. "Where have you been?"

"Why don't you come in?"

"I don't want to come in. I want to know where you've been." The unbridled anger emanated from Charlie's slim shoulders. He wasn't a large kid, but small, narrow, and compact. Ben didn't expect him to ever undertake any heavy lifting for the ranching chores.

"I traveled to Montana. I worked odd jobs. Settled down to working on the oil fields that are all over the east end of the state. Lived in cheap motels."

"How could you just leave?"

"Marcy—"

"Died. She died and we buried her without you. We grieved for her as well as you; we lost both of you. While Dad…"

Ben winced. Leave it to his brother to cut right into it. "Yeah, Dad's not—"

"Dad anymore. You ruined him, you selfish prick. First, you went off and got married without anyone's knowledge and then when your wife died, you chose to disappear? Then the whole place burned up and it took all of us just to keep it afloat. So where were you? *Where were you, Ben?*"

"Charlie." Ben stepped back, almost physically pushed away by the fierce savageness of Charlie's pent–up anger towards him. Shocked by it, actually. He'd been treated so far with compassion and kindness. Most people felt so sorry for him, they could not stand it, let alone lay into him over it. "I've been… screwed up in the head too. As much as Dad is, so was I."

"Because of you, he thinks it's somehow his fault. He thinks he ruined your life. Really though, it was exactly the opposite. You ruined our lives. Our home burned. It's all gone. I watched it smoldering for days and where were you? Nowhere. Nowhere that mattered, anyway." Charlie fisted his hands. His tone wasn't loud, but mean and accusatory.

The door behind him clicked. Ben glanced back and saw Jocelyn, holding *his baby* against her chest. Jiggling Lillian around, she seemed to be following the rhythm of some kind of unconscious, soothing lullaby. Charlie stared past him too. His gaze went from Ben to Jocelyn and back. When he spoke, it was a strangled whisper. "How could you do *that?*"

They both flinched.

All of a sudden, Charlie spun on his heel and ran down the stairs like a bullet. He flashed across the road, heading towards the barns before he disappeared over the horizon. Ben's head dropped. Defeated, shocked, unsettled, and embarrassed, he barely managed to shut the door. Turning to face Jocelyn, they stared at each other.

She shook her head. "He's right. How could we have?"

"He's just a kid. He doesn't understand."

Jocelyn's head shook and fresh tears brimmed over her eyes. "I'm an adult and I honestly don't understand. How could we have done this, Ben? You saw Charlie's reaction. That's going to be pretty much everyone's. Beyond your family, that is what average people will think of us. And her." Jocelyn jiggled Lillian in her arms. "I can't stand people thinking that of her. She didn't do anything wrong. We put her here in this place. That's why I haven't left the ranch."

She dropped her head down. Toying with the blanket over the baby, she shook her head. "I can't even face you."

Something burst inside Ben. Some kind of resolution that made his gut twist and contort. Anger, blinding rage, and self–disgust kept him isolated for months in a near drunken or drugged stupor. Trying to avoid the very feelings Jocelyn was expressing, Ben stayed self–medicated because he could not handle the "sin" he'd committed. How wrong it was. But Jocelyn? She hadn't really done anything wrong. He knew that too, didn't he?

But even Jocelyn looked different than he left her. Everything was different. Changed. Unrecognizable to how it used to be.

But now, her wardrobe was completely understated, underwhelming, and almost ordinary. Even the way she was groomed seemed odd for Jocelyn. He liked the loudness of her former appearance. It was a part of her. What made her unique and different. And part of what he admired in her. Being constrained by societal norms, living up to his dad's expectations, and trying to be proper his entire life, Ben had to adhere to a precise path. To be as free and unusual as Jocelyn? Never. He didn't have the guts to risk that.

But now, Jocelyn looked almost ordinary.

Things hadn't been easy for her. He hadn't given her the credit or concern she was due. But he had no idea of the secret she carried around with her, growing inside her body.

The stress she had to endure, along with the sleepless nights, could have been the source of why she looked so different.

In that moment, he accepted the reality that this was now his life. He wasn't escaping or shirking the responsibility; and he wasn't drifting and doing whatever he wanted. The last nine months were like nothing else in his life and he would not allow his personality to be affected by them. The days of self-medication and drifting around aimlessly while feeling sorry for himself were long gone; he was home now and had to accept all it entailed.

He found no joy or relief in it. On the contrary, it was a heavy, overwhelming burden being set on his shoulders. Knowing that these two before him now depended on him was a large pill to swallow. He had to stay home now. Until he saw his dad and learned about his baby, he dreamed of never coming home. He dreamed of *not* having to ranch again, or live according to the protocol and expectations of his family, specifically, his father. That was his plan after Marcy died. Everything he considered decent inside him died along with her. He wasn't sure if he felt relieved or disappointed when he realized he still had a streak of decency left inside him, otherwise, he would have just left.

He altered Jocelyn. He changed her life forever. He made her ashamed to face her own neighbors. Jocelyn was the most independent person he'd ever known. She didn't seem to care what anyone thought about what she did or said or how she dressed. To find her hiding here on the ranch like a criminal was the antithesis of the girl he thought he knew.

"She shouldn't bear the brunt of... you know, what happened."

"She will." Jocelyn shook her head. "You heard your little brother."

Ben sighed. Trapped again. Marcy trapped him into an early marriage. Now he was trapped by Lillian. He glanced at Jocelyn. She wasn't even trying to trap him. He understood that much about her. She did not expect him to take care of her. She preferred to take care of herself and had done so all her life. Joey and his dad were shocked when they saw where she lived, but Ben had always known. Growing up dirt poor without any advantages, much less help, didn't stop her. All the obstacles in her path never hindered her or made her act out. She worked and got whatever she wanted, and more importantly, she survived. She didn't complain about anything or resent anyone else for having more than she did. Unlike Marcy.

Ben shut his brain off. It didn't help to make comparisons. It didn't matter. He wasn't pitting one versus the other. One was dead. One was alive. Regardless, *he* had arranged it so that he was trapped there forever and had to live and work and die on the ranch. His life loomed before him, long and desolate, boring and mundane, just as it was the entire year before Marcy died.

It was impossible for him to imagine just a few years ago, when he was young, hopeful, and excited about his life. And his marriage. He felt so alive then.

But Marcy tricked him. Claiming she was pregnant, Ben did the right thing and married her according to her plan. To Ben, it was all one perfect package, so why not just get married sooner than later if they were going to be parents? But there was no baby. He caught Marcy putting pinholes in his condoms although she denied it. Eventually, however, in a moment of pride and power, she admitted how she tricked him.

Ironically, the trick was on her. She erroneously assumed once they were married they'd move into the main house at the ranch. But unbeknownst to them, his dad and uncles agreed to convert it and include it as part of the resort. Marcy did not take kindly to that decision, or the lack of influence Ben had; Ben didn't have much authority at the ranch. No matter how many times he explained to her it wasn't his personal ranch, none of it mattered to Marcy. It belonged to his dad and his three uncles in equal shares. Ben had no involvement in the matter at all. She didn't like that.

Fighting over small things, they both suffered from short tempers, anger, and resentment. Knowing about her duplicitous side undermined his subsequent interactions with her. It tainted how Ben once felt about her too. He began to realize that all the annoying things he was blind to before had become intolerable. His attraction toward Marcy started to wane. All the strong feelings he thought would last forever faded in a very short time. It surprised him. He finally understood what others so gently tried to explain to him, that he didn't really *know* Marcy. The scary part was, the more he uncovered about her personality, the less attractive she became to him. He was finding her very unappealing.

But they were married. They had a commitment. It was a done deal. He vowed to make the best of it. More things kept happening. Her stories didn't add up. She'd disappear and he couldn't locate or contact her while her excuses became increasingly transparent. She was lazy, unskilled, and inept. She did nothing at work, nothing at home, nothing anywhere she went.

Jocelyn was the complete opposite of Marcy. Ben trusted his original assessment of Jocelyn. He clearly saw her, *all of her* and had for years. He stepped directly in front of her. At five foot ten, she was only a few inches shorter than he. But Jocelyn was here, where Marcy was not. The only thing he could fix about everything he'd done wrong, was right here in front of him. The knowledge of what he was about to commit to sunk heavily into his gut. He didn't want this. Not for a moment, a day, a month, let alone years. But there was no other choice. He had nowhere else to go, in all honesty, and even he hadn't changed so much he could turn his back on the baby that was his.

She shook her head. "I don't even recognize you anymore."

"That's okay, I don't either. But I'll be here."

"You're not leaving then?" Her face tipped up for a second and then dropped back down.

"No. I'm not leaving. I'm here, Jocelyn. I'll be here for both of you. Do you want me to stay with my dad and Erin?"

"It's your home, Ben. Not mine."

"You're definitely not taking her back to the shack."

Jocelyn's mouth barely lifted in a smile. "Yes, that shack surprised them all."

"Not me. Why did you go back there?"

She shrugged. "Imagine the old bat, Gardner, letting me stay on when she learned I was pregnant. But her house burned up in the fire so it was easier to go back to the shack than look for a new place anywhere else. Miraculously, the shack didn't burn. Besides, Cutter's been gone for so long now, maybe he'll never come back. The shack was only a temporary solution."

"That's so fucked up in this day and age. Anyway, can I stay here?"

"Yes."

"The couch is fine for me."

She nodded and clutched the baby closer to her. Her shoulders sagged. "I'm glad this is finally over. I didn't know how to introduce my unplanned baby to her absentee, proba-bly–hates–me   best–friend–until–I–slept–with–him–one–night father. I have no idea what the protocol is on this."

He laughed out loud and looked surprised. He hadn't laughed so hard in months. He always appreciated that about Jocelyn, she was real. No pretentious bullshit for her. "I was nervous as shit."

"Me too. I've had a stomach ache for hours."

"I had to stop and pound down a few beers for courage."

They shared a small smile. Something nice flowed in his bloodstream. Something close to feeling connected to another. Something close to feeling good. He could not remember any special looks between him and Marcy. Where there had always been between him and Jocelyn. Long before *that night* even. Before they ruined it all.

"So I used to be your best friend? What am I now?"

"Um… I don't know; the baby daddy, I guess."

He snorted. "God, this is…"

"Surreal? Like we turned into different people? Like we are living someone else's lives? Yeah, I know."

The baby started to squirm in her arms and Jocelyn sighed. "Feeding time." She turned on her heel and disap-peared into the bedroom again. What did that mean? Did Jocelyn breastfeed? It almost made him laugh out loud to picture the tomboy he once knew putting a baby to her breast. It seemed so motherly. So feminine, and so not Joce-lyn. He rubbed his head and flopped onto the couch.

Having survived this critical confrontation, now he only had to get through a few dozen more before he could settle back into the life he previously abandoned and live it to its fullest.

BEN'S HEAD ached as if an axe were stuck into it, splitting his skull in half. The incessant crying. Lillian hadn't stopped for hours. Though partially muted by the closed door, the infernal sound could be heard no matter how many times he tucked the pillow over his ears to drown it out. Nothing he tried could muffle it. Nothing helped. She cried and cried. How could Jocelyn stand it?

He sat up, stretching, and rubbing his eyes. He arose, still dressed in the same clothes from yesterday and went to the sink to splash some water over his face. He gulped some into his dry mouth and glanced at the bedroom. Still crying. Fuck it. He grabbed a granola bar and headed outside, pissing behind the building before heading toward the barns.

Joey saw him and stopped dead. They stared at each other across the gloomy space.

"So it's true. You're back." Joey's tone was frigid, like ice cubes could drop off his tongue.

"Yeah."

What? No sympathy? No condolences about Marcy? Nothing from Joey. He simply took the pitchfork in his hand and tossed it towards Ben, who caught the handle. "Stalls are ready and waiting."

Ben sighed. Yeah, some things didn't change. They worked in compatible silence for an hour mucking the stalls. Some required fresh straw and they refilled the water troughs and fed all the horses. Several mounds of hay had to be delivered to the horses by truck or tractor. They visited the various pastures and added barley and a block of sea salt before attending to their personal stable of horses. Jack always required they do it in that order.

"I didn't even know she was pregnant," he finally admitted to Joey after two hours of silence. Erin joined them halfway through before taking off to start training some of the horses.

"You should have checked on her. After that night? How could you not check on her even once?"

"We used a condom. I doubt she told you, but we had protected sex. I had no reason to doubt it failed."

"Jocelyn was *your friend*, before all of it. And that's what should have motivated you to check on her. And us. You should have check on us. The ranch burned up and you didn't even call home *once*. When did you find out about it?"

"This week," Ben confessed, looking ashamed. "I had shit to go through too."

"I know." Joey's voice lost some of its glacial freeze. "But despite that, we didn't know if you were dead or alive. The grieving and all? How could we know how you were handling it? Everyone here was sorry to hear about Marcy, and you're just being a dick if you want to pretend we don't care, or wouldn't give you whatever you asked for or do whatever is necessary for you to handle this. But sleeping with Jocelyn on that night of all nights and then not even contacting her? Not once?"

He gritted his teeth. "I didn't know."

Joey glared at him, throwing down the bag of feed he carried. "She was alone on the dirty floor, giving birth to a baby she never told another soul about. No one. Not even me. She was afraid to tell even me. She's the only woman I've been friends with for fifteen years, and there she was all alone, suffering, scared, and wouldn't tell me because of you. So while I'm sorry about you losing Marcy, there were a lot of other factors in all of this that should have made you contact home at the very least. It wasn't right. It wasn't fair what happened to you. But neither were you being fair or doing the right thing by Jocelyn." Joey pushed past him and left the building. Ben kept his gaze on him before turning away. *Whatever.* Disappointing another family member at this point was no surprise. Nor even that painful.

Ben continued with his self-assigned chores.

After he finished the barns, Ben headed to barn office that used to be his dad's. He found his uncle Ian in there, typing at a computer. Ian halted, lifting his eyes to look at him in a cool, neutral gaze. Ben felt Ian's disdain all the way to his toes. He understood Ian and skipped pleasantries. "Dad's out, isn't he?"

"Out?"

"You're running it all now, aren't you?"

"Not by choice. No one can get him to give a fuck. I didn't steal it from him. I quit a job I actually liked to come back here. For my wife. For her father and brothers, and for my brothers, that's why I'm running this."

"I know. I'm back. What do you need?"

Ian stared at him. "You're really staying?"

Ben sat down, leaning forward and resting his elbows on his knees. "I have a child now. I have no money to speak of and no other prospects. So yeah, I'm staying."

"Jack made it sound like..."

"I might have been fucked up when he found me. I didn't know about the baby. I had no idea. I was trying to forget Marcy. I'm back now."

Ian held his gaze, and his eyes sparked with concern when he said her name, *Marcy*. Getting Ian to show his emotions was a good indicator of how bad Ben's loss was. "I'm sorry, Ben, you know, about what happened to her."

"Yeah, me too. Though it's hard for some people to believe, given what I was doing at the time and what I did to her."

"Ben..."

"Please, let's just concentrate. You, of all people, can do that for me, can't you, Ian? Keep it all business?"

Ian stared at him across the desk. He shuffled his hands over the paperwork. Finally, he nodded. "Yeah, I can do that."

"Okay. Then where are we at? What's going on here?"

"What do you mean? Like for temporary work? Or are you all in for the long term?"

"All in. It's time I was. Maybe I can help make up for some of my dad's apathy."

Ian spent the next several hours showing Ben the books, their insurance claims, and how much they received compared to their losses as well as the latest progress on rebuilding.

Ben sat back finally. "We lost a lot."

"Yeah." Ian's jaw tightened.

"Does anyone else know how much? How tightly budgeted we are?"

"Ah, sure. Shane and Joey have a pretty good idea."

"The exact totals?"

Ian hesitated before he shook his head. "I think we can recoup our losses, keep building it up and get the resort running again. If we can hold out until then, we should be fine."

"I don't think Dad's coming back. I mean, to run this place like he used to. He was talking about rescuing horses, and only training and caring for them. You hear him talk like that before?"

"Your dad isn't the same man since the night you left. Yeah, I heard some of it."

Ben sighed, leaning forward, staring at the tips of his boots. Back in his jeans, cowboy boots, t-shirt, and hat. Back home again.

"I think we have to assume, from here on out, it's Shane, you, Joey... and me."

Ian stared at him, his head bobbing. "You're sure about this? Because you don't have to. We can always use the extra work, but you don't have to volunteer to take on the stress of this place. It's not always a lovely bowl of cherries."

Ben lumbered to his feet. "Ian, I need some stress and burdens to keep my mind busy. Something that isn't about my past. Or my choices. I'm here, right? Where the fuck was I ever really intending to go? All I know is ranching and horses and training. I learned it from Dad. I think I'm ready to step up. How many places can a guy do this stuff nowadays? While traveling around, all I got was grunt work because I didn't have skills in anything beyond those of the ranch. So what else can I do in reality? Get hired as a ranch hand somewhere else? Why? Not when I could do it here. I married Marcy at nineteen, I've now fathered a kid and I'm twenty–two years old. This is it for me, ya know? My life. My place. Better to work for myself and you guys than somebody else. Sure, I can handle it."

Ian stood up and leaned across the desk, stretching his hand out. "All right, Ben. Consider yourself part of the whole operation now."

Ben shook his uncle's hand firmly.

As he turned to leave, Ian said, "Your dad? Not like anyone else when it comes to this place. You don't have to do it to the exclusivity of everything else, like he did. Maybe that's why he burnt himself out. Find balance, Ben, both in your work and your personal life. Your dad had so many years when he couldn't achieve that balance."

Burnt out? Something quivered in his stomach. It almost hurt. Was his dad being put out to pasture when it came to managing the ranch and horses? How could his dad's career end like that?

So Ben went back to work. He slept on the couch of his apartment and listened to Lillian crying all evening and half the night although he tried to drown it out under a pillow. He was always polite to Jocelyn, although they did a damn fine job of avoiding each other. And he worked very hard. His day started when the sun came up and ended when it was nearly dark. It kept him out of Jocelyn's way, and his own. Exhausted by the long hours of physical labor and mental fatigue from learning about the ranch management, the accounts, and plans, Ben stayed busy, constructively occupied, and tired. Feeling tired was good. It meant, at night, when he closed his eyes and turned off his brain, he didn't replay the images of Marcy in the flames or think about his betrayal. Hard work on the ranch did more for Ben than all the drugs and alcohol he used previously to forget the past.

CHAPTER 9

*B*EN NEVER TOUCHED THE baby. Jocelyn fumed as she scrubbed the dishes and rinsed them, her gaze fixed on the rushing river outside. Ben had not once held Lillian or cuddled her or even touched her. He worked long hours. Jocelyn would give him that much credit. Which was a surprise given what Erin had said Jack found Ben like in Montana. Ben was an angry, unbathed, uncooperative jerk. She fully expected attitude from him. And some anger. But instead, all she got was a cold, mechanical wall of nothing. Ben was not angry, nice, polite or rude. He simply existed in the same space as she. He now bathed, groomed and, to her knowledge, didn't particularly drink, but that was about all she could say for him.

Ben handed her a wad of cash after a few days. Jocelyn objected but Ben shook his head and said, "She's mine. And yours. Right?"

"Yes."

"Then I pay for things too. Besides, you're still on maternity leave. God, just let me do this. It's the one thing I can do." Jocelyn assumed that meant the one positive thing Ben could contribute was money. He sure as shit didn't donate his time, energy, concern or do any legwork with their daughter. He left early in the morning and came back late. He ate very little and talked even less. He never asked about Lillian or even glanced her way. Jocelyn expected his being home to be a game–changer, something pretty epic; but all she saw was a fizzling let down. There was nothing between them.

In response to his offer of money, she commented, "I inquired about a job at the River's End Café. They have someone quitting come the end of the summer so they'll let me start taking shifts at the end of July. So…"

Ben frowned. "What? Aren't you employed here?"

"I need to get away from here. I realize that. When I worked here before, I left every day to go home. Now home is here and I can't handle both."

"You like restaurant work?'

"I loved running the café." She shrugged.

"But it burned." He finished her statement. "I didn't realize how much you liked it."

"It was the first job I didn't consider grunt work. So yes, I did."

"But waitressing at the café is basically grunt work."

"To me, it's work."

Ben stopped, hearing her final statement. She turned and headed back to the bedroom to change and feed Lillian.

LATER, fuming with frustration, Jocelyn smacked the dish-towel against the counter, although it had little effect, but it felt good to release some of her anger. Two weeks of living with Ben as an absentee roommate was too much. How could he not even touch his own child? Jocelyn preferred to never see Ben again and simply collect his fucking blood money through the mail. That's all Lillian was to him. A financial burden for the next eighteen years he would kindly acknowledge by sending monthly checks. His only contribution was money and that could be collected from far away. But Ben's family continued to help her and that help was golden to her.

Kailynn brought her meals. Erin and Allison traded off babysitting for her. Ian insisted on buying all her groceries, no matter how often she tried to discourage him. Even Shane and Joey pitched in and allowed her an hour to take a quick jog down the road. She had so much help, she almost felt guilty. One day after Jack and Ben returned to the ranch, Jack knocked on the door. He offered to take Lillian for the afternoon. He said he was just *hanging out;* his words. She allowed him to do it. She was a little hesitant, but also somewhat confident, since Jack had taken care of two babies at an early age and raised them. And besides, he was Lillian's grandfather. When she returned to pick Lillian up, she found him cuddling her and talking away in a soft voice.

After he caught her staring at him, looking surprised, he ducked his head sheepishly. "She likes being talked to. I'm just giving her a brief summary of what the world's all about."

Jocelyn pressed her small, precious bundle against her breast as Jack added, "When you go back to work, I can watch her sometimes. I mean, I'm right here…"

She nodded, rather astonished he would make such an offer. Wasn't Jack ever going to get back to training his beloved horses? She replied that she'd keep his offer in mind.

Leaving the ranch seemed self–defeating. There were so many helping hands, she was spoiled by it. She consulted Allison for all her baby knowledge. Many times, Jocelyn rushed over to her with one question or another. How long could she store breast milk? What was that red mark on Lillian? Was she gaining enough weight? Was that mole changing in size or color? And someone always showed up when she needed them and took Lillian, saving her sanity. Of course, living there seemed the sensible solution for her and the baby. Never mind Ben. The idea of working there, however, left her cold. No, she intended to hitch her wagon somewhere else so she wasn't *completely* dependent on them.

Ben was all but totally useless to her. She gnashed her teeth. After weeks of their odd existence, cohabitating together, he offered her nothing. And he still hadn't even held his baby. Jocelyn did everything; she held, soothed, fed, and cared for Lillian by the hour, day and night. Not even once did he offer to relieve her of that duty. No. He merely stayed on the couch, wrapping the pillow around his head, nearly cowering, to avoid hearing all the crying. As if Lillian *disturbed* him.

Jocelyn spent a lot of time walking outside in the fresh air with Lillian strapped to her chest in a sling. Lillian got fussy sometimes and walking seemed to be the best way to soothe and lull her into sleeping. She saw Ben sometimes on her walks. Yeah, why not? He was always working. Maybe she should have been grateful that the father of her child did so much to provide for her. But that was all he did. She knew in her heart, working was only the means by which Ben could ignore his guilt.

Jocelyn started to tidy up the small living room, kicking Ben's sleeping bag off to the side, fluffing his pillow, and picking up miscellaneous items from the small side table. She nearly fell on her face when her foot smacked into something hard. Hopping around, she cursed as she glanced down to see what heavy item she had smacked her foot on. *Ben's backpack.* She sighed, staring at the culprit before kicking it again in anger, only this time, she was careful not to hurt herself.

The top was open so she glanced down at it. Ben had clothes in the bedroom he didn't use. He only wore the few outfits he brought in the backpack. What was that about? Denial of all things related to his time with Marcy?

Marcy. Her shoulders slumped forward. So often that happened. After building up a good, healthy dose of anger toward Ben, it all deflated when she remembered Marcy. Marcy died, and now here they were. How could she expect Ben to be doing any better?

She flopped down on the couch, rubbing her injured toe. How could Ben resist the urge to touch his own baby? It was... monstrous. Jocelyn didn't know how to reconcile the Ben she used to think she cared about to the Ben she saw now. He was cold, remote, and simply there, taking up space. There wasn't another positive thing to say about him. If only Ben could behave like a normal human being. He refused to show passion or anger or hatred or anything else about the situation. Even to his own baby.

She glanced down again and her eye hooked on the small, round, hourglass-shaped item she saw tossed on top of his clothes. She bent down and examined the small pipe. Her mouth dropped open. Using that as her justification for prying into his personal belongings, she decided to further inspect the contents of his smelly, dirty, worn-out backpack. She dumped all the contents on the floor and gasped when the drugs plopped out after she shook it to empty it. Marijuana, sure. She already gathered that when she saw the pipe. Okay, it was legal now, so not the worst, even if it were still surprising from the once straight-laced Ben Rydell. He didn't even drink until he graduated high school that she could recall. And was staunchly against drugs the whole time she knew him. At least, he used to be.

She picked up the small, plastic baggie of grayish-colored powder with no idea how to identify the substance. All she knew was, it wasn't flour, and of that she was sure.

Ben did drugs now?

Her heart thumped fast and adrenaline pumped through her body. Without another thought, she grabbed Lillian out of the playpen and nestled her sleeping form in her arms. Then she stormed off towards Jack and Erin's house. No one answered when she knocked so she went next door to Ian's. She stomped as loudly as she could with a sleeping newborn in her arms.

She knocked with her fist, releasing her fury on the door.

Ian opened the door wide when he spotted her. He started to smile but stopped when she stormed past him. She saw Kailynn in the kitchen with Erin and Allison. Shane was lounging in the living room with Joey and Jack. The entire family was there after having had dinner together. Jocelyn had been invited too, but she had declined.

She whipped around, holding the disgusting item in her hand.

Erin walked in from the kitchen and Charlie whipped his head up from staring at the TV. His headphones were on and he was playing an online game with Jacob Starr, who was at the ranch visiting Joey with his mom, Hailey, Joey's girlfriend.

"Ben's on drugs."

Jocelyn's blunt statement was so loud, it crashed between them all with the subtlety of a barbell being thrown into the room.

Erin gasped. Charlie whipped his headphones off, staring dumbfoundedly at her. A low murmur of shocked exclamations filtered through the room. Jack? Jack kind of shrugged and nodded as he slowly got to his feet. "Well, I think he's used them in the past. But I don't believe he's *on them*. More of a... a coping agent he feels he needs sometimes."

"Wait? *You knew?*" Jocelyn's voice pitched higher, emphasizing her shock.

Erin came closer too, her forehead wrinkled in distress. "Jack?" she asked in a tone just as horrified as Jocelyn's.

Jack shuffled his feet and shrugged. "Well, I saw them in his motel room. It's just something he used to cope in the past, I think."

"You allowed him to bring drugs into where I live? With his baby? You allowed... Well? What is it?"

Jack cleared his throat. "Heroin."

"Oh, my God!" Allison exclaimed behind them. Erin and Kailynn closed their eyes in disbelief before staring at each other and blinking in horror.

"Heroin?" Erin's screech had Jack compressing his lips as his eyeballs darted around.

"Well, like I said before, I think it was just a—a passing interest. I don't think he's doing it now."

"You *don't think?*" Erin's tone became shrill again, her horror increasing the higher her voice climbed. "What is wrong with you?" She stomped forward. "Where is the man I married? You found heroin on Ben's person, and knowing he was doing it, you what? What did you do?"

"I... Well, I asked him about it."

"And?"

"And what? I just, I don't know; we started talking about other things. I didn't ask about it again."

Erin stared at Jack. Everyone in the room stared at Jack as a weird hush ensued.

She shook her head, then pushed past Jack, leaving her back to him. "You are not the man I married."

Jocelyn glared at Jack. "Why? Why didn't you tell me?"

"I just, hell, you don't know how I found him in Montana.

He actually pulled himself together better than I expected. He stayed, didn't he? His only obligation was to set up support payments. He's working very hard and trying to belong here. I barely convinced him to come back. I told him he at least had to pay for the cost of raising his child. He's doing that—"

Erin whipped back around. "You told your son, he at the *minimum* had to pay for the cost of his child? What did you mean by that, Jack? He could just leave Jocelyn alone and send her his weekly allotment from his paycheck? You sound like we should be grateful he even came back."

"Well... yeah. That's kind of true. You don't know how he looked when I found him," Jack repeated. He sat down, flopping onto the couch. "I think he hoped the drugs would help him forget the tragedies he had to endure for a while. You know? I mean, I could understand wanting to escape pain like that."

Silence followed Jack's assessment. Ian finally spoke. "Marcy isn't Lily, Jack."

"What?" Jack's gaze flew up to Ian. Glowering, he asked, "What do you mean by that?"

Ian glanced at Erin, but hesitated. She nodded, as if saying, *Go for it. Say what needs to be said.* Jocelyn stared, looking unsure too.

"You're comparing Ben's loss of Marcy to your loss of Lily. That's why you freaked out; it set you back. I'm just telling you right now that Ben didn't love Marcy the way you loved Lily. His loss is very different than yours and I think you need to see it in proper perspective. His grief was fueled by guilt. Yours was simply grief. Ben's actions that night are haunting him. Ben can't deal with his poor image of himself and that hurts him more than her death even. Jack, you never had the time to mourn over Lily's death. I think losing Marcy was the catalyst that allowed you to grieve over it finally."

Respectful silence engulfed them. Shane got up and put his hand on Jack's shoulder. "Look, you never had a chance to just freaking *be*. You always had us to look after. I commend you on how well you managed to raise us and provide for all of our needs. Maybe there is a silver lining in this tragedy; it's good for you to stop and take a moment to take stock of your life. And Ian's right; Ben's loss cannot compare to yours."

Jack's jaw clenched. He ignored Shane as he glared at Ian and Erin.

Erin dropped to her knees in front of him. "I understand you want to help Ben. But... you're not. You're not helping Ben in the least. You're just allowing him to find excuses to avoid dealing with his own life. And the life he helped create. He married Marcy before he should have and then failed to make their relationship work. He's not—"

Jack got onto his feet, shrugging them off him and stepping towards the window to stare out with unseeing eyes. "He's here. He's here, isn't he? If Jocelyn hadn't had his baby, he'd have never come back here. I'd have lost my son, along with my parents, my first wife, my home, and half my business. So forgive me if I didn't jump all over Ben the moment I laid eyes on him. He would have loved nothing better than telling me to fuck off. He almost refused to come back with me. Do you get that? I had to bide my time, and wait him out, eventually begging him to just come back and make financial arrangements for the support of his baby. To hear he was staying? Well, that's the surprising part for me."

"He's not doing any more than that either," Jocelyn emphasized. Her gaze was riveted on the sweet little face that had caused all the ruckus.

Jack sighed, leaning forward, his posture sloping in defeat. "I thank God every day for your presence here with Lillian. If not for you two, Ben would have been lost to me.

So what if I don't push him? I'm just grateful he's back." His eyes looked sad and weary when they rested on Jocelyn. "Forgive me, but at this point, I just don't want to lose my son."

The door slammed open and Ben stepped inside. He briefly viewed the occupants in the room before his gaze landed on Jocelyn. She clutched her baby protectively. His jaw locked. "Really, Jocelyn? You had to run straight over here and tell them all? Tattling on me like I was a naughty boy in school? You left everything in my backpack strewn everywhere, so I figured you came here."

Ian stood up, as did the others. "Why don't we give you guys some privacy?" They all filed out but Erin, Jack, Ben, and Jocelyn as well as Lillian.

After they were gone, Jocelyn opened her fisted hand. "Don't you mean, you came running over here for this? Need a fix?"

He sighed, rubbing his hand over the bridge of his nose as if the questions she asked were too exhausting and strenuous for him to even begin to answer. "No. I don't, Jocelyn. I used it sometimes over the last few months. I'm not hooked. Jesus, I'm no junkie."

His lips pursed up and his eyes narrowed, drilling into her, trying to ignore everyone else. "How do you think an addict becomes one, Ben? Why do you think it's called addiction? Most people don't intend to get hooked. Most have a very good reason. You? I suppose you have a better reason than many. But not in my house."

"I'm not hooked. If you'd only asked me, I would have told you I haven't touched any drugs since I got back here." He sounded as if they were discussing herbal supplements and not a dangerous, potent, illegal narcotic. "And it's not your house, is it? It's Marcy's."

A sudden silence followed his angry reply. *"Ben."* Erin stood up, and her low tone was full of warning.

Jocelyn appreciated Erin's protective caring. Shaking her head as she glared up at Ben she said, "No. No, let him speak. Let him actually *engage*. Let us see and hear who the new Ben really is. Perhaps he will allow us to introduce him to his fucking daughter."

She bit her lip, almost wanting to tape her mouth shut. She hadn't meant to let the harsh words be spoken, especially in front of his dad and Erin. The unending stress of living in this soap box of an apartment was constantly drilled into her mind as *Ben's wife's place* and all the drama of tiptoeing around Ben, lest she offend him, when he hadn't even laid a finger out to touch his daughter.

Ben crossed his arms over his chest. "Everyone knows she's my daughter. I wouldn't be here if she weren't. Or I doubted her paternity."

Jocelyn bit the inside of her cheek. Did he think he was doing her a favor by not asking who the biological father of her child was? She clutched Lillian tighter. "You've never even touched her. Not a pat on the head, or her shoulder, let alone picking her up. You don't do anything. You think it's enough to throw some money at me and call it even? She cries, and you leave. She needs to be changed, and you ignore her. You won't even look at her. You know what? Maybe if you *were on* drugs I'd have a reason to blame what is wrong with you."

She sucked in a deep breath. She hadn't meant for so much vitriol to spew forth, but there was no stopping it once she got started. Her hands trembled and her head shook. "Do you want an award for being here? *We* did this, Ben. Not me." Tears filled her eyes, and she sniffled loudly to hold back the runny snot. "She's here now and she's beautiful and she's ours, but you won't even look at her."

Ben's agitation grew as she spoke. His hands fisted, his breathing escalated, and his chest rose and fell rapidly. He shook his head, running his hands restlessly through his hair. "It's not that I don't want to hold her. It's just that I don't know how to. Okay? I don't know how to accept the consequences of what I did. How she came here, and what that makes me."

"A parent, Ben. It makes you a parent. And you're a pretty shitty one, let me tell you. All these excuses. Poor Ben, how hard it must be for you. You chose your path when you chose Marcy. She was never deceptive about her true identity. If you failed to see that, it was your own fault. I don't have time to dwell on it, however, because I'm also taking care of *our newborn*. And it's not easy. It just is. You don't get any dress rehearsals when it comes to dealing with her."

Ben shook his head. He stepped back and looked at her closely.

She sneered, noticing his retreat away from her. "You going to run now? Again? That is all you can do, isn't it? Any coward can run off and what, Ben? Where's the future in that? Are you planning to get hooked on alcohol or drugs? What do they do for you, huh, Ben?"

"I don't know. I just know what I did to her!" he screamed at Jocelyn. "What do you want me to do? I can't undo this baby. But I don't know how to live with it. So yeah, I'm angry. Yeah, I ran. I didn't know what else to do. My thoughts are driving me out of my mind. I might as well have killed her with my own hand."

"It's done, Ben. She's dead. You didn't kill her. I didn't kill her. Lillian didn't kill her. A tragic natural disaster killed her. God. What are you going to do? Let her death ruin your life? What good are you to anyone if you do that? Especially me for that matter? I'm the one stuck with you. For the next eighteen years, you are the co-parent to my baby. So where do I stand in all these pathetic scenarios of yours?"

"You? You were the other half of her betrayal. What do I owe you?" Ben turned and slammed his fist into the wall beside him. It splintered the drywall. "Fuck," he hissed as he jumped back and shook his hand with unmasked pain. "You know what I said to her!" Ben screamed, almost manic now. "How can you, of all people, even look at me after what I said to her? Or let me near your daughter? Huh? How can you even stand me now? You know what I said."

Tears leaked from her eyes and she swallowed the lump in her throat as she stepped further from Ben. His violent outburst was scaring her. She turned her head as if he slapped her.

Erin broke the ensuing cold, strained silence. "What did you say to Marcy, Ben?"

He lifted his haunted eyes, and his mouth twisted in a cruel sneer. "I told her... I told my wife to leave. And only an hour later, she would be burned alive in a vehicle. I told her to leave. I told her to go screw herself and die. I said I wouldn't grieve."

A silence like death followed. Erin and Jack both paused, their faces going pale as their former neutral features transformed into tragic, sympathetic grimaces. "Oh, Ben," Erin muttered. "Oh, God. You poor kid. The guilt you're carrying..."

"Isn't enough punishment. Those were my last words to her."

Jocelyn fisted her hands and let them go. "No one, especially me, thought you meant it, Ben. No one thinks you actually wanted her to die that night." She kept her tone soft and gentle, so unlike the rest of the conversation. "You were mad. Angry. So was Marcy. I heard some of the things she yelled at you over the last few days leading up to that night. It was just… terrible timing."

"You can't call that terrible timing. I wished her dead. To her face. And then I had sex with you. I—"

"Don't you get it? There are no words we can say to undo what we did. It's done. Forever. And now? You just have to live with it. There is no redemption at the end of the rainbow. You will never get her forgiveness because she's dead."

He pressed his head with his injured hand, hanging limply by his wrist. "I fucking know she's dead."

"Yes. But you can't give up on your life just because she's gone. All you can do is try to be better. Live better. Honor her in how you respect the life you have now. But more importantly, remember you are the father of a child. And that has to matter to you more than Marcy. It has to matter more than your guilty conscience or your sorrow. It takes precedence over absolutely everything."

He leaned forward, seeming to grip his head in pain. "I know what I should do; the problem is I don't know how, okay? I don't know how to let it go. I find it hard to do what I should be doing."

"Enough."

The entire room stilled when Jack's voice thundered through it. He stared at Ben, and lowered his tone but only a smidgeon. "That's enough, Ben. All of it. They are all correct. No one believes you meant anything you said. Marcy did not believe you actually meant that either, I know that much about her. But you know what? It's also history. And right now, Jocelyn's telling you just to live with it. You have to take care of the people in your life who are still alive and here now. We… *I* let you do this too. Maybe I lost my way, but you've lost your entire mind. You have a child. A newborn baby. Why haven't you held her?" Jack stepped between Jocelyn and Ben.

Ben cradled his limp hand in the other. "You're lecturing me? You only brought me back to appease Erin. What about that, huh? You didn't give a shit either way what kind of father I was. Or am. What do you care anymore? As far as I can tell, you've given up. On this ranch. On Erin. On Charlie. On me. And most of all, on yourself. So don't even, *Dad.*" His tone was sarcastic when he said *Dad*. "Don't lecture me about how to handle all of this when you haven't handled it any better."

Jack's breathing was as labored as Ben's. They stood almost toe to toe. Face to face. They stood that way so long, Jocelyn had to contain a whimper. She was sure, any second now, one of them was going to launch a punch. That much tension rippled between them. Both of their jaws locked and their neck muscles pulsated.

But then, Jack's expression crumpled. He wiped his hand across his forehead, shaking his head. "No. No, I haven't." His tone was completely different. It fell several octaves, and for the first time in almost a year, he sounded like the man Jocelyn remembered and had worked for over half her life.

"I haven't been myself. I admit that. Losing the house… and you, Ben, really affected me. I thought things I've never contemplated before. But you're right, it's no excuse. None at all." He turned his head towards Erin. "I haven't given up on anything. Not the ranch. Not Charlie. Not you. And not Erin. Myself? I think you're right, I gave up on myself most of all. But not anymore." He reached out and took Erin's hand and she closed her eyes. When she opened them again, they were filled with tears and she blinked her eyelids to restrain them. Jack straightened his back. His focus returned to Ben. "You're right. I did give up on you. I let all my sadness dictate what I expected from you. It was an unparalleled tragedy what happened to Marcy and when. No one's taking that away from you, Ben. What happened to all of us was sad. But tragedy is no excuse to give up. Or abandon those who need us most. And no one needs you more right now than that little baby. Or Jocelyn. She's doing all the work for you. No more. You owe them both a better life."

Ben's gaze held his father's. Still, he cradled his hand. Jocelyn wandered if half of Ben's problems were because of his father, who had always been his beacon. Jack was Ben's model and paragon for how a man was supposed to act, behave, and engage with the world. She knew how seriously before this last year Ben considered his dad's word. Earning his dad's respect was the bar he strived for and he followed his advice when it came to judging his own life and actions.

"Or what, Dad? You had this great revelation and bam! You're back to good, old, reliable, responsible, hardworking, ever–striving–for–perfection Jack Rydell. So what if you realized the error of your ways or worked through your grief or whatever the hell just happened here. Just because you've done so, am I supposed to now? Well, what if I don't? What are you going to do?"

Jack held Ben's gaze before he glimpsed at Erin. They shared a long look. Erin nodded her head in agreement to whatever silent question Jack asked her. He looked at Jocelyn. She had no idea what Jack was thinking. Holding her breath, she was spellbound by this odd, compelling, revealing confrontation.

"Then you'll have to get off my land."

Ben's eyes rounded and Jocelyn gasped. Holy shit. This just got real. And crazy. Jack didn't mean that. No. Not after all that Ben had been through. Hell. What all of them had been through.

Finally, however, something had Ben's attention.

"And before you fling it all back in my face, Ian, Shane, and Joey will go along with what I want. I might have taken a second seat for a while, but I never lost my way, and make no mistake, son, *this is my ranch*. Always has been. Always will be. Until I die, this place is most of all under my authority. And I say get off it unless you plan to step up and properly care for your child. Father your daughter."

"I did what you wanted. I've been working hard. I pay for her care and supplies."

"Yeah? Well, I was an ass to act like that's enough. It's not enough. You start taking care of your daughter like a true father or I will. I can pay your share and provide whatever Jocelyn and Lillian need. I'm not so broke yet. So you decide, Ben. It's on you. Now, I need to work things out with my wife and your brother. In the meantime, decide, Ben. Stay or get out. Your decision, no one else's. But once you make it, I expect you to follow through on it, either way."

Apprehension rippled through Jocelyn. What if Ben chose to leave? Disappearing forever from her and Lillian's life? Jack took Erin's hand and they started to walk out. He stopped and glanced back, just at the door. "This is on you. No one will come looking for you, either way. Unless of course, your daughter comes looking for you eighteen years from now wondering who the hell her father is. Realize, whatever you decide will have long–term and long–reaching consequences. It's just how it is. I hope to God, you decide the right thing." Then Jack walked out.

A stunned silence followed and Jocelyn shook her head. She pushed past Ben and ran out the front door, ashamed for what she said in public. To his family. To him, even. She went towards the beach in the dim light of the June twilight and sat down on a smooth log the river washed up along its banks. She stared at the river and huddled Lillian closer to her chest as she cried and carefully arranged her body to shield her baby. She cried for what she'd done, who she was now, and all the chances, privilege, and choices she lost by having a baby when she did. She cried for once loving someone whom she could hate. She cried because she felt responsible for who and what that man had turned into.

But then again… it wasn't all her fault. There was dual blame here. Yet, he went on with his life and got to ignore their baby as if it were all her responsibility. Which was shit. She and he became parents at the same moment.

She was sorry. She wished with all her heart she could undo her actions that night.

She stayed there for a long while, crying until there were no more tears left. She stared at the river, the mountains, and the sky. Just thinking. Realizing she needed to get her life together. She was no teenage mother. Yes, she was an accidental mother, but no teenager. The only reason she hid her pregnancy was because of the gruesome circumstances surrounding how her baby was conceived. But it needed to stop. She could no more hide Lillian than she could the identity of her father. The facts were what they were.

Gathering her wits, she got to her feet. Lillian needed to be awoken for her next changing and feeding so she didn't stay awake all night.

The apartment was empty and Jocelyn breathed a huge sigh of relief. Quickly, she made herself some dinner and ate while Lillian slept. Then she woke Lillian up while changing her diaper. She talked and cooed at her as Lillian started to stir, moving her hands and legs all around as if she were swimming. Laughing, Jocelyn lay back on the bed and held Lillian up to her breast. Her little mouth shook all around until she latched on with an audibly happy sigh. It made Jocelyn smile as she caressed Lillian's nearly bald head. The peach fuzz she did have had a red sheen to it. Her little arms circled over the top of Jocelyn's breast as if she were hugging a football, making Jocelyn laugh. Her heart melted all over again.

Yes, she was tired and exhausted all the time. But in these

moments, which amounted to dozens every day, her heart was filled with a sense of pride and love that went far beyond her exhaustion. She closed her eyes contentedly as she started to sing a lullaby to her, and Lillian suckled without a care in the world.

BEN STARED at the now empty room. His hand ached and burned. Shaking his head, he walked out the front door. He didn't know what to do or where to go, and the stirred up emotions that were roiling around in his head felt like marbles sliding across an uneven surface and back again.

He stared up the road and saw a figure there. It was Charlie. Sitting on the concrete walkway that led to where the house once stood, Charlie sat with his back towards Ben, facing the empty space that was formerly occupied by their home. Sighing, Ben walked up and stood behind him for a long time before he sat down next to his little brother.

"You miss it?"

Charlie glared at him, then turned to face forward. "I miss a lot of things."

Ben nodded, staring at the blank space in front of them. "Me too."

Silence. Charlie glanced down at his hand, which he held protective–like against his body. It throbbed but he could still move the wrist and all his fingers, so at least it wasn't broken.

"What's wrong with your hand?"

"I got mad about all that stuff and hit the wall."

"That was stupid. What the hell good does it do?"

"None, and my hand hurts like a son of a bitch."

"Yeah, 'cause all that anger has worked so well for you."

Ben's mouth dropped open and he quickly shut it. What

could he say? He knew it was next to impossible to argue with his teenaged brother.

"I'm sorry, Charlie, but no one deliberately sets out to be angry, or acts on it for that purpose. When tragic things happen, sometimes you just can't do any better, even if you know better."

Charlie's back stiffened. "Is that your justification? Just because it's hard?"

He sucked in a fast breath. Wow, the kid didn't give him an inch. Talk about high standards. "Well, yeah, honestly, it is."

"That's a total cop-out. You know cheating on Marcy was wrong."

Ben sighed, closing his eyes. Strangers condemned him. As well as himself and Jocelyn. But so far, not one of his family members had criticized him. Joey had plenty to say about his unexplained disappearance and the way he treated Jocelyn, but not the cheating.

Ben's stomach churned with discomfort. He spread his hands flat before throwing them up in frustration. "I didn't ever set out to be a cheater. I understand what you feel now; and you're right to feel that way. The thing is, I did much worse than just that. I had a baby from my cheating." His brother's unforgiving disdain and anger hit him hard, like an immovable rock weighing him down. "I was wrong. I wish I could apologize to Marcy, or find a better way to do so to Jocelyn, our family, and even myself. But I can't undo it. What do you want me to do? Do you intend to disown me as your brother? Do you prefer that I leave? Will you ever forgive me? Do you wish me dead? How bad is it?"

Charlie took a rock and threw it out over the empty, blackened lot and shook his head. "I don't want you to leave again. That's what made it all worse."

Ben sighed. Nodding. Charlie was right; it did make it all

worse, and especially for Ben. Charlie's anger was probably coming from his absence. He stuck his hand on Charlie's shoulder. "I'm sorry I wasn't here, Charlie, when you went through all of this."

Charlie shrugged his hand off his shoulder and snapped, "You should have been here."

Ben nodded, his gaze drifting over to the burnt field. "Yes, I should have been here." He slowly rose to his feet. "But being mean to Jocelyn or Lillian doesn't make it any better. It only makes you as wrong as I was. Okay? You don't have to forgive me, but remember this: I'm your brother. That's forever and I'm back on the ranch for good." As the words slipped from Ben's mouth, his entire body shot upwards. *Stay.* In response to his dad's ultimatum, he was staying. The shocking twist from Jack, which in all honesty, jolted him out of all his apathy about being back on the ranch. His dad threatening to kick him out? His dad's words rippled through him again. *"Whatever you decide will have long–term and long–reaching consequences. It's just how it is. I hope to God, you decide the right thing."* For the first time in his life, his dad was not going to come after him or help fix it if Ben chose wrong. Something big shifted tonight for Jack... and therefore for Ben. No more allowances or excuses or bumbling mistakes because of his sad circumstances were going to be accepted. It wasn't permission to wallow in his own pity, not anymore.

He had to change. He had to be *here.* Not just physically. But in all ways. He had to work. He had to engage Jocelyn. And most of all, *his daughter.* Or he had to leave. It was a simple and clear cut as that.

And oddly, he realized as he talked to his little brother, it truly hadn't occurred to him to even internally debate it. There was no debate, perhaps there never had been.

He was staying.

Daughter. The magnitude of that concept, and the fact that he now knew what Lillian looked like, changed the entire significance of the word. He hadn't even tried with Lillian. He might not have a clue what to do or how to even start, but the message was clear; he had to start.

He set a hand on his brother's shoulder. Clearing his throat he said, "I only hope that someday we'll be as close as brothers again. But I'll be here, for years if that's what it takes, but someday you'll acknowledge me again and forgive me. I can wait you out." Then Ben walked off, reliving his sin and the ensuing sorrow as well as the never-ending consequences. Life was a bitter pill. Even in his own expectations, Ben had failed and no amount of apologies were enough for some people, no matter how sincere and heartfelt. But there was nothing else he could do. Charlie's words were so true: sometimes everything he did just wasn't enough.

But the point was he could never stop trying to make it right. And before he could make it right, he had to at least start trying to. Right now. Tonight. With Jocelyn and most of all, with his daughter.

~

"I FORGOT YOU COULD SING."

Jocelyn sat up, startled, her eyes flashing open before tugging her nipple from Lillian, who protested loudly at the sudden, jarring interruption of her meal. Jocelyn froze for a long, drawn-out moment before she grabbed Lillian's little body and pushed her back towards her nipple.

Ben. Hearing his voice ended the mental cocoon in which she burrowed. A light from the kitchen poured into the bedroom, falling over Jocelyn, her bare chest and the baby. She was taken aback by the soft, civil tone of Ben's voice.

Her gaze focused in on the way he cradled his hand. It

was unnaturally tight against his stomach. "Did you break your hand?" she asked, nodding towards his right hand.

"No. Just bruised it. I would have deserved to break it though."

"Yes. You would have."

He almost sounded like the Ben she used to know.

And love.

He approached her and stood at the foot of the bed, staring at her and the baby. Suddenly, without a word, he lay down on the bed beside her, placing his head near hers.... And Lillian's. He stared into Jocelyn's eyes enigmatically.

Reaching around behind her, Jocelyn found the baby blanket and quickly dropped it over Lillian's head to hide her naked breast, cursing the blushing heat in her cheeks from her modesty at being with Ben.

He tucked his head on the pillow, his gaze drilling right into hers. "Your version of 'Amazing Grace' is haunting."

She snorted. As if. She wondered what was going on. Was Ben high? She stared into his eyes, looking for signs of it, but they seemed clear. Crystal blue–clear. She had no idea what was going on.

"Something your mom sang to you as a baby?" he asked.

"Never. I don't remember her ever singing to me. Or hugging me. Just some song I heard once. I had to Google lullabies since I didn't know any."

"My mom used to sing 'All the Pretty Horses' to Charlie. I assume she sang that for me too."

Jocelyn shut her eyes and took in a deep breath. What was he doing? Her eyelids fluttered open, and Ben kept his eyes riveted on her. "What do you want?" she asked and her gaze narrowed.

"I shouldn't have said that about not wanting you to live in this apartment."

"Your family has been amazing. That's why I'm here. The only reason I live in this apartment, *her apartment...*"

"Yes, she comes between everything we do, doesn't she?"

"More so now than when she was alive."

"I don't like it here any better than you. Being here brings up so many memories."

"Good ones?"

"Not particularly. Which makes me feel even worse about it."

Jocelyn tilted her head down, avoiding his gaze as she mumbled, "Spreading all the scorn about her that I did... Imagine how bad that makes me feel."

He sighed, reaching his hand out and touching her cheek. "I'm not on drugs, Jocelyn. Alone, while on the road, I did them sometimes. Mostly just to try and sleep. I kept picturing her and hearing her voice. I couldn't stop thinking of her last moments of torture, of her screaming..."

"She died of smoke inhalation. Not..." Jocelyn turned her head into the pillow. She couldn't even say the words *burned alive.* All her tough thoughts and resolutions faded in the face of Ben's honesty. It was so real. So tragically real.

"Anyway, sometimes I took stuff to sleep. I haven't though, not since I've been back here. I won't either. Dad has it all now, and I'm sure he'll destroy it."

"I don't know what to do when you say things like that."

"What things?"

"About Marcy. I know what we did. I know how wrong the timing was. When you describe your guilt and imagining how she died, I don't know what I can do to compensate for your loss."

She almost bit her tongue when his arm came around her and rested on her shoulder. "I don't want you suffering from any of those feelings."

"Yeah? Well, those are the signals you're giving off."

"Maybe I feel that way towards myself, not you."

"Why are you in here?" she whispered.

"I heard you singing. Forgot how pretty your voice was. You don't do it very often."

She rolled her eyes. "I don't feel much like singing anymore."

His hand released her shoulder to pick up the edge of the blanket. He gently tugged it down. Lillian let go of her, placing her little rosebud mouth beside the swollen, red nipple. Something sparked in Jocelyn's stomach, and all of her nerves went on alert. The oddness of the situation and the fact that he was staring at her made her uncomfortable. What? Why? What was he doing?

"They're, like, triple their normal size."

She tugged the blanket back. Careful not to wake Lillian, but trying to cover herself modestly. "For weeks, you've been silent; and now, that's all you have to say?" She whispered, so all the heat and intensity of her words lost some of their potency.

He chuckled. Then his smile dropped. "You hurled a lot of accusations at me tonight."

"I had a right to."

He nodded. "You did. You really did."

"Is it true that you only came back in order to set up child support payments and leave?"

"God, Jocelyn," he said, running a hand over his face. "I don't know. I wasn't thinking at first. It… *she*… All of this seemed so abstract. I'd been lost in a haze of my own selfishness and grief and anger for more than nine months. It was a shock. I know I haven't handled it well."

"No. You haven't handled it at all."

He nodded his gaze sympathetic. Instead of reacting to her angry tone, he said softly, "You're really good with her."

"How would you know? You've spent zero time with us... her."

"I've watched you."

"You don't even know what she looks like. You couldn't pick her out of a crowd of babies."

"Yes, I could. You two sleep a lot. And pretty soundly. At those times, I look at her."

She frowned before picking up a throw pillow and hitting him on the head with it. Then she did it with another. "What the hell is wrong with you? Why would you do that? It's so creepy. Why would you choose to sneak looking at your baby instead of just looking at her?"

He threw his hands up to block her next missile. He was laughing. She stared at him, leaning over Lillian, who slept between them. She hadn't seen Ben smile, let alone laugh since he'd been back. She shoved the pillow into his chest. "You're such an ass."

He took the pillow and his grin started to fade. "I am. I really am. I feel totally inept and don't know what to do but stare at her. She looks so tiny, and fragile. I can't quite get my head beyond that."

"How do you think I feel? Huh? I had to carry her inside me for nine months. All alone. I was terrified, really. Hiding my pregnancy in a town that still, even to this day, frowns on babies that are born out of wedlock. Let alone, adultery. I was present when your family buried your wife, and I pretended she meant nothing more to me than a casual acquaintance. You're not the only one who hurts, or feels unclear about what to do next. But doing nothing is not an option. You freaking man up and deal with it. Now. Figure it out fast, Ben." She flipped the blanket back. "Touch her. For God's sake. Pick up your daughter. Hold her. Hug her when she cries. Just hold her, period. Jesus, even Charlie, a teenager would make a better father than you."

Ben glanced down, and Lillian made a funny face as she stretched her arms and tilted her neck, scrunching up her mouth. For the first time, Ben smiled at his daughter. "What is she doing?"

"I don't know. She constantly moves around in her sleep, making all these funny grimaces. I really don't have any special mystic knowledge. I've never been around kids until now."

His gaze slid from hers, and he stared upwards at the ceiling. "I've been... scared. Okay? I've just been scared. But you're right. I will stop pretending like this all just happened to me."

She adjusted her bra back over her breast and pulled her shirt down. She glared at him, but finally nodded. "Are you going to try to be a crappy father? I'm sick of tiptoeing around you. I'm sick of pretending Marcy didn't die tragically, and we didn't create Lillian the night it happened. I'm sick of pretending. I was raised by a crappy mom, and I won't subject Lillian to it. I mean, not deliberately. If I make mistakes along the way, it won't be from lack of trying to do right by her. Like you."

"I know you had no parents. I was lucky and had good parenting."

"And you're a good person who made a tragic mistake. It doesn't mean you don't get another chance."

He shrugged. "You shouldn't have been put in the middle of what I had going on, nor left pregnant and alone and having to handle everything by yourself. Marcy shouldn't have died like she did."

"You get it, I hope, that your guilt does shit for me. Your anger completely alienates you from everyone and everything. If you really think I don't deserve this, then help me. Be a better father."

He nodded. "Okay."

She released a slow breath. "Are you serious? Just like that?"

He smiled. "I wouldn't say just like that, but yes. How do I start? What do I do?"

"Hold her."

"Okay. How do I do that?"

Jocelyn shut her eyes. Finally. It was something. Effort. Trying. She still wasn't sure she believed him, but it was a start. An offering. She scooped up Lillian and turned towards him. "Cradle her close to you like this, and keep one hand on the back of her neck for support."

She tucked Lillian into his big hands. He visibly swallowed and his gaze dropped down to the tiny bundle in his arms. He drew her close to his chest and stared at her, starting with her forehead, her eyes, and her mouth. "She's so small."

Jocelyn gritted her teeth and replied, "Yes, Ben, I know. That's all you notice or say about her."

His lips curved into a small smile, though he didn't lift his gaze off the baby in his arms. "I meant, she's so fragile, so…"

"Vulnerable."

His gaze pinned hers and he nodded slowly. "Yeah, that's the better word. Vulnerable." He took in a breath and then let it out slowly, blinking his eyes. "When my dad first told me about her, I froze. I didn't expect anything like this, Jocelyn—"

Her mouth opened, ready to interrupt him with a scathing reply. *Neither did I.* But he lifted one hand off the baby and motioned for her to stop. "I know, I know. You didn't either. Just hear me out, okay?"

She shut her lips with a stilted nod. "Fine."

"It was almost… Hell, it might have been as shocking as Marcy's death. I knew we used a condom. It never occurred to me you could possibly be pregnant."

"If you had known before then, would you have done anything different?"

"Yes. I have to believe the answer to that question is yes. You might not believe in me, but I need to believe in me. Okay?"

She held his searching gaze and nodded. He glanced back down and jiggled Lillian gently in a natural reaction to her squirming. It pleased Jocelyn to see him do it without her coaching.

"You really think Marcy messed with the condom?"

"I do. She'd done it before. She wanted a baby. I didn't. Because of our ages and the state of our relationship."

He carefully placed Lillian down on the bed before him, between his legs. She was calm, alert, and making little noises. He listened to the squeaks and squawks as she moved her arms, legs, hands, and feet about. "She's so perfect. So small and innocent that at first, I thought she'd be better off without me. Okay? I felt so dirty. I disgusted myself even looking at her. As if what I did to Marcy somehow tainted her. Not that she is tainted. I am."

"But you're the only father she's got. There's no one else to step up."

"I'm getting there. Or trying to. I know it's not fast enough for you or anyone else. But it's been only weeks since I've known about her existence."

"You're ashamed of this. Her. Me and her."

"Yes." He met her gaze head–on. No waffling. No shying away. He nodded. "It goes much deeper than embarrassment. It's complete shame over the situation I created that night. That's part of it, Jocelyn. I'm sorry if my honesty hurts you, but I'm trying to be candid with you now."

She dropped her gaze and stared at her fingers, twisting them together with nervous fidgeting. Their conversation was so intense, a flood of emotions burst inside her. She almost couldn't stand looking into Ben's sharp, bright blue eyes. She hated to know the shame he felt.

"You seem so lost, Ben. I mean, your dad's behavior over the past year was the perfect precursor to your actions. I look at you and can easily see all that rage still simmering inside you. Combined with your utter disinterest in all this…" She waved her hand around the room. "And I don't know how to even talk to you anymore. Let alone figure out how to parent with you. It happened to me too, Ben. I slept with a man while his wife burned to death. Don't you think it gnaws at me incessantly too? On top of that came my pregnancy that no one could know about. It was terrible. I felt so alone. Talk about feeling vulnerable."

His gaze stayed on her and she didn't look up but could almost feel his eyes on her. "I'm sorry for that. I'm trying to get to a better place. Not be so lost. Maybe I needed what my dad did tonight. Everything that I knew before is gone, destroyed or changed. Even my dad. I'm really going to try harder to find my way."

"First, you need to make your peace with Marcy."

"I don't know how. How did you manage it?"

She licked her lips. "She was born. Lillian was placed in my arms. I looked at her one time and all of it… everything outside of her ceased to matter. Her conception. How she got here. I didn't care anymore. I could get on my knees every single day for the rest of my life and thank God for giving her to me. Then you come home and barely even look at her? And begin saying with abject disinterest *how small she is?* She is a miracle. The miracle we were so *lucky* to create."

He kept his eyes fastened on Lillian. Finally, his chest deflated and he exhaled. His eyes lifted toward hers. "I have no words in my defense. I'm hearing you, Jocelyn. I really am. All I can do at this moment is promise you I won't be a shitty father."

She held his gaze and something profound passed between them. She tilted her head in a nod.

"Good. You're not allowed to be. She..." Jocelyn swallowed the lump that filled her throat. "She's the most beautiful thing on this earth. I can't allow anyone to raise her who doesn't understand and see that first and foremost."

His gaze sought Lillian's face again and he nodded slowly. "I see that."

Tears filled her eyelids. She sniffled. "Good. That's good you finally see that. Because you didn't. Not even a few hours ago."

The smiles they shared meant something big, and strange, and maybe even positive had shifted between them. Maybe it was an entirely new start to the relationship that they trashed and ruined. But now? They needed to repair it more than anything else in the world. For Lillian. They needed to find their way together, and all for the well-being of their daughter.

CHAPTER 10

*B*EN GLANCED INSIDE THE partially open door. Jocelyn was lying on her side with her hand drawn up towards her face. Eyes shut, her dark lashes looked like an open fan against her soft skin. She was sound asleep. Her hair was tousled all about and her shirt was bunched up. The baby stirred, letting out another squeak, which is what first drew Ben to the door. Lillian's hands flashed over the walls of the bassinet, groping all around. Another dissatisfied squeak came from the bassinet, this time with lustier lungs behind it. She was gearing up for a full-on shriek and... Who knew how long she'd cry? He'd already had plenty of proof that Lillian cried... a lot. He stepped inside the bedroom. A nightlight provided the only illumination. Jocelyn shifted and rolled flat on her back, and her breathing was deep and regular. She hadn't slept more than a few consecutive hours in over a month. He should know too; he'd witnessed it plenty of times, but never helped her.

What if their roles were reversed? What if Ben had to take care of Lillian from the very first day? What if he had to feed her ten times a day and change her diapers every hour or so?

What if he had to stay up half or all the nights when she screamed and cried inconsolably? There is no way he could have dealt with it as gracefully as Jocelyn did. And no chance he'd be as patient and kind as Jocelyn was with him.

He shook his head. Once he used to be so different, so kind and giving and positive about the world and finding his place in it. Now he'd gotten so cynical, he'd all but ignored and abandoned his own child.

He stared down at Lillian, whose eyes were wide open. They were a dark cobalt blue, like two quarters in her tiny face. He had overheard several comments on how big and beautiful her eyes were, and how unusual. She had a faint spot of reddish hair. It was no more than peach fuzz, but enough for her to resemble his coloring. She wore purple jammies with footies. He studied her as she stared up at him. His anxiety and nerves made sweat bead on his forehead and set butterflies free in his gut. It should not have been that big of a deal. Jocelyn picked her up all the time. She held her and cuddled her until she looked like an appendage against her body. There was no hesitation with Jocelyn. He could be that brave too.

Jocelyn was like a warrior when it came to mothering, and he didn't know the first lesson in regard to fathering. He wasn't surprised. Jocelyn was competitive and fierce in everything she attempted. She worked harder than any man Ben knew. When she danced, she could've been featured on a pop or rap star's stage. When she took a hike, she rarely stopped until she reached the top of the mountain. She was fearless, strong, tough, and dedicated. She finished whatever she started, no matter what people expected from her. Grunt work was not beneath her and no job was too hard. Her tenacity and stamina were qualities Ben had admired about her for years.

Raised without any worries in his cushy life, Ben always

had his dad and his uncles to care for him. He never had to *survive* like Jocelyn did on a daily basis. He never had to be particularly tough on himself, or do anything he didn't want to.

Until now. For the first time in his life, it didn't go the way he planned. And look how off the rails he went. Yet still, his whiny, entitled ass believed he'd gotten gypped in life. He couldn't get over how unfair it was. Until that night, his life had pretty much been what he expected without any first-hand tragedy. Jocelyn? Never. Life was never fair to her. Ben had an inkling of how poor her family was. He knew her mom ditched her when she was pretty young, leaving her with the cold, mean uncle she detested and the shack she never felt welcome in. He also knew why she spent so much time on his family's ranch.

Jocelyn had been in a much worse situation than he was, physically pregnant, and what did she do about it? She kept working, supporting herself, and saving her money to buy accessories for a baby she didn't know anything about. She practically gave birth to Lillian all by herself. And simply settled in to take care of her for the next eighteen years, at least.

And how did Ben score the first time he was tested? The first time something critical was expected from him? Not so good. He failed, actually. Starting with Marcy, then Jocelyn and now, Lillian.

He gently leaned over and pulled her feather weight into his hands, carefully supporting her fragile neck with his palm as he lifted her up towards his chest. She squeaked and squawked some more, but thankfully, made no huge, gusty wails. He settled her against his chest. Her mouth rooted around and he could feel it open up, warm and wet against the skin of his neck, seeking the nipple, of course. He laughed softly, but was careful to be quiet. "I don't have the equipment you want," he whispered. She grunted and moved her head about some more. Her feather weight settled on top of him and she tucked her legs up against him, curling into his body heat. He sniffed her. Wow! How could such a putrid scent come from such a small creature? This beautiful, angelic little darling? Despite the stink and all, something Ben never felt before released in his chest. His heart seemed to expand as he cradled her in his hands.

A knot of emotions choked his throat. He turned his head, planting his lips on the soft smoothness of her forehead. Rubbing his cheek against the fine bristles of hair on top of her head, he cooed, "Ahh, honey, I'm sorry it's taken me so long to know you."

He whispered and her mouth puckered up as her eyes squinted and she geared up to release an ear–splitting scream. Ben jumped into action immediately, snagging the diaper bag that considerate, always–prepared Jocelyn kept packed and ready. Not that he'd know. He never before now even tried to touch the baby, let alone change her diaper.

He closed the bedroom door, careful to let the knob click shut without slamming it. Lillian let out a whimper–like wail and then another stronger one. Utterly confused whether he should grab the breast milk from the fridge or discard the mess he knew he'd find down south, he opted to satisfy her hunger first. He grabbed a clean bottle off the counter. It was on a drying rack that Jocelyn restocked each evening, providing plenty of them for whatever friend or family member came by during the day to watch their daughter. Ben did his usual work around the ranch. Never once caring for the needs and demands of his child.

Ben observed Jocelyn enough times to remember some of it. Jocelyn didn't think he noticed, but he did. He noticed everything. With almost an obsession, Ben watched them very closely, trying to understand it all. He needed to put everything in context now that his daughter had entered his life.

He filled the bottle with breast milk from the refrigerator, barely heating it up before rushing over towards Lillian. She lay on the couch, working up to another frenzied scream. He scooped her up and something wet and sticky touched his bare forearm. Glancing down, he mumbled, "Oh, crap! Literally." Using the blanket she was tucked inside, he quickly wrapped it around her bottom half to soak up the spillage from her diaper. Then he tried to ignore the foul odor emanating from her. She tossed her head back and forth when he touched the silicon nipple to her mouth. Without any hesitation, she latched onto the bottle and he sighed with relief as she started to suck it down eagerly.

After several moments, he finally scooched his butt backwards far enough to lean against the back of the rocking chair. He ignored her unpleasant scent, becoming hypnotized by the little sucking sounds and the way her lips moved back and forth against the nipple. One little hand came up and she seemed to grip the bottle like a quarterback might hold a ball to his chest. He chuckled at seeing her little arm wrapped around it. "Good stuff, huh?" he asked. She stopped sucking for a moment at the sound of his voice, then continued her feeding.

He interrupted her halfway through and tucked her against his shoulder, tapping her back lightly as he witnessed Jocelyn doing with deft hands and a confident manner. His hands, however, were not so deft. He struggled to keep the blanket around her, lest the nasty package leak some more. He had to work at it but he finally got a resounding burp from her. Strangely, the sound of it made his bloodstream bubble with something good. Positive. Was it pride? He managed to get a burp out of her. Carefully setting her back in his arms, he let her finish the bottle.

He burped her again, but this time, a glob of cold goo flew out of her mouth and landed on the spot where his shoulder met his neck. He jumped at first and then sighed. *Baby vomit.* The faint scent of sour milk reached his nostrils.

He held her out before him with his hands tightly under her armpits as if she were an undetonated bomb. She stared at him with dry eyes, but her mouth had caked milk and spit-up that still dribbled down her chin. She simply blinked and gazed at him, looking much more at ease. "Okay, now both ends are flowing. All right, I'm going in; let's do this, girl."

He wedged her against his side, holding her with one hand as he brought out the plastic-covered changing pad and lay her down on it. He grabbed the clean edge of the blanket and dabbed at her mouth, choosing to clean that orifice first. Rubbing his hands together in anticipation, he said, "Okay, I'm going in deeper now."

Lillian kicked her legs and shook her head, moving her body from side to side. Oblivious to the runny, greenish goo that seeped through the seams of her diaper. He nodded. He could do this. He set the baby wipes close by and jumped up when he remembered to get a new garbage bag, setting it close to the changing pad. He rubbed his hands together and grabbed one tab of the diaper before pulling it loose. Then he did the same with the other tab and held his breath before dropping the diaper down between her legs.

"Oh. Come on. What is that?" He shuddered, leaning back, squinting at all the nuclear waste he found between his daughter's legs. "Oh, wow... How on earth can you make all of that?"

Blissfully uncaring, Lillian just squirmed around and watched him. He grabbed her swinging legs and gently lifted up her tush to draw the saturated diaper out. The toxic goo was all smeared underneath her and even more around her tush, her legs, and halfway up her back. He wrapped the diaper and threw it into the garbage bag. He thought he was prepared to face the sticky mess that still clung to her, but it was no match for barely half a pack of baby wipes. "At this rate, we'll go broke just trying to get all of that off you."

He glanced down and noticed spittle caked on his shoulder and neck, and some dried crap on his arm that was now all over his hands. "Okay, this isn't going very well. Come on, Lillian, we're going to have a warm bath." He picked her up and dashed into the small bathroom, careful to close the door quietly after he turned on the light. He started the hot water and waited for it to warm up.

Gently supporting her in the barely filled tub, Ben scrubbed all the big chunks off her and released the contaminated water before refilling the tub, only deeper this time. She squirmed and got all slippery as soon as she was wet. He set her on the bathmat while he stripped off his feces-smeared, vomit-stained clothing. Holding her tightly against his chest, he stepped into the tub. And sank down into the warm water with a contented sigh. Propping his knees up, he rested her whole body against them.

She kept blinking and squirming, grunting and glancing around, but calmed down immediately in the warm water and really seemed to like it.

Her skin felt as soft as a rose petal against his. He was sure he'd never felt a baby's skin before. He hoped his hairy legs didn't scratch her back. It was kind of nice to be soaking there together.

"So I have some things to learn. We can't bathe every single time you eat and sh—" No. Good Lord. He couldn't talk like that to her. He smiled, chagrinned as he covered his near slip. "You eat and make…" What should he call it? "Little Tootsie Rolls. We'll work on it. Maybe do a few practice runs when you're not packing toxic waste in your shorts.

Though I don't have the nice boobs you like, all full of warm milk, I think we did pretty well with the feeding. Score for us, huh? And a bath too? We got this, huh? Just look at you?"

While he talked to her, her eyes followed his movements and stayed glued on him. How did he fail to notice how carefully she took in every single thing around her? He cleared his throat, suddenly feeling self–conscious. For over a month, she heard his voice, and saw him, but not once did he direct his voice or vision or thoughts toward her. What did she think of him? Judging by the way she stared at him, and connected with him, he was sure she was thinking something. She was well aware of those who took care of her. And that sure as hell hadn't been him to date. He cleared his throat. "Okay, so I've been a sh—" There he went again. Not swearing was harder than he realized. "I've been a big old boob, and not in a good way. I hope you won't remember that. At all. But I can do better. Besides, you're wearing your mom out. Did you hear her snoring in there? All because of you and me. We gotta do better, Lillian."

Lillian made a weird face and squirmed around. He felt something warm running down his legs and stomach. He sighed. "Really?" Chuckling, he splashed warm water to wash it off. "As I was saying, Lillian, you and I have gotta start acting like father and daughter. Huh? My fault, I know. But I'm here, now. Lillian. Lillian Rydell. That's a mouthful to say. Lily would be better, but that was my mother's name. She died. So you'll never know her. But she was actually a lot like your mother. She was tall and strong, and ungirly, just like your mother. My mom was fierce. Just like yours. I don't think I ever realized that until this moment." He shook his head. What a strange thought. How could he not see it? Jocelyn was so much like his mom. So much more than any other woman he'd ever met. Maybe… maybe that was why he was so attracted to her.

"Anyway, back to you. Lily-anne. Ann. Annie. What about that? What about Annie? I like it. We'll test it out. See if it fits. That is, if your mother approves. She's rather opinionated, so we'll have to take that into account. What do you think? You wanna be my little Annie?"

His monologue stopped when he needed to breathe. Lillian was staring at him as he intently examined every single feature about her from her small, half-moon-shaped fingernails that were the softest, shell-pink, to her perfect, bow-shaped lips. Suddenly she smiled right at him as he said *Annie.*

His mouth dropped open. He scrambled to get onto his feet, nearly losing his balance as he pressed his naked, wet, slick baby against his chest. His heart began pumping wildly at the near slip. He clasped her even more tightly to him and released her for only a second to say softly, "I swear, I will never let anything happen to you."

Hopping out of the tub and mindless of their nudity, Ben nearly pulled the door off the hinges as he frantically began yelling, "Jocelyn. Jocelyn. Wake up. She just smiled at me."

But instead of finding her in bed asleep, Jocelyn was leaning against the wall opposite the door. She obviously had to scramble backwards when he jerked it open. Her mouth was agape, and her face was turning red. He stared at her in surprise. "Were you listening to me?"

Jocelyn was suddenly awoken from a deep sleep with a startled gasp. Glancing out, her heart smacked against her chest in fear when she saw the dawn's morning light leaking through the closed blinds. She slept all night. Lillian. Oh, God. Lillian. Something must have been wrong. Lillian never slept that long. Her heart climbing up her throat, Jocelyn scrambled from the bed, kicking the tangle of sheets from her feet as she scooted towards the bassinet, her worst fear making the tears flow in her eyes. *Oh, God! What if...*

But the bassinet was empty. She stared at it, flabbergasted, and hurried out towards the living room, stopping with alarm as she spun around in a circle. What the hell happened out there?

Ben.

Something weird and strange filled her gut. Ben had taken Lillian? She walked out and noticed the bottle left on the table by the rocking chair. There was some spilled milk on the counter. And a disaster on the floor. Poop was smeared on the changing mat. Dirty clothes littered the area. Used wipes were scattered everywhere. It smelled like something died in there.

But... that meant Ben must have tried to change her diaper. *Tried* being the operative word. Her heart expanded and something warm filled her bloodstream. *He tried.*

So where were they now?

She glanced at the bathroom door, which was closed, and noticed the light under it. She walked over and put her ear to the door, jumping back when she heard Ben's voice and Lillian's cooing. Inching closer to the door, she cautiously put her ear against it again, unsure if she wanted to hear what he had to say. But the low murmur of his voice called her in.

"...sie rolls. We'll have to work on it. Maybe do a few practice runs when you're not packing toxic waste in your shorts. Though I don't have the nice boobs you like, all full of warm milk, I think we did pretty well with the feeding. Score for us, huh? And a bath too? We got this, huh? Just look at you."

Jocelyn's head jerked back. Holy shit. Ben was talking to Lillian. Not just talking but explaining things to her. And she must have been content because she was making her usual happy squeaks and grunts. Jocelyn shamelessly leaned back in and listened. Her heart lifted and a strange flutter stirred inside her. He was talking about her, suggesting they give her a break… and about her being like his mother. Holy Mother of all that was holy. Her mouth stayed open, and she was nothing less than shocked. How could this be coming from the angry, rude, sullen man whom she'd been harboring for the last month?

Then… she heard the swooshing of water before Ben was unexpectedly screaming her name. He was rushing toward the door for some reason. She jumped back just as it opened. There stood a stark naked Ben holding a naked Lillian. Only Ben didn't seem to care about that.

His puzzled look conveyed his surprise. "Were you listening to me?"

"Yes."

"Oh." He shrugged. "You'll never guess what. She smiled at me, Jocelyn. Clear as freaking day. Her mouth lifted up and she smiled when I called her 'Annie.'"

Jocelyn stared owl-eyed at the stranger before her. He seemed so excited, in tune, *caring*, that the baby in his arms smiled. He was holding her, cradling her nakedness against his chest.

Jocelyn's voice came out in a monotone only because she was probably still in shock at the turn of events tonight. "It was probably just gas. Babies make faces that resemble smiles."

"NO!" he exclaimed defiantly. His eyebrows scrunched up. He frowned at her, shaking his head as if she seriously offended him. "It most definitely was *not* gas. There was no smell… believe me, and no one can miss her smell. There was just her smile. Her first one for me and I witnessed it."

Jocelyn stepped back, her eyebrows lifting in unison. Ben

seemed so passionate that he saw it. "You said you were as new to this as me. How do you know it wasn't a smile?"

She bit her lip. He was buck-ass naked. In all honesty, she'd never fully seen him naked. *That night* had been dark, and they had been lying down, and there hadn't been much time to really see each other. Right then, his six-foot-three, long, lanky frame filled the small alcove in the bathroom. His penis was unaroused, and he seemed completely oblivious to his nudity right then. Jocelyn was startled to see it nestled against the auburn hair right in front of her. His thighs were ropey with muscles and his stomach was narrow and slim. His arms weren't large, but very well-toned. There wasn't an ounce of fat on his frame. A lot like her actually. There was a dusting of auburn hair that was fainter and sparser on his chest, but thicker on his legs. He glanced down, observing her evaluating him. The light from the bathroom cast a glow over his skin and she almost choked on the laugh that bubbled inside. A bright pink blush stained his skin from his chest to his neck and up into his cheeks. He turned and leaned in, bringing out a towel, which he covered himself with.

"Quit eyeing me up like I'm a side of beef. *She smiled.* Are you getting this? Lillian smiled. I'm not mistaken." And it seemed extremely important to him.

She nodded. "You're right. I don't know. I guess it's entirely possible. If you're sure..."

"I'm sure."

"Then congratulations, you saw her first smile."

He grinned. "It was something." His tone was softer, different than she'd ever heard from him. He cleared his throat and passed by her, going to the diaper bag. He leaned down and squatted on the floor, setting Lillian far away from the mess. Pulling out a clean diaper, he began wrapping it around her. He did a proficient job, and kept his towel half over him, leaving his back end bare-assed towards Jocelyn. And yeah, she might have stared just a bit.

She almost came up behind and told him the diaper was too loose. But she bit her tongue to resist nit-picking. Sure enough, when he lifted Lillian up, the diaper slipped off. "Oh, no. We don't want that. We don't want any spillage out the sides next time." He set her back down and tightened it all up. Then he stood up.

Jocelyn crossed the room and started to grab all the dirty wipes, careful to grasp only the white edges.

He waved at the mess below him. "After she goes to sleep, I'll clean it up. Go back to bed, I didn't mean to wake you."

She paused, considering him. Then she separated her index finger and thumb, letting the wet soiled wipe fall to the floor. Acting like a control freak couldn't help the situation. She wanted Ben to engage... and holy shit. Tonight he did in an epic way. A way she didn't believe she'd see in a year if she were lucky. She had to let him try, to interact, and learn. Everything she knew she had to learn too.

"It's the most sleep I've gotten in a month. I woke up feeling so rested. When I saw the daylight, it scared the crap out of me. I thought... well, sometimes, I worry too much. There are things that can happen, and I get scared if she sleeps too long..."

"I got her."

Jocelyn turned to go back to bed. She rested her hand on the door jamb and glanced over her shoulder. "Did you mean what you said?"

"Said? Which part? Annie and I were having quite a conversation."

She laughed, despite herself. Turning more fully, she crossed her arms under her breasts. They were getting too full again. She needed to pump them and feed Lillian. She should have done it right then, but the break she got from not pumping or feeding or taking care of her newborn in middle of the late night was too glorious to pass up.

"Yes, you were. I'm sorry. I shouldn't have listened, but you have to understand, I had to make sure you were being... you know, nice to her."

Ben looked crestfallen. His mouth tightened and he nodded his head. "Ah, hell. I deserve that. But yeah, I was being nice to her. Though she wasn't so nice to me, what with all the smelly goo she smeared on me."

Jocelyn laughed and Ben smiled. It was a slow, tender smile that was all about their daughter. Sharing a moment about their baby, for the first time, was something to note. "What things, Jocelyn?" he asked after a long moment.

She shook her head, ending the trance she was in. "About me being like your mom."

"Yes. I can't believe I didn't fully realize it before. But yeah. You are."

"Your mom was a tomboy too?"

"Completely. She was taller than you. She was almost as strong as my dad. She worked on the ranch right beside him. Meaning, she did all the physical work. Not inside though. She was more traditional in the way she dressed. You're kind of funky in your style, and my mom was pretty oblivious to how she looked. Any old flannel and grubby pants worked for her. She was destined to have boys, she always said about us."

"So that was a compliment?"

He tilted his head. "The best one I could give you."

She smiled, saying, "Thank you," before she whipped around. She couldn't wait to lounge in bed and had every intention of taking advantage of the rare opportunity. Over her shoulder, she called out, "Hey, Ben?"

He turned to sit on the rocking chair, with Lillian tucked up near his neck. "Yeah?"

"In case I forget to mention it, you have a really nice ass." Her lips lifted into a leering grin as her eyebrows wiggled.

He burst out laughing and she closed the door, smiling for the first time in a very long time, and all because of Ben Rydell.

CHAPTER 11

"*D*O YOU WANT TO go out and get some dinner?"

Jocelyn glanced up from Lillian, who was at her breast... again. She finished and held the baby over her shoulder, gently tapping her back until a healthy burp was audible. It made Jocelyn laugh every time. How could the little package she held create such a man-sized noise? It was enough to make any man proud.

"Uh... sure. Why? What's the occasion?"

"Because you don't get out much."

"Are you trying to be nice to me?"

"Yes, Jocelyn, I want to be nice to you."

Her eyes grew large as she nodded and replied, "Yes. I would like that."

So they started going out to eat. They usually had a quick meal out. Lillian usually sat in her car seat beside one or the other of them. After the fourth time they went out, people seemed to stop staring at them so much. Most were still awkward in greeting them, however. Everyone naturally wanted to see their baby, but Jocelyn didn't miss the odd glances she and Ben received despite how hard the onlookers tried to hide them. It was almost as if the ghost of Marcy was standing between them.

Though it wasn't near as blatantly displayed to Jocelyn when Ben was with her versus when he wasn't. When she was alone, the neighbors and community at large were nearly vicious and overly vocal in their disdain of her role in Ben and Marcy's relationship. It was at times shocking the things said to her and the looks directed her way. But she took it, seeing it as her punishment and her lot in life now after what she had done. So she didn't complain or whine or even mention it to Ben. It became a part of her. It became the status quo.

Still, beneath it all, Jocelyn also still experienced signs of Ben's just–below–the–surface anger. He learned to put it away and temper it down, but there were times she saw it percolating just under his newer politeness, interest, and attitude. Yes, he was trying and was so much better than the man who first showed up as Lillian's father. But there was still an edge to Ben's personality that had not been there before and it was hard for Jocelyn to get used to. His nice-ness, his decency, kindness, and general optimism about the world used to be what drew her to him. Now? He was cyni-cal. Hard. It was a stunning change to grow used to. In all honesty, it didn't draw her to him. But then... seeing him care for their infant reminded her of who she used to know, and that did draw her. It was odd and confusing to live and co–parent with a man she once saw herself in love with. Now? She had no words left to describe what she felt about Ben Rydell.

~

THEY WALKED into the River's End mini–mart to grab some diaper cream when they were on the way home from dinner one evening. Jocelyn carried the car seat with Lillian fastened inside it while Ben waited for her to pick out the brand she preferred. He was browsing through the magazines when a loud voice caught his attention.

"Well, well. If Jocelyn didn't have herself a damn baby. At least we can be sure as shit it's not mine... not this time, eh, girl?"

Ben passed through the aisles until he stopped dead. It was that guy, her uncle, Cutter Johnson. What the hell kind of comment was that? Jocelyn's face went pale and her entire body froze as she clutched Lillian closer to her. "Leave me alone, Cutter."

"Ah, is that any way to greet me? I saw your trail, missy. You stayed in our home, huh? Miss me?"

"Not even for a second. Please, would you just leave me alone?" She glanced over her shoulder, not realizing Ben was standing behind Cutter.

Cutter leaned in and said something to her. She flinched and pushed past him only to run directly into Ben. Her eyes were big and she seemed frantic. "What's going on?" asked Ben.

"Please, let's go now." She cast an eye over her shoulder and Cutter smiled at her with a nasty sneer.

Ben collected Lillian from Jocelyn, whose arms were trembling. He took her to the truck and clicked the infant seat back into its base before turning on the ignition. She huddled inside.

"What was that all about? I take it you're not too fond of your uncle?"

"He's not my uncle," she snapped. "Not for real, I mean."

Cutter's words started to sink into Ben's brain. About the baby *not being his*. What. The. Fuck? "You told me, years ago, that he was your uncle."

"There was no one else for me to live with. Mom ditched

me. He was just one of her guys. He let me stay there. And that's the end of it."

It definitely wasn't. It wasn't the end of it. He realized that. His stomach dropped. "What did he mean, Jocelyn? That Lillian couldn't be his? *This time?*"

She bit her lip, staring outside. "Oh, my God. Don't worry; she's your child, Ben, there's no question about that."

He frowned. "Have I ever once questioned it? No. I know she is. I asked you what he meant by that comment."

She shrugged. "There was never any other pregnancy. He's just an asshole. Someone who likes to make me feel like shit with lewd remarks and sexual innuendoes."

"That wasn't any innuendo. D–did you sleep with him?"

They had arrived back at the ranch. Storming out of the truck, Jocelyn slammed the door. Ben grabbed the handle to Lillian's car seat, clicked the button, and extricated her before coming around the front of the truck with her.

Jocelyn took her from Ben at once. She kept her gaze glued down on the ground. "Please don't ask, Ben. I don't want to talk about him. Or remember anything about my life then."

Remember it? The pig was old. Like, way too old for Jocelyn. Remember it? Like it wasn't recent?

"How old were you?"

"There was no other baby. I've never been pregnant before. He was just being an asshole."

"How old were you?" he repeated and a sinking feeling in his stomach preceded something thick and ugly that began rising in his bloodstream.

She closed her eyes. "Fifteen. Okay? It only happened sometimes. It was just—"

"That fucker molested you?"

"It wasn't molestation. I didn't object. I was just... I had to live there and he..."

"The shit it wasn't. Why didn't you ever tell me?"

"Tell you what? That I had consensual sex with my guardian to avoid being relegated into foster care? It was more important to me that I stay here than it was to resist."

"That's statutory rape. It's not okay. What the fuck?" He shoved his fingers through his hair and started backing up from her. She stepped towards him, and stretched out her hand.

"Ben. Wait. I was young and scared then. I didn't know what else to do. I just wanted to stay here. In River's End, I mean. That's all it was for me: a means to living here. What I did has nothing to do with how I am now."

The anger inside Ben began to grow until red tinged his eyesight. Every explanation she offered only incensed him further. He pictured her at fifteen, when he was thirteen. She was tall for her age, and gangly, her limbs too long for her torso. He always saw her with a smile on her face. And a funky hairstyle. But always very much alone.

Ben shook his head. All the while he knew her then, her childhood innocence was being snatched away by some old, disgusting fuck who forcibly had sex with her? Making her pay for her room and board with it?

"That only went on for a little while. He didn't want me once I developed a bit more—"

Ben went ballistic. He shook her off and jumped into the truck. She ran over to him and asked, "Where are you going?"

"To kill the motherfucker who raped you." His tone was chilling, deadly, and serious. He left no doubt that he meant to do it. Every ounce of anger and rage bubbled over from inside him. Rage sitting there dormant now engaged. His only objective now was to have his revenge on Cutter Johnson.

～

BEN'S TRUCK left Jocelyn in a plume of dust. She swore as she reached down to grab Lillian's car seat handle before dragging her towards Jack's house. Lillian cried as loud as Jocelyn's heart pounded in her chest. It pumped so hard, she feared it would explode. Tears streaming, she ran into Jack's house without pausing to knock.

Everyone jumped up at her sudden appearance. Crying hysterically, she sobbed, "Oh, God, you have to stop him. He's going to kill him. Or end up in jail. Oh, God." She leaned over, bending at the waist as her pathetic sobs nearly choked her.

Erin burst forward. "What is it? Are you hurt? What's going on?"

"No. It's Ben. Oh God, all that anger is still simmering right there under the surface of all his pseudo–politeness. That rage inside him never left. It's still there." She gripped Jack's arm. "You have to stop him. He's going to kill him."

"Who?" Jack grabbed her arms, gently shaking her. "Who is he going to kill?"

"Cutter. He's back. At the shack, that's where Ben went."

Jack released her without a word and was instantly gone. Jocelyn fell to the floor, sobbing, while Lillian kept screaming. Erin grabbed the baby and ran out, saying, "I'll take her next door."

Gasping for breath, Jocelyn tried to make sense of where she was. Hyperventilating, she leaned forward and concentrated until her breathing started to regulate back to normal. By then, Erin had burst inside. "I left her with Kailynn; let's go." Erin's mouth was in a grim line. Jocelyn stumbled back onto her feet. She huddled inside Erin's SUV.

"What is this all about?" Erin asked. She ignored all the traffic laws and roared down the unpaved road, a plume of dust following behind them. Entering the one–lane road, she started climbing up towards the Gunderson Hills.

"We ran into Cutter at the damn mini-mart. He said some lewd comment when he saw Lillian. He insinuated that I used to sleep with him. I don't know why, but Ben freaked out when he heard that."

"Isn't he your uncle?" Erin's tone conveyed she already understood he wasn't.

Jocelyn snorted, crossing her arms over her chest. "No. He was a guy my mom hooked up with before she left me. Cutter let me stay there *on condition*. There was nowhere else for me to live in River's End."

"So it wasn't out of the kindness of his heart?"

"I don't know. For a few years, we had sex sometimes. It was meaningless. It meant nothing to me anyway. I don't think about it anymore."

"And Ben... what? Was overcome by a jealous rage?"

Jocelyn licked her lips. "No. He assumed I was molested. I wasn't, Erin. It was just a fair exchange: sex for a place to live. I got to stay, and he copped a feel once in a while. He was so drunk most of the time, it didn't happen often. I don't even know why Ben reacted the way he did."

Erin glimpsed at her but kept her tone soft. "Because, Jocelyn, it's wrong. But between Ben's festering anger and having no outlet for it, I'm guessing this revelation probably provided the ideal circumstances."

Jocelyn fell silent for the rest of the ride as the vehicle bumped and bounced along the unpaved road. They came to a sharp halt and parked outside the small, oddly built shack that Jocelyn once called her home. They flung the car doors open and quickly jumped out. There, lying on the ground, was Cutter Johnson with Ben straddling his chest. His fists were pummeling Cutter with the speed of a human machine gun. When his knuckles connected with Cutter's face, a jarring, sickening sound of flesh on flesh filled the air. Grunts from both men's mouths could be heard as Jack rushed out of his truck and grabbed Ben. As if he were full of superhuman strength, Ben flung his dad's arms off him effortlessly.

Jocelyn was out of the vehicle screaming, "Stop! Ben! Stop! You have to stop! Now!"

Ben shifted around and punched Cutter in the gut. "You think hurting little girls is okay, huh? Is it fun? Well, let's see how much fun I can have when I hurt *you*."

Jocelyn fell, tripping on the deep wheel rut hidden by the weeds. She got up and stumbled forward, seeing Erin do the same from the corners of her eyes. Cutter's mouth was bloody, and his face jerked every time Ben hit him, spraying fresh blood everywhere.

"Ben! Stop it! Ben!" Jack finally got the upper hand. He pulled on Ben's arm so long and hard that he and Ben slid backwards. Together, they fell off to the side and away from Cutter. Cutter took the opportunity to curl up into a pathetic, moaning ball.

Ben struggled to unglue his father's octopus–like arms from restraining him. He got back onto his feet when Jocelyn grabbed his arm, clutching his bicep. He tried to shake her off and she stumbled. Then she tried to stay right in front of him in order to block his progression. "Stop it! Stop. What are you going to do? Hit me just to get to him?"

Ben stopped dead as Jocelyn's words finally registered. He glanced at her and at Cutter. The strange, wild look in his eyes started to recede. His shoulders sagged as he ran a hand over his face, mumbling, "Oh, fuck. What have I done?"

Jack was back on his feet by then, and he crossed around Ben and stuck his hand flat on Ben's chest. "Son, you need to stop all of this right now."

Ben shoved back from both of them, jerking his arm from Jocelyn. He pushed his hands through his hair, messing it all up. "Do you know what he did to her?"

Jack muttered, "Well, I have an idea, yes."

"That was years ago." Jocelyn shook her head, wiping the tears on her face. "What possible benefit is there for me in you going after him like this?"

Cutter finally rolled over and got to his knees before he staggered to his feet. He was still clutching his bloody, swollen lips and bleeding nose. "I'll see that you go to jail for this," he snarled, spitting a gob of red and white foam from his ragged mouth. "I don't care if you're a damn Rydell, you'll rot in the pen for this."

Ben's entire body strained and he looked as if he might take another swing at Cutter when he heard his threat. Jack stepped in front of him as Jocelyn gripped his shirt. "NO!" she screamed, stepping right up into Ben's face. She was only a few inches shorter than Ben so their gazes were nearly level. She shook her head over and over. "Damn it. You're only making this worse. It's my history and my problem, get it? What happened to me happened to me, not to you. I don't need you doing this..." She spread her hand to encompass the bleeding Cutter behind her. "Now, you are making me a victim, and before today, I wasn't a fucking victim. What I did was just something I did and it's over."

Ben looked at Cutter and back at Jocelyn.

She took in a deep breath and shook her head, fresh tears streaming over her face. She sniffed to hold in the snot. "You're only making everything worse."

Jack whipped around and grabbed Cutter's shirt by his fists, dragging him upwards. This time, Erin was screeching at Jack. Jack merely shook Cutter as easily as a Rottweiler would shake a rag doll. "Listen up, Johnson. You will not report anything; do you hear me? Otherwise, I will personally see that you are brought up on statutory rape charges. You fully deserved the beating my son gave you. But we'll end it right here and now. For both of you. Deal?"

Cutter scowled at Ben, who bristled. He was barely restrained by Jocelyn's hand on his chest and he glanced down at her. She pleaded with her eyes for him to leave it. Ben finally lifted his hands up as if he were giving up. Cutter spat again and smugly replied, "You can't prove anything."

"I can sure as shit try." Jack's voice was very low and quiet. Cold. Chilling. "I'd kind of like to try, actually. But I'm offering you a one–time deal."

Cutter wiped his bloody face with his sleeve. "You're like them rich people, ain't ya? Always buying other people off while your roustabout son roams around causin' trouble."

"No. I applaud my son's actions this time. I might have done the same. But Jocelyn wants this kept quiet; so you'll stay quiet if only to satisfy her." Then Jack smiled softly. "Try me. Let's see how far you get."

Cutter started to hobble off towards his hovel. "Get off my land."

"You ever try and go after Ben with the law, and I'll come after you." Jack repeated to the retreating figure. Cutter simply flipped him off over his shoulder and limped inside before slamming the door.

They were left standing there. Ben glanced down at Jocelyn, then at his dad. "I can't believe you just threatened him like that."

"I can't believe you just beat the shit out of him."

Ben looked around, lowering his head as his entire body wilted. "When I saw him, I got so high on adrenaline." His head dropped down and he cradled one hand with the other. His raw knuckles were bruised and starting to swell.

Jocelyn rubbed away her tears. "What is wrong with you? How could you do that?"

"What's wrong with *him* is a better question." Ben lifted his gaze to hers. "Let's get out of here. I don't relish him coming after me with a gun."

She rubbed her nose. "He just might. And you almost deserve it."

They got into Ben's truck and waited for Erin and then Jack to pull out. He started the vehicle and drove slow and easy over the bumpy, unpaved road. He seemed so much the opposite of his former demeanor in only the last twenty minutes. She leaned her head against the window. Totally disappointed with Ben, and her silence conveyed it.

Ben cleared his throat and gripped the steering wheel. Jocelyn saw his knuckles all raw and bleeding and turned her gaze away from him. She leaned her head on her open palm, and rested it against the door. "You realize this had nothing to do with me. This was about *her*. As everything else is about her. And she is either going to haunt us for the rest of our lives or destroy you."

He nodded his head, disagreeing as he took the sharp turns of the road. "First, she hasn't destroyed me. I'm right here. Getting angry at a pervert on *your behalf*. Not hers. I agree I've been fucked up for the last year. I admit to having huge anger problems and yeah, it's made me cynical where I probably wasn't before. Guilty as charged. But looking back, who wouldn't have wigged the hell out? Those were extraordinary circumstances we both went through. I'm willing to take the blame now and admit my mistakes. I ran off. I didn't face anything. I'm willing to take responsibility for what I failed to do for you and Lillian. I'm working on that. I swear I am. But you're wrong. This just now? This might be the first time in a year that something *isn't* about her. It was actually all about *you*."

"Bullshit. All you do is regret our sordid encounter. Your simmering anger is always just below the surface and anything minor sets it off. And that's because of Marcy. Your wife. Not me. Your accidental baby mama. The baby you never wanted."

His entire body jolted upright and he gripped the steering wheel tightly with his sore hands. He drove over the bumps and ripples of the dilapidated roadway before pulling off to the side with a sharp jerk. Waving his dad forward, Ben rolled down his window and told him, "We need to talk. Will you guys watch Lillian for a while?"

Jack nodded, replying, "Seems a good time to do that. Of course. Take all the time you need." Then both vehicles passed around them and disappeared.

"Did you ever think I might not want to talk to you? Why should I? After your oh–so–charming demeanor when you didn't touch or even look at your own child for weeks? And having to use drugs in order to *live with* that night with me and what it caused to happen in your life? I don't want to rehash it. I know it was a mistake, a tragic night to you… and to me. I know, Ben! I certainly don't want to discuss it now."

Ben shifted into gear, turning up into the hills instead of heading down into the valley. He rounded the corner before he lifted his gaze off the road long enough to glance at her. He suddenly veered off to the side of the road and got out without a word. He walked off the road and went up a small knoll that was covered in aspen trees. Beams of light were streaming in from the setting sun and the sky turned an orange and gold blend, reflecting on the glossy sheen of the fluttering, small, round aspen leaves. Their trunks glowed like white beacons against the emerald green foliage. She sighed and opened her door before following him up the knoll.

He stood overlooking the valley, and she saw where the fire hadn't burned as much acreage. Above the valley stood the peaked, rocky tips of the Cascade Mountains, and much closer were the rounded, rolling hills of the Rydell River Valley. Browned and barren now, there were occasional spots of color still. Like in this aspen grove. The trees on the edges were completely burned and some were singed nearly halfway up the trunks. Only a center strip, which was over a creek, remained green and unscathed.

She stood there, watching Ben stare over the distant valley. "Today wasn't because of Marcy. Everything else has been because of her, but this wasn't."

"What you did back there was completely unacceptable."

"No. It wasn't." He stared into her eyes and his gaze traveled lower. Jocelyn fought the urge to wrap her arms over her chest and deflect his perusal. "What Cutter Johnson did to you was totally unacceptable."

She turned away. "You don't understand."

"Then help me understand. That man took advantage of you when you were a child, only fifteen; how is that not wrong? What if it were Lillian? I mean, wouldn't you want to kill him for doing that to her under such circumstances?"

"Of course I'd kill him if it were, Lillian. Because *no one* like him will ever have access to my daughter," she spat.

"No. They won't." Ben spoke in a calmer voice. He was somewhat collected and serious in response to her volatility and anger. He seemed to be the saner one now. Not the wild heathen that was pummeling an old man on the ground. Then he continued, "Because she has us, Jocelyn. She has us to protect her. We'll look out for her. And feed her and clothe her. *We* will teach her. *We* will guide her. *We* will love her so she will know her true worth and find someone who is worthy of her."

As he spoke so gently and calm, his tone bought tears to her eyes. She kept her face turned away so he couldn't see them. "What? Unlike me? Who doesn't know better?"

"Yeah. Because there was no one to look out for you, or help you, or teach you, or protect you, and love you."

"You don't either. You don't love me. You don't look out for me. You don't do anything for me except blame me for seducing you when you fully intended to cheat on your wife. So don't stand there and pretend my childhood upsets you or protest about it on my behalf." Bitter anger laced her words.

"I'll admit I have anger management problems, right now. But I remember you at age fourteen, fifteen, and sixteen. I know what made you smile and laugh and what you did for fun. And I can't stand knowing that he hurt the girl I knew and cared about." Ben leaned over and oh–so–gently touched the tip of his index finger to her cheek, brushing off her wet tears. "I had no clue it was happening. If I did, I would have punished him then. I would have tried to help you."

She stiffened in response to his tender touch. Pulling back, she rolled her eyes and sneered, "It wasn't that bad. It was just sex, Ben."

"It was extortion. He had all the authority in the relationship. I don't regret what I just did. And it wasn't about Marcy. It was about *you*."

She turned her head as if he just hit her. "You were never as volatile as that. Not until you tapped into this insane rage that you've retained since the night of the fire. You're rewriting history now to justify your anger."

He snorted and tossed his injured, swelling hand through his hair. "I can't rewrite it. What do you think I spent the last year trying to do? I tried to forget it. I tried to forget *you*, Jocelyn. Drugs. Running. Anger. Rage. Everything I did was to escape all this. Before I knew about Lillian, all I kept remembering was that I deliberately set out to do what happened that night. And unlike what you persist in thinking, that night was all about you, not Marcy. Which is where my guilt enters the picture. None of it *just happened*. I wanted you that night."

"So you were going to use me to do it? To take your revenge against her?"

"Honestly? I wish it were that simple. Wouldn't that be

easier to explain and justify? But it wasn't a random hook–up. It was with you. I wanted to be with you."

"Oh, my God. You're so full of shit." She lifted her hand with the intention of slapping his lying face. He jumped back, his eyes rounding in shock as he instinctively lifted his other hand to catch her wrist mid–air.

"What the hell?" he yelled back. "Why did you just try to hit me?"

Her cheeks flushed in heat. "None of that was about me! How dare you!" She was overwhelmed by the anger flowing through her blood, and stumbled over her words, "How dare you mock me? To pretend your anger last year was about your feelings for me. It was all about *her*. All of it. The only reason you're even here anymore is because your dad threatened to evict you."

"It wasn't any threat. He finally meant what he said. It was necessary. I needed to take a long, hard look at myself."

"And yet, here we are just having pulled you off another man and then your dad threatening him not to press charges against you."

"He deserved it. It wasn't a random assault."

"Well, at least you see it was assault."

"It was justice."

"For you. Not me. Which really doesn't count, because he didn't do anything to *you*."

He took in a deep breath. "So… it didn't at all make you feel something? Redemption? Like he got what he deserved finally?"

"No. I choose not to give Cutter Johnson any power in my life. I don't think about him or it. All you're doing is digging into stuff I have made my own peace with. You don't have to understand it, but I do. That anger of yours? How instant and unreasonable it was? I won't live with it. Do you understand? This?" She lifted her hand and spun it around.

"All of it is totally unacceptable to me. I won't subject my daughter to you flying off the handle and acting how you want and then justifying it."

He shut his eyes and his pain rippled through his features. "Okay, okay. Maybe you're right. Maybe some of this reaction stemmed from anger I harbor. But what Cutter did to you? I grew up with you. I loved you as my sister and best friend for years. How could you think I wouldn't react to this?"

She sighed, running her hands through her hair. "You could have just expressed your general sympathy and concern."

His hands slipped from her shoulder and he bowed his head forward for a long, pronounced moment. A serious moment. She waited for him to blow up. Or begin his recrimination... but surprisingly, he started chuckling. Laughing out loud, actually. Frowning, she wondered if he were losing his mind. Maybe all the stress from the last year, combined with his guilt and anger were giving him a mental breakdown. "I couldn't handle any situation the right way, not even if someone put a gun to my head demanding it, could I?" He fell forward, laughing even harder. So hard, tears rolled down his face.

Horrified, Jocelyn stared at him, but he kept laughing. Finally... she started to chuckle too. Through her own laughter, she shook her head and replied, "No, you really can't."

"I just..." He kept laughing, "I just wanted to fucking hit someone. The entire last year."

"I think you managed to finally beat up someone."

They laughed until they were both crying and gasping and exhausted. Then silence descended, an amiable, strange, and easy silence that affected both of them. It was like they finally released years of unexpressed stress. He put his hand out towards her finally, palm up. "Friends again? Will you be my friend again, Jocelyn Jantz? I promise not to beat anyone up to defend your honor again. I promise I'll try to direct all of this anger somewhere constructive. Like maybe toward my job at the ranch. I promise not to hurt you again."

She stared at his hand for a long moment before lifting her hand from her side and sliding it into his. He squeezed his fingertips around hers. She compressed her lips into a flat smile. He smiled back. Maybe… just maybe, they found the link they thought they lost, the connection that for so long cemented them as the best of friends.

It was wrong, and Ben knew it. But unlike the night of the fire and his choice to cheat on Marcy… this time, Ben wasn't sorry. Much of his pent-up anger was released. And fuck. Any child molester in his eyes deserved the worst punishment ever. But the best part of that day? The only part that vindicated him was when he opened the door to the apartment and found his brother standing there.

"Heard you beat the shit out of Cutter Johnson."

"Yeah," Ben said, eyeing his brother. Previously, Charlie had rejected every attempt Ben made to engage him while he was working on the ranch. "Dad said you found out he molested Jocelyn and lost your shit."

"Yeah."

Charlie eyed him up, and this time, Ben eyed him back, without cowering or apologizing. It was so odd hearing Charlie swear. Charlie wasn't the same kid Ben had left here. Charlie finally nodded his head. "Cami had a bad upbringing too. I'd go ape-shit too if I found out what was done to her and knew the man was right up there, staring down at our ranch."

Ben held his breath. Would his brother, maybe, finally talk to him? He nodded. "You wanna come in? See Lillian?"

"I've seen her already. Dad and Erin have her a lot. I see her then."

Ben squinted his eyes at his brother. "Do you spend time with her?"

Charlie finally smiled a small, smug grin. "Yeah. Cami thinks she's the greatest thing since a kitten or puppy, or even better, she claims. So yeah, I have and I do."

Ben smiled wider. "I knew you weren't the unfeeling little shit you've been acting like to me. You wanna come in and hang out with me? Watch a game, or something?"

Charlie shrugged. "Why the hell not? Got nothing else to do."

Ben was relieved. After all these weeks, he and his brother were watching a game on TV together. He asked politely, "So you and Cami… That anything? You seem to spend a lot of time with her."

He scowled. "She's my friend, okay? We practically live together here. That would be too weird."

He held up his hands. "Okay. Okay. Just saying. She's pretty cute."

"You intend to sleep with her too?" Charlie retorted. Ben paused, hurt and surprised at Charlie's snappish reply. When did his brother become so sarcastic? Kind of edgy? Not so much the little kid he fondly remembered? Ben nodded, realizing his brother had also grown up while he was off in his own drama. Ben was stunned to see how much he missed.

"No, dickhead. I just wondered if you did, or perhaps, you want to but were denied and that's what's making you so fucking cranky."

"I'm not a little kid who gets cranky."

"Sure about that? You've been a little pissant since I came back."

"You deserved it. You left as a dickhead and returned as a pissant." Charlie took a pillow and smacked it at him, but not as nicely as Jocelyn did. It freaking hurt. Ben did it back before they were off. Intertwined in a wrestling match, their arms and legs made them both fall to the floor with grunts and moans of real pain. But when Jocelyn walked in, she paused at the doorway, and they looked up in a near choke-hold on the other.

She rolled her eyes. "Men are so stupid. I'm glad I had a baby girl." Then she walked into the bedroom. They grinned at each other before they continued.

Maybe not all was lost and his brother could eventually forgive him. Ben sensed a new understanding between them. They were still brothers and loved to smack the shit out of each other, but all in fun. They talked to each other in ways he'd never talk to anyone else. They hit each other and wrestled and acted like they were still twelve years old. And that's what was so freaking special about it. Now, however, they talked like they were twenty. Charlie had changed significantly; he had matured and grown up. It made Ben feel old to realize sex and real issues bothered his brother now. When he left the valley, before the fire swept through, Charlie was still just a little kid. Not so anymore. Ben knew they had a lot more to learn about each other now. Which meant more changes. But maybe, he was starting to understand not all changes were bad. His daughter. Jocelyn. And a brother who was more an equal? Yeah, those were the good kind of changes.

CHAPTER 12

THE GENERAL CONSENSUS OF the valley seemed to be that Jocelyn—bad, motherless, white-trash Jocelyn Jantz—must have seduced Ben and purposely gotten pregnant by him. Who knew how long she'd been scamming to get Ben? Maybe they had a long, ongoing affair. Whatever. She was the cause. It was a well-known and publicly observed fact that she and Marcy had a ceaseless running feud. It was not entirely impossible that others observed the giant crush she had on Ben prior to all this too.

The strangest part was that now that they had a baby together, and practically lived together, Jocelyn didn't have a crush on him anymore. She was too tired to contemplate sex or romance or desire. It seemed a long forgotten activity that had very little relevance to her life now. Which was fine with her.

She was growing more confident in her abilities to handle Lillian and fulfill her needs. To avoid growing stir-crazy, she left the ranch daily to do errands. She quickly learned how to haul Lillian everywhere and change her diapers, provide feedings, and allot times for napping while she did all the other things she intended to. At first, she was hyper aware of all her duties toward her daughter, but that soon became second nature. By the time everyone knew that Jocelyn had a baby and the baby's father was Ben Rydell, Jocelyn had become a very proficient new mother.

She had to suffer through the cashier prattling on and on at the River's End mini-mart. She insisted on giving Jocelyn a long talk about the Rydells being "such decent folk" and scolding her because "she tainted their entire reputation." Then she saw the two mothers who sniffed and passed her like a couple of snobs when she came into the grocery store aisle for diapers. One pushed her shoulder into Jocelyn, shoving Jocelyn back. Not a word or apology did she offer. Sighing, Jocelyn straightened herself up and didn't say anything. After choosing an economy size of diapers, she paid and escaped the traumatic scene. There were many more slights. She didn't fail to miss all the whispered conversations that fell oddly silent when she passed through a restaurant, gas station, shopping center or hardware store. It wasn't her imagination.

When she stopped in the café to let Sheryl, the owner, know she'd be happy to start her new job next week, she was told with a sniff of disdain that they no longer needed her. She was told no explanation, nor was it offered. She bit her lip, staring in shock at Sheryl, but finally nodded, blinking back her tears. No way would she let any of them see her cry. Spinning on the heel of her shoe, she stomped out and headed home. Allison was watching Lillian and Jocelyn quickly gathered her up to go home.

"What's wrong?"

Jocelyn shrugged, avoiding eye contact. "Oh, nothing, really. I didn't realize how petty this valley was until I became the girl who ruined Ben Rydell and the Rydell name, in general."

"What do you mean? Are people giving you a hard time?"

"Yes. Just lost the job I thought I had. I guess Sheryl figured out Ben was the baby daddy." Jocelyn held her hand up to Allison's face, who was turning red and about to go off in Jocelyn's defense. "It's okay, Allison. I slept with a married man and his wife died that night. It's an ugly story. With ugly consequences. I have to deal with them."

"It's really not okay. It's no one's business but yours and Ben's."

Jocelyn tucked Lillian into her arms, kissing her forehead. "I don't care. I'm glad I have her and that's all that matters."

She waved goodbye and thanked her for babysitting before retreating towards the river. She walked beside it for a while until she came to the graveyard. She stifled a groan. Only this family would have their own goddamned grave-yard on their land. Some of the dates on the headstones went back to the mid–eighteen hundreds when the first Rydells settled there. The tombstones were the big, old slabs of concrete that stuck up all creepy–like. Ben's grandparents, mother, and wife were buried there. Right there on their land.

She sighed as she wove her way around the fence and gate before finally reaching the bench and sitting on it. While gazing at the dead, she reflected on her life. The grass was always mown and the bushes lining the fence were trimmed regularly. Miscellaneous flowers in full bloom showed up on the more recent graves. She didn't know who the people were or when they died, she just noticed the fresh flowers. She often walked past here. Why? Maybe it was some kind of perverse way for her to punish herself. For Marcy. Always back to Marcy.

She slouched down on the bench. Marcy's fresh grave had

a sparse layer of grass growing over where it was mounded last summer. She came there frequently without knowing why. To remember her sin? To pay her respects? To simply say she was sorry? Oh, she was. She was so sorry for how she treated Marcy now that she could find no way to fix it. She was sorrier still that Marcy died. But she realized she didn't actually kill Marcy. She didn't murder her or wish her dead. Sometimes, when her stomach knotted after a day like today, in which she was blamed, or just sickened by her own history, she came here to remember none of it happened on purpose.

"Jocelyn?"

She stilled. Ben's voice was quiet and deep behind her. She peeked at him over her shoulder. "What?" Her tone sounded sharp and probably as annoyed as she felt.

"What are you doing?"

"I'm staring at Marcy's grave, Ben," she answered simply, keeping her tone crisp. Matter-of-fact. Duh. Could he not see that?

"Yeah, I get that. But why?"

"No, the question is why don't you? Have you even visited here yet? Paid your respects? Said you're sorry? Goodbye? Anything?"

He was on the other side of the fence and his face wrinkled up in disdain. "I don't think talking to a pile of dirt does any of those things."

She scoffed. "No. You're afraid to face her, even in her death. You refuse to accept it. Do that and you might just find a way to live with it."

"Have you?"

"What?" she snapped, facing forward again.

"Found a way to live with it?"

"How can I when people keep throwing rude remarks in my face? Telling me what a home-wrecking slut, white-trash, gold–digging, dyke bitch I am, who led poor Ben Rydell right down into the path of hell."

She didn't bother to face Ben and was stunned when a few seconds later, he was standing right in front of her. In the graveyard. His hands were on his hips with his elbows poking out. She had to stare up against the sun at him. "What are you talking about?"

She scoffed. "The usual scuttle around the valley. Come on. Like you haven't heard it too."

"No. No, I haven't. No one said a word to me. What are you telling me? You're being taunted by rude people?"

She cleared her throat. Typical. She was being vilified for the act, but the man who conceived Lillian with her? Nope. Nothing. She was the woman, after all. So naturally, the general consensus was it all her fault. She performed a miracle and managed to impregnate herself, it seemed.

"Yes. Just lost my job today. Sheryl must have heard my baby's father wasn't just anyone, not a stranger, as so many assumed when they first saw me with her. Gossip started that day, especially since I moved to the ranch. At first, they assumed your dad only allowed it because I worked for him. Until the truth became known."

"You lost your job? They're blaming you? Only you?"

"I guess I assumed you'd understand that."

His frown was deep. "No. No one said a word in front of me. That's not right. I mean... I'm guiltier than you."

Well, yes, but she bit her lip to keep the snarky thought inside. At least she hadn't been the married one.

"That's fucking bullshit."

She blinked and jerked back when Ben suddenly turned around and kicked the nearest gravestone. It was a relative who died in 1934. She flinched in surprise at the level of loathing in his tone. And the anger in his sudden kick.

"Well, it's reality. I'm going to go talk to Ian about a job. I guess I'm back on here again. If that's okay."

His facial expression softened. "Yeah, yes, of course."

She got up and dragged Lillian with her, her heart heavy as she started towards home.

BEN WATCHED Jocelyn cross the road and head towards the ranch buildings. She was holding his daughter. He shook off his odd feeling and slowly turned around. He was right in the middle of the damn cemetery. The place he vowed never to come to. But his anger had blinded him from paying attention to where he was. Seeing Jocelyn's misery, now he stood where his wife was buried.

He sighed and walked towards her grave. It was the newest, freshest, most recently disturbed plot. Others were lush and green, blending in with the landscape. Marcy's was mounded and still half bald. He stared at her gravestone. So young. Twenty–one years. She only lived for two decades. A knot lodged in his throat. He hadn't cried, not once, since she died. He cleared his throat and finally squatted near the stone. *It's just dirt,* he repeated in his head.

But in his heart, it wasn't just dirt.

He set his hand on the sun–warmed headstone of Marcy Beth Rydell. He stared at her birth and death dates before closing his eyes. It overwhelmed him. The feelings inside his entire body thrashed and plowed through his organs and bloodstream, causing acute pain behind his eyes and in his heart.

He sat there for a long time. Long enough for the sun to touch the horizon. He finally cleared his throat.

"I'm sorry," he whispered. "I'm sorry I cheated on you that night. I'm sorry you cheated on me, too. I'm sorry you died.

I'm sorry we weren't nicer to each other. I'm mostly sorry about that. But I… I have a child. And she needs me now. I am so sorry, but I also have to take of Lillian." He could have gone on for hours perhaps, itemizing what he was sorry about, including her actions towards him. But maybe it was more than what he'd done. Maybe his sorrow was over what they'd done to each other.

He let his hand rest on her gravestone, tracing her name several times as he sat on his haunches. He lifted his face towards the sky and hot tears fell from his eyes. There were only a few. He took in a deep breath and blinked repeatedly until they were gone. He nodded, wishing somehow Marcy could speak to him and let him know he was forgiven. But that absolution could never come. The thing he most sought and the person he most needed it from could never be. Not for real. And Jocelyn was right, he'd just have to learn to live with that.

"Ben?"

His shoulders wilted. It was his dad.

"Both of you were unhappy. Marcy cheated too. I know she did. I know she could have been caught as easily as you were. It was tragic timing."

"It was, Dad," Ben acknowledged. He rose to his feet and turned towards his dad, who stood back a respectful distance.

"I saw you down here. You… you hadn't been here yet?"

"No. I came to check on Jocelyn. Oddly enough, I found her sitting here."

"I've seen her here several times over the last year."

Ben nodded and kicked a rock at his feet. "What a fucker of a year, huh?"

His dad was silent. Ben glanced at him. Jack was staring at Lily's grave, then at Marcy's. He nodded finally. "It has been a fucker of a year."

"I held her."

Jack smiled. "You know Erin talks to Jocelyn daily. I knew the day it happened."

"Why didn't you say anything to me?"

"Because you call me Jack," his dad answered simply.

"You threatened to throw me out."

His dad's smile was quick. "And you deserved it."

Ben chuckled, finally sitting down next to his dad on the bench. They stared out at their dead wives' graves together. "Odd fucking thing to do. Sitting here in a cemetery."

"Yes. Weird damn thing to be doing together as father and son. No one's denying how much you lost. But with a baby, there has to be a timeline on the length of your grief and dealing with it. The baby has to come first."

"I hold her all the time now. It's—it's so easy now. She's pretty funny. She makes all these faces and noises. I think I might even be helping out Jocelyn."

"Yeah, I heard that too. She's completely puzzled by your sudden interest."

Ben held his gaze towards the horizon, sucking a deep breath. "So am I. I'm confused by every single thing that my life has become."

"Well, welcome to parenthood."

Silence fell between them. "You lost your shit because of me last year?"

"Pretty much," Jack answered as he leaned back, stretching his legs out. "Some of it was because I'm just so damn tired of losing things. Of things changing. Of bad things happening. We're considered so lucky in this valley, but sometimes having the money, the land, and the privilege we have keeps others from seeing the hefty price our family often pays."

"I think… I'm starting to understand the father in you. I look at Annie and she's so small. So helpless. I can't imagine letting her loose in this chaotic, violent, scary world. She'd be better off living out her life locked inside our house."

Jack shifted around and his smile was huge. He slapped Ben on the shoulder. "It doesn't change. Not when they turn ten or sixteen or twenty–two. I want to keep you still safe in my house. It's hard to let you go. When things happen…"

"Yeah. I think I understand now."

"Can I ask you something?"

"What?"

"Did you have feelings for Jocelyn? Before the fire, I mean?"

Ben nodded, staring ahead. "Yes. I didn't know what to do about it. Then, Marcy and I had some real shit going on that had nothing to do with anyone else but each other. I didn't intend to cheat on her. I wasn't sure how to respond."

"I figured that. I do know you, Ben. Even with the epic bender you've been on for a year. I know what's inside of you. The thing is, Jocelyn doesn't believe you. She can't believe you wanted her. I know Jocelyn that well. She'll deny you could feel such things for her."

Ben nodded. "I don't know what I feel now."

"You should take some time and think about it."

"Are you still disappointed in me? In my life? I know you didn't want me to be married so young, and now I'm a young father…"

"It's done, Ben. There's no going back. No, I obviously didn't want any of this for you. You will eventually understand how it feels to want your child to have every opportunity in the world. But then… that isn't real life either. You were bound to make mistakes. You have also been taught well how to live with your decisions and take the consequences. Life happens. So no, I don't think I disapprove of how your life is turning out."

"Did you know the people in the valley have been giving Jocelyn a terrible time?"

"Yes. You didn't know?" Jack asked, his head tilted.

"Fuck no. Why didn't you tell me?"

"Well, son, we don't exactly talk to each other."

"Sheryl won't let her work at the café. That's just bullshit."

"I agree."

Ben swept his hat off and put it back on his head. He couldn't change much but he sure as shit could change that. He moved past his dad. Jack was startled and asked, "Where are you going?"

Ben paused, then said, "We're the Rydells, right? Got some kind of status here. Maybe nothing outside of River's End, but in this valley, our name means something, right?"

"Used to."

"It still does. Well, I'm going to use that to my advantage."

"What are you going to do?"

"Tell Sheryl I'll shut down her café if she takes that shit out on Jocelyn. I can make sure every single patron of her establishment doesn't come in. People will do it because of my say–so, exclusively, so I can organize a substantial boycott of her business. Go ahead, Jack, and tell me not to, say I can't do that."

Jack shook his head. "No. I say go for it. Small–minded, prejudiced bigots. You have my permission to play dirty. Can I watch?"

Ben laughed, surprised his dad agreed so quickly. Together, they set off towards the café.

When they walked into the diner, they were greeted warmly. Ben declined a table and asked for Sheryl, who came out of the kitchen. "Ben. Jack. Hello, how goes things?"

"Not so well, I'm afraid. Did you give Jocelyn a job and then tell her it was gone when you found out I was the father of her baby?"

Sheryl's smile dissolved. "Well, er, I mean, yes. It's such an ugly story. And I don't need that in here."

"You mean my daughter? Are you calling her 'an ugly story'?"

Sheryl's eyes darted around in visible anxiety so Ben stepped closer. "I don't take kindly to women who would bully another woman about her personal life and her personal business. Jocelyn's daughter has nothing to do with her work here, does she? You hired her only because you know what a hard worker she is, right?"

"Well... yes. But Ben, I mean, it's..."

"Hear me out. I will shut this place down. Not another Rydell, or those of our extended family, will cross this doorway. I'll personally make sure anyone who does business with us gives no business to this café. I'll blackball you, Sheryl, for the prejudiced, mean–spirited, small–minded woman you are." He kept his voice low for her ears only. Her eyes widened in shock and her mouth dropped open.

"What has that... that woman done to you, Ben? I can't believe you'd threaten me like this."

"Oh, that's no threat, Sheryl. This is for real. You bully her, and we bully you. Now call her up and explain how sorry you are and convince her you didn't mean it."

Sheryl's gaze was as evil as Ben expected. He smiled pleasantly before turning and walking out. His dad trailed him to his truck. Once inside the cab, he said, "Tell me why I was always so fucking good all my life? That felt kinda wonderful."

Jack shook his head. "I know I should not be telling you this, but she had it coming."

"She did. You know what Jocelyn would detest most about it?"

"What?"

"That men had to intervene on her behalf. We really should have sent Erin."

Jack nodded. "Yeah. Now, that you mention it, we should have. We had to strong–arm the bully, but coming from Erin, it might have been more effective. It might not have been legally right, but sometimes, you just have to stand up and fight against the shitty things in life that cross your path."

When he got back to the ranch, he and his dad shared a drink before Ben went back to the apartment. Taking the stairs two at a time, he entered to find Lillian in the bassinette, staring up at the spinning mobile. She moved all around, seemingly enraptured with the simple toy. He dropped a hand to her forehead and kissed her cheek. Then he glanced at Jocelyn who stood folding a load of Lillian's clean clothes and blankets.

She turned at his entrance. "Holy shit. You won't believe this. Sheryl called and apologized to me. Said she realized she was being 'short–sighted and unfair.' I can start working there next week. We'll have to figure out childcare, but…"

Her smile pleased Ben. For once, he liked being a total and complete ass. Using his family name and privilege was something he'd never done before, much less willingly. He always tried to negotiate and compromise. Now? He was glad he could do it and was thrilled it had worked. He felt satisfied too that for the first time in a year, he acted on behalf of someone else, and for no other reason than because he cared about them.

"She should have. It was a shitty thing to do to you. No one should blame you. Or throw your personal life in your face at work."

She shrugged. "Well, at least I get another chance."

"Everyone deserves that."

She stilled and looked up at him. "You're right, Ben. They do."

"Even me?" His voice perked up, hopeful. Wanting.

She swallowed. "Even you, Ben."

"I'd like to help you more. You know, do the laundry, maybe some cooking, and take turns caring for Annie. But mostly, I want to do it because I want to be her father now. Not just her monthly support check."

Tears filled Jocelyn's eyes. "Th–that's… yes! Yes, you can do all of that. But her name isn't Annie."

He smiled and tears almost filled his eyes but he blinked them back, clearing his throat. Annie started to cry. "It is to me. She and I both like it."

A laugh temporarily stopped her tears. She wiped her eyes. "You and she both like it…"

"Well, a girl needs all the advice she can get. Who better to give it to her than her… daddy?" His voice choked up, stumbling over the word that he was ready to assume as his new identity.

Jocelyn nodded, hesitating, and also choked up. "No one better."

BEN STARTED to live in the present again. He was not just functioning and following the old routine. No. He was actually engaged with life, as well as with Lillian and Jocelyn, who found it rather disconcerting. Ben became much more involved and kind.

The best part for Jocelyn? Listening to Ben's incessant, running monologues with Lillian. He talked to her anytime he held her or took care of her. He got much more proficient at changing her too, even the poopy diapers. No more baths just to get her cleaned up. He could feed, bathe, dress, and diaper her in less than an hour. He helped her fall asleep too. He often made her smile. Jocelyn had to admit that she was definitely smiling now, and maybe he was the first one who saw it. He got plenty of smiles from Lillian during those funny, one–sided conversations.

Lillian lay on the floor where Ben spread out a blanket. He sat beside her, stretching his long legs out before him and rolled her onto her stomach. She kept lifting her head and then laying it down, turning her head to the side as if it took all her concentration and energy just to lift and lower it. He patted her diapered butt. Interactions like those were increasingly often, growing more spontaneous. Jocelyn's heart quit thumping so hard whenever she witnessed it.

He was slowly melting all of her carefully fortified walls. The ones she had erected around her heart to protect her against falling for Ben Rydell. If he continued to show so much love to their daughter? Well, she feared her already vulnerable–to–Ben heart would have to take the dangerous plunge and fall madly in love with him. And what was sexier than a grown man being enamored with his baby? For that night, the night he finally engaged with Lillian, seemed to change Ben's entire life.

Before that, she was a burden in his mind. A mistake. A consequence to regret. But after holding her that one time, and spending one night together, he obviously started falling in love with her. Now he was all over her. He carried her. He held her. He moved her little body all around to exercise it and gently kept her entertained. His tenderness and the way he touched her with his large, callused hands made Jocelyn's heart swell. She felt it thump harder each time she witnessed it. He smiled at Lillian all the time and in return, Lillian smiled at him. He talked to her all the time too. Each day, after working on the ranch, the first thing he did after washing his hands was pick her up.

If she happened to be feeding, he paced the floor impa-tiently. If she were sleeping, he'd go so far as to wake her up a time or two. He could not wait a second longer than necessary to be with her.

Jocelyn asked him, "This isn't some kind of situation where she's like a new, shiny toy that has suddenly caught your eye, is it? All your help, dedication, and attention make it seem like you really care and actually like our baby. Will that grow old for you at some point? You're not going to disappear again, are you?"

Jocelyn's tone was grumpy and perhaps she had no right to ask such a question, but before she could truly trust him, and know she could rely on him, she had to be convinced he was all in. He was staying. He really did fall in love with the baby too. And not the fickle kind of love that was new and exciting before it waned and dissipated in strength.

His entire body stiffened and he jerked back, glaring at her. If lightning bolts could have shot from his eyes at her and thunder boomed from his mouth, she was sure he'd have commandeered nature to emphasize his reply. He was so offended by her questions and innuendo. She shrugged at his glare. She had a right to know the answer and he *was* a terrible father *at first*. That was his fault. Not hers. "I won't disappear," was his terse reply.

She took a deep breath. After three months of existing together like roommates, for the entire summer, sharing this odd bubble of an apartment at the ranch, they were now living together. No longer just buddies, friends, or two people who merely hung out together for recreation, now they were figuring out how to raise their developing newborn.

Jocelyn returned to work. Oddly enough, Jack babysat Lillian more than half the time. He was crazy good with her too. He held her and talked to her and seemed utterly bonded with her, almost as much as Jocelyn. Erin and Allison also pitched in. They were all more than willing to take care of her. Jocelyn received her work schedule for the café and they all got together to divvy up their time. When she offered to pay for an outside babysitter to free them of their responsibility, they looked at her with icy reproach and replied, "Why?" With more than enough volunteers on the ranch, she was not surprised that no one supported that idea.

Ben worked with his uncles and Erin while Jocelyn waited tables at the café. Ben slept on the couch too, and never once complained. There was no schedule for who took care of Lillian. Ben tried to take her half the time. Without asking Jocelyn, Ben eventually figured out what to do. He helped with the dishes, the laundry, and all the other household chores, letting Jocelyn sleep as often as he could. He was, in fact, exemplary. The polar opposite of what he'd been when he first came home. It was like he could only be all bad or all good. It was crazy. They lived together fairly easily. Thankfully, they didn't fight and he didn't drive her nuts. They took Lillian to the beach, and walked around the ranch, visiting the horse barns in the evenings. They hung out together by choice, almost like a real family.

One evening, Ben asked, "Why don't you dance anymore?"

Jocelyn was pumping milk, letting the machine suck away on her boob. Her gaze was unfocused when he asked her that question so randomly. Lillian was asleep and he'd been watching a baseball game on TV. The day was hot, and they were cooling off inside with the air conditioning on.

"Ummm. No reason to, I guess. It was just a way to pass time in my youth, you know? Fun. It's not like I quit so much as why would I do it now?"

He leaned forward, pausing the TV. The silence was louder than the game. "You're all healed up, right?" He waved towards her body. "South end, I mean."

She grunted and a small smile slipped over her lips. She

finished pumping her milk. "Yes, Ben, I know what you meant. Yes, I'm all healed and fine from childbirth."

He grimaced. "So... why don't you dance anymore? You don't even sway or tap a finger when the music you like comes on. That's all you used to do. You were never without your ear buds and you always danced. Why don't you ever play your music anymore?"

"Hard to hear a baby crying through ear buds."

"Like right now, I'm here. You could, you know."

"I just don't feel like it anymore." Growing agitated, she stood up.

"Is it because of me being here? Though that seems stupid, since it never stopped you from bouncing around and dancing at all kinds of odd times before."

She stowed the breast pump and placed the milk in the fridge, slamming it shut before she whipped around. "That was another lifetime, Ben."

He stared at her, frowning, as she was seemingly lost in thought. "So I ruined that about you too? You loved to dance. Now, you don't care? And while we're on this, why don't you look like you anymore?" He waved his hand towards her again.

"What do you mean?"

"I guess I didn't even know that you had dark blonde hair. I haven't seen your natural color in years. Where are all your piercings? Why is your hair growing out? The only thing you can't undo is those tattoos." Her arms had many of them, along with her back and hip.

"No kid wants their mother looking weird," she quietly replied.

His eyebrows furrowed. "She can't even see clearly across the room at this point. I highly doubt she's sitting there criticizing how her mother's hair is done. Come on, Jocelyn, what's this really about? The one thing most distinctive about you was you always had your own style. From the time we were in elementary school. You mentioned being a tomboy when talking about my mom. She was a tomboy. You might have been a tomboy, but you always had your own style. It was an edgy style, but all your own. What the hell? Now it's just gone?"

"It was a delinquent's style. I'm twenty–four years old, Ben, time to grow up."

He squinted his eyes at her. "For crap's sake, Jocelyn, I don't think anyone could accuse you, or even me now, of not growing up, especially at our ages. You faced motherhood on your own, and squarely faced off a scandal that would have sent lesser women running scared. There was nothing wrong with your style. You were... always unique. You were your-self. Now you can't be? That's bullshit."

She sighed, flopping down on the couch. "I have enough stacked against me that I don't need to add dressing weird. People will hold it against Lillian too. Besides, you should be glad I don't look like that anymore."

He turned to face her. "I came onto you when half your hair was shaved, did I not?"

She averted her gaze. So rarely did they bring up *that night*. But never did they mention it so casually. "What? You want me to shave my head?"

"It felt kind of cool. Bristly." He brushed his hands through his hair, a habit that increased whenever he was nervous, annoyed or angry. "I always admired you for being different from anyone around here. Why would you stop that?"

"Because you fit in here. You wear the clothes of a horse rancher and it works. I live in a small, rural farming town and I dressed like I just walked off an inner–city neighbor-hood bus. It doesn't belong here. Never did." She dropped her gaze and added softly, "I want to belong here, Ben."

"You *do* belong here. You were born and raised here. You belong here more than most."

"I want to be part of it. And not as the weird girl. The tomboy. The girl that people call names. And trust me, Lillian will not want me to be that woman either."

"You love her. You care for her every need, no matter the time of day or your mood, even if you're exhausted. You talk to her and look after her and your entire heart is all wrapped up in her. I mean, any idiot could see that. She isn't going to care how you wear your hair or your clothes."

"Thank you for saying that."

"It's true. Look, the night we made Lillian might be all tainted as shit and make us 'bad' but you know the reality? The reality is, I could not have handpicked a better woman to mother my child. Marcy could never have been half as loving, adoring, disciplined, and well–meaning a mother as you are. I'm not even insulting her. That's just the truth. And you're right, now that I have her, I would never want my life to be otherwise. You know where I lucked out? Having you, Jocelyn Jantz, as her mother. It was a complete accident on my part. I never considered the kind of mother you could be."

She snorted, crossing her arms over her chest. "Well, duh."

"Yes, duh. But you being the accidental mother of my child? Best stroke of luck that ever happened to me."

She eyed him warily. Then she stared down at her short fingernails and picked at the dried skin on her cuticles. "Thank you for saying that."

He threw his hands up. "You don't believe me. Jocelyn, where is the girl who believes in herself? Knows herself inside out? Where are you in all of this? You don't have to abandon the past because you had a baby. Even the disgraceful and shocking way we did it. Because I did that too. But I still get to be me and do all the things I love. Why can't you?"

"Please drop it, Ben. It's just better this way."

"It's not right."

She scoffed. "Since when has 'right' described the reality of our situation?"

He muttered and returned to the game. She took that to mean the conversation was over.

$\mathcal{H}$E, HOWEVER, KNEW THIS conversation was just beginning, and definitely not over.

Ben didn't like hearing that the trauma involving Jocelyn and him had altered her entire personality and appearance. Changing her hair to a soft dark blond that swooshed around her chin in a smooth, straight bob, she had no spikes, bangs or layers. Just soft hair that framed her face. She rarely wore makeup. She had a nice forehead, and evenly-spaced, whisky-colored eyes that were huge with dark eyelashes. Blessed with a long, regal nose and a small, bowed mouth, she was always thin, and had an amazing body. Even if he had been a monk, he could not have missed that observation over the years. Relegated to being her "friend," he never failed to notice her body. She had a desirable figure that fashion models might long for. Funny, because her personality was so far from flaunting her figure. Even her long, thin arms were defined in toned muscles. She had shapely, slim legs with strong thighs and calves that only accentuated her long, narrow, elegant torso. Her breasts were no more than a handful and she had a heart–shaped tight little ass. She could move with the litheness and confidence of a panther or a cougar. She always had. Ben found it hard to take his eyes off her.

Before this, however, she looked... different. Not as in *weird* different, but *literally* different. She changed her look every few months. Her hair color changed as often as she changed her sheets. First a Goth brunette, then a redhead, then a platinum blonde and then a brunette. Sometimes multiple colors, including purple or blue, and even a sedate brown. At times, her hair was really short, crazily styled or shaved; and at others, she went for a smoother, almost prim effect. There was no guessing. One day, she could be wearing saggy pants three times too big for her and a jersey that drowned her thin body; and the next, she could show up in a sexy little jean skirt with neon–colored cowboy boots, studded with rhinestones. Completely transforming herself was an obsession at times. And hell, Ben didn't always like her newest choice. He found comfort in familiar things and was not very comfortable with change, but knew it wasn't his decision. And that was just how she was. Now? Nothing like she used to be.

He couldn't stop wondering why she never danced. Before Lillian's arrival, she always danced. Jocelyn was born to dance. It made her visibly happy. Music and dance. Perhaps, if she lived anywhere else, or had any kind of role model or support, she could have done great things; he felt sure of it.

But at least she found something she liked and did it. Now? She never did.

Another thing he had destroyed and ruined for her.

He fisted his hand. He was tired of ruining things that mattered to those he cared about. He hated being the cause of other people's pain, disappointment, and frustration. But he knew how he could fix this one thing. He could help find a way to make Jocelyn dance again.

A few weeks later, after much searching and work, Ben came up with the answer. He wouldn't give Jocelyn the chance to say no or back out.

"Hey, can we run into town? I need some things."

Jocelyn had just returned from work and was still wearing the uniform from the River's End Café. She smiled with a tired sigh and nodded. "We?"

He already had Lillian in his arms with the diaper bag slung over his back. Once, it would have been a backpack filled with drugs, now it was a baby bag full of diapers, rash cream, and baby wipes. Ben liked the diapers much more than the drugs.

"Yeah, I want you guys to come with me."

She shrugged. "Okay, I guess." Her odd look showed she wasn't used to hearing such a request. She came out in her jeans and a plain, black tank top with a vest over it. He narrowed his eyes. *Is that outfit appropriate to dance in?* He wasn't so sure. But to say anything about it would only bring questions. And provide her with a reason not to go.

So Ben said nothing. He strapped Lillian into her infant car seat and snapped it into the base that was already securely belted in his truck. He'd been driving a truck that was owned by the ranch and formerly used for maintenance. He intended to purchase his own soon. He wanted to get a big, safe one, what with all the precious cargo he now had to haul around. Jocelyn slipped into the passenger seat, clicking her seat belt. She rubbed her hands on her pant legs and went still, suddenly nervous in his presence. He started the truck and drove past Pattinson before getting on the interstate.

Her head whipped around. "Where are you going?"

"Somewhere new. It's a surprise."

She frowned and picked at a frayed spot on her jeans. "Why?"

"Because I want to." He kept his lips tightly shut. She folded her arms over her chest in a huff but he ignored her. Pulling into his destination, he turned the truck off. There was a long, exaggerated silence before her disapproval nearly exploded the entire cab.

"What is *this?*"

"Exactly what it looks like: a dance studio."

"Well, I can freaking read, Ben. Why are we here?"

"So you can dance."

She rolled her eyes. "Even when I did dance, I never once stepped foot in a dance studio. Besides, I'm twenty-four, not fourteen. These studios are mostly only attended by kids under eighteen. Not adults."

"Well, not this one. It has students of all ages and all dance styles. Once a week, an outside instructor comes by that does hip hop and you are booked for a private, hour-long session with him that starts in five minutes."

She kicked the dashboard. Startled, he glanced at her.

"What are you doing, Ben?" she nearly shrieked. Her frustration rising, not towards him Ben believed, but being at a dance studio. However, her gaze kept glancing towards it with something close to longing in her gaze. The gaze made him double down on wanting to do this.

"Making you dance again." He stared out the windshield. "I think I inadvertently took that away from you too. Along with everything else. Your future. Your ability to marry and have kids with the man you choose, at the age you choose. I turned you into the valley pariah by having a child with me. For which I cannot forgive myself. Of all the things I took

231

away from you, the one thing you cherished and adored and loved to do and what made you *you* was dancing."

Her gaze studied his face. And her angry expression melted. "You didn't take all that from me. I was there too, remember? We did it *together*."

"Whatever. Please do this for me."

"I haven't danced in over a year. I'm so out of shape and practice. No way could I keep up with an instructor. I've never had a minute of real training."

"Which only makes your abilities all the more amazing and why you should have proper coaching."

She shook her head. "It'll embarrass me."

"No, it won't, and it might remind you who you are."

She scoffed. "What's the point? It takes over an hour to get here. I can't keep that up. If I want to dance, I can just do it at home for free."

He turned and faced her. "No. You won't. You work long hours as a waitress and then drag yourself home to take care of a newborn. Your life is too hard. Without enough fun. Maybe I just want to make sure you don't grow old before your time. I don't want you to become cynical, jaded, and bitter. You need something outside of what your routine has become. I don't want to be blamed for you forgetting the things that make you happy. This"—he threw his hand towards the studio—"dancing made you happy. I see you smile at our baby. But otherwise? Not so much. Believe what you want of me, but destroying your life will not be on my conscience."

She tilted her head, rolling her eyes. "You're being way too dramatic."

He rolled his eyes back to her. "Well, so are you. It's just a class. An hour. I'm sure you could spin circles around whoever they asked to teach it."

She swallowed and then stared at him hard, with her eyes

squinted. Finally, in a low tone that was very intense, she asked, "What are you doing, Ben?"

He smiled easily, sure of this one motive. "Trying to be your friend again." Her eyes grew weary. He shook his head. "I'm just trying to make up for how my thoughtless actions interfered with your life."

She turned forward, scoffing, "You don't even know what good dancing is. Let alone where I fit in."

"I know enough to understand you are clearly amazing. Please, Jocelyn. I already paid for it. You don't want to waste my money, do you?" He all but fluttered his eyelashes.

She gritted her teeth and grabbed the door handle. "Fine. But just this one time. Because this is so stupid."

She slammed the truck door and he almost fist–bumped himself. *Yes!* He persuaded her to go inside, at least. He grabbed Lillian from the back seat. She was wide–awake with her big eyes staring all around.

He checked Jocelyn in, but Jocelyn stood back, her gaze not connecting with anyone. Her resentment towards Ben and being there nearly radiated off her. The interior was painted black with crimson splashes and cherrywood furniture nicely arranged around the reception desk. They were directed towards the back, to a studio with hardwood flooring and a whole wall of mirrors.

Ben almost had to push Jocelyn through the door. She scowled at him, her reluctance showing in the set of her shoulders and how her hips resisted his shove. The instructor was squatting near a computer and plugging into the stereo system. He stood up at their entrance. He was a large African–American man, bald with huge muscles and an even huger smile. "Jocelyn Jantz? You my next private session?"

She rolled her eyes. "I guess."

"I'm Tareq. Go ahead and start stretching." He waved at Ben in an obvious message to leave.

Ben sat down outside the room before he attempted to unbuckle Lillian from the car seat. "Wait until you see what your mama can do. Coolest mom ever. She just doesn't know it yet."

Lillian blinked and stared vacantly towards the two-way mirror, catching her own reflection.

"That your boyfriend?" he heard the man ask. "He was pretty excited to find me. Said you were some kind of marvel at hip hop."

Jocelyn just stood there with both of her hands deep inside her pockets. Placing a foot up, she barely leaned over in the lamest stretch Ben had ever witnessed. "No. He's my baby daddy." She scoffed. "As if. Look, he's just trying to be nice. I haven't so much as spun a circle in over a year. I never had five minutes of instruction."

"Yeah? Well, twenty years ago, none of us did. There weren't any real teachers back then. We all learned like that. Let's see what you got."

"What the hell are you doing around here then? No one dances like this in the valley."

"You'd be surprised. It's becoming pretty popular. Little kids wanna do what they see on TV. I'm from here and come to visit my family once a week. I work on the west side mostly, though."

"Full time? As only a hip hop dancer?"

"Yeah. *Only.*" Tareq smiled. "As a teacher. Choreographer. And sometimes a dancer. Sure."

Music started and the deep bass boomed. The door was shut and Tareq walked towards the front of the studio. Jocelyn stood there, her head lolling back and forth. She made even a head roll look like something special. She captured the smallest details like her shoulder moving up and then down. She could twitch a finger and turn it into a dance move. Ben knew he wasn't full of shit. The girl could move. But she hadn't even tried yet.

Ben couldn't hear their conversation, but he saw the instructor smile and nod his head. He waved at her, and Ben suspected he was challenging her. Making a small move with his arms, he did it almost like a wave but slower and more fluid. Jocelyn rolled her eyes, but repeated it. He could see her face in the two–way mirror and she looked bored, almost to the point of being insulted. Tareq nodded with a grin and dropped his arms. His feet shuffled and dropped, going back up and left and right, then around and another drop. She raised an eyebrow, but grinned and seemed curious by the obvious challenge from Tareq. She mimicked his move and added some. The teacher clapped once and laughed, his body language getting totally relaxed as he got into it. He hooked his arm in the air as an obvious gesture of acclaim over what she did.

Ben saw the exact moment when Jocelyn engaged. She was annoyed and embarrassed at first and her mouth was set in a grim line, always protecting her fragile confidence that made her doubt she was really talented. Never mind that everyone who saw her was stunned by her performance. She could follow this guy, and Ben was sure of it. He started out with several of the usual moves; even Ben had seen them before, the staples. His legs going out, and touching, then the other leg sliding in as his body looked bouncy and loose before sliding into the next move.

Then he nodded, smiling as he progressively increased the sequence of steps before moving aside as if to say "Your turn." And each time, Jocelyn's confidence grew as she moved her body and showed off her skills. It took a while. The music changed and the beat was faster. Finally… she smiled a huge grin Ben hadn't seen in… hell, a year. It was different from when she was staring at Lillian. Those smiles were for Lillian's benefit. Watching the smile that curved her lips, and dug into her cheeks until it reached up to her eyes, Ben clearly saw she was thrilled. She merely survived before this and she was *fine*. But happy? Oh, hell no. He nearly set his hand on his side of the glass. Until that moment, Ben could not articulate what was missing from the Jocelyn he'd always known and cared about. It was this. Jocelyn's smile. Her *real* one. Her smile that looked as big as the fucking planet when it was aimed at you. The twinkle in her eye. The mischief he saw there. Like right now. Rising to the instructor's challenges and seeing what she could do made her *alive* again. Back to the funny, challenging, confident, smart, wild, sweet girl, no, woman, that she was.

The same way she was *that night*. The night they betrayed Marcy and the night they made Lillian. He was starting to add that distinction when thinking about *that night*. It wasn't just a night of sin and betrayal; it was also a night of caring and creating a new life. He might have been drunk but he was very much aware of Jocelyn. He clearly remembered her dancing and laughing, tilting her head back and roaring with unbridled abandon. The music completely filled her with joy as her body moved to the rhythm. She was so cool, so smooth, so in control and so beyond anything Ben had ever known or seen before. He had always liked watching her.

She was his conduit into a world that went far beyond their limited valley, and privileged, small-town world. She dressed like a bold, crazy, fun, young, amazing, alive woman. She was crazy hot then, and she didn't realize it, which made her odd, eccentric package even more appealing. There was an underlying sweetness and vulnerability of needing to fit in. The sad part was, in many other environments, she would have had no trouble fitting in and belonging. She could have been the one everyone wanted to know and emulate. But not in this valley. That night, Ben was intrigued and intoxicated by her wild abandon and joy, and hell, knowing she shaved her hair. He'd never known anyone, guy or girl, with as much guts as she had.

Ben's life had been lame, boring, stressful, and lacking in personality. He married someone who was typical and ordinary as soon as you got beyond her looks. All that filled his chest that night was unadulterated regret. His youth blinded him to the man he really was and the one woman he really wanted. *Jocelyn.*

He was glad he stayed to watch Jocelyn dance. Seeing her smiling now with the instructor because she was finally doing what she always loved to do, felt like some of the wrongness from *that night* could start to be put away.

He sat back, pressing Lillian against his chest. He was glad for her solid presence. It reminded him that it wasn't *all* a mistake.

Because of *that night*, in his selfishness, Ben ruined the most genuine, kind, confident, amazing woman their valley had ever produced. He singlehandedly turned her into average, ordinary, and unsmiling.

She was as lost as he felt.

But watching her now, for the first time in a year, she didn't seem so lost.

The hour went by and she pointed at the computer, at the time, no doubt, but the instructor shrugged his shoulders and started moving his body again, sliding his feet around and back, and inviting her to join him. And she did in almost perfect synchronicity. Ben stood up and stared in awe as they continued improvising something together and running through it over and over again. He knew she could keep up with him. She'd never believe it unless she did it.

Eventually, a half hour longer than the lesson, the music finally ended. Jocelyn leaned over and wiped the beads of sweat off her forehead. They shook hands and talked some more before she came out. Her entire body radiated with energy. She stood taller, held her shoulders squarer, and something positive was emanating from her. She grinned at Ben. Then her gaze dropped to Lillian, who was sleeping in his arms. Her smile dimmed for just a moment, but he saw it.

She had some kind of hang-up about being herself versus being a mother. As if liking to dance and smile was not part of motherhood. He'd just have to find a way to get around it.

They stood a few feet apart. Then she passed him and he nudged her shoulder. "I told you you could do it. Who was teaching whom?"

Her face dropped, but he did notice the beginnings of a smile. A confident, proud smile. A knowing, she-kicked-ass-at-it smile. "Not me. But yeah, I can still keep up."

"You can do much more than keep up." He strapped Lillian in and hooked her car seat into the base. They headed back to the ranch.

"You're coming back, right?"

She shrugged.

"You had fun. Admit it. I saw you. You can't deny it." She didn't confirm or deny. He finally leaned across the cab and tucked his hand against her side, right under her armpit and tickled her. He knew she was crazy ticklish there. He used to do it to her anytime he was trying to get her attention or to shut her up. She used to rib him and annoy him, trying her best to purposely irritate him. He missed those interactions. She clamped her arm down to her side tightly and tried to stop him.

A smile escaped her even as she wanted to scowl. "Okay. Okay. I had fun."

"Then you'll come back? Besides, I already paid for it. I'll bring you again next week."

"Whatever."

But it was so much more than *whatever.* He caught her over the next week... dancing. Not like the old days, but with little, subtle steps here and there, and only when she thought no one was looking. She put her earphones in a few times too, while holding Lillian, and moved around with her. He even saw her at the beach doing the combination of steps he witnessed at the class. Something huge shifted in Ben's chest. He wanted to pound his fist in the air and say *Yes.* There was a sparkle in her again. A sparkle that he was completely responsible for. He had allowed his guilt over a dead woman to impede his bond with his child and her mother. What he'd done to the woman who was still alive, Jocelyn, made her just as much a victim of his actions as the dead one.

The dance studio became Ben's favorite place to go. He sat there, entertaining Lillian, who had plenty of volunteers to watch her but he politely declined their services. She needed to watch her mother. And her mother needed to enjoy the things which she loved to do and defined her *and* have a daughter. Plus, it just made him happy. He loved to watch her smile and see her excitement. Not to mention the straight-up awesome dancing. Jocelyn and her instructor made a striking pair. They choreographed a duet that was sexy as hell in the way they moved around each other, without any touching or grinding. The instructor was a huge guy and all muscled up. Her slimness and easy grooves complemented his heavier stomps and bumps.

Tareq high-fived Jocelyn and grinned, pulling her against him for a half-hug. "You, girl, are unreal."

She smiled, and her sheer pleasure erased all the shyness from her face, filling it with confidence. Ben watched her remember she could do this and he knew to stay back. She was really touchy about him watching her. He had to be discreet. Still, he could hear them practicing clear as day.

"Come this weekend."

"I don't know. I have Lillian and work and it's not like it's close."

"You got the baby daddy. Let him babysit."

Ben bristled. He knew Tareq often referred to him as the *baby daddy*. He didn't know why, but it annoyed him.

"Well, I'm the baby mama, so..."

"You're wasted here. In this place. You get that, right? I could hook you up. You—"

"River's End is my home. Nothing more to discuss."

Then their voices dropped and Ben missed the rest of the conversation.

He followed her outside without a word. The drive home was quiet but finally, he had to ask. "Where did he want you to go this weekend?"

"Oh. Just some club. On the other side of the state. No way would I."

"To dance?"

"Yeah."

"Nothing else? You don't think he wants anything else?"

Gripping the handle over the door, she turned towards him. "Like what?"

"Like a date? Sounded to me like he was asking for more."

She laughed. "I highly doubt that."

Quiet filled the truck cab. She shifted her butt around and gazed out the window. They started heading into the ranch. "Maybe we should talk about that."

"What?"

"Dating. I mean... how we're going to do all this. At first, we were just trying to survive and I didn't want you to do everything all by yourself. But... you know, we've settled things down a bit. We're... being mature. Handling things like adults. I guess it's time we address what we should do about... our lives. I mean, I'm not looking to date. Maybe never again with my track record. But... you..."

"I'm not looking to date either, Ben." Her voice was low and she kept her head tucked down.

He sighed, turning the truck off. They were within a few steps of the stairs to the apartment. "But you should. You can't pretend your life is over. You... you deserve to be happy, Jocelyn. You deserve to have whatever you truly want. We're going to take care of her together, no matter what, right? I mean, I feel like we agree on that much."

"Yes."

"Okay; maybe not now, but at some point, it's only natural to want to date, have sex, and find companionship and love." Or at least, she could. Ben felt burnt out on it; enough to last a lifetime.

"Ben, you went from your dad's to living with Marcy to now living with me. The only time you were alone it sounds like you managed to spend it high or drunk and nearly nonfunctioning. Maybe what you need to do is figure out how to be alone. Figure yourself out. As for me? I've always been comfortable alone and with my own company. There's nothing to talk about for me."

"There will be. Given enough time."

"Maybe. But not right now. I'm not looking to date Tareq."

"Just if you wanted to, we could work it out is all I'm saying."

"Okay. I appreciate that, but not yet. I've had enough drama, changes, and upset to last me a few lifetimes. It's nice not to wake up with a stomach ache or my head pounding with stress. I could use some calm for now. So far, it's working, can't we just let it be? We've worked pretty hard to make it so."

"Good point. I just wanted you to know..."

"What?"

"I did a lot to hurt you last summer. If there's anything more I can do to fix it, tell me and I will."

"You could help me the most by figuring yourself out. Not trying to figure me out. But thank you," she said softly, looking at him. "Right now, doing nothing would help me the most."

CHAPTER 14

HE JOB AT THE River's End Café was a bitter disappointment to Jocelyn. After spending the last several years working for the Rydell River Resort, she had complete autonomy and trust. No one micromanaged her. In fact, she managed all the others. To be relegated to waitressing and being supervised was tough. Plus, Sheryl was nasty to her. There was no rhyme or reason about what ticked Sheryl off. She got mad when Jocelyn took the initiative to handle a patron's complaint, and a few days later, yelled at her in front of the entire establishment for requesting her assistance about a customer's concern with their bill. Sheryl accused Jocelyn of never being able to do her job too, and said she wasn't there to hold her hand for every little thing. Jocelyn descended from being the boss, manager, and near owner to a grunt employee again, and it was a tough transition. But she didn't complain. Maybe it was what she deserved. Plus, she liked to get away from the ranch now that she lived there. She needed some outside interaction.

Usually.

Until she looked up at the customer who just walked in, her mouth dropped open.

Marcy's dad.

She bit her lip, and tried to swallow the lump in her throat. She might have just deserved it. He glanced up and gazed at her from her head all the way down the front of her. She ignored proper decorum. "I'll get you another server." There was simply no other choice. She would not subject Marcy's father to her presence. She understood why.

"Wait."

She took in a deep breath and forced herself to turn back. His finger come out and he beckoned her forward. She stepped next to the table and met his gaze, suddenly feeling very weary and resigned. Whatever he said, she'd let him say it.

He hadn't been a decent father to Marcy. Jocelyn knew that. She knew how much he drank. And that he was never home. Or kept track of Marcy from the time she was nine years old and on. There was no mother in Marcy's life either, just some brothers who were in and out of jail. She knew he used to hit Marcy on occasion and called her names. He even shoved her into the wall once. And that's just when Jocelyn was still friendly with Marcy. She'd seen plenty of bruises on Marcy's arms. There hadn't been much kindness or love in Marcy's life. Perhaps that was the reason why she had so little to give. Except for Ben. Jocelyn hoped Marcy achieved some love in her short life from Ben.

"You killed her!"

His voice echoed through the establishment. It was harsh and loud and meant to draw plenty of attention. The diners stopped eating, holding their utensils in mid–air. An unearthly hush filled the place. Jocelyn finally nodded her response, whispering, "Yes, sir."

"You're a slut. A whore. A cunt. Not fit to carry her shoes.

That baby of yours? It'll never be anything but white trash. A goddamned mutant of society. Should have aborted it."

"Yes, sir," she mumbled again, keeping her head down, staring at the edges of her brown shoes. She licked her lips and tried to keep his words from affecting her demeanor. He was angry. And hurt. His daughter was dead. Jocelyn could forgive him for whatever he needed to say to her. It was understandable.

He slowly rose up, reaching across the aisle behind her. Confused as to what he was doing, Jocelyn glanced back only to see him grab a full milkshake off the table. Then something thick, cold, and creamy smacked the top of her head and oozed down her hair, her forehead, her eyes, nose, and mouth, dropping in clumps off her head to her shoulders and shirt and skirt and finally to the floor. He upended the entire milkshake on her. She stood there with her head still bent and didn't say anything. She didn't even flinch. She didn't dare move. She just stood there and let the gooey substance slide down her body and pool onto the floor.

He shoved her aside as he passed her. She shut her eyes as the cold ice cream filled her eyelashes. The silence in the café was thick. Using her sleeve to clear her eyes off so she could see, she looked around but no one spoke. When she dared to look anyone in the eye, they dropped their gazes and stared at their tables, plates, and each other, but not at her.

She leaned forward and used a napkin to wipe off her face and the extra milk and ice cream that saturated her.

"Well, what did you expect?"

Glancing up, she was startled to find Sheryl standing there. "Clean it up. And tell your precious boyfriend I didn't do that so he needn't come back here and start yelling at me about it."

Puzzled, she took the mop handle Sheryl flung her way. Along with the bucket. She didn't say anything but started mopping up the mess and wiping down the table. The restaurant slowly started to ignore her and people began talking, in whispers at first until they were using their normal voices finally. A few walked past her but not a word was said. Humiliation unlike anything she'd ever experienced overwhelmed her. She finished cleaning up before Sheryl told her to leave. She still had ice cream all over her.

Jocelyn kept her composure and didn't say anything or reveal any feelings. She didn't cry or cringe even.

Not until she pulled into the ranch driveway. Then she leaned her head against the steering wheel and let the flood of tears fall as a cry escaped her lips and her shoulders shuddered. The names kept repeating through her brain. Names she called herself over the course of the last eighteen months. But to include Lillian in his tirade? It made the area around Jocelyn's heart literally ache. No! Lillian could not be blamed for her birth. For her parents' sins. Oh, God! Would her momentary lapse in judgment haunt her, *them,* always? Sighing, she finally opened her car door and headed up the apartment steps.

She stopped dead in the doorway. Ben was holding Lillian and she glanced up at his mouth, about to say hello when all her words failed her. He jumped off the couch, and placed Lillian down. "What the hell happened?"

She bit her lip and tried to find the words. But his utter shock at seeing her drew out her emotions. "M–Marcy's dad…" She started to cry again.

"Oh fuck," Ben muttered. He stepped forward and pulled her against him, mindless of the sticky ice cream still clinging to her. Her head was tucked against his chest, by his neck. She sobbed against him.

"I should have gone to him. I kept meaning to go see him… you know, to apologize and pay my respects. I never did. I'm sorry. So sorry. Oh, Jocelyn, I'm sorry. I should have prevented this. It's me he's angry with…" He kept repeating his apology as he patted her shoulder.

"No… no, it was me too. I deserved it. I—"

He pushed her back so his face was right in hers. "No. Damn it. No, you didn't deserve this, not while you are working. What did Sheryl do?"

Jocelyn sniffed and rubbed her nose. "She told me to clean it up."

Ben's jaw tightened in displeasure. "She what?"

"Well, it was a huge mess. She also mentioned something about telling you *she* didn't do it. What did she mean by that?"

He sighed. "Come on, why don't you take a bath and we'll talk afterwards, okay?"

She let him lead her into the bathroom. He ran the bath until it was super-hot and poured in bubble bath, letting it foam up. "I'll leave you alone now, but know this, you will not be treated like that again."

She stared at him as he started for the door. "You can't stop it."

"I sure as shit can," he mumbled as he slammed the door.

She sighed, feeling too dejected and heartsick to ask what he meant, for right now that is. She glanced at the mirror and winced. "You deserved it," she said after glaring at her reflection.

Sinking into the bath, she closed her eyes and tried to pretend this day, and the last year, hadn't happened.

BEN PACED. Lillian lay there, gurgling away and looking at something she found intriguing against the couch cushion. It usually made him smile to himself in pride and love and amusement when she interacted with what seemed like nothing, but right now, his stomach was pinching in pain. He phoned Kailynn and told her what happened. Then he asked her to find out whatever she could about the scene at the café today. Kailynn had worked there many years ago, but was still friends with one of the longtime waitresses, a girl named Rhonda.

Kailynn called back minutes later. "It's bad, Ben. He called her a whore and a slut and screamed out that she deserved to die. He even said that Lillian should have been aborted before he dumped the milkshake on her head. Then Sheryl had the gall to make her clean it up. All the patrons in the entire place went completely silent. Jocelyn just took it. She didn't say a word in her own defense. She let him pour the whole thing on her without even stepping back to avoid it."

"Thanks. I just needed a clearer picture. She won't tell me anything."

"Yeah? Well, I don't blame her. That's not easy to admit. What do we do? How do we make sure this doesn't keep happening to her? Or you. Or Lillian?"

"I don't know. I don't care about me. But those two? She could start by not working there."

"I agree. If she or you need anything, I'm here."

"Thanks."

He paced some more. It was almost an hour before Jocelyn came out, freshly scrubbed, her hair pushed off her face. She was wrapped up in a robe and she grabbed Lillian off the couch and cuddled her, kissing her head, face, and eyes. She sniffed the hair on her head and rubbed her cheek against Lillian's. Fresh tears filled her eyes as she took in Lillian's innocence and purity. Ben knew what she was thinking. He fisted his hands.

"You convinced Sheryl to hire me back, didn't you?" Her voice was soft and flat. "I've been thinking about what she said. She nearly spat her words at me. Talking about my boyfriend needing to know 'this wasn't her fault.' You gave her no choice but to allow me to work there, didn't you?"

"Yes." Ben kept his gaze squarely on hers, unashamed for doing so. "She was wrong to act that way toward you. And Lillian's birth has nothing to do with your work there."

"No, but it's a small town and people like to talk. A lot. About us. She couldn't bear the disgrace of me working there. She didn't want things like what happened to occur. What did you say to her to persuade her to rehire me?"

He shuffled his feet. "I threatened to blackball her business. And being a Rydell, I could make that happen."

She gasped. "You did not!"

Agitated, he started pacing... again. He fisted his hand. "I sure as shit did. I'd do it over again. She had no right to treat you so horribly."

"Oh, my God. Your father's going to freak if he hears you used the family name like that." She spun around and started towards the kitchen, anxious to disperse her own agitation by moving about.

"My father was right there beside me, Jocelyn. And nearly cheering me on."

Mouth agape, she exclaimed, "He was not. No way. He doesn't operate like that."

"Well, you know what? Maybe we both do now. Maybe we aren't as nice as we once were. We got the name, the history, the resources, and the power around here. So why not? I used it for a good cause and I'd do it again too. When it comes to Lillian... or you. You two, now you're my family."

She sat down on the rocking chair, looking dejected. "You shouldn't have done that. You should have at least told me. I wouldn't have walked in there blind, and thinking things were okay, when she was secretly seething with anger and resentment toward me. Believe me, it came out anyway in subtle actions. But not so blatantly that I could totally call her on it. It was worse, Ben, than just knowing."

"That wasn't my intent. You deserved that job. I didn't want to see it ruined because of me. I can't stand having you treated with so much discourtesy."

"There's what should be and what is. You won't do anything about this. It'll only make things worse. Come off it, we of all people learned something, didn't we? We can't force some people to accept our actions. And I'd rather know who those people are going in than be blind–sided like that."

Ben dropped his head, looking deflated. "I didn't think of it like that. My only intention was to help you. This time I wasn't working out my residual anger by pummeling a complete strangers on your behalf. Like I did with Cutter. I… I did it to make your life easier, or so I thought. Not harder."

Her facial expression softened. "I guess I understand that." Her gaze skittered off. "Do you mind if I just… I don't know… go to the beach for a while? I just wanna…"

He waved her off. "No, not at all. Go."

She stood up, and pressed her lips together. "Thank you, Ben. I know you were trying to help. But you can't help me like that, okay?"

He nodded. "Okay."

She walked into her bedroom and came back out moments later wearing shorts and a tank top. He and Lillian stood at the back window watching her walk down the road. She had her ear buds in. That was good. She'd been doing that a lot more lately. That was how Jocelyn always dealt with her problems in life before, with music.

So he screwed up…. again. This time, however, his motivation wasn't driven by anger. Or at least, not on his own behalf. He was mad because of someone else. Someone he cared about very much. His heart swelled, picturing Jocelyn standing there, still and quiet, as angry, terrible words were hurled at her before having a milkshake dumped over her head. He could imagine her grace and dignity, taking what she considered her justified punishment. But why? All because of the compassion she felt for the man doing it. He lost his daughter, and no matter how shitty a father he'd been in the past, Jocelyn forgave him.

Lillian sucked away on her fingers and Ben kissed the top of her head. From the very start, Jocelyn handled everything with poise, grace, and dignity. Everything that was lacking in him. Something pinged in his heart. She symbolized strength and love and caring. She was everything missing in his life and she made him realize he and Marcy never spent a single day sharing things with each other like he did with Jocelyn.

He tucked Lillian into a light coat and arranged her in the front carrier that Jocelyn liked to use when she walked around the ranch. He started towards the beach, but stopped when he saw Jocelyn. His heart lifted. She was dancing. Her steps were subtle. And her feet scuffled through the sand. Barefoot and wearing her earphones, she did all the moves he recognized as the same ones she did with Tareq. He stayed back, watching her more closely. She did it by memory at first, and then with more energy. In the end, she was moving through it so fluidly, she was fully ready to present it before a crowd. Her movements grew more confident, more involved, and meticulously precise. Sweat beaded off her. Ben smiled and felt genuinely happier. She stopped suddenly and started talking on the phone.

It was Tareq. Speak of the devil. Sitting down on a log, she continued talking to him. Annoyed, Ben stepped forward to avoid eavesdropping or appearing like a stalker. He let her know he was there right away. She waved at him and talked for a few more minutes, laughing at something Tareq said.

"Couldn't have been as bad as mine. I had an entire large,

chocolate milkshake poured on top of my head." She nodded as if he could see her, laughing out loud. "I shit you not.

"What did I do?" She glanced at Ben and quickly shifted her gaze away. A small smile filled her face. "No, it wasn't for bad service. He was the dad of a girl I wronged. So it was kind of justified."

Silence as she listened to Tareq speak before she said, "Look, I'll see you tomorrow night. I gotta go. Yeah. Okay. Bye."

She pressed her phone screen and withdrew her earbuds. With a big smile, she leaned forward to tickle Lillian under her chin.

Ben nodded to the phone. "You two friends now?"

She glanced his way. "Yes. Does that bother you?"

"No. I think he's good for you. You share a lot in common, makes sense you'd connect. Besides, you need to replace the friends you lost, don't you? What happened to all your friends anyway? You don't mention them."

Jocelyn pulled her legs up under her. They stared out towards the river as the sun dropped behind the rounded hill across from them. It trailed orange across the river like a path, drawing them to the horizon. "It's a hard story for people to know what to do about," she said quietly.

"You lost your friends?"

"Some. Didn't you?"

"No, not really. Besides, Joey has always been my best friend. He and I are repairing things. I never fit into the big, popular groups like you did."

"I only fit in after high school. High school I was the outcast. Like I am now."

"But now? It's because of us? That's why you quit dancing and hanging and listening to music and being you. All the things that made you so edgy. Huh?"

"Partly. That, and I was just so tired. So sad. All the things you were. However, may I remind you that I've never done hard drugs or run off across three states. Who's the edgy one now?" She shoulder–bumped him and it made him smile.

He nodded. His eyes left hers to gaze at the river. "I was. I was free to go off and be angry and horrible and try to work out some of it. You, however, never got that luxury."

"I don't miss it, Ben. If that's what you're asking."

"I am." He took in a deep breath. "I am asking you that. I'm asking if you want to leave. Here. This valley. Should we maybe go somewhere else and start all over? Fresh. No sad story following us? No Marcy. No prejudice being cast onto our innocent daughter? I'm asking if you want to go somewhere with me and start all over?"

Her entire body startled and her breath came in short gasps. "Ben. What are you talking about?"

"*You.* I'm talking about finding the best way to do what's right for you. And Lillian. Maybe we can't live this down. Maybe Lillian will grow up and be called names. I can't stand the thought of that. I can't stand knowing I did that to you."

She shook her head. "It was just a bad day. Put it in perspective. Jeez."

"Do you ever think about leaving?"

"What? Us? Together?"

He tilted his head, his gaze landing on hers. "Always. Don't you know that whatever happens from here forward, it's us in some form? I mean, she needs both of us." He gently tilted Lillian towards her. She had fallen asleep, and her body was a welcome, warm little bundle against him .

"She does. But no, I don't want to leave, Ben. I haven't lived any other place but here."

"So what? How about we go west? To the city. You saw how Tareq reacted to your dance moves. He wouldn't be the only one. Maybe you could finally do something with that talent and passion of yours. Maybe meet the right people who appreciate it enough to help you succeed. God knows it's wasted around here. You couldn't have been raised in a more old–fashioned, hick, backwards town."

A quick, small smile flashed across her lips. "Part of me doesn't fit, I'll admit. But in other ways? I do. It's my *home.* I can't imagine starting over anywhere else. Besides your family... Lillian needs them, and in some ways, I need them too." She picked at her fingernails. Staring at them, she shook her head. "You know, I always thought of you guys as my pretend family. You just didn't know it."

He covered her hands with his. "We *are* your family. But most especially, I am."

Her eyes filled with tears. "I can't believe I lost friends over this." She lifted her gaze to his, and it nearly shredded his heart. "But the one I missed the most was you. I lost you in all this."

Choked up, he nodded. "You did for a while. But now? You have me. Now and for the rest of your life."

"Trapped. Marcy would be proud. I accomplished something she couldn't." Her eyes widened and she slapped her hand against her mouth. "Oh, my God. I shouldn't have said that."

Ben leaned forward and Jocelyn glimpsed a grin as a short laugh escaped him. "Probably not. But... it was kind of true. I mean, what Marcy would do. The thing is, I'm not trapped. Are you? I mean, technically, we both should feel trapped. But I don't. Do you?"

"No." Her gaze took on a sad, unfocused quality as she looked out towards the water. "The moment I looked into Lillian's eyes, I felt like I'd finally come home. I belonged to someone. Perhaps mothers shouldn't need their babies, but I need her. I wasn't connected to anyone, not for real. Now I am. And I don't regret any of it."

"Do you feel trapped with me?"

"Ben…" Her gaze drifted away. She gulped loudly before she licked her lips. His eyes were riveted on her face. He took in all the details of her features. From her small mouth to her faintly arched eyebrows above her eyes. No detail was lost in his gaze. "You…" She took in another deep breath.

"What? Me what?"

"You were the one I always wanted. It's hard to feel trapped when you finally get what you always wanted."

His heart lifted and renewed hope spiraled through his body. She kept her face tilted from his gaze but he could see the pink infusing her cheeks and neck. The toughest girl he'd ever known was so different with him. Shy. Unsure. Blushing. He touched the tip of his index finger to her cheek and tucked her loose hair behind her ear. "How come you never told me?"

"Because you had Marcy. Because you saw me only as your friend."

"I'm sorry," he whispered. He leaned towards her, his lips touching her hairline and hovering over her ear. "I'm sorry," he repeated, peppering his lips below her ear and down to her neck. "I'm sorry I didn't realize it sooner. I'm sorry I didn't see it. Or feel it. I'm sorry when I finally did, I was married. But I'm most sorry that I let it taint something that could have been… *everything.*"

Jocelyn set her shoulders in a stiff line and kept her head high. Tears tracked down her cheeks. "You don't know what it would have been. It could have been nothing too."

"I think I do. The connection we shared was something I've never shared with anyone else." He withdrew from her and lifted his hand to cup her face, turning it towards him. "I know what it is now. We've put this back together. Correction, *you* put us back together. You are so tough and capable; you accept life and all of its responsibilities with strength and integrity. I didn't do anything. You did all of it. You forgave me and allowed me into Lillian's and your lives again when I had no right. No one could have faulted you if you refused me."

"You're her father."

"And look what I did with that at first. Look what I did to you."

"I want to forget that. I want to just move forward."

"Even when stuff like today happens?"

"Yes. Today was just a bad day. It doesn't make me want to leave here or run away or change my life. I just want to feel justified by being pissed off and hurt and then I'll get up tomorrow and forget about it and continue with my life."

"I have a lot to learn. I hope to learn it from you." His mouth touched hers, hesitantly at first. Their lips met in a soft sensation of warm flesh. She pulled back. So did he. Their gazes locked. Something deep and full of feelings traveled through Ben, making his skin extra sensitive and glazing over his nerve endings. Really, good, intense, turned–on feelings. But also, something more. Something deeper.

He leaned in again and pressed his lips on hers. Long moments passed with their lips touching, caressing, pressing, and tasting. Then he lifted his hand and cupped the back of her head. He tilted her head for more access to her face. Their lips fit together like a key fits into a lock. Perfectly. Her mouth softened as his tongue gently touched the rim of her mouth. She reached up and her fingertips explored his face and cheeks before sliding down to grab onto his shoulders. Her mouth opened up to him. His bloodstream started to rush as it swooshed and boiled inside him. More than a year of celibacy had his body reacting to her slightest touch. She moaned and her grip on him tightened. He leaned down and kissed her harder. He started to pull her up against him when Lillian intervened, although she was totally oblivious and still strapped to his chest. Startled, they both separated before a slow smile spread on both their faces.

Shaking her head, she said, "Talk about birth control."

He grinned too, patting the top of Lillian's bald head. "That'll do it," he agreed.

She cleared her throat, looking down. "What now?"

His hand cupped gently over his baby's head. "I don't suppose you'd let me unstrap her, and set her down somewhere safe, make sure she's clean and maybe fed... and then continue where we left off?"

She smiled at his lame joke and dropped her head, her shoulders shaking. She finally shoved his arm playfully. "You're so dumb, Ben."

He laughed too. "I am. I haven't been in a long time." Then he caught her hand. "What if we go out?"

Her eyebrows rose. "Out?"

"On a date. Like we could date each other."

"We live together. We could just go back and have sex."

"We could." He nodded. "God, knows I'd like to do that. But..."

"But?" Her eyebrows rose.

"Everything started out all wrong. I want to do it all right now."

"Do what, Ben?" Her eyes dimmed, and a general sense of weariness overcame her. As well as disbelief.

"Try to date."

She jumped onto her feet. "Stop. You can't come out here after the day I've had and talk to me like this... or *do this.* It's not fair."

He stood up too, but much slower so as not to wake Lillian. Lumbering somewhat clumsily, trying to balance the bundle he had strapped against him, he nodded. "I get that. But I have feelings for you. And I'd like to go on a date with you. So I'm asking you out."

"Again, Ben, we live together."

"But we are *not* together. So what could it hurt? I'll ask my dad and Erin to watch Lillian and we could go out. For real. I'm not married now. We're both single. Lillian is too young to have a clue what's going on, so we're not hurting her by exploring where this might lead to. Seeing the possibilities."

"It would hurt her if we ended up hating each other. Like your last marriage." Bitterness tinged her words.

"Right. Yes." He cleared his throat. "But we might end up doing just the opposite."

"And if it goes wrong, there you are, back on the couch. And there I am, in your old marriage bed."

"Okay, so nothing is ideal."

She snorted. "You think?"

"Look, if it doesn't work, we figure out what's next from there. If we can deal with what we have so far, and you have to give us some credit: we're pretty amazing so far. What if—"

"What if you're afraid to be alone? What if all this is because you still don't know how to be alone?"

"What if I'm not?"

She squinted at him, nearly tapping her foot impatiently.

He smiled. "I had a thought about that anyway."

"What?"

"Shane and Allison just finished their house. Joey plans to move back into his house in a week or so. What if I stayed with him?"

She started to bristle but he raised his hand. "It would give you some privacy. Some breathing room. And give me the space I need too. But the good part is, I'd still be close. Very close. I'll take Lillian as usual and vice versa. I can still stay overnight. But it would be a lot less pressure on both of us. Maybe... maybe we could find our way to normal somehow."

"I guess going out would be nice. Just to get away from the ranch for a night."

His heart nearly leapt out of his chest. Smiling, he had to remind himself to be less intense and pushy. He knew she was looking for every reason for this to fail. She couldn't trust him yet, so he could not afford to give her any basis to confirm that belief.

BEN SPENT the majority of his time working at the ranch by helping to maintain the horses and the land. Now that Jocelyn considered him as a date, he believed she was right about the need for space and not having it as long as they were living together. It was an odd place for them to be together, and not, but maybe they wanted it to be.

He believed Joey was his best solution and they hadn't spent any time together in too long. Carrying two beers, Ben walked towards the fence where Joey stood, watching the horses frolicking and bucking inside. Joey glanced up when he approached. He jiggled the bottle in a signal for him to take a break. Joey grinned and walked over, taking the beer.

"Hey."

"Hey."

"Did you get the new pump done?" For days, they'd been working at putting in a new water pump in the river to irrigate the orchards and fields. Ian was the one in charge of that. He had all the technical knowledge of the expensive equipment. AJ and Ben were the muscle.

"Yes, Uncle Joey, I finished my chores."

Joey shoved his shoulder. "You're such a dick." He often called Joey that when he wanted to annoy him. Joey took a long drink and wiped his mouth on the back of his sleeve.

"Damn, that tastes good. So, how's that baby of yours coming along?"

"Getting huge. She gained five pounds already. We took her for a well–baby check a few days back. She's turning over now too. It's like she gains these new skills on a daily basis. Amazing."

"Amazing to see you like this about her, considering how you were when you first got here."

He winced. "You ever going to let me live it down?"

"You didn't even witness what Jocelyn went through," Joey said, his tone cut and dry.

"No. But she told me all about it."

"She's way nicer than you deserve." Joey leaned on the fence and Ben did too. They stared at the horses now running in a wild circle and started encouraging the other dozen to follow along.

"Can I live with you?"

Joey glanced up, raising his eyebrows in unmasked shock. "What? Why? What about Jocelyn?"

Joey was insanely protective of her. And Ben was glad now for that. "It's *for* Jocelyn."

"How do you figure?"

"She thinks I need to live alone for a while, seeing as I went from my home here to Marcy to losing my shit on the road and then living with her. She believes I don't really know how I feel about it all because I never spend any time alone, or away from them. But I can't move far away… there's Lillian. Not only do I want to be with her, I don't want Jocelyn doing it all on her own. But if I lived with you, I could save money, and she could have the whole apartment. The way things stand, I'm pretty much still right here, but living apart."

"Do you think maybe she's right?"

"Yeah. In many ways. Things have not gone easy for us.

I'd like to see them improve. Maybe become… normal. I'm trying to get her to date me. But who moves in after their first date? That's in many ways where we're at right now. But then again, we have this whole history and past connection. Maybe this could relieve some of our stress. Unless Hailey's moving in?"

Joey shook his head. "Nah. Not now. Her kids…" He sighed, brushing his hair back off his forehead.

Ben nodded. "Yeah, I really get that now. I didn't before. Wondered why the hell you were bothering…"

"Things change when you fall in love." Joey straightened up. "I have to tell you, I can't wait to stretch out in my own house again. But you'd be welcome."

"Do you hate it? The distance between you and Hailey?"

Joey shrugged. "I don't know. We were new too, last summer. We had issues, like you and Jocelyn. Just different ones. There were her kids and her ex and she felt a bit like you, needing time on her own to figure herself out too. Our arrangement allowed her that. So sure, Ben. You can stay with me, but be forewarned, Brianna and Jacob often come with her."

"Be forewarned that so will my baby. And she's *not* quiet. I love her to death, but God! Does that girl have a set of lungs. Doc tells us she's colicky. So…"

Ben tipped his beer towards Joey and Joey clicked his. Joey added, "So not how I ever pictured you and me as roommates, with three kids between us, ranging from an infant to a teenager and a couple of moms that we're trying to make it work with."

Ben grunted. "Shit." He shook his head, glancing up at the mountains above the ranch. "But when was the last time anything I planned turned out the way I planned it? Flip it, turn it over, shred it, and re-tape it together: that's how my plans end up working out."

Joey drank a long gulp of beer. "Yeah." He glanced at Ben from the corners of his eyes. "Jocelyn's right; a separation right now might do you some good."

Ben nodded. "Yeah, I realize that. I've had some... pretty intense, messed–up issues. Believe me, I know. I know she's right. It'll be a damn miracle if I can ever convince her to be with me on a permanent basis."

Joey's head whipped around. "You want that with her?"

Ben drank his beer, remaining calm and casual. "Yes."

Joey narrowed his eyes and seemed to be studying him from his forehead down to his ankles. "You seem... absolutely sure about this?"

Ben shook his head. "No. I was sure about Marcy and look where that got me. I want to try. I had feelings for Jocelyn before the fire. Before Marcy died. I have feelings now. I'm trying to figure them out. So is she. Try doing that with a screaming newborn and only a sad particle door to muffle it."

"Kind of like keeping it up across half a state and dealing with a teenage girl who thought I was the worst thing that ever happened to her mom. I hear ya about hard circumstances."

"You've made it work though."

"Honestly? If not for the fire, Hailey would have left and we'd have never spoken again. We ended it because of Brianna. Long story. Bottom line is, I left here to fight the first fire that broke out, believing Hailey was never coming back. She needed to be a mom first before my girlfriend. Only with the fire breaking out, she stayed on to make sure I was okay, and then she realized she could figure out a way to have both."

"So... the fire did bring some good then?"

"I don't think like that. There was no good to come from that inferno."

Ben shrugged. "I don't know, thinking that something good happened makes me feel... I don't know, glad. Glad something positive came out of it." Joey's gaze was different. He nodded and put his hand out. Ben shook it, asking, "What is this for?"

"You're in there still. Welcome home, Ben."

Ben's throat swelled with emotion, making it hard to swallow. He didn't say anything, but nodded as they faced forward, quietly drinking their beers and watching the horses.

CHAPTER 15

*J*OCELYN KEPT RUNNING HER hands through her hair, styling it back. She squinted in the mirror. Wow, she looked so... normal. So typical. She should have kept herself like this in high school. She might have even been accepted by more of her peers. Out of high school she made friends and grew to be well liked. But in high school? It hadn't been easy being different.

Her hair was a soft, subtle dirty blonde. Straight as a bone and all one length now, she shook it back from her forehead and it fell around her face in perfect, silky strands. She tugged on some leggings and an oversized shirt with a pair of boots she hadn't worn in over a year. Maybe longer. She looked like what she was: a typical woman on her first date with a guy she'd had her eye on for a long, long time. Except sometimes, the woman staring back at her in the mirror seemed like a fraud. Nowadays, however, she looked almost motherly. Just what Lillian deserved. Even if Jocelyn actually didn't feel like it.

She took in a breath and finally jerked open the bedroom door.

Ben jumped up. He'd been on the couch; channel surfing, if the remote he still held in his hand were any indication. He wore slacks and a button–down shirt, and his hair was all combed and styled. He had taken Lillian to his dad's and got ready there. It was awkward all day. Coming out this morning, they discussed the mundane details of getting through the day: their schedules and their chores. Then came more work for him and baby care for her; after all, she didn't have a job now. Anyway, that left her preparing for a date.

And odder still were the butterflies that fluttered around her stomach. She was excited about it, which was either crazy or sick. How could she be? After the destruction and strain and regrets their one and only time together managed to cause, how could she be so eagerly anticipating this time?

Ben stared at her and she stared back at him. Only the din of the news on the TV could be heard. Taking his arms from behind his back, he held out a single rose in his hand. Jocelyn recognized it from Jack's yard.

"You look great."

She took the flower, her heart blipping. It was thoughtful. "I look normal, you mean."

His eyes sparked. "Who asked you to? If you don't want to be normal, don't."

She scoffed. "As if Lillian doesn't have enough stacked against her without a freaky mother."

He stepped forward, wrapping his arm around her. Shocked at his close proximity and finding herself in his embrace, she began to withdraw so he leaned closer, placing his lips right over hers. "Our daughter doesn't have anything stacked against her. She has everything going for her. My family, this ranch, even this valley and *us*. But most especially, she has *you*. So if you choose to look this way, you can blame it on yourself, not on her. She isn't telling you how to be or anything else. You are. And for that matter, neither am

265

I. Give yourself the credit or blame, not us, if you decide you need to look more... typical."

She leaned her head back and a laugh escaped her mouth. "You're saying you think I want to look like this? Like... I've somehow grown up all of a sudden or something? All at once, I feel an urgent need to fit in or something?"

He shrugged, releasing her and smiling too. "I have no idea, Jocelyn. I'm just saying you're accepted by us unconditionally. So—"

A smile made her lips twitch. "I don't think I decided I wanted to look more... normal."

"Maybe it's just a phase for you. If so, you'll be done with it at some point and shave your hair off again. Nothing is out of the realm of possibility with you."

"And what, Ben? If I did? You'd like that?"

He took her head in his hands and tipped her face up towards him. She rolled her eyes as he squinted his, as if he were assessing the shape of her head. "Well, you do have a nice, round, small head. So at least you *could* pull it off. Maybe not my first choice of hairdos, I admit. But knowing you could very well do something like that on any given day, makes me realize I kind of like that part about you. I'm so predictable. So routine. Conventional. Except for the last year, I was totally unoriginal. I could never take chances. You can though. You can be unpredictable, impulsive, wild, and crazy—"

"Used to be," she interrupted.

"Used to be," he repeated. "You're this unique and perfect combination. You're like the salt of the earth, working hard and consistently because of your own integrity. Unlike Marcy, who was lazy and thought any kind of work was beneath her, I love how hard you work and that you accept any kind of work. But then again, you have that crazy side. The side that has no problem keeping up with Tareq's moves.

You could soon outdo him. And suddenly dye your hair purple and flash me a new tattoo or… I don't know, you have the kind of excitement that I lack."

Something weird blipped in her heart. "You see me like that?"

His smile was crooked. "I see you like that."

They stared at each other for a long moment until she cleared her throat. "Should we go?"

"Yes, we should."

They went into Pattinson for dinner. Sitting together, they stared at each other across the small table with one lit candle and a little jar of flowers. "This place is nice."

"Shane told me about it. He took Allison here when they started dating."

"We're not dating," she instantly corrected.

"Excuse me, but we are on a date," he pointed out, his eyebrows rising in challenge.

"One date doesn't mean we're dating. Too many obstacles for us to date."

He nodded, drawing a long drink from the ice water before him. "We also have a lot going in our favor. Like a beautiful daughter. No small commodity."

She rolled her eyes. "Ben, women don't have to be married to raise a child anymore, even if they stay together. Your predisposition for getting married is crazy serious for one so young. I'm not going to marry you for Lillian's sake."

"I know. That's what I like so much about you."

She nodded toward her menu. "Just figure out what you want to eat," she grumbled, despite the smile he saw on her face.

They ate in silence, forbidding any talk of Lillian. At first, it was stilted and awkward, until they started discussing the people they liked and didn't like in the valley. In learning of their huge scandal, some people were awful, while others were quiet and understanding, willing to at least give them a chance. In no time, they fell back into the familiar rhythm and humor they had always shared, starting from long ago when they were only friends. The *best* of friends.

Leaning back, Ben crossed his arms over his chest and the conversation fell quiet. His eyes sparked with something as he assessed her. His sudden scrutiny made her nervous. She grabbed a glass and crunched on some ice.

"What?" she finally asked.

"You know what we need most?"

"What?"

"Fun. We should go have some fun. Do fun things like we used to. Wasn't that why we were always together? How easily we always had fun together."

"Yes," she said softly. Remembering. Longing squeezed her heart. It used to be so easy for them. Before everything got so tainted. "It used to be easy."

"You know why I enrolled you in those dance classes?"

"Why?"

"Because I hated seeing you without the spark that made you Jocelyn. You have this endlessly restless energy about you. You have it still. You work and take care of Lillian, but there's nothing left for you. It's like what happened stomped all of that out. I couldn't stand seeing you so flat and crushed."

She crunched more ice. "If I hadn't stopped doing that, it would mean I was a sociopath, don't you think? Anyone with a conscience would have to change after what happened."

"I know. I'm not trying to deny it or forget it. Let's make our amends with it, and yeah, move forward."

After he fell quiet, the bill came and Ben paid for it. Finally, Jocelyn nodded and said, "Fun. Yeah, I would like to have some fun."

His quick smile brightened his whole face and her heart lifted as they stared at each other and she grinned back.

So they decided to have some fun. When they eventually drove back to the apartment, the ride was quiet. They chose to spend a few hours bowling, of all things. They found a bowling alley with four lanes and only one other group was there. Both Jocelyn and Ben were awful at the game, which made it even more fun, as they laughed and cracked jokes at how bad they were.

Ben walked up ahead of her to the front door when they arrived home. He stopped, and put his hand on the knob, since they didn't bother to lock it ever. Country living with lots of acreage around their place had its advantages.

"I think I'll stay over at Joey's tonight."

"What about Lillian?"

"Dad and Erin wanted her for the night. You should sleep in. Lounge around tomorrow. Enjoy some time to yourself."

She was ashamed to realize that sounded more appealing and comforting than she and Ben having sex. She wasn't sure about it yet.

"You're good with that?"

His smile was quick. "If we figure this out, I want it to be out of... choice. Not because we could or should. I want passion to be the source of our decision, because we *want* to do it. No other reason. Nothing else between us."

She nodded. "That sounds hard to find."

"But maybe we can find it."

He released the doorknob, turning towards her and drawing her closer as his lips brushed over her mouth. He kissed her softly, only grazing her lips and she was almost on her tiptoes to follow the heat of his mouth. Then he drew back and opened the door behind her. "Good night, Jocelyn."

"I'll see you tomorrow morning when I come to take care

of our daughter," she muttered to remind herself of the situation.

"That you will. But for tonight? My date is over. Good night."

He left her there and she watched him as he walked the short distance down the road. She felt odd as she closed the door behind her. The apartment was so empty and silent. How oddly decadent.

She hadn't been so alone in ages. Or if she had, she was full of self-recrimination. Now? She could just be herself. She took a long bubble bath, enjoying for the first time in months one of Ben's beers. She wasn't nursing tonight, and Lillian had plenty of milk she'd already pumped for the feedings.

She lay down on the sheets and slept all night. No waking up early. She lounged until nearly ten the next morning, which did so much to revive her. It was exactly as Ben had said earlier, *fun.*

Which was Ben's entire point, she believed. He asked her out on more dates. And they both enjoyed them. By day, they parented Lillian. Some evenings, Ben went to stay at Joey's house and Jocelyn stayed at the apartment. Sometimes she had Lillian, and on others, he did. She got a few nights more of pure rest, which did a lot for her moods. Ben kissed her a few more times, but nothing more than that. He left her blood zinging through her veins and her frustration growing. Yet he held back. They were both unsure. There was still so much at stake. And for once, they were taking the time to figure it out and not risk what they had already built. Fun became a goal that they purposely tried to achieve. It was better than dwelling on raising their baby. Fun took some of the pressure off. Fun cemented the connection that used to exist between them.

～

ONE DAY, they went to a bar together on another date. "Shot? Beer?"

Jocelyn smiled, delighted. "Yes. Both. I haven't drunk much alcohol since nursing. I'm going to tonight and just pump out the milk and discard it."

They were in a bar in a town over an hour away that Tareq told them about. He had become a friend to both of them, always calling Ben *baby daddy* and never his real name. Ben gnashed his teeth the first few times he heard it, but eventually accepted it was just Tareq's way. He was a big, easygoing guy who might have wanted Jocelyn for himself, except he sensed that Ben wasn't *just* the baby daddy.

He chuckled. "A long time ago, words like that would never be exchanged so easily between us."

She laughed too. When the shots of Cuervo 1800 came, they each licked salt off their wrists, then clinked their glasses together and gulped them down, leaving a slice of lime stuck in their mouths and making funny faces at each other. Jocelyn smacked her lips together. "Oh, my God. That's good tequila."

Her face was already flushed from the single beer she started with.

"You're going to be a lightweight, aren't you?"

"First for everything." Cheekily, she grinned and raised her eyebrows.

He tilted his beer towards her in a toast. "Here's to firsts of everything. Here's to maybe it can be good again." His tone was serious despite the din of the bar.

Their gazes locked and a huge smile filled her face. She tapped her second beer to his. "Here's to firsts." Then she added, "By all accounts, I'm thinking your tolerance is probably at an all-time high."

He dropped his smile as he stared down. "Yeah, you could say that."

"How about women? That at an all–time high too?"

His head jerked up, his eyes smoldering as they stared deeply into hers. "No. Just you. You were my last, Jocelyn." His voice was quiet, and what he said rippled through her. Her blood was heating from the alcohol and making her skin flushed.

"No one else?" she whispered.

"Nope." He stared at his hands, and peeled off the label on his third beer of the night. "There has only ever been Marcy and you. Sleeping around was never my thing. And after that night, I couldn't even get it up. I was never drowning in sex, I was trying to drown out everything else. Sex was the last thing on my mind."

"I didn't mean to make it an issue. Not right now."

He shrugged. "It's okay, isn't it? To bring it up and talk about it? It is between us. More than anyone else in the world, shouldn't we be the ones to bring it up? Can't we talk about it together? Help each other through it, by going over it and remembering it? Because I don't see any other way."

She licked her lips, her heart skipping. "I never thought about it like that. Maybe. Yes."

He smiled, and his eyes dimmed. Then he shook his head as if he were ending the subject and the sadness that lingered around it every time it was brought up.

"So, what about you?"

She almost spat out the drink in her mouth. Her eyebrows jutted upwards. "Uh, just pregnant then nursing. Doesn't speak sexy."

His smile was quick. "I meant, what's your history? I actually have no idea. I never heard much about you. Was there just…"

"No. There were more than him. There was just never a boyfriend per se. You want names?"

"I'm thinking not, judging by your tone of voice."

She nodded. "Wise choice. It doesn't matter now. But not that many, not really." She tilted the empty shot glass over and then turned it back up.

"You're pretty good at it."

Her entire frame jolted in surprise as her eyes met his. "You can't even remember it."

"I remember it."

"It's hard to describe what that night was like."

He shrugged. "Just saying, I remember liking it." His gaze skittered away. Nerves? Yes, almost like he was a virgin. He licked his lips. "Did you? Like it... I mean, before it all went so wrong?"

A small smile finally tugged her lips up. "Ben, I wanted to be with you for... way too long to mention. Yes. I liked it. Before... before it went so wrong."

He nodded. "Strange we could be sitting here like this, isn't it?"

"Yes."

"But here we are."

She smiled. "Yes, here we are."

"Come on, let's dance."

"You can't dance. I know you can't," she said, her eyes sparkling in fun, and even flirting. "Well, that's not true; you can line dance. I saw you doing that before. But this isn't that kind of place."

He pulled her up and nearly growled at her. "You're such a comedian. I know this is your thing. Doesn't mean I can't stand out there. Come on; show me what you got."

A laugh bubbled up inside her chest and escaped from her mouth. It had been so long since she consistently laughed and smiled... and had *fun*. It was kind of epic to do so now.

Alcohol also made it easier to fall back into the familiar place they used to be. To talk effortlessly with each other without the whispered presence of *Marcy* coming between them. Jocelyn's hips instantly started moving to the music. The bar's dark interior and strobe lights made it pulse and beat like she remembered. She smiled. She was finally dancing again, free and lost to the ordinary routine of her life and even herself. The music had the same effect it always had on her. Warm, lovely thoughts filled her brain induced by alcohol, relaxing, music, dancing and even Ben. Ben's presence made her feel happy. He tried to dance, but mostly just shuffled around. It was funny to Jocelyn. Seeing Cowboy Ben in an environment like this, so urban and close to a city–scene. It made her laugh as she moved closer to him to try and save his pathetic dancing. She could make any partner look good when she danced with them. Always had that one talent. It meant nothing and did nothing for anyone, not even herself. She often wished she'd been blessed with some other talent, one that could make her money, or establish her significance in the world at large. Maybe if she were born somewhere else, she could have channeled it, and perhaps it would have mattered more. Instead, all her talent managed to do was make her happy. And after the last year and a half, hell, maybe it was the most important thing of all. To experience pure joy again.

And she did.

She approached him, her body dancing closer to his. He responded, trying to mimic her movements. A smile flashed over her face when she saw how hard he tried. He smiled back, completely understanding how funny his attempts must have looked. She liked that about Ben; his ego didn't stop him from dancing horribly and knowing it but still doing it. All to please her.

Well, perhaps the alcohol facilitated some of that.

His hands wrapped around her waist as he pulled her closer to him, trying to make their bodies move in tune. She leaned towards him and looped her arms around his neck, letting the complicated dance moves go and leaning against him. And he against her. Their gazes met and they ground their bodies together. The music was pulsating around them, preventing them from speaking. Allowing them to forget and just be in the here and now. It was glorious. Liberating. They were young and sexy and together and openly feeling each other. They were lost to the moment, which was hot and intense. His head tilted and his lips fell on hers as they started kissing. It was deep and long, and his hands cupped her face as his tongue explored her mouth. Forgetting to dance, he leaned more over her to deepen their kiss.

When they finally disengaged their lips, she blinked up at him, looking completely entranced. He smiled and rubbed his thumb over her lips. Then he pulled her against him and they danced some more. She clung to him, letting their bodies bump and grind. She was glad they kept dancing for so long, over another hour. It was exquisite torture and just them. It was the unparalleled experience of their bodies feeling each other. It was... fun. They were turning each other on and not feeling wrong about it. Their first time having sex was suddenly irrelevant and nearly forgotten.

At that thought, Jocelyn pulled her head back. Maybe they should *replace* that memory.

She took his hand and pulled him towards the edge of the dance floor. When they were far enough away from it, he could hear her voice over the music. She tugged his ear closer to her mouth. He leaned down to hear her. "Let's go home, Ben. Together."

Ben drew back, his eyebrows furrowing. "You mean..."

She nodded. "Yes, I mean..."

"Are you sure? Maybe it's just the alcohol talking. I don't want any regrets. Not this time."

She shook her head. "I'm not even close to drunk. Are you?"

"No," he said softly. She felt goosebumps breaking out on her arms by his intense eye contact.

"Your dad has Lillian again? All night?"

"Yeah."

"Then... let's go home."

CHAPTER 16

HEY WERE SILENT ON the drive home. The headlights flashed on the shop and their apartment over it. Ben cleared his throat and that drew her attention. They stared at one another. She eventually broke, grappling for the door handle and jumping out.

They entered the darkened apartment. Lillian's baby paraphernalia cluttered the room. Swinging around, he grabbed Jocelyn. They weren't chickening out. They weren't going to delay it... and most of all, this wouldn't involve the fire or Marcy or that night. Or even Lillian. It was only about them. Now. Here. Tonight. And their mutual feelings, the real ones that were good and honest and about time. It was overdue for them.

He put his hand to her cheek and stroked it. "I love you."

Her eyes seemed wary and big, shining with fear. Fear that he'd hurt her? That he didn't mean it? That he was still wound up with Marcy? He wasn't sure why she was afraid but he understood. Ignoring Marcy finally, Ben knew Jocelyn deserved to know how he felt about her. She deserved the words perhaps more than anyone else.

He leaned down and kissed her. Their lips locked and tasted each other. Hot tongues slid over each other and she moaned when his hands dropped to the hem of her shirt and he scrunched it up in his fists. He pulled it up over her head as their gazes stayed locked, their faces solemn. Her breasts were still swollen from nursing and her nipples were huge brown circles. He ran his palm over the end of one nipple and felt something warm and wet on it. She pulled her face away from his. "It's milk…" she whispered.

He leaned forward, kissing the top of her head, moving his lips through her hair as his hand rubbed her again and he smiled although she couldn't see him. "Well, duh. I see you nursing my daughter only about a dozen times a day."

Her nose wrinkled. "Doesn't it bother you?"

"Does it feel good?" he asked, moving his hand to the other one. He liked flicking and playing with her hard, brown nipple.

"Yes," she said, her breath catching. "But they tend to leak sometimes. That isn't sexy."

He knew that too. He had to bite his lip to keep quiet. He'd seen her leak before. Usually, she wore little pads in the cups of her nursing bra, which was a fascinating thing in itself. It had panels that easily dropped down so she didn't have to undo anything. Sometimes, she didn't realize he was *right there* for almost every interaction with Lillian. Yeah, he missed the first few weeks but since then, his attempts to make up for that became almost manic and obsessive as he watched her with Lillian. He saw her tired and frustrated when she'd lose her temper and later, grab Lillian from a dead sleep and hug her and kiss her over and over as she apologized for losing it. Of course, Lillian wouldn't remember the slight annoyance in Jocelyn. He also watched her nurse for hours and hours. He caught fleeting glimpses of her breasts and nipples and his baby sucking on them, well, hell, a lot. It was intriguing at first. And sexy in a confusing way. Not when the baby sucked on them. He shuddered. No. Seeing her nipples and her breasts as Jocelyn got ready to feed before the baby was latched on evoked an odd, tugging sense of tenderness and protectiveness in Ben.

By now, he'd seen her in almost every way there was to see a woman: from attractive to sexy to tired to exhausted, to messy, to angry, to happy, to tender, to gentle, and finally, to looking so beautiful, she broke his heart. So... yeah, a few drops of milk didn't bother him.

"No, it doesn't bother me." He kissed her mouth again as he dipped his other hand into her pants and ventured down the front of her panties. They were already wet to his touch. "This is wet too. Don't worry, it doesn't *bother* me. Unless you care to explain why these are wet too?"

Surprisingly, his comment did exactly what he intended. Jocelyn started to laugh and let out a huge sigh of relief. She finally appeared to be relaxing. When he moved his finger gently along her opening, she gasped and bit her lip. Her eyes grew big. "No. I think you have a grasp on wh—" She gasped again when he sunk his fingers inside her. She closed her eyes, her breath coming out in intermittent pants as she finished her sentence. "... on what my body is doing."

He pushed her backwards and explored her, rubbing her clit with his thumb as his fingers manipulated her. She opened her eyes and stared into his. He couldn't look away and neither could she. All at once, she closed her eyes and her expression contorted as she grabbed his hand. "Ben..." She was breathless.

"Come for me, baby," he whispered in her ear as he kissed the side of her face and then her mouth. She responded, reaching up and sucking his tongue inside her mouth as deep as it could go. She suddenly pulled her mouth off his and cried out as her body went tense before she convulsed around his hand. She nearly wilted afterward. He withdrew his hand and caught her, holding her close to him as she turned into jelly, collapsing and nearly boneless.

She glanced up with a shy look on her face that melted his heart. Jocelyn was not a typical girl, never had been. Seeing her vulnerable or shy always surprised him. "It's been awhile."

Didn't he know that? Exactly how long it had been? She dropped her gaze down. "I was kind of afraid I couldn't..." She cleared her throat. "Well, having an unplanned baby and figuring out what to do next doesn't make a girl feel exactly sexy."

He dropped his head so he could kiss her and looked into her eyes. "You are so sexy. As a mom now and before too."

She smiled and shrugged, always uncomfortable with compliments. She took his hand and led him into the bedroom. Ben hadn't used it as a bedroom since Marcy. Same room. Same bed. Things were sometimes so twisted. But it wasn't the same bedding. Or the same girl. Much less, the same circumstances.

She held his gaze and discarded the rest of her clothes. She still had a rock–hard body. Her free time was usually spent jogging down the road or doing sit ups, push–ups, and the like. She could have been stronger than Ben was. He wouldn't have doubted it. He did plenty of physical work outside but not since high school PE had he participated in a "work out."

Jocelyn looked nothing like Marcy. Marcy had large breasts and pink nipples with a slender, soft build. Her tanned skin did not have a blemish on it. Jocelyn had a hard, thin body, with wide shoulders and narrow hips. Her barely-there boobs were noticeably larger now because of nursing. She had a toned, muscled body and tattoos that covered her arms, her shoulders, her lower back and right over her left breast. This was the longest time he'd gotten to look at her naked. It wasn't like the first time, when they never had a moment to take in the other.

He reached out and traced the tattoos of a soaring bird over her breast. "I like this one."

Withdrawing his hand, he stripped off his own clothes. Pushing his shoes and socks off, then his jeans and shirt, he dropped his boxers. Her gaze followed every motion. He was long and lean, and freckles dotted most his skin. He had auburn hair on his legs, that grew thicker there than it did on his chest. His thighs were well developed, but he didn't have huge arms. He wasn't as well-proportioned as some guys. She reached forward and touched his chest, sliding her hand along his stomach, then towards his shoulder to trace the skin over his clavicle. "I like how this feels. I like how it feels *not* regretting it this time."

He swallowed and tugged her closer to him. "Me too."

She smiled and the tension dissolved as their mouths touched and their hands explored each other. For a long time, there was nothing sexual. Their soft lips pressed against each other and they enjoyed the feeling of bare skin to bare skin as if meeting each other for the first time.

Her hand gradually slid down to address his erection, which strained towards her. His breath caught at her hand; it felt so soft and gentle on him. She tugged on him and he followed her. His mouth was still on hers until she slid her mouth off his and whispered, "Sit down, Ben."

Nodding, he stepped backwards, keeping their mouths engaged until he felt the bed hitting the back of his legs. He lowered himself and she followed him, getting on her knees. She let his mouth go while both of her hands touched him and played with him, tugging and gripping until it seemed like all the blood in his body was collecting there. He watched her with heavy-lidded eyes. Still on her knees, she lowered her mouth to the end of his penis that rather resembled a flagpole as it strained towards her open mouth.

His breath faltered and he groaned when the wet heat of her mouth engulfed him. She glanced up at the sounds of his pleasure. Her gaze was dark and intense. He touched his fingertips on the side of her face, rubbing the soft skin of her cheek. It felt like a rose petal against the pads of his fingers.

Lowering her gaze and head, she took him even deeper inside her mouth. She started slowly, using her mouth and tongue to work his bulging knob before she slid him further in. He had to resist the urge to come as all the blood in his body seemed to boil and he ached to release himself into her mouth.

Momentarily lost, he leaned back, lying flat, closing his eyes. Jocelyn moved upwards to stay on him as he pulled on her arm. "Jocelyn…"

She lifted her face off him and kissed his stomach as her tongue glided over his sweat–slicked skin. Her lips peppered kisses between his nipples and his neck until she finally got up to his mouth. Their tongues met again and she lifted her eager opening above his straining, anxious erection. She slid onto him. Weeks earlier, they discussed different kinds of birth control and decided on an oral kind that may be taken while nursing. They hadn't said *why* they were doing this, but they had made sure to keep another unplanned pregnancy from occurring.

So Ben could slide bare and free, skin to skin, deep inside her. He moaned as all that wet warmth surrounded him. She was so slick and welcoming, she accommodated all of him. Then she straddled him, spreading her legs over him, connecting their bodies completely. She stayed like that for a long moment before releasing his mouth and adjusting her position until she was sitting straight up. With her eyes closed, she squeezed his member inside her vaginal walls and he groaned in response. "Ahh, God." He sighed out loud. "Yeah."

She moved her hips up and down. Again and again. She was so at ease. Very slow and controlled. He lifted his hips upwards, aiming towards her heat, and arching his back. She let out a soft groan and then leaned over him as her mouth found his. She bounced her body over his fast and hard for several moments before suddenly halting. He groaned and his eyes popped open. She was staring at him. "I used to love you too."

His brain was heated to the point of boiling. Steam should have been blowing from his ears, that's how hot he felt. She went still but kept staring at him. He nodded. "I know."

He let go of her butt, which he'd been squeezing to push her harder against him. He touched her cheek, cupping it. "I know I about broke your heart last time."

"Don't do it again." She lowered her forehead so his lips were touching it. "Don't break my heart again."

He closed his eyes, sucking in a breath. "I won't. I swear to God, Jocelyn. I won't hurt you again."

She tossed her head up and her hips began to move again, only slower this time. He used both hands to cup her face before planting a kiss to match their body movements. She sighed, letting her eyes roll back in her head. "Then, maybe I *could* love you again."

He nearly gasped at her words. "Then, maybe I could be happy again."

Closing her eyes, she seemed to relax and abandon herself to their love making. She moved slowly at first, but then harder and faster before flipping over. Now that he was on top, she opened her legs wider, cradling him against her. Pushing inside her as far as he could, he pressed his face against her breasts until he felt her straining around him. He could so easily lose himself in her. For the first time in ages, sex not only was a release, but a high. It filled his chest up with warmth and happiness. He felt real love for the woman he was doing it with. In the last months with Marcy, sex was cold. An act they fulfilled by rote. With Jocelyn on the night of the fire, it had been wrong. Sullied. Sad. Wild. Tainted. Coveted. Sizzling. Hot. Stressed.

Not like this. This was so much better.

It was so right. This time, it was all right. And being with her felt right. He held her close to him and wrapped her up in his arms on the bed. He loved feeling her body relax as she snuggled into his and he pressed her bare butt against his crotch. Nothing was wrong, and he had nowhere else to go. Nothing else mattered now but staying right there together.

THEY LAY IN BED, staring at each other, their heads on a pillow, lying on their sides, with their hands under their cheeks. They slept some, and had sex again, but it was completely different. Not so tender. Not so tragic, and very healing. It was just hot.

Now, morning was nearly here. The room was barely lit with the whiteness of dawn. There gazes held each other, transfixed. They were still naked, but covered with a sheet. He looked at her long and hard just because he wanted to. And now, he could.

"Do you ever think of all the things you could have done with your life?"

He shrugged. "Occasionally. But it has an abstract quality about it now. You know, having me at such a young age didn't destroy my dad's life."

"No?"

"No. You seem to think it did mine. I just don't think so.

I'm okay, Jocelyn. Here. With you. With Lillian. Planning on staying and working. There's nowhere else I want to be."

"But there might have been."

"What? And pretend there isn't a Lillian? You can't do that. You can't picture life without her now. So it doesn't matter what *could* have or *might* have happened. Because I wouldn't want that now. There's Lillian." He smiled softly. "And you."

"I just think sometimes what if you had the opportunity to leave and live somewhere else? Maybe…"

"Maybe I'd be happier? I'm happy right here with you and Lillian."

"It's handy sharing a child. What if that's the only attraction?"

"No." His tone was definitive. Sure. Confident. "The big feelings rolling around my heart and head often confuse me, but they also inspire me. Tell me you don't feel that too."

"I always have though. But when all those feelings started to hurt too much and got so tainted, we sort of lost our way. How? How can we go back?"

"We don't go back. We go forward. Us. Together. Doing our best. Just like any couple does. Like my parents did. We deserve to have a life still. We didn't lose ours. As you pointed out, we didn't mean to hurt anyone. If we did, I think we hurt ourselves most of all."

"People will think it's only because of Lillian."

"Not my family. They see it… and know us. But who cares? We know the truth. Lillian will know the truth from her parents and seeing how much they love each other and respect each other."

"If we make it."

He smiled. "*If we make it.* But I think we have as much of a chance as any other couple."

"It seems impossible we could succeed though after the

bad start we had. I don't want to tell anyone about our... trying."

He leaned forward, his lips touching hers. He looped a tendril of hair around his finger and pulled it from where it was stuck to her lips. "Okay. No one except my dad and Erin need to know we're trying."

"What if it messes everything else up?"

"What if? I just don't see how it could be any worse than it was in the beginning. If we can make it through that, we can probably handle other unforeseen circumstances if us being a couple doesn't work."

She nodded, her eyes clinging to his, and her doubts still unconvinced. He leaned out and touched her shoulder, squeezing it with his fingers. "I believe in my heart this will work out. Not because of Lillian. Or Marcy, for that matter. But because of *us*. That is, if we let it."

Her nod was infinitesimal, but still, it was a nod of affirmation. "Maybe, you're right. Okay. We'll try this. For now."

CHAPTER 17

INALLY, BEN DECIDED IT was time to address the subject of the ranch. He spent a lot of time thinking out his latest idea and did a lot of research, as much as he could. Having been such a mess for the last eighteen months, he wanted to make sure he approached this in a responsible, well thought-out way. He couldn't afford to turn anyone off or consider his idea another rash, crazy brainchild from Ben. He wanted to move forward toward the future, and not dwell on the wife he lost and the life he nearly imploded.

The entire family went to his dad's house. Many meetings had taken place there over the last few months, but Ben had shown little interest. Only recently did he tune in and consider the future of the ranch. Fairly recently, he decided to become part of it, and because of his involvement, his dad decided to join in too.

Pockets of casual conversation bounced around the room, until Ian said, "So I think we need to decide what to build with the money we got for the house." That was the topic of this meeting. Ben cleared his throat, meeting his uncle's gaze and drawing all eyes on him.

"Are you planning to stay on here, Ian? Or are you going back to Seattle?" he asked his uncle.

Ian's surprise by his odd question reflected in his gaze. "Well, no. We're pretty committed to staying here."

"I mean, for good. I know you and Kailynn gave up a lot to come back here. Is that temporary or for good?"

Ian and Kailynn glanced at each other. "For good." They said it with some regret, as well as resignation in their tone.

He nodded. "Yeah. You ran a pretty impressive part of the company you worked for, right?"

Ian frowned, obviously puzzled and wondering where Ben was going. He hoped Ian humored his questions. "Yes."

"And you, Kailynn, have a degree and accounting experience?"

"Yes," she answered, her expression just as puzzled.

Ben flipped his gaze to his dad next. Others were intrigued by his line of seemingly unrelated questions, and anxious to see his purpose in asking them. "And Dad, you don't want to run things anymore, right? I mean, you're fine with delegating the business end to Ian, right?"

"Yeah. I am," his dad said finally with a shrug. "I guess…"

"And Shane, you'd be happy just working at your shop, right? Now that your house is ready for your family to occupy. Your end goal is Rydell Rides, isn't it?"

Shane nodded, tilting his head. "Yeah, but only if I'm not needed elsewhere on the ranch."

Ben glanced towards his stepmother, who was biting her lip, her head tilted, and a frown conveying her perplexity in all this. "Erin, you could be in charge of the horse care, right? All of it?"

She shrugged. "Well, most of it, if I had some help."

Looking towards the back of the room, he nodded and

asked, "AJ, you're staying on for good, right? You could assist Erin with the horses?"

"Yeah, I do whatever needs doing." AJ's tone was confident and firm.

"And Kate, you know how to do marketing, right? You understand the big picture when it comes to doing business."

"Sure. Why? What is this?" Kate asked.

Ben ignored her question as his eyes landed on Joey. "And, for the foreseeable future, you'd be willing to start up the resort again, yeah?"

"Yes. Where are you going with all this, Ben?"

Ben glanced at Jocelyn, ignoring Joey. "And you'd like to run a café or restaurant again, right?"

She blushed uncontrollably as she hissed, "*Ben*. What are you doing?"

Ben glanced around the entire room. Even Charlie was watching him, his curiosity piqued.

Ben nodded. "I have an idea, but I need to know who is staying and willing to be involved before I describe how I think this could all come together."

Jack's solemn gaze hadn't left Ben's. "Okay, son, you have my undivided attention, all of our attention. Where are you going with all this?"

"Years ago, Ian had a pretty progressive, forward vision of expanding our ranch. Adding the resort and then the café because our family was changing and growing was a logical move. No matter what, our family is different from most. Change was a good thing. Ian had an excellent idea but unfortunately, it burned up."

"Duh," huffed Charlie.

He glared at his little brother. "I don't think we should use all the insurance money to rebuild the main house. I know that's what most everyone was thinking of."

A wave of discontented surprise swept through the room,

including a few startled exclamations of denial. "Why the hell not?" his dad asked. "What else would we build?"

"The house that burned down can't be rebuilt. We can't recapture what was lost. We can't bring anything back. It's all gone forever." His eyes scanned the crowd, meeting the stares of several people who firmly understood what he meant: his dad, Erin, Charlie, Shane, Ian, and of course, Jocelyn. She knew better than anyone. Certain things could not be recaptured.

"Well, we can't just turn our backs on it," Joey muttered.

"No, but we could alter the plans to better suit our needs *now.* I've read through all the stuff Kate presented about the business models for our ranch and resort. Before, we were working with what was already set up. Our existing facilities and such. But now? We have the unasked for and unfortunate circumstances of starting from scratch, right? That's what's eating away at everyone and freaking us all completely out."

Kate nodded vigorously. "Yes, he's right. This place has huge potential. Some of the more profitable avenues would have required more significant investment for the expenditures and the facilities. More than the family wanted to risk at the time. What is it you're foreseeing, Ben?"

Ben flashed a grateful grin to Kate. She ran a consulting company out of Seattle and thought "big" in ways none of the others could. "When I was working in Montana, I passed several huge spreads like ours. But unlike ours, these had arenas." Ben pulled out a drawing he made. It wasn't a great rendition of his concept as he had zero drawing skills, but he tried to visually explain his plan because they needed something concrete before they would be convinced.

"They are multi–level facilities, with dozens of horse stalls inside them. They also had offices, conference rooms, even restaurants and living quarters. And of course, the main arena."

"Inside? You're talking about putting the arena inside?" Ian asked as he leaned forward and his gaze scanned the sketch. His interest was serious. "You're talking about a million–dollar building here, Ben. Maybe more."

Ben held his uncle's gaze. "I know I am," he acknowledged quietly.

"Putting horses inside takes it to a whole other level. You gotta have huge HVAC systems to ventilate an indoor arena. Horses inside create an excessive amount of humidity. That could cause crazy problems."

"Not if it's done right."

"How the hell do you have a restaurant in a horse arena?" Shane asked, crossing his arms over his massive chest.

"The few I saw were completely walled off with glass. From the mezzanine, it feels open, with views right over the arena and stalls, but no horsey smells or unsanitary issues. The sound is also muffled. It actually creates a nice ambiance."

"My question is, why would we?" Jack asked.

Ben sighed, knowing his dad didn't want that. But he didn't want the other changes back in the beginning. "Because it's really not your ranch anymore," he said quietly, dropping his gaze to the floor in deference to his dad.

Everyone else exclaimed their opinions at him in quick succession. Most were shuffling and grumbling in anger at his suggestion. But his dad tilted his head, and a small smile appeared. He was remembering their conversation on the way home from Montana. When they were both so lost and disillusioned. His dad held his gaze. "No, son, it's really not mine anymore. You're thinking…"

"I'm thinking you could be free of it if you wanted… *Dad*."

Ben's tone was quiet and respectful, so unlike what it had been for so long toward his dad.

Jack shut his eyes. His chest lifted and expanded as he exhaled a deep breath. Erin exclaimed, "You can't take this place from Jack. God, Ben, what is wrong with you?"

"He's not going to," Jack interrupted softly. Everyone's gaze focused on him as if he shouted. Ben smiled too. Naturally, everyone still looked to Jack for leadership, guidance, and approval. That might have diminished somewhat, but it would never change. Especially for Ben, he finally acknowledged. He needed his dad's support and approval. For fuck's sake, there was nothing wrong with that. He finally saw that it didn't make him weak or immature or too inexperienced to use the resources at his disposal. That included a loving, decent, knowledgeable father. Jocelyn would have killed to have such a father. Hell, he hoped to create the same bond and relationship with his own daughter.

"He's trying to give me a second chance."

"What?" There was a round of puzzled glances.

"Dad prefers to run the ranch less, and have nothing to do with the resort. He would like to start training more often but not for shows or rodeo tricks. Dad wants to rescue horses…" Ben drifted off.

Erin gasped, then smiled. She shook her head, holding Ben's gaze. "I'll be damned," she uttered softly. "You really are back, aren't you, Ben?"

"Yes, ma'am. I am."

Erin glanced around. "Jack has always dreamed of that. Running a rescue organization for horses that he could retrain and resocialize, especially abused horses, as well as the wild ones culled off the range by the BLM. He also thinks our horses would be amazing therapy animals for handicapped people or at-risk youth to meet and experience. Until now, he couldn't pursue any of that because he's been so busy for his whole lifetime keeping the business and the family running. What Ben's providing is an opportunity: if Jack wants to hand over the reins and concentrate on his own passion, he could finally."

"Yes," Ben added with a nod at his dad and Erin. Their faces were shining with relief, love, and pride. They were proud of him. His heart swelled and his chest puffed up as his spine seemed to lift even higher. Yes, pleasing his dad still mattered very much to him. With a huge amount of relief, Ben crawled back into the skin he had occupied for two decades. His self–image soared. His family, their burdens, and their expectations all contributed to his sense of self. Best of all was the love and support they offered him. The steadfast anchor to a chaotic, violent, scary, and unfair world.

"What about this arena then? You taking over?" Shane voiced what others must have been thinking.

Ben shook his head, grimacing. "Oh, God, no. I'm not capable of something like that. I'd be willing to do whatever needs doing... even an errand boy. I wouldn't mind learning something about business and whatever else I can pick up, but I have no clue of the logistics or how to make any of this work. I just came up with the idea."

He turned his head and looked toward Ian and Kailynn. "I was hoping you two could take the reins. You both have plenty of schooling and experience for something like this. I know that being here and living here wasn't your first choice, or anything you planned on. Maybe this could offer you something more. Like a challenging career comparable to what you would have found in the city."

A soft smile slipped over Kailynn's face, reflecting pure pleasure. "It just might. And thank you for not telling Ian he could do it all. Because you're right, I can do it too." She glanced at Ian and they exchanged a silent message before nodding their agreement together. "You're right, we could do this."

"We'd be taking a huge risk, however," Ian added. "The insurance money is enough for a decent down payment for what you're proposing, but it by no means will cover everything. We'll need some hefty business loans to cover the rest of it. Much of the project will have to be financed. How do you foresee our business profits after this investment?"

"The arenas ran horse clinics, pulling in different events and all kinds of avenues. Things like barrel racing or reining. Reining, by the way, is huge on the west coast, and we've never even looked into it. We were all about boarding and basic training. What about attracting people who are more interested in the sport of riding? We could offer jumping and dressage and even 4–H clubs and the like. They all need places to meet and practice and show. Why not us? I've checked already, and there's nothing like that in a two hundred–mile radius. Nothing. On the west side of the state, you'll find a lot more of them, but on our side of the mountains? Not so much. We could create a new market and bring in new business. It could be a selling point of the resort that would increase the numbers and types of people staying here. World famous trainers could host clinics for people from all over the state. I saw one going on that was about centered riding when I passed through an arena outside of Billings. They had full classes being taught by a certified instructor. There's a ton of potential and all kinds of uses for a building like that. We have the land. We have the access. We have the horses. We have Dad. I'm sure he'd have to help at first." He threw a glance toward his dad, adding, "You know so much about the horses, we would need your guidance and design ideas."

"It's not like I'm moving away. I'm right here. I just don't want to do what you're proposing Kailynn and Ian manage. And Joey. I don't want to work for the resort."

"And Jocelyn can handle the restaurant?" Joey asked, his eyes sparking with interest as he nodded his approval at Ben.

Ben smiled, crossing his arms over his chest as Jocelyn shrank down in her seat. "Yup."

"Yeah." Joey grinned back. He turned and with good humor patted her shoulder. "You'll never be anyone's target again or the subject of loose gossip. Not here."

"No. And we're self–contained as well."

Silence followed until his aunt Kate leaned forward. "You willing to bet the family's entire future on this?"

"Yes," Ben said without flinching. He held her gaze, and Ian's, and of course his dad's.

She grinned. "That's why I love youth. Too young to be cautious and scared. But in my professional opinion, I think it's got huge potential. I can study it more, but my initial gut reaction? I think it would be a game changer for this family and this land, while honoring the memory of the first Rydell River Ranch *and* the Rydell River Resort. But mostly, it'll be a game changer for the Rydell family."

Jack grunted. "Yeah. It's certainly far beyond anything I've ever conceived, let alone knew how to bring it about." He lifted his gaze to Ben's. "Game changer, huh?" They exchanged a long look, both remembering their initial discussion about what constituted a *game changer*. Back then, Ben felt incapable of overcoming the *game changers*. "The fire was the ultimate game changer, wasn't it?"

"Yeah, and some of us lost everything…" His words trailed off as his gaze clung to Jocelyn's. "But maybe we could rebuild something better and gain so much more than what we lost."

Allison spoke up. "I think we need more information, like actual architectural drawings, and all of us deserve to voice our opinions of what we see for such a facility. In the meantime, Ian, Kailynn, and Kate could calculate the cost to finance, insure, and then execute the project. Kate could help us with the marketing so we target the right people. We can't do this based on gut reactions, or what we miss, or because we are trying to recapture more than what we lost. I agree we need to do something so big we can gain back some of the prestige that made us the Rydell River Ranch. Recreating what I first found here can't happen. Ben's right. But I think we could accommodate different ideas and find something new. There will be a lot of kids running around this place as the years pass by, far more children than Jack had to deal with. Consequently, we have to make this more than what we had before to give them all a fair chance of being part of it."

"Eloquently said." Erin nodded. "And I agree."

The conversation proceeded into details and assignments of work. A new energy started to envelop the room. Voices rose and fell, and an argument broke out between Kate and Jack only to end in laughter when Jack threw his hands up as if under arrest, admitting he was mistaken and Kate was right. Ian was anxious to get a preliminary architectural drawing of the proposed arena with the mezzanine facilities. Kailynn wanted to research financing, insurance, and costs. The room had become a hive of excitement. A buzz of energy, voices rising and lowering... and underneath all of it? Hope. There was a renewed sense of hope now flowing through a family that had been beaten, depressed, and sad for too long.

Ben found Jocelyn standing next to him. She stared at him for a second as he straightened up on the bar stool he'd been sitting on. They said nothing for a long, intense while. The din of the room rose and fell around them, but in some ways, it practically faded out. It felt like the room contained only them.

Throwing her arms around his neck, Jocelyn hugged Ben. Her head leaned against his shoulder and her hands clung onto his neck. He tucked his face into the crook of her shoulder and slid his hand up to her neck, entering the base of her hair and cupping the back of her head. He tilted her face back far enough that he could see her. "Hey, what's this all about? Not that I'm complaining."

When she pulled back, she was blinking through her tears. A tiny smile tilted her lips. "Because you're still you. I thought it ruined you. I thought you'd never be *Ben* again. I couldn't stand that you were lost to your family, especially your dad, to the world really, but worst of all"—her voice dropped several octaves—"to me." His entire family was in the room behind them. From his little brother and Cami to all his uncles and their wives and kids and his own daughter, who lay gurgling up at Cami. She preferred playing with Lillian more than listening to all of their schemes and proposals.

So rarely did Jocelyn open up to him. Her light brown eyes were wide and soft, almost liquid with feelings. He raised his other hand and brought it up to the side of her face, cupping it in his hand. "I don't know where all this is going, but wherever and whatever the future of this place and this family is, I'll be here. With our daughter, and I hope"—he paused for effect to illustrate the gravity of his meaning and stare into her eyes, smiling as he finished —"with you."

Her face crumpled up in tears and she sniffled loudly. She glanced down and back up, nodding her head once. Then again. And again as she started crying harder. "I love you, Ben." Her voice was soft and breathless.

He held her cheek in his palm and stared into her eyes. "I love you too."

She grabbed his hand in hers and held it against the side of her face. She glanced down and bit her lip. Releasing his hand, he lifted it and placed his knuckle under her chin to raise her face to his. She let out a little laugh, almost a half cry, shaking her head. Their timing? Just nearly a dozen people and a toddler and two babies were sitting behind them. Who knew if they were listening or witnessing any of this? It seemed like such an impossibility after the journey they went through, to finally end up together here.

He threw his head back as his own eyes filled up with tears, enough to match hers, and they both smiled tremulous, watery smiles. She lifted her hands from his shoulders to his face and gripped both sides of it, bringing his mouth to hers. Their lips met in a wild, tight, closed–mouth kiss that felt like an exchange of pain and grief and joy and love. All the emotions that nearly drowned them both and nearly ruined them both had somehow rebuilt them both.

She pulled her mouth from his and threw herself against him again, clinging to him in ways she should have the first time they made love. Or if he stayed around when she found out she pregnant. Or when he came back. Or when their daughter smiled. Or when Jocelyn began to dance again. Or after he found a way to forgive himself as well as Marcy.

Someone must have noticed something because the room suddenly fell quiet. They separated and dropped their arms off each other, but kept their hands linked. He squeezed her fingers in his. They glanced at each other and smiled with almost shy, contrite expressions before Ben merely shrugged his shoulders. He heard a little giggle and knew it was Cami.

"Uh, want us to keep Lillian tonight?" Erin finally asked. When his gaze lifted to hers, she grinned wider. Her eyes were sparkling.

He glanced at Jocelyn. She grinned widely but shook her head *no*. He tugged on Jocelyn's hand. "Nah. Thanks, we're good," he said as he leaned down and picked up Lillian, tucking her against his chest. She squirmed all around; her little neck was much stronger and her head bobbled around. She reached out her hand like a claw to grab his hair, squealing in delight when she accomplished it. He chuckled at her as he took Jocelyn's hand and pulled her with him to leave.

They left the room and stared at each other. "You want to come home?"

"I want whatever you want."

She nodded. "I want you to come home with me... with us. For good."

He grinned back. "I can do that. I can finally do that, Jocelyn."

EPILOGUE

"*Y*O, BABY DADDY! HOW'S it hanging?"

Ben turned towards Tareq with Lillian in his arms. She was bigger now, and her head whipped around with his.

At three and a half years old, she smiled and reached out toward Tareq. "T! Hey. Can you take me backstage?"

Tareq patted Lillian's head. "No, I wanna watch your mom's show." She stuck her tongue out and he laughed.

Ben rolled his eyes towards Tareq. "You know, you could just call me *Ben*."

"I could. But what's the fun in that? Your girl ready for this?"

"What do you think? She fretted all day and half the night. She's convinced she should not be doing this."

"That girl isn't half as tough as her looks promise. She's ready, all right."

Ben nodded his agreement as they turned towards the stage. It was a large performing arts center that was attached to a community college in north Seattle. Tonight, Jocelyn's dance class was performing a sold–out Halloween concert.

Amazingly, it was finally happening. In the beginning, Tareq charged Jocelyn for his time during the first six months she danced with him, but by the end of that year, they simply met whenever they could just to dance together. They fed off each other, both of them growing. Tareq was nagging Jocelyn to instruct a class for little kids between the ages of three to five. She resisted his suggestions over and over. After more than a year of dancing with Jocelyn, Tareq finally convinced her to start her own class.

"I'm not even trained. I can't teach a class."

Tareq just rolled his eyes. "It's not public school. You don't need a master's degree to prove what you can do. All anyone has to do is watch you."

Ben kept prodding her until she finally relented. She was so nervous at dealing with the preschoolers, he feared she might throw up at her first class. He went with her, and stayed outside the classroom for moral support. But come on. It was only a small group of three– to five–year–olds, preschoolers; how intimidating could they possibly be? Jocelyn claimed she wasn't afraid of them, but their mothers. But Ben was in the hallway and he heard some of them praising it as Jocelyn was lining up the girls and beginning her class. Her quick, easy smile charmed the little girls and one boy, just as she charmed Lillian. Jocelyn was amazing with kids. She swiftly launched into a thirty–second dance sequence, showing off just a little bit. Right off, her audience must have thought she did have a master's degree in dance, judging by their reaction.

So she agreed to start teaching. Mid–year, Tareq assembled an older recreational dance class of eleven– to fifteen–year–olds. As usual, Jocelyn said no initially, but finally gave in again once Tareq begged her for long enough.

"Girl, hip hop is the hottest thing nowadays. It's gaining more and more acceptance as kids see it on all the reality shows and music videos. Now, it's as accepted as any other form of dance. But there aren't enough teachers, or people like you that are willing to spend time as instructors. And it doesn't matter how you were trained or got to be that good: all that matters is *you are*. So embrace it."

She started teaching the older kids after those words of persuasion. By days, she worked for the resort as soon as it reopened. Six months ago, the arena was finished and the restaurant moved to the second–floor mezzanine. It was now under her management entirely. But she reserved two nights a week and two hours on Saturday during which she taught dance classes at the studio. It made Ben's heart swell every time he saw her dance. He was so glad she could share her love and talent of dance to inspire others. But he mostly felt a debt of gratitude to Tareq for having the tenacity and insistence to convince her to return to it. In no time, he could see the light it brought back to her eyes.

It took two years for Tareq to persuade Jocelyn to perform onstage with him. She had never done such a thing and nearly had a panic attack. But the entire place instantly erupted in cheers, whistles, and cat–calls for an encore. At first, the shows were performed for the dance studio's parents and students. But eventually, they took the acts to Seattle, Tacoma, and nearby outlying areas for paid perfor-mances. The other venues were showcasing hip hop crews and teams of all ages, styles, levels, and numbers; from duos to trios and large group performances.

It didn't pay well, of course, not any of it. But the joy Jocelyn received from it transformed her. And the reward Ben got from seeing Jocelyn doing something she loved was pure elation and awe.

Of course, little Lillian, Jocelyn's daughter, could dance like no one's business too. She followed her mother around, moving, grooving, popping, and locking with surprising speed, skills, and learning that rivaled Jocelyn's. She was enrolled in Jocelyn's three-year-old class, of course, but she could dance like the kids in the five- to eight-year-old class.

Jocelyn's days of wearing the grunge and urban streetwear of the genre was reserved exclusively for dance classes and performances however.

But for their daughter? Jocelyn had a completely different standard. From the very first day of Lillian's life, Jocelyn brushed Lillian's barely-there hair. Now it was long, bright, and carrot-colored. Yeah, she got the Rydell genes in that department, but thankfully not the Rydell dancing genes. Jocelyn loved to comb their daughter's long hair until it shone like a halo. She styled it in various versions of pigtails and braids, using bows, headbands, clips, and curlers. Lillian mostly wore little pink and purple dresses or girly versions of capris and shirts or shorts and jeans. Never did Jocelyn allow her to dress the way she herself had.

One day, Ben softly suggested, "You know, it's not the worst thing if she prefers to dress like you. What if she doesn't want to be girly-girl?"

"Well, of course, I won't force her. I'd never try to make her be anything but who she really is." Jocelyn frowned at him. Then her facial expression changed and almost tore out his heart. Thinking of Cutter Johnson and the mother who abandoned her, she added, "But if she would rather not be like me and chooses to be like most other little girls, her life will be so much easier and better."

Ben got up and took Jocelyn in his arms, causing her to release Lillian's hair from the braid she was working on. "Don't forget: Annie has us. She won't be judged by the way she chooses to dress. And she won't feel alone and lost for being at the mercy of some old, pervert bastard. Nor will she ever be ridiculed or bullied by anyone. We won't let that happen. Her childhood will always be one of love, growth, and adventure."

Jocelyn surrendered to his embrace. Sometimes, it surprised Ben that she could be so clingy and vulnerable, while on the flipside, she had no problems handling guys like Tareq and the staff and crews. "I know. I just want so much more for her."

He leaned back, kissing her forehead. "She already has more because she has you."

"Us," Jocelyn corrected him. She touched the side of his face with a tenderness that contrasted with her appearance. "She has us."

Jocelyn stayed "normal looking" (as she called it) for about a year. After that, little changes began to appear. It started with small items. Different styles of clothes. Bigger earrings. Then no earrings. Different makeup. Then none. She started wearing the bandannas and hats sideways and backwards. Her real affinity, however, had always been changing her hair. It was shoulder–length by then, and smooth and quite pretty. She started by adding some red to it. From there, it went through several shades of brown and auburn before going back to blond and then to black and on it went. Ben came in from the fields one day and found her crying in front of the mirror.

"What's wrong?"

Sobbing so hard she couldn't talk, she pointed up at her head. "Look what I did," she exclaimed before hanging her head down.

He slid his hand into her hair, pushing the silky strands aside and chuckled. She cut the hair at the bottom of her hairline close to her scalp. Why? He had no freaking idea. But he wasn't alarmed, in fact, it almost encouraged him; maybe she was finding her old self again.

He merely kissed the top of her head and started to walk out of the room. "It'll be a few inches long by year's end."

After he walked out, she called out after him, frustrated. "It will not!"

But of course, it did. She returned to wearing her hair in various degrees of short to suddenly growing it out, and trying a new color. The hairstyles were endless too. She refused to wear any of her piercings despite Ben's frequent request for the tongue stud, which he was dying for her to put back in. But her prim sniff to that idea instantly shut him up.

"It was not for any man, Ben, it was for me. Let's forget it." He sighed, disappointed. But she did pierce new things. Things no one else but him could see and touch and experience. He liked those.

Almost as much as he liked the woman who felt the need to have them.

Ironically, Ben's daughter was always the neatest, best–dressed, prim and proper young girl.

Except when she went out to the stables to ride the horses. Or played in the dirt from one of the fields. Or went off grooving her little tush like her mother.

Jack and Erin, along with her countless uncles and aunts, often took Lillian riding or allowed her to pet the horses. Uncle Charlie eventually came around and turned out to be her favorite. Zeroing in on Charlie when she was about eleven months old, she melted his heart and that was that. She followed him around and nearly bounced off her butt to get his attention. He couldn't resist her, of course, and now the two were nearly inseparable. Their bond rivaled that of Ben and his own uncles.

Tonight was the first performance that Jocelyn had choreographed. She chose the most advanced dancers from their studio and devised a dance for them to perform as a duo. She was strung tightly as usual with anxiety and nerves. Backstage, Ben knew she worried that everything would crash and burn, and the crowd would boo her and accuse her of being a fraud, which she always worried she was.

But no. Cheers and applause had the crowd on its feet, stomping to the heavy music. Tareq slapped her back in congratulations, saying, "See you for practice on Tuesday, partner."

"See you, Tuesday, partner," Jocelyn answered, eyes shining with pride, her hair again short.

Jocelyn then rushed towards Ben, who held Lillian. She took Lillian in her arms and let Ben hug them both. They stood that way for a long moment before Ben slipped back so he could see her face and smiled gently. "So, how about we celebrate by getting married?"

Her smile faded. She licked her lips, glancing at Lillian fiddling with the edge of her favorite blanket. "What?"

He shrugged, putting his strong arms around her waist. "I know, it's a weird place maybe. But it's where you're happiest. I like seeing you happy all the time. I don't have to feel insecure about it either because you love River's End too. And you love Lillian to death. And you also love me."

Her eyes were wide, studying him. He took her hand in his and kissed the back of it. Then he slipped a ring onto her finger as he glanced at her. "I happen to love all those things too. And I would sincerely like to ask you to be my wife."

Her eyes closed. *His wife…* He knew exactly what her brain was thinking. The wife he had before. The only woman who was briefly known as Ben's wife: *Marcy.* The cruel taunts rarely happened anymore, but it was always something they expected. She stared down at the ring. It didn't look anything like Marcy's. It was something that actually fit Jocelyn's personality: a thin platinum band with small diamonds in a row. Not too big or flashy or girly. Nor could it catch on anything while she was working or dancing.

"It's time now, Jocelyn. It's been more than long enough. This isn't about Marcy or the fire or even Lillian. This is strictly about you and me. I love you. I want to share my life with you for as long as we live. Now do you want the same thing that I do?"

Her gaze found his, and he seemed to be clinging to her. She nodded, biting her lip as tears filled her eyes, smearing the dark black eyeliner she drew to highlight them.

"Then marry me."

She exhaled as her fingers curled around his. "Yes. I'll marry you, Ben Rydell."

Exactly four years and one month after their daughter was born, Ben and Jocelyn Rydell were married on the site where the Rydell family house once stood. Now it was a lovely flower garden with a view of the river. Off to the right of that stood a brand new, over–one–hundred–feet–long indoor riding arena, with a restaurant, barns, and assorted meeting rooms. It was just like Ben first imagined and described.

The resort instantly drew the attention of potential visitors from all over the Pacific Northwest. People called to ask about their facility, their resort accommodations, the affordable packages for families, and the luxury cabins for those with a thicker wallet. Several world–class horse trainers flew in to host clinics and workshops. Naturally, the people who came for the clinics booked the accommodations at the ranch. Business was booming on a scale far beyond their previous model.

And all because of Ben's idea. It never failed to amaze him whenever he glanced out and saw the arena. It featured custom–designed sliding barn doors on one end and dozens around it that were fashioned to look like old wooden barn doors, but in reality, they were comprised of expensive top–of–the–line steel. They appeared to be timber and green roofs with faux siding that mimicked the log cabins of the resort.

The gardens were open to allow the guests of the resort to stroll through, but they were really planted for the family. It was a symbolic remembrance of what the Rydells lost as well as what was gained. It was a new beginning and a new reality for everyone. But for Ben and Jocelyn and Lillian, it was a new family.

ABOUT THE AUTHOR

Leanne Davis has earned a business degree from Western Washington University. She worked for several years in the construction management field before turning full time to writing. She lives in the Seattle area with her husband and two children. When she isn't writing, she and her family enjoy camping trips to destinations all across Washington State, many of which become the settings for her novels.

Made in the USA
Monee, IL
17 May 2020